Before the POISONED APPLE

LS DUBBLEYEW

outskirtspress

DENVER, COLORADO

To:

My great, great grandchildren. Read this story and you will have met your great great-grandpa and ma, uncles, aunts, nieces, nephews, cousins and our great, great, grand-friends, who are every bit a part of your family.

I hope you have as much fun reading these words as I did writing them. Don't forget… families are to be remembered!

Thanks:

To those of you — and you know who you are — who helped me. Not only with semicolons and commas, but with simplifying the thoughts and clarifying the visions of a mind that easily wanders.

For:

My beautifully scrumptious wife Jackie, our wonderfully silly children, Rachel and William, and various pets — some that died during the course of writing this. Your magic made this possible. I treasure your lives and love you very much!

Chapter One

Lightning Dust

She adored her father.

At her wits end, she acted upon his last urgent words, cried to her right before he was killed... "Fear not the light, eat the dust, call to them—they will come!"

The tired young maiden brought the silky soft pouch to her mouth, tilted and poured. Like the sweetest of sugars, the powder coated her tongue. She screamed for help, screamed for hope from an unknown hero. The tinny heat of the lightning tingled her tongue as a jagged bolt jumped from her mouth. She watched it fly and smiled as it rose. Another flash— her world went gray. A spear sliced through her throat.

The stalking beast that speared her watched the flashing light fly from her mouth. Frightened, it chose not to take her, so it ran. After all, its leader, the *Kig*, would have fresh human babies to eat.

In those brief moments while her life-light dimmed, a crescent moon and her mother's last soft words haunted her... "We make babies because they have special magic that we need in our lives." It was an answer to a child's question. It was the last day of her fairy-tale life. And she broke the last promise she made to her mother... "Momma, I *will* save her. And I'll save the other one too!"

On that day, all the cities and towns in the West Fields, that special place within The Reach, where her family had lived for generations, were over-run by monsters. The army of beasts had gathered in strength and couldn't be defeated. The children were protected as best as strong parents could, but the evil was too much. The forest she once played in was misty with smoke, and muffled screams of fighting poked through short bits of quiet.

As she lay dying, she barely remembered what happened only one minute before— that she stopped for only a clock tick to grieve...I'm an orphan? Or that only two minutes before, as skilled as a seasoned warrior, she pulled a lance from the chest of an ogre and thought...I might need this again! There was a quick thought...survival *must* conquer sadness. And a voice..."Fear, one of life's most natural forces, has a *might,* all its own."

It was only three minutes since she realized the place where she hid her sister and the other baby, a cubby she once played in, an old knothole in an enormous tree, was empty. Could they have crawled to escape? No! They were infants, not able to crawl, barely able to roll. They had been taken.

Darkness came to her while her father sang..."Your shiny green eyes, your strawberry hair...the Kingdom's most beautiful, a princess so fair." It was his song to only her.

Meanwhile, young Angus Grimsdyke watched in horror as the town fell and the land burned. He cringed watching deformed ogres and other mindless beasts torch houses and crush out lives. He hated his family. His useless leech of a father first tried to use Angus as an offering, then as a shield. But Angus was too squirmy; he broke free from his cowardly father and happily watched when Papa lost his footing and was caught by an orc with tusks. His mother screamed at Angus to come back, but he would not. He knew she too would try to use him as bait. He ran, but knew not where to go. He didn't care what ate his mother. Scattering about the woods, darting from tree to tree, he remembered and breathed hard, "The fort!" and ran further into the woods. Angus jumped up the ladder to the tree-fort castle that he was never allowed to play in. He lifted the ladder in; nothing could climb up. He prayed that ogres couldn't fly.

From his perch, Angus watched the woods. Every now and then, there were screams and grunting calls of attacking creatures. The town was gone. He was truly alone and just about to cry uncontrollably, when he heard a shriek. Looking down, only a short distance from him, he recognized the beautiful little red-haired girl with green eyes running through the forest. He'd seen her before, but she wouldn't recognize him; there was no reason for her to have ever known him or his family. He was just about to call to her, to let her know that she could be safe with him, when he spotted some type of creature hiding behind a tree. He couldn't scream out, it would come at him. Angus could only watch as the ogre followed the girl. Suddenly, she made lightning fly from her mouth, and the creature threw its spear. Angus whispered hard, "She made lightning-speak. She's calling the dragon-elves!" He watched the attacker's spear hit the pretty little red-head's neck, and she tumbled to the ground. The attacker ran away. "It's afraid!" he quietly cried out. Angus quickly looked around and saw no other beasts. He climbed down the ladder, knowing that dragon-elves were coming and that he'd be saved. He sprinted from tree to tree, looking to the spot where the little red-head lay twitching. He dashed to, and stopped at a row of hedges; he smiled, thinking it a perfect hiding spot.

He was too shocked to scream as a beast's thick, scabby hand shot out from the dense hedge and grabbed his face. A powerful clobber to Angus's head made his world go black.

Cries

Dagon, an old dragon-elf, rested uncomfortably on a dusty peak and watched smoke rise in the distance. Some of his friends also rested;

from other peaks, in treetops, and some watched while hovering within clouds. The battles were being lost. Armies of ogres and other ferociously foul monsters sprouted from the ground, attacking, killing and eating everything. Dagon wondered…why do they leave their lands? And who, or what, leads them to attack the good folk? Another dragon-elf, Zeck, glided down near Dagon, and spoke while landing, "We need more help. I'm sendin out our fastest, to da north and south. He'll find friends. Humans can't last long." He looked at his elder— "Dagon, you hear me?"

Dagon was lost in thought, but aware of all happenings around him. The air had been tense for too many moons. The Spirits had warned him of this time, of their destinies being entwined, humans and elves. But it didn't feel like destiny to the weathered old dragon-elf. It felt like their demise. The mutants and fiends grew in strength and number, and Dagon questioned fate. He rescued the golden goblet, as was demanded of him…but why? All he knew was his kind and their friends were dying. And still, the Spirits' thin, wispy voices said confusing things… "Find the Scrollsssss….Babiesss, must live!" Dagon reached far back into his ancient mind for clues to the riddles the spirits had been whispering to him for decades. And Dagon *had* searched, but where are they? And babies? What babies? The spirits last screamed in his mind… "Their cry will be clear!"

And clear it was. Before Dagon could answer Zeck, a distant silver flash exploded and flew from the ground, shot like an arrow; its path was obvious. Homing in at the source, Dagon's eyes didn't move. The jagged white lightning passed close enough to singe the hairy scales on his head. Zeck dropped to the ground while Dagon jumped up and screamed, "We fly!" His leathery, bat-like wings unfolded; strong flapping thrusts stirred the dusty ground.

Zeck, slower to react, called out while running and taking flight, "Wait— not alone." He flew fast, but couldn't catch his stronger friend. Dagon kept his eye on the spot… must fly harder! He saw an ogre, but couldn't kill it. The source of the lightning must be found first.

The large ogre that speared the young girl heard flapping high above and looked up. Surprised to see a dragon-elf, it ducked and dropped the human it held—Angus. The ogre watched Dagon fly past and thought… must not'v see me. It didn't want to take a chance; it left Angus and ran away.

Zeck flew hard, seeking Dagon, but spotted that ogre running. He thought…Dagon didn't attack it? Well, I will! Zeck's long claws were fully opened as he dropped from the sky. The ogre ran; its back was to Zeck. The much smaller dragon-elf landed hard on the ogre's head and back, his thick talons embedded into its skull and neck. The surprise and forceful attack made the ogre buckle. Zeck was thrown as the monster hit the ground. He rolled once and stood at the ready. The grounded ogre clutched its head and saw its attacker. Before the ogre stood, Zeck, with clenched hands, blew his strongest fire-breath at the monster's ugly head. The powerful blast of heat met the ogre's surprised gasp; daggers of flame seared deep into its eyes, nostrils and throat, instantly blinding and choking it. Before taking flight, Zeck spat one last bit of fire and sneered, "Suffer!"

The ogre, crumpled in a fetal position, could only take short, quick sniffs of crispy breath while it waited to die.

Meanwhile, Dagon had found the lightning source. Cradling the badly wounded girl, he whispered, "Stay strong little-un."

Hearing his words, she faintly spoke… "Save them please." She prayed she wouldn't die, she needed to say more.

Startled, Dagon asked, "Save who?"

"Babies… save babies." Dagon's heart beat faster. The girl whispered the word "mountain," and fell silent.

The elf's mind raced…*babies!* His mind screamed…the Spirits said *"babiesss must live!"* He pulled the spear from her neck, lifted her and took flight. Before clearing the treetops, he stopped and floated in mid-air. He thought he heard something... a cry? He looked around, but the smoke was thick; he saw no one and flew on.

Angus Grimsdyke woke just in time to see a dragon-elf fly from the ground with the limp, pretty red-headed girl. He was amazed to be free of the ogre and prayed that the only scream he could muster would be loud enough for the dragon-elf to hear. The elf stopped and hovered, Grimsdyke punched the ground and screamed again, "I'm here, I'm here." And when the elf climbed hard and fast and flew away, Grimsdyke still heard his own cries, "I'm here. Please. I'm here." And when he could no longer see his savior, he still cried... "Please. Please. Pleeeeese." Then Grimsdyke passed out.

In mid-air, Dagon met Zeck, threw him the girl and said, "To da nest, let her drink from da goblet. I'm not done yet. I'm going to da mountain." As Dagon flew away, he screamed an ear-piercing cry to his brothers, a call to fight! For the first time in decades, Dagon flew with a different purpose; he needed to find babies.

From all points of a compass, his warrior-elf brethren heard his cry.

Grimsdyke woke to being dragged by his feet along charred ground. His head bounced along bits of rock and rubble, his dangling arms and hands were useless. He saw ogres dragging others, they looked human, but it was hard for him to tell from his position. He was thrown into the back of a cave guarded by two beasts. Bits of skulls, bones and old clothing were scattered about the rocky, sandy floor. He wondered... where were the others dragged to? He knew he would be eaten alive and prayed for time. He hoped...maybe—just maybe he could find a way out of there. To no one he cried, "He saw me! That dragon elf saw me." His head pounded with a fierce headache. His anger began to fester.

At the dragon-elves' nest, the wounded little redhead was surrounded by young and old: mothers, fathers, and children—all dragon-elves. A beautiful golden goblet was taken out of a pouch and filled with water; a drop of the young girl's blood was added— dripped into it. The goblet was lifted to the girl's mouth. Drops of the magic water moistened her lips and found her broken throat. In the background, Zeck heard the elders chanting their ancient healing songs. Within a few clock ticks, her wound bubbled and steamed, the girl gasped, coughed, then let out a soft cry. She opened her eyes and quickly grew scared, but a gentle caress followed by a soft voice calmed her... "Tis ok, little-un, we watch-over."

The girl rubbed her speared neck. She thought...I *should* be dead. I should be a spirit. "The babies? My sister?" she sadly asked.

The dragon-elves looked at each other. "We don't know," Zeck answered, "but our strongest went ta da mountain where da monsters live. If they's there, he'll save-um." The girl passed out.

A huge monster came for Grimsdyke. Was it an orc? Perhaps an ogre? It didn't matter. With their mottled skin and matted, weed- like hair, they looked similar; only they themselves bothered sensing the differences of their kind: the fatter ogres, the slimier orcs. The beast that lumbered up to him smiled and muttered grunts of hunger. Grimsdyke could only cry and think of his happy place, by his pond, with his fishing cane. For the first and *only* time, he was filled with regret. He was sorry for hurting his younger brother; he was sorry for hurting a little bird. He was just sorry for everything. The beast reached for him, Grimsdyke cried, and a flash of green light blew up in back of the ogre. A grayish mist followed the flash, swallowing the beast. Before his eyes, the ogre just melted. In its place stood what

Grimsdyke immediately knew to be a hag-witch: greenish, tight skin— cadaverous looking features, exactly what he envisioned a witch to look like.

"Come with, boy," she demanded. "Dat dragon-elf, ee did see ya's, ee jest waasn't gonna save ya," she cackled, "not like me, I can save ya. Ya wants ta be saved?"

Grimsdyke looked at the witch. Numb with fear, he could only nod slowly while saying, "Yes please."

"An that little girl, she with green eyes an' pretty red hair. She alive I'm sure, an' she tells him ta let ya's get eaten by that!" the witch pointed to the pile of green ogre slime.

"But...I...I saw her die," the young boy said, "She was killed, an ogre killed her."

"She aaain't dead," the witch mocked, "an I'll tell ya's why." Angus looked beyond her, sure that ogres and orcs would soon be running into the cave to try to eat him.

"Don't ya worry 'bout them, they won't hurt ya now that I'm with. Anyhoot, them dragon-elves, they got somethin' should be mine. They's stole it. If ya help me, I helps you." The witch walked up and put her face close to Grimsdyke's, "If ya don't help, then I don't need ya."

Scared, hurt and lonely, he said, "I can help."

"Good," she said, "call me Myrtle. We gonna be good friends. I have somethin' fer ya." She fumbled in her pocket, then brought her hand up to his face and opened it. In her palm was some sort of flower. They both looked at it, and poof!- the blossom twinkled and became a little star. She moved her hand away, and the star floated at eye level with the little boy. Grimsdyke smiled at the tiny bit of magic. So did Myrtle. He thought...she *saved* me! With a simple suck, the witch inhaled the tiny star, then spit at his face. But what came out of her crusty mouth was not a breath, but a blast of wet heat, sending young Grimsdyke to the ground holding his head in pain. She screamed at him… "They stole me goblet and ya promises ta get it back! Don't care 'ow long it takes, da longer it takes, da more misery there be. Drink from da goblet an' magic fills you up. But you… you mine!" Myrtle grabbed Grimsdyke by the face and lifted him off the ground while chanting her spell…

"Never to love, your kind, your heart,
The wicked men to fall will start,
Your pain will show your truths to bear,
A darkened spirit within your lair,
Every tick the time to take,
Your spirits flame, your soul to bake,
A master's bidding, a master's bidding."

Myrtle continued to mumble and chant, then threw Grimsdyke to the ground and said, "Go east. Look to da weeping crescent. The beasts won't hurt ya. You'll see me agin, I'll finds ya." She skirted out of the cave, but before leaving his sight, she turned to him and screamed, "IF YA'S DON'T HELP, THEN I DON'T NEEDS YA. YOU OWE ME SOMETHING!"

"I'll help, I promise," he answered back. A nervous jolt made him shudder; he had just lied to a hag-witch. And Grimsdyke first wondered… how *does* one kill a witch? He sat up and lightly rocked back and forth. He wasn't afraid. "A magic goblet," he whispered and thought… I bet it's made of gold; it should be mine, *will* be mine, not the witch's. He didn't know what she meant about the weeping crescent, he didn't care. To no one he said, "And her—red hair, pretty green eyes. If she's alive, I'll find her. I'll kill her. Leave *me* to die? I'll save her pretty green eyes in a jar. And I'll kill that dragon-elf." Grimsdyke was furious. He couldn't help but to believe the witch. But he wasn't afraid.

Myrtle heard Grimsdyke speak to no one. She smiled and disappeared.

Seven hours later, the young, green-eyed girl rescued by the dragon-elves woke. Sleeping next to her were the two babies she couldn't save. Somehow, they had lived. From behind her, Dagon said, "You ok now, but we have ta gets ya far, far 'way from here. Far east. To da other side of da Reach." He stepped into her view. He was bigger than the others. She wasn't afraid. She had been told of this special race of elves. Her mother once said, "You'll come to love the look of them." The girl thought she already loved the one named Dagon.

While caressing and touching both babies she said, "My name is Zee, this is my sister, Rose. I don't know his name."

"Plenty a time for makin' names," Dagon said, "Rest a bit more. A long, long way we have ta go."

Zee stroked the babies. And staring at Dagon, her eyes moist, she simply said, "Thank you."

He smiled. "No need fur dat, spirits say ta save ya, dat's what'll do." Smiling, Dagon patted the infants. "Least 'til they grows up a bit." He looked at Zee. "See, these two babies, they special—like you. They gonna marry. Don't know why yet— suppose da Good Mother has her reasons, just has ta be."

Zee paused, she thought of their future. "Thoran," she said. "We'll call him Thoran."

Chapter Two

To The East

The next day, a score of dragon-elves flew in wishbone shape heading east, over the immense lands known as the Naturean Reach. The Reach is vast, with oceans bordering east and west, and mountains, deserts, valleys and rivers to the north, south and in between.

Protected by the formation, on the inside were two elves, Dagon and Shida; and each held a baby. Zee traveled with another named Durt, who was a bit of a troublemaker, but was strong and held a perch that Zee sat on. Flying higher than they ever had, to an end farther than most knew even existed, Dagon and his friends were doing the Spirits' bidding—saving the little-uns.

"How we gonna know where ta take 'em?" one in the pack asked, again. "The Reach is huge. Right?"

"Don't you worry, we'll knows," Dagon answered, "you jest look ahead an' fly true," he said.

They flew over far reaching forested peaks, colorful rivers and hidden lakes. Every now and then they spotted a burning castle, a smoldering cluster of cottages, and smelled smoke. They glided through humped valleys and seemingly barren deserts. The further east they flew— away from the armies of ogres and beasts that ripped their Mother Earth apart, the calmer the world became.

After a fortnight, they crossed a great river. A small town was far below them. "That town's alive, down there," Shida said, her sharp eyes spying streets that bustled. "The beasts haven't come this far." She whispered to Rose, "Hope they never will."

Zee had always wondered what a city was like. Oh my…she

dreamed... the cities I've read about, with people and things to see. Father was always afraid of them...why? Zee got teary at her brief thought of Papa; he spoke in her mind... "Always watch. Be careful," he'd say, "Like most of life, there is always something more than that which is within only a whiff of our sights." Papa had *never* taken them away from their cottage.

The pack slept mostly in treetops, and took cover when lightning filled the air, or if rains beat too hard about their wings. Only Dagon seemed to never sleep. He would sometimes scurry about the woods, mumbling, or he'd fly around, scouting the land. The elders in the group knew he spoke to those who watch-over.

After thirty some odd days of their trip, two elves on the tail of the formation, Ornald and Thum, broke from the crowd, flew into the middle, and to Dagon whispered, "We're being followed."

"I know," Dagon said, "devil-hawks—they huntin'—been back there fur days." Dagon gently flipped and flew backwards to scour the skies. "They jest waitin'."

Another elf, Faert, heard them and broke a bit from formation to look back. "So?" he said, "Those tiny things—we'll eat them f...f...fur dinner."

"Those little things are thrice da size of ya," Dagon said, "they's jest far away—they spit fire too, they can gives us a heap a trouble." Then to everyone, he spoke loud. "Spread outs a bit."

They had been lucky; they had had no trouble and were getting close to the eastern lands. They had traveled across most of what was known within the Naturean Reach. The faintest whiffs of salt from the Sea of Algaen tickled their noses. But luck could run out in a flash of lightning. They had to be careful in daytime—and more anxiously, at night.

On the thirty-seventh night, scattered amongst the tops and in deep knotholes of giant redwoods, they rested uneasy. A nest was built only for Zee and the babies. On that night, the babies slept soundly, as did most of the elves. The next morning, all woke to the sounds of hungry babies—all except three.

From a large hole, Faert blasted out, "Where's Ornald? An' Thum? They were right next to me!" Another elf cried, "And Burth? There's blood on da branch we slept on. Ee's gone!" At the sound of panic, the babies cried.

Dagon knew that the devil-hawks had begun their feed. "Need ta get goin," he said, "tis ok, no screamin—ermember our task." Grumbling spread throughout the pack. If the hawks gained in number, there was no hope. The elves took to flight. Dagon and Shida flapped their wings hard. The others quickly followed.

"Our task?" Durt complained loud while fighting the wind. "Our task should have been to stay with our land, fight with our kind." Zee looked at him and knew it best to stay silent.

Dagon also heard him, "You go back anytimes ya want!" Although he said no more, Dagon made a decision. Dropping to the rear of the group, he called to four of his kin to follow. Dagon still held a happy baby Thoran. The five dropped far back from the main bunch.

Durt screamed, "What's he doin?"

"Silence!" Shida hissed at him.

Zee said nothing while baby Rose cried…looking for her friend. Dagon came back after a few minutes and joined Shida at the inside of the pack. Dagon cried; he knew he had sent loved ones to their certain deaths. But it was necessary, for they desperately needed something they were running out of—time. The graveness of their predicament created quick, hard tension amongst the pack. Some stole nervous glances backwards. After only a few more minutes, in the far, far distance, roaring shrieks could be heard, unmistakable sounds to those who know the cries of battle. Dagon still held Thoran, and again dropped to the rear of the group, and called to four more of his kin to follow.

Rose watched Thoran being taken again; she stopped giggling. Her little lips pouted while Shida hummed to comfort her. Rose was just about to cry when Dagon returned with her friend. Durt said nothing, even though he wanted to scream at Dagon, to remind him how few dragon-elves were left. To calm the little-uns, Shida spoke softly, as a mother would. "Our friends—your friends, they already built you a cottage in a fairy-tale woodland. It's gonna be your home—forever and ever. It has two windows for eyes, two awnings for brows, a door for its nose, and its glassy eyes will sparkle for you." Rose fell asleep while listening to Shida's smooth voice. Thoran played with Dagon's chest hair. More roars, coupled with faint screams were heard in the distance. The devil-hawks were getting closer. The dragon-elves flew quicker. Dagon and Shida swapped a simple stare; Dagon and two more of his friends dropped to the back.

Durt couldn't keep his mouth shut. Speaking loudly he said— "I hears amongst that woodland are things. Little furry things, an big, scaly, angry things." Zee knew Durt was trying to scare her. He continued— "An *things* are always hungry. Some a da things have a hundred heads that guard treasure, an some are spidery things, with lots a eyes that always see, never sleep, with heads and eyes taking turns ta rest, while others watch."

Zee looked at Durt, smirked and said, "So?" Zee had seen *things,* run away from *things*, and killed *things*. "I'm not afraid," she said. Dagon heard Zee. He smiled and thought... no, you're not.

Closer roars sounded like thunder. Dagon, Shida and Durt stole quick glances behind. The hungry flock of devil-hawks could now be seen. They playfully tossed heads and bits of dragon-elves amongst themselves. For the first time, Durt was speechless. He looked to Dagon, his eyes began to tear. Dagon turned to those that held no child and quietly said, "Da Good Mother waits. Fight like never before." His friends smiled, nodded and dropped back. To his last companions, Dagon said, "With da wind," and they fell from the sky with fury.

Far below, scattered townsfolk from the little Village of Laban looked up to the sky. Puffs of flame, black smoke, and far-off sounds of anger were heard. The sky battle was too far away to be fully seen, but concern filtered through the crowd. "What's that noise?" a child asked. "Why's that little cloud on fire?" Not wanting to scare the children, someone said, "Never you mind. Let's go about our business." The parents looked up one last time, then at one another, and thought it best to tell the town's council what they had seen and heard.

Meanwhile, Shida, Dagon and Durt flew along the treetops. It was only a few clock ticks before they felt the heat from the hawk's laughing screams. Great shadows darkened the sky. In his mind Dagon heard the flying devils speak to each other… eat the babies first. Coming over a small mountain, an amazing crescent-shaped lake opened up before them. To Shida, it looked like a claw, yet Dagon knew it meant life! They landed hard in a field next to the lake; their feet didn't miss a beat, running at the moment of impact with land, their wings folded in. Rose was jolted awake; she began to cry. Thoran, not rattled, still giggled. Zee jumped off her perch and ran to her sister, grabbing her, then Thoran, cradling them both. She wished she had a weapon. The three dragon-elves formed a shield around the children. Clenching their fists, they prepared to battle the circling devils dropping from above.

The first blast of fire came at them; Durt swung his wing, hitting the fireball, bursting it into smaller bits that scattered about. The largest devil-hawk swooped in. Shida and Dagon blasted it with their own daggers of hot breath. The hawk laughed and swatted away the two smaller blasts with each of its wings. Then, from the woods came a sound. A sharp, pointed scream, followed by a glistening, bright spear. The spear flew hard into the hawk's body, sending black feathers exploding. A shriek of panic came from the devil-bird. From its wound came white hissing smoke, and the bird fell into the claw-shaped lake where a great commotion came about. Whatever was in the lake began to ravenously feed.

From the woods they came, scores of small, fuzzy creatures, each holding sparkling spears. The devil-hawks above screamed with anger, flew haphazardly about, but did not further the attack. Throwing their weapons at the hawks, the new, little attackers screamed back in anger. The devil-hawks retreated in defeat to their far-away nests. The battle was over.

The small army of fuzzy beings greeted the dragon-elves, "The Good Mother always tests, doesn't she?" one said, "Welcome, friends, I am Shuran, leader of our family of wood-sprites." And motioning to those with him, proudly he said, "We've been expecting you." Staring past the elves, he walked to Zee and held out his hands. "Come little brave one. Let us take your family home." Zee smiled. Rose began to calm down. Thoran still giggled. Turning to Dagon, Shuran said, "Even to us, she tests. We've had those ice-spears for many years— never knew what to do with them, and they never melted, they just stayed cold!" He laughed and shook his head. "An' imagine. Our worst hunter—that little one over there," he said while pointing at a small goofy sprite that pointed back, while picking his nose, "Ee screams and just throws that thing with all his might. Hits that devil right in its heart, eh?" Shuran laughed and shook his head, "Odd, odd stuff," he said while scratching a tuft of hair.

A bit of rustling came from the wood sprites, and a small cart was brought out, obviously for the babies. The wood-sprites themselves were slightly smaller than Thoran and Rose, and much smaller than Zee. All stared at the beautiful surroundings. For the first time in what seemed like forever, Dagon, Shida and Durt could rest. Speaking to Dagon, Shuran said, "You've done well. We'll watch-over them now, my friends."

Dagon reflected. "I know you will," he said. "Dangerous tiems we do live in," he nervously chuckled. The speed of the battle, the loss of their friends, the defeat of the hawks, the normally talkative dragon-elves had little to say.

"It's time to say goodbye," Shuran slowly said. "For now. We'll see you in a few years." Shida and Dagon smiled; both hoped to visit the babies as they grew into children, but they knew they had to fly back west, to help their kind do battle. Without further fuss, Dagon and Shida kissed the babies, hugged Zee, and watched the wood-sprites and the children walk to a path in the woods. Then they were gone.

Afraid to speak earlier, Durt, the troublemaker said, "That's it?"

Dagon smiled, "Maybe we do a little fishing, eh?" He and Shida walked to the lake's edge, holding hands.

In the meantime, young Angus Grimsdyke was making his own way east through The Reach, from the place where he was born. But he walked; there was no one to fly him the great distance. He left right after he met Myrtle. And she was right—the ogres didn't bother him. He knew the creatures had spotted him, but they'd just grumble and walk the other way. He thought…maybe I smell funny. The first few days, he watched flocks of dragon-elves flying high above. "On their way to attack, defend and try to take back the lands, no doubt," he'd say to no one. Grimsdyke always talked to himself. He was his own best company. He didn't care what happened to any of the towns within the West Fields. He didn't care about anything, except for going east. As he kept going, he saw less and less of anything—man or beast.

On a clear night, many days on his trek, Grimsdyke stared at the crescent moon. A small cloud in the shape of a teardrop floated at the bottom point of the crescent. "Look to the weeping crescent," he said to the still forest. "That's what the witch said." He decided not to sleep that night and walked, keeping the moon in front of him. When the teardrop vanished, a memory washed into his mind. He remembered his father beat him for no reason. On that night, Angus dreamed it was he that killed his father. When he dreamed of killing, his head seemed to ache less.

Angus came to a small cluster of thatch-roofed cottages separated from him by a river. He looked to each side; the river rounded away from him. To the inside of the round canal were thick hedges with few breaks; only the upper cottage floors, chimneys and roofs could be seen clearly. He stood at the edge and stared at smoke that came from stone and mortar smokestacks. He started to walk the perimeter; the little village was actually surrounded by a moat. It was an odd little island, and he was impressed at the inhabitants attempt to protect their dwellings. He couldn't swim and saw no way in. But the smoke carried with it the scent of bread baking and Grimsdyke was famished, having eaten only berries and bark for many days. "Oy!" he screamed, "Anyone there? I say, IS ANYONE THERE?" He walked and screamed again. "PLEASE. I ASK, ANYONE? HELLO?"

"SHUT UP!" someone startled him. "WHO ARE YOU? GO AWAY!" a voice from across the moat and within the hedges screamed. And from the hedges came two men, each holding bows with arrows drawn. "Your name and your purpose!" one said, then quickly, "Who are you, child?"

"I mean you no harm, sirs. I am from the farthest town in the West Fields. I've escaped the killings and am only seeking a bit of bread." Grimsdyke paused. "Please sirs, I've been traveling for many days and only seek a bit of kindness."

"He's just a boy," the other man said, speaking to the first.

"No outsiders...no exceptions!" The first man said. "Keep to the woods boy—now be off!"

"He's just a boy!" the other man said sharply. "Surely we can give him a night's rest and some food."

"NO," the first one said. "We bring no outsiders in! No one to be trusted. That's our law! That's how we survive." He turned to Grimsdyke and said, "I'm sorry son. That's just the way it has to be. This is the world we live in now."

"Please sir...I beg, just a bit of bread." Grimsdyke said pathetically.

He sounded distraught, but sounds can be deceiving, as Grimsdyke was seething with anger inside. How can these maggots not help a poor child in need—preposterous! The two men stepped back into the hedges, Grimsdyke heard them arguing; he fumbled in his pockets. Within the bushes, the second one said loudly, "It's just some bread!"

The first one came back out, and to Grimsdyke he shouted, "He'll bring you some food, then on your way. It's just the way it has to be." Grimsdyke looked at the man with disgust. The man went back into the hedges to hide.

From the side of the little island came the second man rowing a small boat. He docked in front of Angus and pulled out a sack and a bedroll. "I'm sorry son, I'm outnumbered here. This'll last ya bit, tho'. There's some bread and cheese. And here's a blanket."

"Thank you sir, it's more than I had." Grimsdyke reached out with his left, to shake the man's hand. The man, with *his* left, awkwardly went to complete the handshake. In Grimsdyke's right hand, he held a knife. As swift as a snakes' strike, young Grimsdyke plunged the knife through the friendly man's throat and twisted. The man gasped, clutched at the knife and pulled it out. Grimsdyke snatched the knife back while grabbing the man's face before a scream could leave his wounded neck. Grimsdyke plunged the knife into the man's chest, and let him fall. The sound of a horn startled the quiet air. Grimsdyke looked across the moat; the first man blew a horn and fumbled with his bow. Grimsdyke grabbed the sack, the bedroll, and the kinder man's bow and some arrows, then ran—smiling. The first man screamed in anger and sounds of other's shouting filled the distant air.

He had just killed for the first time and was sure he would be followed. Angus was proud of himself. And his headache was gone.

Chapter Three

Some Words on Witches and Families

When most think of a family, reflections of love, silliness and even frustration jump to their mind's eye. Then there are those whose eyes, minds and spirits are blind to all that is good, and the word 'family' might as well be struck from language all together, replaced with colder words, like clump, or lump. To some, families are just disgusting humans, lumped together, their only purpose to cast aside the most helpless of souls.

When most think of a witch, they think of evil, and they're right to do so. Oh, there are good spellsingers and sorceresses, those that use their powers and what they've learned for decent, happy purposes. But we really *don't* think of them as witches, do we? When the good ones are born, their parents aren't afraid of them. But *proper* witches are only to be feared; for they are the rare seventh daughters *of* a seventh daughter. And those special babies, instead of being a family's center of attention, cuddled and tickled, they're cast away—all of them. For those little ones start their lives belonging to a race of evil creatures—the blood-trolls.

Smelling the unique scent of the seventh, the blood trolls only come out seeking these rarest of infants. Throughout history, some families resist. But they all lost, were killed and most likely, eaten. The newborns are allowed to live only to become slaves. The blood-trolls torture, starve and beat the sevenths… it's not only how they amuse themselves, it's what they live for.

And when old enough, after years of being emotionally decapitated, despair having grown into the darkest of hatreds, the seventh little girl will dream *only* of others' misery: long, painful, agonizing, misery. And her dreams fester and boil. Then her hatreds and dreams grow into her natural strength. With cunning delight, she'll snatch the weakest troll, dig her hand hard and deep into its chest, and pull out its heart, bringing the still beating muscle to her parched lips.

The first bite is the best. It's the one that will unleash her growing power. As the heart meat slides down her hungry throat, it passes close to the young hag's heart. And as it passes, the juice from both hearts join, creating a great need—an ache: an ache cured by eating the rest of the troll. It's a hag's first, truly satisfying meal. The other, stronger trolls always scamper away, cursing their continued stupidity. And if they're not careful, they'll be the first that she will make suffer. So the trolls wait. Wait in the dark for many years for the rare scent of another seventh of a seventh. It's a bizarre tale, the birthing of a true witch; it's as natural as the male black widow expecting to be eaten by its mate. And you really can't blame the little hags for detesting any family.

A new, *proper*, family was growing; they just didn't know it yet. Two days before their seventh birthdate, they played at the foot of the Shortcliffs that dipped into the Sea of Algaen. Thoran barked, "I'll throw this shell up. See if you can smash it with a rock. Okay, Rose?" She ignored him— she just wanted to find pearly shells. She was tired of smashing and shooting at things. He, on the other hand, wasn't.

The wood-sprites raised the young family with strength and love.

Shuran sat with Zee. They watched the children play in the waves, discussed life in general and planned for the upcoming return of their dragon-elf friend, Dagon. "It will be good to see him," Zee said, "hard to believe it's been seven years. And all this time, all he's done is battle."

"The western lands have paid a heavy price," Shuran said, "as have those that protect, and live within. That part of the world is said to be mostly wastelands now." He paused and touched her arm lightly. "Don't question him about it. Let him only speak about it if it comes up...naturally." They sat and watched colorful gulls drop to the water and feed.

"What if she grows up and doesn't want to marry?" Zee asked, "Not all girls want to marry. In Laban I met two sisters that lived together for seventy years without marrying. And they were very happy. What if they both want to visit other parts of your *Naturean* Reach? What if they want to explore lands *outside* the Reach?"

"It's not *my* Reach!" Shuran barked. "It's where *we* live. And no one goes out of it. At least not our eastern lands. There's no need; the Eastern Reach is the only world good folk need to be concerned with."

Zee looked at him. Was he angry? He calmed down.

"They can choose what they wish for their lives...it's their choice. But look at them," he said. Zee watched her beautiful sister and Thoran. She knew they were already in love. Shuran kicked a bit of sand on Zee's feet, then shook the sand from his little shaggy foot. "You also have choices. You can stay in Laban for a spell, if ya want. Meet some young'uns, same as your teen-age."

"Maybe," Zee said. But she wouldn't, and she knew she was never going to. She made a promise to her mother a long time ago, and was very happy to honor it. She liked visiting Laban, but hated being away from Rose, even for a day. As for Thoran, well, she just liked to have fun with him.

"Come you two, get a drink; you'll pass out from the heat." The two children ran up to her and she handed them water pouches. They drank quick and ran back to the waves, as they had just started building a sand castle. Shuran picked up the pouch that Thoran drank from. "I wouldn't drink from that," Zee warned Shuran.

He looked at her and shook his fuzzy head. "Why? What have

you done?"

"Watch," a smirking Zee said, nodding and pointing at the children.

Quickly, Thoran clutched his stomach, not in pain, but in pure panic. He looked to Shuran and Zee, and screamed, "I have to go!" He looked for a place to relieve himself, and ran to a bulge of nearby rock—the only place he could remotely think to do his business; he didn't make it. In front of the rocks he stopped and was able to at least grab hold. And before he did it, he turned to Rose, smiled and said, "Excuse me," then contorted his face, and started to burp—long and loud. Rose was shocked. Zee started to laugh. Shuran shook his head. In the middle of his act, out from Thoran's mouth came a yellowish gas that first twirled in the wind, and then swirled into the form of a smoky, laughing dragon's head. "AHA!" Thoran screamed and laughed. The gassy, smiling serpent head blew towards Rose, who ducked while screaming in disgust. Thoran wasn't done. With pure joy, while laughing, "Ahahuhauhuha," he tried, and succeeded, in creating another blast, that turned into another laughing serpent's head. "Stop that!" Rose screamed, as he laughed and strained himself, still trying to continue.

Zee laughed so hard she rolled off her blanket, onto the sand. Shuran looked at her. "D...d...dragon wind! He's got the dragon wind," Zee screamed while laughing. Shuran began to chuckle. Rose heard her sister and ran at her.

"I'll have to keep a better eye on you when next we go to Laban," Shuran said, "no more trips to the herb shop."

"You did that?" Rose said in a squeaky voice, holding her stomach and looking horrified at Zee. Steps away, Thoran still tried, but could no longer make the fierce breath; the storm had passed. Rose threatened, "If that happens to me, I'll..."

"Relax, little sister, your squiggly hair will straighten from worry," Zee chuckled, wiping sandy tears from her eyes.

Thoran walked to them, rubbed his belly, saying, "*That...was fun.*

Any more?"

Rose was just about to scream, when Zee spoke. "I promise no gas shall pass from you, Rose." Zee laughed. "Now go on, we'll be leaving soon. We have a party to plan for!" Rose and Thoran ran back to the waves, hand in hand. For a short spell, Zee and Shuran watched the ocean spray the air, and slap at the Shortcliffs. The tide was coming in; salty wisps mixed with floral whiffs heightened their already grand mood. The sun was high overhead. "You know," Shuran said, "they'll soon be old enough to play tricks on you! You'd better be careful."

Zee looked at her friend and smiled. "I look forward to the challenge. But until then, I plan on having loads of fun." She dug at the sand with her feet. "I'll soon be nineteen years old." She shook her head. "Nineteen. The picture of her as a baby is still so clear. And yet, we talk about them being married. Need to figure out how to slow time down." Zee said, "It'll go too quickly."

Shuran laughed, "Well good luck with that."

"You want to laugh at something?" Zee asked, "Just wait a minute." Shuran looked at her, again confused. Quickly, Thoran screamed with delight, "AH.Ahahhahaahahh." He stood there pointing and laughing at Rose; she had grown donkey ears and a tail. With her hands on her hips, she scowled at Zee, "I *will* get you!"

Zee laughed while saying to Shuran, "She'll make a pretty little donkey-bride, won't she?"

Shuran laughed and wondered how many practical jokes the three of them would play on each other during the rest of their lives.

Chapter Four

77 Years Before
They Met Snow White

Deep in the forest, minutes before a setting sun cast its last ray, an unusual seventh moon phase began. On the seventh day of a special seventh month, in the Year of The Fiery Stars, warm sweet night-winds lulled crickets and cicadas to combine into song—a rarely heard tune. The sky melted into purple-black. It glowed, dotted with speckled stars. It welcomed a new crescent moon that shone brightly. Almost as bright was an aura surrounding a cottage— *their* cottage. A small stray cloud in the shape of a teardrop hung from the southern point of the crescent. The cloud followed the moon, slowly, as only a moon could move. To those that are good, the weeping crescent is embraced. To those that thrive in darkness, the crescent angers.

On the seventh tick after seven o'clock, their first son was born. His cry cut through the chirps, clicks and screams of the forest kin, silencing all. Acting as a mid-wife at Rose's bedside was Zee, who was now an aunt. She handed Thoran his first-born; he was now a father.

The new papa cradled and just stared—such a beautiful, simple life. A rose-colored flush painted Thoran's cheeks. Chiseled under his nose was a broad smile of bone-white teeth and his chin was moistened by the tiniest of streams from teary, tired eyes. A prouder papa there could not be. The baby's little eyes were wide open; he quieted down, stared back at the large, happy thing holding him, smiled and wiggled his ears.

Rose was tired. "A boy," she happily said. Drawing in deep excited breaths, preparing, she exhaled, "Our little Ayell." They loved the name.

Aunt Zee reached for Ayell. "A little elf he is, and a beautiful little elf. Come,meet your momma." Thoran gently placed his baby back in Zee's arms. She gave a quick wipe with a soft cloth and gently slid Ayell into his mother's arms.

Close to her beautiful flushed cheek, Rose held her first born, capturing his sweet scent. In a hushed voice she said, "I'm not done, my love." Thoran raised his eyebrows and inhaled slightly. Smiling, Aunt Zee took Ayell and placed him next to his mother on the large bed.

Their second boy also cried hard when born, just as the first. And as proud, Thoran held him and stared; the little one stared back at his father with a puzzled, wise look of somebody older than just minutes born. "A thinker we have here," Papa said.

"A wise one," said Zee.

"Alvis he shall be called. A healer he might grow up to be." Rose loved that name. In the same hushed voice she said, "I'm not done, Papa." Thoran again raised his eyebrows. A quick wipe by Aunt Zee, a quick cuddle by Momma, and Alvis joined his brother on the bed.

Their third boy looked and cried at the large thing that grabbed and held him, yawned, stretched his arms and drifted to sleep. With a warm chuckle, the father said, "His long journey still weighs upon him—Yawnel should be his name." Momma and Aunt Zee loved it, both whispering, "Yawnel."

"I'm not done, Papa."

With raised eyebrows, Thoran tilted his head slightly to his wife. The next child came with a softer, sweeter cry than the first three. The angelic voice belonged to a little girl; she cried a melody— a song to Rose, Thoran's and Zee's ears.

"My word," Thoran breathed, "I can't describe my feeling," he sighed, almost afraid to hold her, "Look at her. This is truly magic."

Zee held the baby girl and looked at her tired sister. "She twinkles like a star, sparkles like a diamond."

"A little gem she is," Rose smiled, whispering, "Little Gem." Thoran watched his wife and her sister; he knew his little girl's name. "It's beautiful," he said, caressing her soft cheek, "Our Little Gem." They were taking turns holding her when Rose quickly said, "I'm not done."

Their fourth boy giggled and laughed when born, as if he had been tickled with a feather. They chuckled with excitement.

"An ancient name for happiness, Joyal suits this little treasure," Aunty said. Momma and Papa loved it.

"I'm not done, Papa." Thoran's eyebrows edged upward a little higher than the last time. This time his nose also seemed to follow.

Their fifth boy squirmed out and clutched his father's arm, in desperate need of attention. "There there, little one. As cute as you are, you'll never want for a cuddle." They hugged. The little one blushed, seemingly embarrassed. Rose said, "Little... Shyel, come join us on the bed." It was another beautiful name. "I'm not done, Papa," she said. Thoran's raised eyebrows never lowered.

Their sixth boy was born with a stern look of someone that was mistakenly left behind, grunting, letting everyone know of his unhappiness. "A little lion we have here," Papa said. I'm sure everyone will know what you're thinking."

"Grumel," Rose said softly, "we shall call him Grumel." Aunt Zee and Thoran couldn't help but to also love that name. Gently wiped and cuddled, he was placed next to his siblings. "Papa?" his wife asked.

"Another?" Thoran asked—amazed at how his bride hid the little people in her little body for so long without a clue to their number. He smiled at his wife. They were fat with happiness, glowing with love. On the bed were seven naked babies. The heat of the night, the love in the room, the babies were warm and quiet. All had their eyes on the mother. Softly, the father said, "As many as your little body will let go. Six boys. One girl. My, my. Perhaps we'll be blessed with another little girl, to help keep all these little men in line."

"Only one more my love," Rose calmly proclaimed.

Their seventh boy was born without a fuss; his only cry being the breath of life. While his father held him, he watched his siblings squirming on the bed, playing with each other's hands and feet and thought… *I* want to be over there. Without warning, his little nose crinkled, one eye half closed, the other wide open, his mouth squiggled and he let out a sneeze that sent a cloth draped over Thoran's shoulder flying through the air landing on Aunt Zee's head. The family burst into a fit of laughter that echoed through the forest.

"Bless you, little one," his mother and aunt said while the rest stared at him.

"Achoo" said a sweet, faint voice from the bed where the remaining seven cuddled each other. The grownups looked at them.

"Now who said that?" a grinning father questioned. "Isn't anyone going to take the honor for naming your youngest brother?" The seven babies looked at him and smiled. Only Ayell made a sound—a deep, long bottom burp that sent them into another fit of laughter. And that special laughter, that pure sound of joy, carried throughout the land. The woodland creatures heard their laughter and joined in their happiness, smiling and chuckling in their own woodland way.

And that special laughter woke something. Something dark. Something deep. Something evil. Something that had rested for a very, very long time.

Only Seven Days Later…

Rose, Thoran and Zee woke to a sharp, single cry. A cry of panic? Sadness? Confusion? It was a cry an infant shouldn't have been able to make. They jumped out of their beds and ran to the nursery where the children's cribs were set in a circle. It only took a few clock ticks for them to reach the nursery, but by that time the children were lightly sobbing, all but one. One little voice was silent; one little body wouldn't move— couldn't move.

In a flurry of panicked activity, the elders tried anything they could to summon a simple breath— to bring back a little life. Yet no magic was to happen that night.

Rose couldn't get a thought out of her mind... of her child possibly sad, trying to grab a breath. Rose passed out while Zee held her.

There is no sense to a child's life being taken before that life had a chance to shine. It can't feel...fair. Yet, there is no choice; The Good Mother is forgiven, her reasons are naturally just. For seven days, their lives had been perfect.

Weak with sadness, Rose and Thoran leaned on Zee for support. Zee would constantly remind the parents that their child went to the spirit world smiling, not in pain.

Grieving and helpless, seven infants pleaded as infants only could, with teary sobs and fierce clutching when held; they knew one was gone.

Thoran would finish the eighth rocking horse, but only after a long period of grief. Rose would not wash away the scent of her daughter from the blanket the baby last cuddled.

The single cry from Ayell, the last sound he might ever make, would haunt Rose's dreams forever. Though she would never tell her husband.

Chapter Five
Far, Far Away

Deep, deep in the crusty earth where caves and crannies are always warm, monsters hid. Survivors and offspring of those that battled long ago, they huddled in craggy caverns of rock and mud, their days and nights were one. The walls glowed gray in the great chamber where most gathered, and echoes of breathing, strange ticks, and tiny drips broke the still air. The creatures rarely showed themselves, for they were afraid—of storm demons, dragon-elves, dwarf lords, and all those who always wanted them gone. Of men. They hated men, but craved to eat them. They only came out when there were no more sick or weak among themselves to eat. They hid for so long, it was the only way they knew how to live.

Near the mouth of a cave, on the stormiest night ever, a group of ogres watched lightning battle the dark rain and wind. The great storm wouldn't end. The flashing wet had been there for months. They were hungry, needed to feed, and one of their own would die soon if the lightning didn't stop and something couldn't be found to eat. They looked at one another and schemed...who would fight the least?

From the flash of a giant bolt, something was left. Something that stood, hobbled into their cave, and came up to them while mumbling. Being stupid creatures, they first just stared at the strange, crusty female that shuffled to them. She didn't smell human—they tried to eat her. When they touched her, their fat fingers burned and they screamed; she laughed, hard and scratchy. They had never seen a hag-witch, but they knew the stories; they became very much afraid. More of their kind came from within the deep to see what was happening.

She spoke… "Found ya's. Ha. Don't be ascared of me, ya help me an I help yous. You be strong agin, rule the world," she lied, "ya help me and I help yous."

An elder orc gruffly asked, "Hhhow?"

"Our master—*our* King, Ee's gonna make things right," she said, "an ee's gonna find me mirror, me mirror that talks ta me, tells how ta kill things… mens. Oh yes… plenty a them about. Far, far away, but ya's be eatin' them soon enough. Ya just have ta listen. I needs some ta come with."

"Why?" asked another, younger orc.

"Don't ya worry yur pretty little faces," she answered, "ya want ta eat youunnglins?" Those words made them rustle with an agitation that started in their stomachs and ended in drops of spit that dribbled from their mouths. Even though most had never tasted the sweetness of humans, they *needed* to eat younglins, as did their ancestors. Their craving for human blood was inherited. They didn't care about a magic mirror. They were driven by hunger. And the ugly little female that stood before them gave them something they never had— hope. For even the most stupid are driven by sparkles of hope.

"I need some… eight of ya'. Who's coming with?" she asked. The ogres just stood there. They didn't know what to do… they couldn't count past one.

Well to the east, close to the coast of the Algaen Sea, Angus Grimsdyke had long since settled down near the little town of Laban. When Grimsdyke fled the monsters that attacked the lands of his birth, he traveled *only* east for years and had walked what seemed to be the whole world. He knew not the names of the forests he cowered through, the mountains he scaled, nor the rivers he crossed. He took shelter in little hamlets when snows arrived, sometimes staying months on end. And to those who were kind to him, he usually killed, as he always wanted what *they* had. He followed the weeping crescent, when seen, and Laban was where he wound up. There is a great city on the sea...Thundor, where Grimsdyke first thought to reside. But Laban was more—comfortable. It seemed an easier place to—control. The people there seemed—stupid, to him. He had worked hard and gained local prominence. So much, that he had been nominated to succeed as the Council Master for the town, after the unfortunate and untimely death of the last Council Master—Phelep Garsoon. In fact, it was Grimsdyke who was chosen to lead the investigation into the death of Garsoon. A fortunate choice, as it was he who had killed Phelep.

All the while, Grimsdyke had been searching for something that was proving to be elusive. His mind *always* raced back to an old hag-witch screaming at him..."YOU OWE ME SOMETHING." Oh, how he hated those words. She wanted what rightfully should be his. Every now and then, he also thought about the little girl with green eyes and red hair. And it seemed that the only time his head didn't ache was when he thought about, or succeeded in, killing.

And Angus Grimsdyke made a friend. An unlikely companion at first glance, as his new friend, Max, looked more the part of a pirate than good neighbor. Grimsdyke treated Max like a dog, so much so that he only let him sleep in a barn with Grimsdyke's horses.

One fine sunny day, Grimsdyke said to Max, "Can I count on you to help me, Max? Help me take care of those who have hurt me very badly? Are you hungry, Max?"

Max didn't understand what his master asked of him. But with a sinister lisp he said, "Yes Masther," anyway, as he was just happy to have someone feed and take care of him.

Chapter Six

The Fairy Door and a Hag

Seventy fingers, seventy toes, never idle, never slow. The adults were outnumbered. Tho' stronger and wiser, their six arms were no match for those seven babies. Ayell was strong. Alvis was smart. Yawnel was silly. Joyal was happy. Shyel was quiet. Grumel was anxious. And Achu? Well—he was always scratching himself. At any given time, either separately or together, the babies could be: giggling, pooping, drooling, yawning, crying, burping, grabbing, flailing, sneezing, spitting up, spitting down, standing up, falling down, grumbling, stumbling, grappling, gurning, and all other delightful little things that babies do.

By their second birth-date, the seven were out of cribs, sleeping in their own little beds and had become swift walkers. "Before we know it, they will be swift runners," Aunt Zee would say, "and then, we build them a cage."

"Better be higher than their cribs," Momma added. "They learned too quickly how to climb out of those!"

The first night of sleeping in their little beds, something happened. Earlier that day, their father gathered them, told them to close their eyes, and brought them to a corner of their room. He sat them on the floor, smiled and happily said, "Open your eyes." To the boys' delight, at the foot of their wall, along the thick skirting board, their father had built a little fairy door out of twigs and twine. Somehow, he made the teeniest of door hinges and the tiniest doorknob for the slightest of fingers. Thoran knew his son's favorite bedtime poem was:

Fairy door, fairy door, twigs and twine,
Open when I sleep, close just in time,
To dream a wish, a world so bright,
Protect our kin, with all your might.

They couldn't open it, because only fairies can open fairy doors, and fairies get huffy and offended if anyone other than a fairy ever tries to open one. The boys were fascinated with fairy-tales and were too young to realize their father glued the door to the baseboard, so it really couldn't open.

But that night, a light hissing sound woke Ayell. Looking around, he saw the fairy door was ajar. He punched Alvis awake and pointed to the little opening. Alvis mumbled in baby-speak, "How open?" Ayell shook his head and shrugged his shoulders.

"Shhhhh," Shyel tried to whisper, as he was also now awake. The simple commotion woke the others. Ayell jumped out of bed and walked up to their fairy door, smiling and pointing. It opened slightly more, a light amber glow seeped from it. The boys were amazed. Careful not to make a noise, the rest lightly hopped out of their beds. Ayell bent down to get the first peek into the magical fairy world. He crawled a bit closer.

His brothers couldn't save him as a slithery, forked serpent tongue shot out of the little door and wrapped itself around Ayell. And as quick as a flash, Ayell was pulled, shrank and sucked through the door. The little door slammed shut with a little pop!- and six boys screamed while jumping back.

Thoran, Rose and Zee bounded up the stairs and flew into the boys' room: panicked, demanding, "What's the matter?" The boys, yelping, ran and grabbed at the adults. Rose instantly saw Ayell was missing. "Where's your brother? Where's Ayell?" The babbling infants pointed to the fairy door. "What do you mean?" Thoran asked, forgetting for a moment as all the adults did, that the boys couldn't speak yet. Zee ran to the closet and looked in. Rose ran to the window, but it was locked tight.

One heavy knock came at the front door. The adults shared a quick, puzzled look, ran out of the room and down the stairs. Thoran pulled hard at the front door, opened it, and there sat his first born, little Ayell, smiling at the woods. Thoran thought he heard a heavy slithering crunch in the woods, if only for a clock tick. Ayell looked at his father and tilted his head as if asking... "What took you so long?" Thoran ran outside, Rose ran to Ayell, scooped him up and brought him inside. Zee kept the other six from venturing outside.

A few moments later, Thoran came back. "Nothing. I don't understand." He looked at the boys, walked up to and picked up Ayell, "How'd you get outside, little man?" Ayell just smiled and stared at his father.

"Let's get them back to bed," Zee said, "I'll sleep in their room tonight."

"I'll stay up for a bit, you get some rest," Thoran said to Rose.

"Hardly," Rose answered, "but I'll try."

The lot of them went back to the boys' room. Before jumping into their little beds, Alvis, Grumel and Achu pointed and grunted at the fairy door. "Take away?" their father simply asked. All except Ayell shook their heads yes. The boys happily watched as their father pried the door off. After the strange little door was gone, they quickly fell back to sleep.

The next morning, the little ones seemed to remember nothing, as if it never happened. It was the day of their second birth-date. It took two years, but after one said "achoo," on the day they were born, the next proper word spoken was "ouch," and that was by Alvis, after Grumel bonked his hand with a rattle. The others repeated "ouch," together. Except Joyal, who was fast asleep on the floor. Tho' he would have said "ouch," if he was awake.

"Grumel, do not bonk your brother or I will let him bonk you back," his mother said. Grumel folded his arms, giving his mother a look as if to say... I'll give him a what-for if he does! Alvis, tending to his pretend wound, thought…I'll get him! Yawnel, who was all smiles, grabbed his favorite ball of yarn and rolled it for anyone to grab. Shyel chased the ball, grabbed and held it. He didn't want to share. Joyal woke up and pointed to the ball of yarn. Playfulness quickly turned into a child's anger. Shyel hugged the ball and thought…mine!

All pointed to Shyel. The battle lines had been drawn. Alvis called to arms all warriors with the command, "HEEEEEAYOOOOO YIDGIT!"

Five little boys formed a line to attack. The sixth held the magic yidgit. The seventh, Ayell, peacefully minding his own business, now took notice of the commotion and came running to fortify the line. But first, to test their balance, he ran into them, unable to stop, crashing with a mighty thud! The other five went flying, landing in a twisted heap of arms and legs, and screaming five variations of ouch: oooch, eeoouch, yowwwch, houuwwsh, and a new one, wooohowoosh.

Spying the mess that Ayell made, sensing an escape route, the keeper of the yidgit dashed for safety. Must protect it… Shyel thought. A quick turn and Shyel found himself face to gam with his father's one thick leg. His father's other leg was strong, but not as thick. Realizing a new danger to the yidgit, Shyel backed away. With his hand out, Thoran demanded— "Please give me the ball, Grumel." Rose corrected him, "That's Shyel."

Ayell ran at Shyel. In a desperate move, Shyel sought out the only person who would value the yidgit as much as he—wonderful Aunt Zee. Throwing her the golden yidgit was the only way to save it. He paid no mind to the slop bowl she carried to feed the goats. With a mighty toss, the magic yidgit flew. In slow time, the yidgit bounced off many sets of little fingers before resting at the feet of Aunty Zee.

With the force of a waterfall, the six of them attacked the ball. Without time to react, Thoran could only scream, "Rose!" as all flowed into Aunt Zee, sending her well off balance. The slop bowl flew out of her hands, perfectly upright, as if in a trance, and hovered magically over Thoran's head. It turned over and thunked down, splatting thick goop on most of his head and shoulders.

It should have been funny, but there was no laughing throughout the woods. By his stare, no one could tell if Thoran was angry, happy, or embarrassed. As he stood there dripping with slop and smelling none the better, a goat wandered through the front door, looked at all and wondered… are we dining in tonight?

Momma alone started to laugh so hard, it echoed through the forest. Her laugh infected everyone and they joined her with hearty, pure, fun laughs that carried through the woods on sweet, swift winds. The sounds filtered far, far into the lands. Far past the warm, earthy colors that surrounded little babies, to a thick, dark world of hollowed out, dull and dead trees with scraggly, tall, leaf-less arms that reached to the sky, as if they sought help to pull them from the diseased land.

To where *she* lived. And *she* heard them. And she smelled them— and hated them. She wanted to end it, slowly and with misery.

She was another hag-witch—and the far-away, happy sound of the young family burned her ears. At her cave, she clenched one fist, while picking at her old skin covered with boiling warts and flea-like, fungal bugs called clivets. Her cave was well hidden. So well hidden that people didn't realize how close they came to being her pet's dinner. Though some did realize it, just much too late. For after being tricked, they'd wake up in a strange dark room, thick with an aroma of must and mead. The scared hostages had hope. That is, until they felt the breath of a faceless beast. The first bite was almost too shocking to be painful. The second bite brought reality. Their flailing and screaming made her laugh. She never watched her beasts feed, didn't have to.

Her name was Seena. And like Myrtle, Seena cringed at the sound of happy. It made her sick—and not the kind of sick that witches like.

"Little ones, little ones, tasty and fresh," she muttered as she grabbed a gritty, old, cracked wooden bowl. "Smalls and tasty, and bloody's they flesh," she cackled with a smirk and grabbed dead plants from a pocket. A stone pestle lay on the ground near the mouth of her cave. Seena scampered about while holding her bowl, fiddling with bits and adding them in. She scurried into the mouth of her cave and scurried back out, holding a small cage of trapped small animals, mostly mouselings and bats. She shook the cage; their tiny squeals threw tiny echoes. Her fingers cracked as her crusty hand reached into the cage and grabbed a small, nearly dead bat. Seena crushed its last breath and threw it into the bowl. Pieces of her remaining fingernails also fell in. More spices were sprinkled; then a mouseling—a very alive one. Alive until she squeezed its juices out. Into the bowl it went with more herbs.

Smiling, she spit, and what came from her mouth began to boil when it hit the muck. While smirking, she picked up a pestle and pushed it in the bowl chanting: "Seven little hearts, seven bloody meats." She paused, sniffed the air and continued:

"Slight of life, sick to linger, to their brain, from the finger,
Hearts to stay, so true for fear, of loss and pain, a bitter tear,
An infant smells of misery, the little ones to stay shall be,
Smaller and smaller, their hearts to be, wither away, the moon to fear."

Seven minutes after Seena heard the joyous laughter of seven little ones, a potion was made. Finished, she cackled with pride and spit into the bowl of grindings. In a shrill voice, she called to an empty sky, "Heeeere!" Quickly appearing, fluttering and jerking, came a long necked grackler—an ornery, funny looking little flying creature with small, thin wings.

The orange bird-thing fluttered up to Seena, who grabbed it and shoved it into the bowl, coating it with her gooey potion. She dropped the bowl to take hold of the grackler by the head, to open its mouth. With her thin pinky, she wiped a gob of potion off the grackler and shoved it down its throat.

"Go," she said while throwing it up in the air.

Seena closed her eyes and stopped breathing. In her mind, she could see the grackler fly away. Over the woodland, she watched as it flew. Over the treetops, Seena's eyes saw what the bird saw. She watched as it flew far to the cottage where the happy laughter bubbled out; the grackler stopped and floated above the happy homestead. Sometimes breathing, sometimes not, Seena smelled the smoke coming out of their chimney. She watched a soft rain cloud stray over the scene and a mother, pretty as a rose, walk from the cottage holding a pitcher to fill from the nearby well. The mother smiled to the sky, a smile that widened when she saw the colorful rain-cloud, high above. She didn't notice the grackler. The mother looked forward to a sun shower and laughed as the puffy, pink and grey cloud opened, gently letting go of its water. It would be her last laugh for a long time. Raindrops, passing over the grackler, grabbed bits of the potion and fell. Smiling, the mother held the pitcher up, as if to catch a tear from an angel above.

One drop was all it took. Seena knew the little ones would drink from the pitcher.

Chapter Seven

Fever

The first day they had the fever was the first day none of the seven could eat. By the second day they couldn't get out of bed. On that second night their eyes barely opened. Thoran rode hard and fast to fetch the doctor from Laban.

He came with his medicines, but they didn't work; so he could only try and comfort them. "I've never seen a fever as such," he said, "the damp from your cloth steams from their foreheads. And these rashes, they look like…moss. I'm baffled." The kind doctor stayed with them, but after only another day, he said, "We need a more… *powerful,* healer."

That same day, he went to implore the King's help. The King allowed counsel with his Grand Wizard, Sidaelf, of the Elden. The grand wizard, who rarely met anyone, asked but two questions of the doctor… "Did you say there are seven? And do you know if they were born on the night of the weeping crescent?" The doctor answered "yes" to the first. "And if it brings you to their cottage, then—yes, to the second." The answer of *seven* was enough to intrigue the old wizard. Sidaelf was as enlightened as any human could be, a sage, if you will. But still he was a man. Although the Spirits did not whisper to man, he knew there to be a prophecy of The Seven. That *"seven shall save all."* In his long life, he had never seen seven, nor had any of the known wizards met seven. Sidaelf's mortal life would soon be over. He was tempted by the doctor's tale, so he went.

The Grand Wizard wrapped himself in his simple gray cloth made of angelsilk and gently grasped his staff of dragon bone. "Come Neelie," as he called it a she, "Let us see if we can heal." To the doctor Sidaelf said, "I will ride with you. Give this herb to your mare, and with the wind, we will fly." He handed the doctor a pouch. The doctor was unsure how his horse would react to not only having two riders upon his back, but to whatever herb was in the pouch. The horse greedily ate the herb and the two healers mounted the horse. The horse ran so fast, it felt as if it flew.

While the doctor was gone, Rose, Thoran and Zee, were in pure distress. A mother and father who had lost so many: in the womb, many born still, and one Little Gem that wouldn't wake. They agonized. Rose would ask over and over again, "Oh Papa, why don't they wake? Why can't their eyes open? What have we done?" She knew that her strong husband had no more answers than she, though she needed to ask, as if an answer might come from the sky. Seven little hearts did all they could to continue beating. To live! Seven little boys couldn't see fear on their parents' faces, fear when little eyes barely opened as a shaky finger gently caressed a soft cheek.

Fear that a slight cough might be a last breath.

Sidaelf walked through the front door without knocking. He could only think of the prophecy as he went right to the boys' bedroom. As he entered, an essence of light followed him. Rose and Zee wept, while they hurriedly patted soft linens on the infants' foreheads. Thoran met Sidaelf with only the look of exhaustion. To Zee, the Grand Wizard said, "The aroma of lightning becomes you." Her eyes opened wide, and she sobbed harder.

"We don't know what to do," Zee cried, her mind thrown back to the day she made lightning speak. "I can't save them!" She grabbed her sister, "I'm so sorry, my love. I can't save them!" Thoran rushed to the girls, put his arms around them and pleaded for them to be calm.

Sidaelf went to each child and rested a hand on each forehead, nodding. His lips lightly moved, though he said nothing—he whispered to himself. He asked what their names were; the parents told them and he slowly spoke them. He looked to Zee again, then to the parents. "This reeks of evil!" He looked to the window. "Who else has seen these children?"

"No one," Rose said, "No one since they've been born."

"Only the doctor," Thoran added.

The wizard smiled and began to fumble in his pockets. "I can help," he said to the worried family. The wizard again thought of the prophecy. He remembered reading in old scriptures that the Good Mother's wisdom is just. "Flowing water," Sidaelf said. "We must take them to flowing water. I smell a stream. We must take the children to it." He picked up Ayell.

"Do you think that wise?" Rose said, reaching to touch Ayell, very concerned that any movement would surely cause them pain. "They're so...little." She wept harder. "I'm so afraid, sir. I don't know what to do."

Cradling Ayell, the smiling Grand Wizard showed him to Rose. "I can help, child," he softly said. Then harder, "This smells of a curse."

All gasped, and at the same time Thoran said, "But." Rose said, "No." Zee said, "How?"

"Sometimes we just don't know. Evil is...crafty. Tricky." Sidaelf answered, "These rashes. They don't seem natural. But we can't question right now. We must act! To the stream!" The old wizard had his suspicions that it could be a witch's curse, and he didn't wish to scare the parents any more than they already were. But before him, seven babies were still. And if they were the seven of the prophecy, then he had no choice but to help save them. He would use the rarest herb he had. There was but one pinch of it left, and he'd never have any more. He had held it for decades and chose to use it now.

Thoran, Rose and Zee each grabbed two babies, the wizard the seventh. The limp children barely uttered a sound as they were moved around. Once outside, at streamside, the wizard handed Ayell to the doctor and fumbled in his pockets, brought out two pouches and proceeded to pour them into the stream. From one pouch came only the smallest amount of powders. The shallow waters churned and turned a bright orange.

"They must be washed in the healing waters," Sidaelf said, "The Good Mother's tears are strong." He opened his hands to the sun. "Her light warms." He stepped into the stream, and motioned to all— "Come, hold them above." Quietly, the adults waded in and sat in the slow current, holding the babies so their bottoms were in the water. The old wizard generously splashed each child with the cool, orangeness. He rubbed the waters on their lips and on their noses. He took out a small parchment and read from it:

> *"Through her tears, through her,*
> *to coax a word, from the wind,*
> *for heart's song, for love's color."*

At once, the mossy rashes on each child started to fall off in bits. But still, the boys lay quiet. "The evil in them is strong," he said, "this *will* help."

Meanwhile, Seena stirred her boiling kettle and smiled; that is, until the slop in her kettle turned bright orange. She jumped back from her fire as if it burned her and looked around, expecting something to come at her. It was the first time it had ever happened; her potion was spoiled. "Curses," she spat and spat. "Curses an' curses!" She screamed, "What's dis all 'bout?" Confused, she walked around mumbling. The hag went to her cages where she kept beasts. "Sometin' happn'd. Sometin' messed wit my spell. MY SPELL!" she screamed. "Somebudy playin with." Her beasts stirred and growled in their cages. "They's gonna live," she seethed, "but I'll gets 'em. Don'ts wurry. They's gonna know misery. They's gonna know it but good."

Thoran and Rose dried the still sleeping babies and wrapped them in soft blankets. Their eyes would not open, but their breathing was better, and their skin looked healthier.

"Who could want this to happen?" Zee asked.

"Are they cured?" Rose asked.

Sidaelf looked at her and shook his head. "I'm sorry my dear, I don't know. Mayhaps there was something in what they ate, or some type of foul mist from the sky. Mayhaps we'll never know. And a curse? Could well have been. But they bathed in the most powerful of waters. They won't die from whatever they had, but I can't promise the fever won't come back." Sidaelf caressed the babies. "Let them rest. They'll wake when they're ready." The wizard thought...if these are *the* seven, the parents will know when the Good Mother sees fit. But I should only heal, and that's what I did, so let the family be a family, and I won't fill their heads with prophecies that may, or may not, become their fate.

Their fevers would cool, but the potion would stay in the boys' little bodies forever.

Meanwhile Council Master Angus Grimsdyke and Max had just finished putting a corpse in Grimsdyke's basement. "I don't know why you don't like it down here, Max," the Council Master said. "It smells a little, but it's a nice—homey room. Don't you think?"

"Air feelths wrong—don't like looking at them. We hurt them," Max answered.

"*They*—hurt me Max. Remember that. They... hurt... me. And that means they would have tried to hurt you. Let's see, there's Mr. Ferden—he looked at me wrong one day and I feared he would have attacked. And Miss Schlagel over there? Oops—Mrs. Shlagel, she

was a newlywed, lovely ring she had— she was going to steal from
us." Looking to his left, Grimsdyke snickered at a corpse with a sock
shoved in its mouth and said, "And how are you today, Mr. Loudmouth
Lennifer? My, you were a beast to bring down. Do you remember
him, Max? Do you? Do you remember *his* crime?"

"Yes, Masther," was all Max wanted to say. But Grimsdyke pressed
him.

"What did he do wrong? Max!"

"He was slow to feed your horsth, Masther."

"*HE*—was going to KILL my horse Max. Don't you remember?
How can you forget that? Think, Max. Don't be so stupid. Remember?
He was going to steal from me and kill my horse so I couldn't catch
him." Grimsdyke laughed. "You really are stupid, Max. Go upstairs and
get your scraps. Eat them out in the barn. Make sure no one tries to
kill any more horses."

"Yes Masther." Max climbed the stairs out of Grimsdyke's 'special
room' thinking...I am stupid, but I don't like it down here. Max also
knew that none of the corpses committed any crime, but he was too
afraid to say anything; Max did as he was told.

Grimsdyke shook his head in disgust and walked up to ol' Basilton
Cline— his oldest corpse. "Hello, Bazey," Grimsdyke said, "I brought
you another companion. This one had a whole pocketful of gold."
Grimsdyke's right hand tossed up a pouch holding his victim's gold
chips and caught it with his left. To his dead friends he said, "Now, let's
see who else will be trying to hurt us."

Chapter Eight

A Hairy Stranger

Neighbors were far and few between, and visitors to their cottage were rare. Most stumbled onto Rose and Thoran's home while traveling along the ancient road to the coast from Laban or other towns. Some just hoped for a meal. After the boys were with fever, the doctor from Laban would frequent their cottage. Sometimes a surveyor might show up to collect the King's fee, or to keep woodland folks up on goings on; or a holy man might visit to deliver a sermon on the virtues of loving your family and respecting the Good Mother above. There were no nearby families known to Thoran; the children played with no others.

Rose and Thoran were always polite, but they never wanted strangers staying too long. Thoran, always wary, always watching, had at least one hand ax strapped to him—always.

One day, Ayell heard strange rustlings and sounds coming from the woods— clanking and squeaks. He wondered why no one else could hear them. Animal sounds and a voice were heard. The sounds became louder, as did the voice, and they came from the front trail to their cottage. A very large man came to visit. He came traveling on a large mule, with a second, smaller donkey towing a cart filled to the brim with all sorts of odds and ends that jangled as he clomped towards the cottage. "Keep up, Spike!" the man screamed.

Hearing strange words and clanging, Thoran popped his head out a window, recognized the man immediately and bellowed, "Stanley Shniggleton! It's good to see you my friend."

"Thoran!" the man answered excitedly. "I know you have your

hands full, haven't seen you in a while, so I hope you don't mind—but I brought my store to you!"

From inside the cottage came excited shouts and calls. Within a few clock ticks, a flood of a family gushed out the front door. Seven little boys rushed to greet the stranger and his strange stuff. The boys had never seen a mule before. Rose, Zee and Thoran followed.

"What's that?" Joyal and Shyel asked, speaking about the weird looking horses.

"Boys, girls, meet Mr. Stanley Shniggleton, the master potter," Thoran said with a bit of pride, and not answering the question just asked. A master potter is what Mr. Shniggleton had become in his later years; his youth was spent battling, killing and be-heading any beast that threatened good people. The seven boys stared—as he was a big, burly sight to be seen.

"We've met on one occasion, Mr. Shniggleton," said Zee. At the same time Rose said, "The pleasure is ours."

"He's a very, very hairy man papa," said Grumel.

Zee gasped and screamed, "Grumel! Mind your mouth!"

"He's a hairy potter," Achu laughed.

Before Rose could reprimand her child, Stanley said, "No, no, young lady, quite alright. The boy is right. I am quite the gruffly one," and turning to the rest while parting his hair so his eyes could be seen... "Boys, I *am* a hairy potter. Stanley Shniggleton is me name and friends call me Shniggles," he paused, "I hope you will too." Everyone smiled. "I have a shop in Laban, but I had an idea to cart some of my wares to the folks around. And this is a stop I *must* make. To my good friend Thoran! Gather round little men. There just might be something in me cart for ya's." The boys ran to the cart. "Look to the very back," Shniggles said, "There's a set of knock-em pins and a ball. Go set the pins up and try to roll the ball to knock 'em down. It's one of the favorites." The boys grabbed the set of wooden pins and the ball and quickly took to this new game.

While the boys played, Shniggles noticed that Ayell had not yet found his voice. He looks like he's laughing, Stanley thought, but he makes no sound, so he asked, "Don't you like the game, little one?" Ayell shook his head up and down furiously, but offered no words. "What's the matter, can't you speak?"

With a broad smile, Alvis answered for his brother, "He don't know, he ain't never tried. Don't matter none, we know what he means." And that was a fine answer, so Shniggles never wondered about it again. From that day on, Shniggles would become one of their best friends.

"Come," said Thoran, "a quick tour of the cottage. A castle it's not, our four rooms are just enough."

Rose added, "Our cottage is a member of our family, every bit as important as an arm, leg or a nose."

Inside the cottage, Shniggles admired their favorite painting, The Seven Castles of Elberon. "A gift," Thoran said, "to my aspiring artists." He bowed to the girls. The painting hung true on the staircase wall. It was not large, and the minute detail of the seven castles nestled in a lush forest enthralled the seven little ones. Each boy had claimed a castle of his own in his little mind. Tiny windows stared at them. Teeny, but grand staircases led to magical doors that begged opening. Quite often, each of them would sit and stare at the artwork, lost in simple, but deep thoughts.

The boys came bursting in, screaming, "Wanna see our horse?" He couldn't resist. Shniggles followed them outside.

Pointing to a pool near a stream in their backyard, Yawnel said, "That's our bathing hole where Momma scrub, scrub, scrubs us clean," Grumel laughed.

"An Papa's teaching us not to sink," Shyel added.

"It is important not to sink," Shniggles laughed.

After a bit more of touring the garden, Zee asked, "Can you stay for bit?"

"I must be moving on soon, more to visit, more to see," he said.

"Oh, but before I forget, I'm to let you know the head of the Laban City Council, Council Master Grimsdyke, might pay folks around here a visit. He didn't tell me when or why."

"Who?" Zee asked.

"What's a Grimsdyke?" Alvis asked.

"It's a *who*," Stanley said, "The council makes the rules for the city. He's like the leader of it, but all members are important. It's called, politics... you'll learn about it someday."

"Wonder what he wants?" Thoran wondered.

"Watch out for that Grimsdyke, never trusts him, he's a bit— curious," Stanley said. "The visit could come next week, or next month. He wanted me to tell everyone I visit, that he might stop by. He didn't say why, he just asked me to send the message."

"Well, we'll keep a lookout," said Thoran, "and he is a curious sort of guy," knowing full well what Shniggles meant. "I remember first meeting Grimsdyke—the man with one crimson eyetooth, or 'the red fang', as the town's children call him. That fang makes him look a bit— off. Wouldn't you say?"

"I would say," Shniggles laughed.

"A fang? Like a tooth?" Shyel asked.

"Yep. A dark, red one. Looks a bit— off," Shniggles said, while winking at Thoran. Thoran remembered that day well, as Grimsdyke had stared at him, even as he walked away. And every chance meeting after, he would catch Grimsdyke staring after him. The Council Master was always polite, but creepy. "Probably looking for money of some sort," Thoran said.

"Well, can't expect the King to pay for all the towns' services now, can we?" added Shniggles.

Yawnel asked, "Where's the King live?"

"Ohhhh!" Stanley enthusiastically said, "Your papa never told you, eh?" Thoran raised his brow, shook his head, and motioned for Shniggles to continue. "Well, the King, he lives amongst the

Thundorians." The boys became very interested in his words. "You see, there're small towns like Laban, Geiselton and Skeersabolski— each with their own fun little flavor of people. But the greatest of cities, at least in my opinion, is Thundor-on-Sea." Shniggles became animated… "Rising from the depths of the Algaen Sea, higher than the highest of mountains, are the Cliffs of Mauleron, and carved, chiseled and sculpted into the steepest of the cliffs is the fortress city itself— Thundor-on-Sea," he said with clenched fists shaking in the air. "The city has never been breached."

"What?" three of the boys asked. They didn't understand all of his words, but they loved the way he talked.

"Uhhhh, broken into," Thoran said. Stanley continued.

"Thundor reaches high above and deep into the cliffs. And the Thundorians are storied to be descendants of the ancient high-beings, with powerful mysteries running as deep as the city's tunnels. And chiseled into the highest of walls is the decree handed down by the ancients." In a deeper voice, Shniggles commanded, "And it reads— a humankind civilized society shall have a fair and justly satisfied majority, and of this majority shall not oppress any humankind minority nor friendly beings to beasts, all shall be loyal for the good of our society. Any and all horrible acts against humankind and of the friendly ones shall promptly be rewarded with like kind act and or death. It is written…it is done." Shniggles clapped and said, "Well… I'm off!"

"Whooaa, whoa, hey!" seven boys screamed, "What do ya mean!" The seven spoke on top of each other, asking questions that couldn't be understood.

"Stop," Zee screamed, "one at a time."

Grumel pleaded, "Tell us more about the Thundorians."

"Your father will take it from here boys, I really have to get going. I'll be back someday."

Their hairy friend gathered his bits. Ayell stroked Spike the mule and sneezed the loudest sneeze ever. A flood of boogers and spit flew from his face, splattering three of his brothers. "Oy! Cover yur face when you do that!" screamed Shyel.

Without thinking, Alvis said, "Yeah, you got that shniggly stuff all over us!"

The boys stared at each other and burst into laughter. They hoped their new friend hadn't heard them, but he had, and he too laughed, as he realized the seven little ones just renamed their boogers, 'shniggles'. And that was just fine by him.

Chapter Nine

Getting Older

The seasons changed, and the boys embraced the shifting temper-
atures with the enthusiasm of getting a new toy. It was always
warm around the time of their birth-date, then frosty mists would
come, bringing fresh, cool winds that would stiffen the grasses and
make icy-skin on the trees. "One day," Thoran said to them, "we'll take
a trip to the mountains where there's snow as high as you all."

By four years old their playing became intense. Their running,
climbing, and throwing, quickly turned into all out war. They still liked
the knock-em down pins that Shniggles brought them, and they really
enjoyed bucket ball. It didn't matter what they played, everything
always turned into a seven-boy brawl. So a game of bucket ball quickly
became 'bucket-brawl'. And knock-em pins became 'knock-him-
with-a-pin'.

One day, while Rose and Thoran watched their children play, she
said, "It's time for them to learn their letters and numbers. We shall
prepare them well, so they'll flourish when we take them to the Islands
of Learning."

"Still a few years away from that—let them play," Thoran added,
"The great halls of Wormwood's Mysterium or Tegeders' School of
Enchantments, or Sorcery or, uh... Survival or...whatever it is...can
wait."

"I know," Rose half-scolded, "but they're never too young to learn."

Reading and writing would be as competitive as a sport to them.
Their spongy little minds were amazed when they first realized
that "letters," as Zee would say, "when planted, sprout into words,

with limbs that grow into sentences, and everything flourishes into a paragraph. And a family of paragraphs blossom's into a story." To keep their young attention, most stories involved battling dragons and other beasts. Things that terrify men, children are only curious about; things that frighten those with experience fascinate those with none.

"As long as they are learning *something*," Thoran would say.

By age five, the boys were building castles made of mud, branches and twigs—large enough to hold them all and strong enough to thwart attacks from the mightiest of foes.

During that time, the boys were given special axes Thoran made especially for them; mighty little hatchets to chop down massive trees, to build stronger castles. On their own, the boys began to make crude weapons and tools for play. And every couple of days, they drew blood. Though never on purpose—mostly. They ran fast, climbed high and threw hard and far, for just pure fun. Throughout their young years, they learned from and of the forest; they became one with the woodland, and claimed it as their own. It was Achu's Angry-Land, or Ayell's Dark Magical Land, or the Mysterious Woods of Grumel. Yawnel nicknamed his part of the woodland Grimm's Forest, a name that all of them liked, and frequently used as their own.

Their sixth birthday was most special. At daybreak, they woke to a ruckus of clomping and snorting. Their hairy friend, Shniggles, brought seven ponies of all different colors. It was amazing when the excited little horses each chose a boy of its own.

He also brought them a new game. "This, my boys, is your first Grimmage Clan," he said while unpacking some very interesting things from the back of his cart. Grabbing bits of wood, he said, "The ancient sport of building, defending and destroying castles. It's very popular in the towns and schools. These are for the towers we'll build." He threw them to the side, fumbled around, and said, "These flags mark the 'lines of reckoning.'" He threw them aside, fumbled again and said, "And here's the scrumble!" He pulled out a strange ball, the shape of a watermelon, seven and one-half inches long. He threw it to Grumel, who caught it and looked at it curiously. The rest, also curious, picked up the other bits.

Shniggles explained the purpose—to defend your castle before it is destroyed— but the boys barely listened. They quickly took off and made up their own game while he set up the playing field in the front garden. The 'castles' were simple wood beams set up on four legs. Two were made and placed at opposite ends of the field. "They look like your sawhorse's Pa!" Achu screamed.

"In the bigger games they make bigger castles," Shniggles said, "but the main thing is that each castle must have two turrets."

"What's a turdet?" Shyel asked.

"A turrrr-et," Alvis corrected, "that's the small bits on top of the bigger bits, right?"

"Very good young man," Shniggles said, and he placed two small blocks on each end of the top bit. Flags were placed in front of each castle and Shniggles said, "In the big area between the flags, the scrumble can only be kicked with your feet—no hands! Throw us the ball." Grumel threw the scrumble to Shniggles, who stopped it with a foot and quickly began to lightly tap, tap it towards a castle. "This is called 'dribbling', boys."

Achu laughed, "Ha. Joyal dribbles when he talks!"

"I'll dribble your head!" Joyal answered.

The ball couldn't roll true because of its shape. It waddled like a duck. Shniggles continued dribbling towards one of the castles. "Two of you go stand in front of that castle," he said. All seven ran and stood at the ready. "Now," he said while lightly tapping the ball towards them. "When you pass the line of reckoning," he said while pointing at the flag, "only then can you pick up the scrumble," which he did. "Once you pass the line, you try and destroy the castle." Stanley Shniggleton ran the last few feet hard at the boys, screaming. He scared them. When they moved, he threw the scrumble hard at the castle, completely missing it. Shniggles smiled at them. They got the point.

Shyel ran and grabbed the scrumble. He threw it at the castle, hitting one leg; half the castle broke and fell. Part of it remained.

"Very good," Shniggles said, "but you have to completely destroy the castle. Okay. Form two teams of three. One on each team stay in front of your castle, the other four start the game in the middle of the field. Don't use your hands until you pass the lines."

"That's only six," Alvis said.

"Aha," Stanley said, "that's a fun little twist when you have an odd numbers of players. The odd man is the prisoner. He can escape and run onto the field. The prisoner is like a wild man. He can destroy either castle. And if he does, both teams lose, and he wins. So if you play with a prisoner, watch out for him."

To the boys, Grimmage was grand. And between Grimmage and their new ponies, their sixth birthday was the best birthday ever. Until the next one.

Seven Years Old

Their seventh birth-date neared, and one thing was obvious—their wonderful growth in every aspect of life, reading, writing, throwing, climbing, did not carry over to their height. The boys were—short.

The parents knew their boys would grow stronger and wiser. And only rarely did the parents consider that the fever the little ones suffered through such a long time ago had any effect on their height. And they couldn't even begin to consider that an evil hag-witch's spell cast from a single drop of rain lived within them.

"Perhaps they will be late sprouts," Aunt Zee would say. In his travels, Thoran took notice of other children. He and Rose knew their boys lacked only height and nothing else. "Perhaps they will, Zee. Though height will have no bearing on their happiness," Thoran said... a thought shared by the three adults.

Thoran was a tall man by the standards of the day and Rose was of a mother's height—smaller than Thoran and larger than the boys. Zee was the same height as her sister, but it was difficult to see the resemblance as her flowing red hair and striking green eyes were miles away from Rose's deep blue eyes framed by her thick, long waving locks of dark hair. Her *squiggly* hair, as Zee and the boys would joke. Ayell especially loved twirling his fingers within his mother's hair, because he had none. He wasn't envious of the tangly-looking stuff that grew atop his brothers' noggins. But momma's hair was something special to him.

On their seventh birth-date, Thoran woke before sunup to gather all things necessary for what he had been waiting seven years for— their first fishing adventure! He was eager and overjoyed just thinking about sharing this day with his offspring. He whistled while packing sacks with bits and gubbins, tackle and food. Rose hoped to wait until the boys were a bit older, but Thoran persuaded her they were old enough for the adventure.

"You will be careful? Do not let them out of your sight!" Momma half-scolded... "Do not become a child yourself. And please..."

"Honey," he interrupted. She stared and waited for him to start his sentence so she could finish it.

"My love, no harm will come to our little men." For three ticks of silence, they stared at each other.

"Children," she said, "they are children. They know little of the forest. They don't know what to be careful of. Angling or fishing or whatever, they can't..."

"Their instincts are strong," Thoran again interrupted, and a bit louder, "And they *can*. You know I hate that word— *can't*." At the same time he cupped her hands in his and pledged, "We'll return with a grand feast."

With a quick, reluctant nod of her head, her eyes slightly closed, it was settled. "Wake up boys," she said while walking up the stairs.

Twelve eyes were open before their mother and father walked into their room; they overheard their parents talking about them. Joyal was always the last to wake up. He seemed to truly never fully wake up and it amused his parents how he performed all chores asked of him with his eyes typically half closed.

"Fishing?" Grumel asked. They had heard Papa talk about this, he was usually excited.

All at once, six boys asked—

"Where we goin' Pa?" asked Alvis.

"What we doin' Pa?" asked Yawnel.

"When we eatin Ma?" asked Achu.

"Who's goin' Pop?" asked Grumel.

"What's goin' on?" Joyal asked while stretching.

"How we…oh never mind," Shyel finished.

The simultaneous questions made it impossible for one answer. Ayell was already out of the bedroom, down the stairs and ready at the front door, clapping his hands and jumping up and down. Thoran could barely contain his own excitement, "First a quick meal. Then we're off!" The boys were buzzing and restless, they quickly ate hearty bowls of sugared porridge and milk. Their chatter was layered with bits of anxiety about the unknown. It was the first time the boys and their mother would be apart. They never had to hug goodbye, and when the time came, it felt awkward. When the 'goodbye' happened, at least twenty-one "I love you's," were said.

They decided not to take the horses, walking would be more fun.

Rose and Zee watched the boys head into the seldom used back path. Quickly the little men were out of their sight for the first time.

While crying, the two sisters went inside to prepare for their return.

Chapter Ten

The Dragon's Claw

Seven boys jabbed hiking sticks into mossy ground while swinging little sacks filled with bread, apples and nuts. Their father had a larger sack and two water pouches slung on his back. He stayed at the end, keeping watch to the front and sides. After seventy or so paces, the boys were further away from their cottage than they had ever been. As they walked, they looked back in quick turns, amazed as their home shrank. Fourteen little eyes were wide with curiosity.

"Now will you tell us where we goin' Papa?" Grumel quizzed.

"How long will it take us to get there?" asked Achu.

"Is it scary? Will we see elves or gobles?" asked Joyal.

Ayell pulled on his father's shirt and rubbed his little belly, smiling.

"We've just begun, it's too early to eat," Thoran said. "Now hush up all, and listen, I've a story to tell about where we're going."

"Will we see trolls or ogres, Pa?" asked Shyel.

"Or dragons, giants, witches or grimlers?" asked Alvis.

"How do you know about all these things?" Thoran asked surprised. "Did Shniggles say anything to you at his last visit?"

Alvis confessed, "We hear you and Momma talk about things, but we only hear bits a what you say."

"We don't hear much, but we hear that ogres and them lot ain't good," added Yawnel.

Thoran looked at his boys and wondered... what could they have overheard? They'd told them tall tales and bedtime stories of some harmless creatures, maybe a dragon here or there, but they were careful not to bring too many monsters into their stories. He and Rose decided they would have to start talking about these things, agreeing the trip to the Claw would be their first proper discussion. Thoran knew he could have fun with the boys, talking about monsters and things; just not too much fun. "Please do not say *ain't*. Speak properly," he said.

The boys looked at him. A proper speaking lesson was the last thing they'd pay attention to, he thought, smiling. He continued, "There's always a chance of meeting up with anything in the woodland." That got their interest. "Though it is a warm, dry, bright day and orcs an' those sort mostly don't like this weather." Thoran looked around, "The sun burns them, not good weather for beasts and monsters. But if it gets cloudy..." The boys looked to the sky. Puffy clouds were far away.

Together, six asked, "Where we goin' Pa?" Ayell shook his head.

"Well, we're going to the Dragon's Claw."

Together, the boys said, "Whoaaa."

"And as the tale was passed on to me, it was built by the ancient elves and good folk to trap ogres, trolls and mullogs that came to battle." That was enough to stop fourteen little legs in their places. Inwardly, Thoran laughed; outwardly, he maintained a serious look.

"Trap?" three of the seven asked.

"Trick them?" Alvis asked.

"Keep walking, boys." Their father continued—"For years and years the good people feared an attack from outside the Reach by ogres or other beasts. The ogres had already eaten an elf queen. And men, women and children were snatched from their sacred home-lands and never heard from again. Tens upon thousands of good folk and beings had been taken as slaves for the ogres. No one, or thing, was safe—as the story goes." Thoran paused and looked around.

"That's the storied history of the unknown lands outside of The Reach, boys. Throughout ancient times, most battles were against the ogres and other evil kinds as they tried to conquer all." The boys again stopped, stared at each other, and digested what they were hearing.

"Keep walking," their father commanded. The line moved. "So the elves, with the help of men, dwarves and other good beings, planned to use the forest as their weapon. Elves had special beasts of burden, called' em aligars. They'd..."

"Beasts of what?" Alvis asked.

"Burden," Thoran answered. "Strong beasts they used to move things. And carry things. They went to war with them, too. And the elves and others rode them—like horses. They were fast. And they were loyal. Most would have only one master for their whole lives.

"They were bigger than horses, much stronger, much smarter. They had long noses like the tuskers, and strong mouths. Anyway, the goodly folk, with the help of the aligars, moved earth, gouged and dug out a ginormous hole to trap their enemies. The hole was in the shape of a crescent, though the woodland folk said it looked more like a dragon's claw— hence the name. They moved trees and brush, making natural looking trails leading to the empty, claw-shaped hole. I was also told they dug trap holes throughout the forest, deep pits of no escape. And a massive underground tunnel was dug, a tunnel that just about connected a river to the giant hole. If the plan was to work, the ogres would be drawn into the claw, the mighty river would be unleashed and those caught would be drowned."

Again, the boys stopped and turned to their father, all with the same thought voiced by Grumel, "So there're dead ogres where we're goin'?"

"And you want us to eat something out of this lake?" asked Achu.

Smart... Thoran thought. "Well, the main point of the story is that the ogres never came." The boys stopped walking again, looked at their father with a bit of disappointment and pondered that last revelation. "No wars. No battles. No eating of anyone," their father proclaimed. At least not here... he thought. "They were defeated long before they ever got around to these parts. Now let's keep moving."

"What happened to them?" asked Joyal. Ayell was shaking his head.

"Who cares what happened as long as they're gone," said Alvis.

"What if they're not gone?" asked Shyel.

"What if they're hiding and just watching and waiting to trap us!" asked Yawnel.

They turned to look at their father, four of the seven asked "Are they gone Pa?"

Confident, Thoran answered, "Yes. They're gone, now keep walking." With that statement, a father closed his eyes and quickly drew in a quiet breath, exhaled and sighed. His first lie to his children hurt him. Thoran didn't know if all ogres and their like were dead. He suspected they were not. At this point in the boys' young lives, he, Rose, and Zee thought it best to tell the children there were no ogres. Along the eastern Algaen seaboard, no monsters had been seen; they were defeated centuries ago. Oh, there was a witch or two, a small dragon here or there, maybe a warty troll, but no ogres. That's why he and Rose were brought there as babies.

Joyal asked, "When you said they eat everything, Papa—"

"Would they eat people?" Alvis and Shyel finished. All stopped and turned towards their father, looks of fear spread on their little faces.

"How 'bout people Pa?" Yawnel asked.

To that, Thoran wouldn't lie about. "Yes," he simply stated, "but don't you worry, they were killed a long time ago. And if one rears its ugly head, well, I'll do this—" and Thoran quickly ran to the nearest small tree, jumped up on it as high as he could, grabbed its wooden arms and attacked it whilst screaming the silliest of sounds. Surprised at their father's silly anger, the boys burst into full belly laughs. Seeing their father clearly outmatched, they ran to help kill the evil tree ogre. Attacking the tree quickly led to attacking each other and after only a few clock ticks, a full-scale brawl happened. The boys threw sticks and brush at each other. Thoran beat upon the tree with mock anger.

Achu screamed, "The family that slays together stays together!" The others shouted their approval. Thoran thought…that'll take their minds off ogres. After the evil attackers were defeated, the boys calmed down and got back into formation.

Joyal asked, "What's that, Papa?" as he pointed to a small plant with no leaves, just a light brown bulb on its top.

"That's a brown wart plant, very poisonous. When they get older, they turn a dark red. Never touch 'em, especially when they're red. Like that one," and he pointed to one whose stalk was definitely older and whose head was red.

"Look at those," Grumel said, pointing to a patch of dark yellow flowers that opened and closed as if keeping time like a clock. The boys thought they were butterflies, but then realized they were plants.

They walked and talked about animals and creatures of the woodlands. And as they walked, the boys' world grew. Faraway vistas magically sprouted from pockets of land without trees. They quickened their pace. New colors, odd sounds and different smells greeted them at every turn, sometimes silencing them. Everything seemed different from those around their cottage. Trees, grasses, bugs were all—different.

Sensing their wonder, their father said, "The woodland is always changing. Every time you walk past the same tree or rock, it will probably look different to you. That's what happens as you get older." The boys sensed sadness in their father; it lasted a few clock ticks.

Around one turn, a sight stopped them; they bumbled into each other with grunts of "Woah!" A massive tree with odd, braided limbs stood before them. The tree was in the midst of bushes filled with purple berries; it was the largest tree they had ever seen. It only had a few leaves, however those few leaves were enormous, each as large as their cottage. The leaves were splashed with colors and had golden veins in their center. And its great, coiled limbs reached out — to other trees, to the clouds, to all around. In awe of the magnificent tree, Alvis asked, "Can we climb that Pa?" The others quickly answered, "Yes!"

"Another trip boys. Keep moving."

"What kind of tree is th…th…th…th… thaaaaaachoooooo…That?" asked Alvis while wiping his nose on his sleeve.

"I never found out its proper name," Thoran answered, "I keep meaning to ask about it in Laban. Beautiful, isn't it?" Beyond the enormous tree with huge leaves, a small hill rose. It was off the path they were on. Smallish trees and thick brush were scattered about this hill and a faint, sporadic rumbling could be felt.

"It kind of makes my feet tingle," Alvis said.

"Grumblers Hill, I call it. Probably has an underground waterfall or something," their father said.

When Grumel asked how that could be, Thoran answered, "Well, remember there's more we don't know about the woodland than do know. As much as we can see, there's much, much more we can't see." Their father's words made the boys wonder. Shyel envisioned a vast underground world of caves and creatures. Yawnel pictured an underground castle. Ayell felt his stomach rumble, but was preoccupied with the wonderful sights.

They walked and talked about giants, ogresses and dragons. They saw their first grimler, a small one, rooting about the ground. "What's that?" asked Grumel.

"That, boys, is a grimler. See, they're like pigs, but they grow to all different shapes and sizes. The largest one I caught weighed over seven hundred pounds. The smallest can fit in your pocket. They're not friendly and they can make sounds like other beasts. That's how they draw in their prey. And they eat anything. Let's keep walking and hope its momma is *not* around." Thoran squeezed his hand axe.

They joked about snakes, slugs, bumblers, and saw a large winged insect with many dangly legs flit around, then land on a small tree in front of them. When it landed, it folded its wings and blended into the tree, mimicking a branch. Thoran quietly walked up to the strange bug and grabbed it. The boys yelled, "Hey!" Before they could express more shock, their father brought the bug to his mouth and bit what they thought was its head, quickly crunching, smiling and swallowing. Unable to speak, they looked at their father as if he had three heads. "It's delicious," Thoran said.

"That's terrible!" Shyel said, "Why'd you do that?"

"Those bugs are called twiglets," Thoran said, "and they're one of the few bugs you can eat. They're very good. Wanna try?" He thrust the 'twig thing' in front of them; his boys backed away. "No way," they all screamed.

Except for Ayell. He was hungry. He walked up to his father and put his hand out. Smiling, Thoran placed the insect in his hand, "Just take a little bite, it's good, you'll see."

Ayell sniffed the bug and defiantly looked at his brothers. He bit the bug with gusto and chomped. Then he spat it out all over the place. He spat and spat and spat. His brothers laughed. Ayell stuck a finger in his nose and pretended to pull out a gob.

Alvis laughed, "He says it tastes like a shniggle!" they all laughed, even Thoran.

"Never mind. Well, there's no other bugs that look like them, so in a pinch, you can eat them." Ayell still spat.

That little episode led Thoran to continue talking about what could be eaten and what, under no circumstances, should be touched. The boys paid close attention, but there was too much for them to grasp in that first outing.

Thoran started whistling a song he knew, a song he sang when he went to the mines. Whistling always intrigued the boys. Papa said that whistling while you walk or work makes both go quicker, so it was time for them to learn. Seven little men puckered, spit, drooled and blew; they made every sound except a whistle. They tried for quite a spell, until they were bored and all puckered out.

Through winding trails they walked, scuttled and hopped; over fallen branches, through spongy patches, near edges of land that dropped down and down. Coming upon a slight incline that led to a wide-open expanse of colorful valley, the vast land before them moved and breathed, quieting the boys. In the hazy distance, mountains covered with rainbow colored forests gently shimmered. Closer to them were trees that seemed clothed in flame. And what looked like specks floating across blue-green skies, were actually flocks of birds, also swaying with unseen gusts of wind. The boys knew that the trees in the horizon had to be huge, but to them, they looked like blades of grass.

Far into the valley, though not as far as the mountains, glistening pools or rain puddles sparkled. As if reading their little minds, Thoran said, "Those aren't puddles boys. They're the Wells of Magog. Anything that falls into them turns into a horrible creature. Poisoned pools they are."

"Are we going there Pa?" asked Yawnel.

"They're many, many days away," he said, "legend has it giant serpents swim in them. Magic tongues they're storied to have. *'Brew the serpent's tongue, always stay young,'* so the tale goes. No, we'll be staying straight ahead." They looked at the inviting path back into a forest.

While walking, the boys scoured the forest, wondering... are we being watched? There were many places where things could hide, many sights, definitely unseen. It sure felt like something was watching. They mostly stared up and around as they walked. They didn't notice below them the trail became thinner and thinner. The forest subtly crowded upon them. Branches and leaves started to tickle them. Although it was still early morning, the sun poked its finger-like rays all over, and shadows covered the ground. Through bits of sky that peeked through thick treetops, flashes of fluttery things were seen. Birds? Bat-wings? The boys couldn't tell. Walking in a huddled line, they frequently crunched into each other, sending either those in front, or those in back lurching. Only Thoran and Ayell heard the slight sound of babbling water. They came to a small opening and stopped—a large rock formation blocked their way, save for a slim passage through the craggy hill.

"They built that, didn't they?" Shyel asked, "Them gnome things."

Alvis screamed, "It's a trap, Pa!"

Joyal blurted, "I'm not goin' in there."

Their father surveyed the area. "Well, there's no other way in, we have to move forward." The boys looked for a way around the blockage; they hoped not to have to trek through the sliver of darkness between two small mountains.

"You go first," five of the seven demanded as they pushed Ayell. Their quiet brother sneered at his cowardly siblings.

"I'll go first," Thoran said. Then quieter, "Stay close men, for no one knows what luurrrrrks beyond yonder wall of stone." Into the dark passage they went, seven little men led by one large. "This *might* be a trap, make sure you keep a keen eye to the sky and ground. These are old passages, built a long time ago, careful of loose rocks." The seven looked up. "Careful of holes." They looked down. "Careful of what's following." They looked back.

Shyel said, "Yu...yu...you're just trying to scare us, ain't you Pa?"

"Braaaaaaaaackkk," came an angry squawk that made them yelp and jump forward, all but knocking down their father.

"It's only a grackler, nothing to worry about, boys."

They slowly crept through the passage. Around a sharp corner, a bright white blocked their view. Their father, knowing what was ahead, said, "Well this certainly must have taken them a long time to build." He picked up the pace, the boys followed... "and tireless hours of pain and hardship must have been endured." The boys thought their father's tone a bit odd, and more than a bit scary... "Can you feel it?" he said. They couldn't, they were only feeling nervous. "Can you smell it?" The boys sniffed, but smelled only dirt. Bursting out of the passage, their father screamed in a loud, booming voice, "Fear not, me boys, for the Dragon's Claw awaits," and with a wide sweep of his arm, as if flinging a wizards wand blasting bright colors, a magical sight opened before them. A sight that made seven boys exclaim slowly and deeply, "hhhhhhooo." And no one realized it, but the usually silent Ayell participated with a gasping exclamation.

A magnificent, glistening, sparkly lake, surrounded by thick, colorful mountainy cliffs lay before them. Even from a distance, they saw water lapping at enormous, chiseled-stone walls built into the foot of the hills. Its odd, crescent shape became clear. The boys held their breath for a clock tick, and watched as the sight came alive.

Trees bordering the water stood guard in perfect position, their leaves waving hello. Flocks of blue-white starlings, green and greener sparrots, and fire-orange hawks squealed and flew in patrols, barely above the water, upward into the forest and sky. Broad arrows of sunlight beamed from above, bounced off the water and shot back into the forest, landing where no one could see. The sound of a running river was heard. Water slapping the ground along edges of the Claw made bluish bubbles float…then quickly pop! And the water—oh did the water have colors! Blues, greens and blacks melted into each other forming ever-changing hues, with hints of gold and silver—or were those fish darting just under the surface? It didn't matter, the colors were playing. Pointing to the center of the lake, their father said, "This path leads us down to that clearing. That's where we'll set up camp for the day."

They ran to the lake, Thoran walked briskly, all grinned with excitement. At the clearing, faint rainbow colors noticed from afar were actually lush grasses along the shoreline. The boys tread slowly on it, savoring its soft, pillowy feel.

The clearing ended at a thick rock wall holding in the great lake. They ran to the wall and jumped on it to peer into the water. Their father commanded, "Boys!" He paused while they turned to him. "Beyond that wall lies cold, deep water. And within that water are creatures that I know little about. Most of them are tasty. Some are dangerous. Do *not* enter the water. Over there is a shallow beach area where we can wet our feet."

"Look!" Shyel screamed, pointing to their left where the retaining wall sloped down and met the slapping water. What he saw was a large dead tree, upon which sat a gathering of orange, big-toothed terrapins that slowly turned their heads to hear what was disturbing their serene surrounding. The dead tree was the terrapins' station, a resting point on their way to deeper water.

"Look at those teeth!" Joyal said.

"Do they bite Papa?" asked Achu.

"Only if you roll around in dead fish," Thoran answered.

Grumel made a sharp move, and with heavy plunks the colorful terrapins scattered into the water —slight swirls followed.

"Now," Thoran said, "I'll unpack the gear and we'll soon be ready. You can explore a bit— but stay within sight of me and do *not* go into the forest. I won't take long to unpack." He pointed to the nearby forest that began at the point of the crescent. With those words the boys took a half step back, looked around and at each other, smiled and scattered in seven different directions, excited, screaming. They quickly regrouped to explore in small groups.

Thoran watched and smiled. He stared and just took in the sights, drifting into a happy memory of the first time he was brought to the Claw. Their wonderful, loving caretakers, a very special family of wood sprites, first brought him here. That day, he came without his future bride; she was on her own adventure—to the coast of the Algaen Sea. He wasn't much older than his boys and he had explored in the exact same way. And quite possibly, those same terrapins sat on that same log. Sadly, the wood-sprites left shortly after that happy day.

Enough daydreaming, he thought. He unpacked his sack and laid out all the bits and pieces needed for the task at hand. During their walk, he explained how hooks, nets, and hand lines were all made from different portions of the ginkash tree—a tree known for its strength. Strands carefully pulled from its wet bark were tied end on end forming line of any size. Not only were nets woven, but also longer lengths were made so a baited hook could be tied to it and dropped in the water. Thoran had been making line and carving hooks for many years, an art he would soon teach to the boys. With all his bits laid out, Thoran called out to his boys.

"This is a hook," he said, while holding one up. "The hook will be attached to a line, we are going to put something on this hook, throw it in the water and hopefully fish will eat the hook and we will catch one. Get it?"

"Won't that hurt him?" asked Alvis.

"Won't it bleed?" added Grumel.

"How do we know it's a him?" asked Shyel, "what if it's a girrrl?"

"What goes on the hook?" Achu asked. A concerned Ayell looked at his brothers while they asked questions, as if he himself was the questioner.

Joyal tried to ask a question, "Wha, wah, wah, wah—waACHOOOOOO,"—he sneezed scattering the fishing bits all over. They bombarded their father with questions, speaking on top of each other.

"Stop!" Thoran screamed. "I don't know if it hurts them, boys, but it's the only way I know how to catch fish." He quickly added, "But I was told that it doesn't." He watched for a reaction. They concentrated on his words. The boys were taught not to harm any creature. Although it didn't bother them knowing that chickens were killed for Momma's fired chicken with sweet sauce, their favorite meal. Wait 'til they taste roasted fish…he thought… they'll soon not worry about those either.

"Will they eat apples?" asked Joyal.

"Or how 'bout bread?" Achu added.

Their father smiled and answered. "Well, let us see." That was enough for Shyel. He ran to his sack, pulled out a piece of bread and ran to the water's edge. He broke off a large crumb and tossed it.

Before the crumb hit the water, a large, blue-green picklefish burst up, grabbed it in mid air, and slammed back down into the water, sending a splishing splash that covered Shyel's face and shoulders. Speechless, Shyel stood soaked. Stunned, his brothers grinned. Ripples of water started to smooth out from the spot where the fish attacked the flying bread.

"That's dinner boys, try some apple," Papa said to anyone. The seven fumbled with their sacks— apples and bread were quickly ripped to pieces.

"Save some to eat, you *will* be hungry soon." Each boy tossed a piece of something into the water. A frenzy of colorful tails, fins and fishy mouths erupted. As quick as something was thrown in the water, it was viciously fought for and eaten. It was all very amusing to the boys, though they couldn't fully appreciate the voracity of the feeding fish. "Now to catch our feast; we'll catch enough fish to feed an army!" Thoran declared, thoroughly enjoying the moment. "Come here boys." Reluctantly, the seven stepped back from the retaining wall while watching the mesmerizing ripples on the surface of the Claw. Thoran had a hand line with a hook attached to its end. "A piece of something please," he asked. All offered. "Just one, thank you."

"Can I be first?" asked Achu.

Five others asked at the same time... "No me, me." Ayell pounded his chest.

"There's enough line for everyone. First, I'll show you how it's done. Then everyone will have a turn." Thoran grabbed an apple piece from Ayell and plunged the hook into it.

"Some fish are very strong boys, they can break hooks. They can even break these strong lines. Don't let them pull you in, else you'll be *their* dinner."

"Really?" six boys asked at once.

Thinking for two clock ticks, he said, "No, I won't let that happen." They knew he was just joking. "But some battles will be lost with strong, angry fish—but not for lack of trying. We never give up. That's the fun of it."

Thoran walked to the edge and flung the hooked apple into the water; it hit and was quickly eaten. He held on—the line went taught. "These fish must have grown since I was last here." He pulled and in turn, something pulled back. The boys watched their father grunt and pull what was on the end of the line. He was dragged a bit along the waters edge. Watching, they were not as eager to trade places with him. Close to their father, each lightly touched him.

"Easy, Papa," said Joyal.

"Don't let go," Yawnel added.

"It's a big one, huh Pa?" asked Alvis.

"What kind is it?" asked Grumel.

"Don't know yet." Thoran grunted while slowly bringing the hand line in. Then snap! As if shot from a bow, he went flying back and landed on his rump with a thunk!

"What happened?" asked Shyel.

"You hurt Pa?" added Alvis.

Thoran popped up and tugged at the now limp line. "He got off, probably bit right through the hook. We try again."

"Bit through it? How big was it Pa?" asked Achu.

Ayell tugged at his fathers arm and handed him another piece of apple. Smiling, Thoran said, "We try again." He walked to the edge, still retrieving the line. It snagged onto something. A couple of tugs and the line became un-snagged. But there was something on it. "Strange," Papa said.

"What Papa?" asked Grumel, "Something still on the line?"

They gathered closer to see. Thoran brought the line out of the water; they could see the hook had snagged a large branch. "Dead branch," their father said, smiling. He went to grab it, and their whole world turned upside down.

It wasn't a branch; it only tried to look like one. It was a creature—

a creature with a wet mouth that was opening, showing a broken set of bloody, jagged teeth. A terrible mouth with a tail, some of the boys thought. It surprised Thoran; he hesitated for only one clock tick. One painful, terrible clock tick. The creature whipped itself at its enemy. Its teeth found their mark, angrily latching onto his arm. His children watched in horror and shock as a slimy tail snapped and twisted while jagged teeth burrowed into their father.

Thoran screamed a cry of pure agony. The boys had never heard such a sound, couldn't conceive one ever existed. They shuddered as he dropped to the ground. He grabbed at the creature, its poison already weakening him. "Boys," he cried, "don't let it bite you! Get it off! By…any… means!"

Scared but not frozen, they searched for help. Grumel and Ayell were first to grab their walking sticks and stab the creature. "With all your might," Papa weakly said. The remaining boys were quick to follow. They all beat, smacked and speared the snaky creature. In only seconds that seemed like minutes, the creature stopped wiggling. Ayell grabbed it as the others shouted "No!" And with a mighty pull, it came off. He heaved it into the water where it landed with a splashy commotion. It was quickly eaten by something much larger.

On lush, cushy, short grass, curled into a fetal position, Thoran thought… I should have known. "It's a poison slug," he barely said above a whisper, "need to find a green leech, in rotten trees… drawn out with…." And he was gone.

"Papa?" his sons asked quietly.

"Papa?" they screamed, "Papa?" They shook him, they cried. Frantically, Shyel screamed, "What we do?"

"We need to find a rotten tree," Alvis and Achu said together.

"Poison's real bad, real bad," Joyal said, tears streaming down his red cheeks.

"Two stay here, the rest search!" said Grumel. "Into the woods!"

"Is he dead?" Shyel cried.

"No," cried Yawnel, "he said we need to find a green leech, leeches are put on wounds, they suck out poison, remember Papa said?"

"We don't know how to get them," said Joyal.

Again Grumel commanded—"We have to try, we have ta find 'em. Ayell, Joyal, stay with Papa!"

A smooth, confident voice filled the air—"Blood." The boys stopped in mid-panic.

"Who's there?" Alvis quickly asked. "Please, we need help!"

At the edge of the forest, it stood. "Da leechis come out of rotted treess wit blood," it said, while hopping towards them, "You be quick, your pap's snot dead, but he will be. Find's a tree, cut yurself, drip blood on a tree, they crawl out. Grab 'em when they comes out—by da tail, put 'em in yur sack. Bring 'em back. Dead trees over there," it pointed, "Make HASTE!" it shouted, and they moved.

"Grummy, Ayell, stay with Papa," Alvis said while running at the woods.

"No needs for that, I'll watch-over," it said.

"So will we." Grumel said. He backhanded Ayell's arm. They walked over to their father. Ayell un-strapped Thoran's hand ax, Grumel stroked his head and whispered, "Please Papa, don't die, stay with us." Thoran's eyes were shut. Beads of sweat covered his brow. To Ayell, it looked like he was crying; his father's breath came in simple, short, quick gasps. When Grumel looked up, the others were gone. He and Ayell were alone with it.

Thoran's struggled breathing was the only sound. They studied the creature; it did the same to them. Ayell thought… this thing is old.

The creature thought… these are his offspring, lots of them ee's had.

Grumel thought… it looks like a strange bird. Ugly. No wings.

They won't be as tall as their father, none of thems would. "I know yur father," it said, startling the two brothers.

Ayell and Grumel looked at each other, eyebrows arched, unsure how to respond. With a slight tremble Grumel asked, "Are you an ogre?" Ayell stared suspiciously at the creature that talked funny.

"Why? Does I look like one?"

"Don't know, we've never seen one," he answered. Ayell nodded in agreement.

"Well, I has, an they's ugly," the old creature answered. The dragon-elf studied Grumel and continued…"I help'd yur father a long time ago. He needs me help agin. So I come back. Hopefully in tiem ta help ya's."

Grumel stroked his father's forehead— hot to the touch. The boys felt helpless as they stared at their father's pale face.

"Poisin works quick. Hope yur brothers come quick, not much time. Sun's hot, can't stay out long."

"How did you help Papa? Who are you?" Grumel asked, not feeling threatened for some reason. The other boys burst out of the forest, each carrying a wiggling sack, their right arms were bloody. They ran to their father, stopped at his side, unsure of their next move. They stood over him.

"Must tend ta Toran now," the dragon elf said, "hands us a sack."

The boys stood, confused at everything that was happening. With blood dripping from self-made wounds on their arms, the five looked at Grumel, who quickly asked, "How do you know his name?"

He stared at the seven while saying slowly, "I *am* a friend boys, you'll see…lots a leechis yo!" No more questions, they all pushed their sacks at him. "You call me Dagon."

It now had a name.

Dagon snatched a sack, reached in with a four-fingered hand and grabbed a squirming leech the size of a banana. "They don't like me blood. Too old," he added while holding the bright green bloodsucker over Thoran's wound. He dropped it. The parasite grabbed on with gusto. A second one was quickly placed next to the first, then a third. "No more," Dagon said, "too many'l hurt 'im more."

Standing over their father, snatching glances between Dagon and the sucking leeches, the boys worried as the leeches quickly got fat with their father's blood. They prayed that the poison was being sucked out.

"They sorta look like the slug that bit him," Alvis said.

"They not," Dagon said. "Leechis have good spit stuff too," Dagon added, "cleans blood. Oh dey ugly, but leechis good. Slugs are black. Leechis nice and green."

What seemed like many minutes was only a few clock ticks. Their father groaned. Quietly, so as not to wake him, his sons asked, "Papa?" Thoran's breathing went from short, pained gasps to deeper, smoother sounds. A few more moans and his eyes fluttered open. He stared at the sky, he silently prayed. Sunrays that normally made him squint, lit-up his soul; a soul that only moments before floated in darkness, a sad soul that heard whispers from the spirit world. His eyes sought his boys— his beautiful boys, bleeding from their arms. He stared at the leeches, he saw his old friend Dagon, and cried. His sons were too happy to cry.

Dagon smiled, "Yur boys are strong," he tapped his own head, "strong up here. This the last time I come, Toran. You brung apples?"

Thoran smiled. "My brave, brave sons. I don't know what to say— I love you so much."

"Leechis are full up, pull-em off boys," Dagon interrupted. There wasn't much wiggle left in them, they were too fat with blood. Ayell, Grumel and Achu tugged at the slimy tails. They came off their father's arm with a slurping, pop! Thoran grunted. Blood splurted out of the sucker-like mouths. Three bloody O's were left on Thoran's arm.

"Throw them in the lake," their father said, stronger, more sure of his command. The leeches were heaved into the lake. With great commotion, they were devoured by the unknown.

"No swimmin here— ever!" Achu said.

"Ever!" they all agreed.

"Water?" Dagon asked, pointing to a jug. "Pour some on yur cuts.

Bleedin's stoppin tho'. Let's cut a sack an' wrap yur father's bite. After, we walk ta that river, da water's good. Fresh, faster — too fast for slugs," he said. "Clean up a bit, we sit fur a spell. Rest next to yur papa, boys, let da soft ground comfort you. Close your eyes and rest a bit. I'll watch-over." His voice had softened, was smooth, soothing, comforting. They trusted him. They quickly tended to their wounds and curled up next to their father. The warm ground and lush grass reminded them of their beds. Their weary little bodies needed a rest, their weary little minds needed to stop thinking, needed to stop being afraid. They were very tired. They really never had to deal with any emotion other than happiness before. They were never afraid, and couldn't remember truly being scared. Their father almost died. Died! Now they knew a deeper happiness, one that started as their deepest fear. And that made them more tired than one could imagine. Before Thoran closed his eyes, he stared at Dagon, his friend. He couldn't speak he was so tired. His arm had an ache the likes he had never known.

The dragon elf said, "It's okay my Toran, you rest. I'll watch-over." Thoran and his sons were sleeping before Dagon finished talking. Dagon hoped they would rest peacefully, with no scary dreams.

Seven and a Half Dreams

The first one...

Walking through the forest, our bows are ready for battle. We're being quiet, because our quarry is also hunting us.

It's a beautiful sunny day—but not a day to be eaten.

"Hello boys!"

"AHHHHH, who are you," I screeched, he scared me... and us.

Shyel screamed, "Who are you? Where's Momma? Where's Papa?"

"I'm the only Papa you need to know," he said. "Remember me boys, I'm the King...and I'm coming for YOU! Have you ever seen a unicorn's horn?"

I screamed at Joyal to stop crying...

The next one…

It's never been this dark since I can remember. I'll call out for Momma.
She'll come and light a torch. I do not like this dark. Why are there no night
sounds? What's that noise? Who is that?

"Little one's, little one's, tasty and fresh…"

Who said that? I'm running away. C'mon Grummy. Grummy?…

The half…

"Find the Scrollssss. Find the Sssscrollsss!"

Who's saying that…over and over again? It's annoying. What's a scroll?…

And the next…

"She's more than just the Lady of the Lake," Dagon said, "The Mother to us all.
Her spirit is within all."

I watched the golden hair of the Good Mother trail in the current beneath our
boat. Her image flowed through the waves. I stared into the water. I first thought
the sun was playing tricks with my eyes. Her gentle face drifted through my
world.

"Don't' be scared, Ayell," Dagon said, "for what you see is only the reflection of
she who dwells among the sky and land. To glimpse Her is an honor, and only
few have ever done so."

"I can't wait to see Momma," I thought…

Another one…

"That man, he said he's a King. Why's he chasing us? What's his name…Terrin?
He can't see us way up in this tree. Grumel, look at Ayell, Yawnel look at Joyal,
Shyel look at Alvis, search the forest."

"Look at me!" screamed Ayell… and he jumped up a branch and grabbed onto
a higher one.

"Watch this!" Shyel shouted… and like a squirrel, he ran along a branch,
jumped and flew onto the tree one over.

"Try to do this!" Grumel hollered, scurrying up a tree trunk so quickly, so high *that he barely could be seen.*

Joyal was crying. "What's the matter?" I asked.

"Papa died," he said. From way above, Grumel screamed and came crashing down, hitting every branch. I watched him hit the ground, he's not moving...

Still another...

Finally, we made it home. Where is everyone? Papa? Momma? Aunty Zee? Grumel? Yawnel? Alvis? Ayell? Joyal? Achu? Dagon? Where's the front door? Who's in our house? I smell fire. Why is my hand bleeding? Papa? Papa's hand is hurt. I hope he's ok. Is that Momma in the woods? Over there! That's not Momma...

The sixth one...

"Who is she? How can she float like that?"

"I don't know, Achu." Alvis said. "But she sure looks... soft."

"I know what she's saying... but her lips aren't moving. That's strange. Right, Yawnny?"

"Why does she keep whispering... 'save the scrolls'? Save'm how? What's in them scrolls that's so important? Must be some kind a magic. Right Achu? It's a shame that Aunt Zee's gone."

And finally...

I watch my boys. We're so proud of them

"So am I!"

"Who are you?" I cried. It sounds and feels like I'm crying.

"Do you know why I'm proud of them?" he said. "Do you, father Thoran?"

"Because they're strong!" I barked at the stranger. "They're stronger than you!" Why did I say that?

"Doubt it. That's why I'm going to kill them. Go! Run away!"

A Mother's Lot

Rose had an uneasy feeling about the whole fishing trip, though it was a trip she knew her husband must take. The time of the year, the weather…it is a perfect day for it, she thought. Still, she worried. Without the boys there to mess about, the housework was done by mid-morning. The cottage, the forest, all was so quiet. Too quiet. Rose wondered if they thought about her. Soon they'll be off on their own; it made her sad to wonder how empty her life might be without them. She stared deep into their forest. "There's so much they need to learn," she said. She knew this simple trip would set in motion a new craving in their souls; a craving only satisfied by getting dirty, getting wet, and getting lost. They'd break branches, bleed a bit and get to know all that could be taken from the woods. Rose thought she was actually jealous, she smiled.

Aunt Zee looked at her sister, "It probably is time."

Rose remembered the wood-sprites joking with Dagon when she and Thoran were seven years old, the only time she remembered playing with the dragon-elf. That's funny…she thought… I haven't thought of him for a long time. "Curious," Rose said out loud, fishing for a conversation.

Aunt Zee bit, "What's that? And please be to the point, I know you," she smiled.

"I was thinking of our old dragon elf friend."

"Oh? Funny. Me too. So many years since we've heard from him. Though I trust he'll be poking around sometime. He did say he would return someday, 'whens da tiems right,'" Zee said, trying to mimic him. They both smiled, they loved him dearly. "You were probably too young to remember all his babble and worries about ancient terrors. Never really understood him about that stuff," she said, staring hard. Then her brow softened, "Well, whatever he talked about, I pray he's wrong. And his visions *were* vague, even he doesn't know what might, or might not happen. We're safe, we're strong," Zee said.

Rose sighed, "Dagon," and laughed, "He must be over two hundred and seventy years old."

Our Time Will Come

Far from seven little boys, their father and a dragon-elf, eight ogres sat deep in a cavern, and looked at each other while pulling pieces of meat from a carcass. The younger were careful not to get in the way of the oldest. Large clivets and fleas bit their faces and jumped about. The older ogre's eyes burned red, blood dripped from its hands. It stared at the ground. It didn't care about a mirror that talked; it only cared about the last words that came from the witch's mouth… "Younglins. Head east, find the one called Grimsdyke. Don't eat'm! He'll get you the younglins'… all you can eat!" she cackled.

The oldest simply grumbled, "My time ta come." With a crude axe, it swung at the carcass, taking no care, as it hacked off not only the rear leg of the great buck, but also the right hand of one of the smaller ogres. The small ogre knew enough to run away, quickly and far. For if the feed was still on, it wouldn't be spared.

Meanwhile, in a dead valley where it was never sunny, old hag Myrtle stirred a kettle set above embers that had been hot for decades. She stared deep into its muck. The congealed slop in her pot was thick with the boiled skulls and bits of animals and people who never deserved to be killed, let alone boiled. Old skulls and old bits. "Anyting boilt long 'nuff turnt to soup, aye," she said loud, to no one listening. She watched something that hadn't happened yet—but it soon would. And swatting her hand at nothing she shouted to no one, "A puppy… fehhhh." She mocked Angus Grimsdyke… "Can I still conjure, hah! Stupid maggot, always been. I knows ya too well little Angus. Ya owe me somethin."

A growling moan came from a hole near her shack. A hole covered with a heavy wooden grate. A grate that held back her very angry, hungry, pets.

Time to Go

Dagon let them rest long enough. "Up, up, up, up, up boys. Sleep time done, tiem ta go," he barked, "lots ta du." They woke, startled and groggy. Their dreams *were* scary, and all were unsure if they were truly awake. The boys looked to their father, relived he was alive. Thoran looked to his sons, praying his fears stayed in his dream. He needed to show only strength to his boys.

In a sling made of a giant leaf, Thoran's arm was wrapped tightly to his chest. "Had ta mend ya a bit, Toran— salt and spider plant," Dagon said.

"Papa?" Joyal asked.

"You okay?" three other boys asked.

The seven stared at their father, glanced at Dagon, who was busying himself, and back to their father who said, "He is a friend, boys. The most special friend Momma and I could ever have."

"He's not like us, Papa," Shyel whispered.

"He looks different," Joyal mumbled.

"Where's he from?" asked Alvis.

Ayell looked at Dagon. He mouthed, "Thank you." Dagon returned his look with a crooked smile. It didn't matter if Papa's friend looked, talked, or smelled differently. It didn't matter if his th's sounded like d's. At least he talks, Ayell thought.

"Do not judge by looks alone boys," Thoran said, "Judge by actions."

"He saved your life, Papa," Alvis said. The seven looked at Dagon thinking thank you, but for some reason they just couldn't say it aloud yet. Dagon busied himself around a fire he made and looked at each boy for only a clock tick, smiling.

"I think all of you saved my life," Thoran answered.

"Dat's what happen boys," Dagon said, "you don't see my arms all cut up."

"Momma knows him?" asked Alvis.

"Does Aunt Zee know him too?" asked Achu.

"Does he know magic?" asked Grumel while Ayell stood near, shaking his head up and down, smiling.

Looking at Ayell, Dagon asked, "Dis young'n don't speak?"

Smiling, Achu answered, "We don't know— he ain't never tried." Ayell nodded his head up and down, smiled and shrugged his shoulders.

"Never mind fur now, gettin dark, for we know. Yous eat," Dagon said while pointing. The boys looked and were hit with a wonderful sight. On a wooden spit above a low flaming fire, a large fish, once colorful, was charred and smoking. Dagon turned the spit and the fish flipped. A mouth-watering scent hit their noses. Sweating its juices, the fish dripped clear drops onto the fire, and each drop that landed, sizzled, fizzled, and erupted into puffs of savory yumminess that slowly trailed to seven little noses. That wonderful scent triggered feelings, both ravenous and exciting.

Thoran looked at his boys and thought…they're so hungry, they actually look—angry. He smiled and said, "Our attempt at fishing wasn't as successful as yours, my friend."

"But ya sure know how ta catch a slug," Dagon joked and they all nervously chuckled. "Go gets 'em fish." Next to the fire were large leaves, the same kind wrapped around Thoran's wound. Using their knives, the seven boys attacked the fish.

"Tell us about your friend, Papa," asked Yawnel.

"How do you know Papa, Momma and Aunt Zee?" Alvis asked Dagon as Ayell stood near, shaking his head as if he asked the question.

As they feasted on the roasted fish, Thoran told his sons a simple story of his friend Dagon. The boys were in a trance as they ate and listened to a shortened version of the rescue of the boys' family, long ago, and how it was Dagon and other special friends who taught them about the forest. Dagon chose not to interrupt Thoran, but Thoran wouldn't have minded, as he missed hearing his old, scaly-friend spin tales.

Dagon thought…He'll tell them what he wants them to know. "Here, you take dis back for sweet Rose," Dagon said, holding up a sack filled with what they knew was fresh fish, "salted an' wrapped good." Achu grabbed the sack.

In a deep breath, Thoran said, "We'll come back again. I'm sorry that I've ruined what should have been a fantastical outing. We'll come back and I'll be more careful." He stared at the sky; the boys thought he was sad. "By the look of the sun, we should just about make it home afore dark. Even in the best of health, I don't want to wander the forest with you so far from home in the dark."

His boys formed a circle, whispering to each other; Shyel broke out and said, "Papa, this has been one of our best days ever."

"And you're okay— that's the most best part of it," Joyal added.

"We'll come back and catch the biggest fish in this lake!" Grumel exclaimed.

"Can Dagon come home with us?" asked Alvis.

"Just to watch-over for a spell," Achu said, smiling.

"Course me coming. Get to know you little banshees. Can't stay long tho'," Dagon said, looking at Thoran.

"Why? Where you have to go?" asked Yawnel.

Seven little heads tilted with curiosity, and looked at Dagon, who looked at Thoran.

"Well, this da last time we meet Toran, almost done. Goin ta me last place ta rest boys."

Dagon's simple answer stopped them cold. They weren't expecting it, a shiver of sadness went through them as they realized what he meant.

"Are you ill, my old friend?" Thoran asked.

"I'm just old, an' it's just me tiem," Dagon said, "we know when done is done. And I'm done." He paused and looked around, at the forest at the sky, "Not so fast, not as strong. Still smart tho." A quick pause and a chuckle, "an prutty good lookin," he said. They all chuckled.

"When you goin?" asked Grumel.

"Don't you worry 'bout that," he answered. "Now say goodbye to da fish, you'll see 'em again, I promise." With little enthusiasm, they did as they were told. The feeding frenzy of throwing the bones of the fish they just ate into the lake lost its excitement; they were tired—and sad. They just met Dagon and not only would he not be with them long, but he said he was going to die.

"Come, let's go home to our girls," Thoran said, more excited. "They're going to be very happy to see you," he said to his old friend. Thinking of their mother instantly made the boys feel better. Everyone would be excited to see each other.

Dagon poured water on the sweet smelling fire. It steamed and sparked, colorful plumes of smoke dissolved into the air. The boys gathered their bits, their sacks and quietly started walking back the same way they came, frequently looking back at the lake, still lost in thought. The sun, high overhead, already started on its well-worn path in the sky, eastward, to brighten up some other world. The lake teemed with activity— fish popped out of the water, bugs flit and flew everywhere, and gaggles of colorful birds circled high above its center. Every few clock ticks, a far-away hawk would drop from the sky to the lake. Like an arrow they aimed for fish, or anything else edible. The boys looked around, and then to each other...we'll be back, they thought.

It took them three hours to walk back to their cottage. Dagon led the way, Thoran brought up the rear. They barely uttered a word.

Chapter Eleven

Home Sweet Home

From the woods came screams—"Momma! Momma! Momma!" Rose and Zee ran to them. Wide-eyed and yelling, the boys ran up the path—panting, smiling, and babbling, running into and grabbing one another. The only words she could understand were "Papa," "Dagon," and "blood." Rose looked right at her husband's arm, and then to his eyes. She saw he was in pain. Although overwhelmed with joy, she didn't hide her concern. Her eyes met Dagon's; she wasn't surprised; the dragon-elf gave her a wink—*hello.* He gave the same subtle greeting to Zee.

"Papa," she said with a hint of sarcasm, "I take it your adventure was exciting. Must have been to bring our old friend out." She looked at Dagon and smiled while stroking Thoran's wrapped arm. "What happened here?"

"A little run-in with an angry slug. It will be sore for days, but I'm here. Thanks to our boys—and Dagon."

"Last tiem I can help me little rose in da meadow, I make it a good 'un, can't stay long," the dragon-elf answered. She hadn't been called that in years. Thoran forgot how she loved to be called it.

Rose and Zee walked up to their old friend. They hugged. It was obvious to them that their elven friend wasn't long for their world. His eyes still sparkled with color, but they sunk more deeply into his head. His body was more hunched than they remembered. Thoran didn't notice it until he saw his wife's subtle, crooked smile; a smile she saved only for sad moments—like when the boys had found a broken little turtle, and it died in Shyel's little cupped hands. "We're so happy to see yous and yous just stay as long as yous want," Rose said, smiling while mimicking her friend. Dagon hugged her again. The boys watched the happy embrace.

"He's going to die, Momma," said Joyal. Rose's smile only slightly wavered, her brow only slightly arched.

"He won't tell us how to help," added Alvis.

"No needs ta help little'uns. Like I says— I'm done. Tis a good thing. Me part of da story is almost done. Next parts are right here."

Rose sensed where this conversation was going and decided to end it for now. "Well, boys, he's a stubborn old elf. Let's talk about this later, today we celebrate. We're going to have a party!"

Excited, Aunt Zee added, "A birth-date celebration for our returning heroes. It's a wonderful idea." So a party began. Rose and Zee had already planned a feast, now some fun would be added.

Their father cheered, "Boys go get the fifes, zithers and bong-bongs. Let's make some music!"

The next hours were spent in and out of the cottage. A large outside fire was lit. Sweetbread, fresh fish, soup and fired-chicken were devoured and everyone took turns blowing, plucking and banging instruments. Dagon made whistling sounds as pretty as any songbird. The boys took turns telling their mother about their adventure. Those not talking or trying to make music ran around or danced. No serious talk happened that night. The boys treated Dagon like one of their brothers; there were no questions asked; they were just happy to play. Afore long, the fire burned out, the food was eaten and droopy-eye dust fell from the sky. Dagon whispered to the elders, "You all go ta sleep. You rest, we talk tomorrow. No dreams, just sleep. You go. I'll watch-over." They went into the cottage. Thoran lightly caressed his dragon-elf friend's shoulder while walking past him. Zee looked at Dagon, smiled and shook her head.

Rose shuffled the boys into their room and onto their little beds. Each was given a kiss and a silent prayer. Thoran was sleeping before his head hit the pillow. Rose went to the parlor where Dagon sat, wanting to ask one question before settling down to rest. She sat next to her old friend and whispered, "What's going on?"

He looked at her and lightly smiled. "Rest now, we talk at sunrise," he said, "I'll watch-over." He turned and hopped out the front door. Rose was unhappy, but knew he would guard them with all his might. That night, they all slept soundly.

Chapter Twelve
A Dragon-Elf's Tale

Dagon sat high in a tree and watched the moonlight filter through branches and leaves, always studying the difference between subtle movements of wind and the purposeful movements of things. His body was failing, but his mind was sharp. His eyes— still keen. He sensed something was watching from afar. It was time to tell his friends all that he knew, or at least all that he was told. The sun would soon wake them.

Rose, happy she woke first, lay next to her husband and timed her breathing to match his. Something very bad almost happened yesterday, she thought. Nothing else could have made him so tired, this she knew by his breathing. The sun shined and he lay there in as deep a sleep as she'd ever seen him. "It's okay my love, you rest," she whispered. His arm worried her; it was dark and bruised. It would need proper cleaning and fresh ointment, an infection was more than likely. It must be closely watched else the limb could be lost. He was able to move his fingers—a good sign. She slipped out of bed to greet the day.

Her boys slept deeply—a hard day on them also, Rose thought. She went to see her scaly old-friend. Aunt Zee boiled a pot of sassafras tea, Dagon stood by the open front door. All eyes met and softly, slowly they blinked.

"I'll leave soon, Rose," Dagon said, a bit sheepishly.

"Why?" she asked, "our boys need some— we'd love some time with you."

Aunt Zee handed both a cup of sweet tea. "Seems we still have a couple of games to play— or have you forgotten?"

"Furgit? Firget? How can me furget you beating me's sevunty-sevun times in a row. I haven't played counters since. Barely rolled dem dice da last games. I only quits cause you beat me da last'uns so bad me didn't get a counter off da board! I'll stay back from that gammon-game thank ya very little!"

"Calm down, calm down, you'll wake the dead with your carrying on," Zee said, "I just wanted to see if you'd remember."

"Ermember. Yes — I ermember it all, Zee," he smiled and winked.

"Are you hungry?"

"Any apples?" he asked.

Zee went to the back door, "I'll pick some fresh."

Rose stared at her old friend — he knew what she wanted to talk about. "They should learn from you! You're the teacher." Rose said.

Dagon smirked as Zee walked back in with fresh orange apples, he looked at Rose, "Tis what it tis, sweet Rose. Yous know more'n I'll ever know."

"I doubt that," Rose answered. She looked at him. "It's been thirty years since we've last seen each other. What brings you back?"

"Time for them ta know what they's might be up against. After they wake, we sit in da shade, tell ya's everyting I know."

"Almost everything," Zee added, "some things they just don't need to know."

"They's strong, Zee. They's never flinched, even when Toran lay on da ground, not moving like. They scared— ho yeah. Didn't freeze up tho'. They's strong. Just like you. They can handle it. Their blood is thick," Dagon said, "Like Toran's head." They both smiled.

Zee knew the fear the boys felt a day earlier, memories sometimes hurt. She looked up at blue-gray storm clouds that grew bloated and puffy in the sky, thunder coughed in the distance. It brought her back to a memory. A promise...Mother, I will save her. She rubbed her throat where a monster's spear went through, many, many moons earlier. "Your timing is curious sir dragon-elf— just out of nowhere you appear."

"Brave Zelda, is it *sir* now?" He smiled and half-walked, half-hopped to her. Gently stroking her hand, with no hint of sadness he slowly said, "You were da first one I met. And you must be da last one I see so I can sleep in peace."

"Is it true you're dying?" Zee asked.

"Dead…not da right wurd," he corrected, "drift aways more like it. Need ta wake da mens up. Time ta talk."

Reluctantly, with a sigh, and in a simple melodic tone, Rose sang "Ho boyyyyysss."

Rustling, fumbling and clunking came from their room. Then voices—"Wake up-ugh. Wake up!" Then—a different "uhg," a small crash, and a louder stomp. "Hey, stop that!" A grunt, "Hey, move it!" a grumble and "stop it!" Then came wrestling sounds, laughter and finally they sprang from their room, hair disheveled, eyes puffy-tired.

Coming down the stairs, staring at Dagon, questions from the boys came quickly, and all at once. "Momma I'm hungry. Dagon, how old are you? Where do you live? Do we have any cheese? Do you know magic? What do you eat? Where's Papa? Do you have any children? Are you a boy? Can you—"

"Hold it, boys," Thoran loudly interrupted, scratching his head with his good arm. "Stop. We'll get to the questions, first let's wake up."

"Tis okay Toran, questions are all good. Little'uns need ta know stuff, so they ask."

"How'd ya learn how to speak like us?" asked Alvis.

"Well dat's easy. We dragon-elves are pretty smart," he said while tapping his head. "We pick up others speakin pretty easy. We talk most of da speakin's of da land. You be surprised how many kinds speak like you. We calls it *common tongue*. Even dem stupid ogres. What little wurds they knows—you'll unerstand'm."

"Talking ogres?" Joyal asked.

"You've seen them? Talked to them?" Alvis asked. But all the boys wondered…why would we be speaking to ogres?

Dagon turned to the boys, "Let me talk a spell, lots a answers in me talk. I'll jumble bits around, but lots a answers for you."

"Sit boys," Rose said, pointing and nodding at Dagon, motioning him to sit at the table's head. She turned away to gather some food, "We can eat while we talk."

Dagon grabbed an apple and started crudely chomping at it while Rose placed bowls of honey-porridge in front of her boys. Dagon coughed and started, "Well, far, far away an a long time ago, we took yur momma an papa from some nasty ogres. Zelda was the first human person I ever touched." The boys stared at Dagon; there was a lot to grasp in what he just said. They looked at each other, then at their mother, to their father, to Zee, and back to Dagon. All they could say was, "Whaaaaaat?"

"Zelda?" Alvis, Grumel and Yawnel asked together.

"Me!" Zee said. "Actually, my full name is Grizelda." She slowly looked around at her nephews and said, "Tho, you'll only call me Aunt Zee—right?" She was hoping for a chuckle from them, but it never came, they were dumbfounded. The boys never knew their aunt's real name and what Dagon just said baffled them. For the first time in their short lives, they felt differently about their family, a realization that hit them hard. They didn't know what to say, a feeling swept over them and just hung in the air, like a lingering scent.

The elf continued… "So Zee made lightnin' speak an' we found her. Then—"

"Woa, hey!—what's he mean?" Shyel asked anyone.

"Nothing subtle about you, is there?" Thoran asked Dagon.

"That's for a different day boys, let him speak," Zee said.

"But wait," Achu pleaded, "saved you from ogres? Made lightning speak?" He looked at his aunt. "Can you do magic?"

Zee answered with a sigh, "No, and let's just say I was attacked and Dagon saved me. I'll tell you the rest someday, just not right now."

"But how'd ya make lighting speak?" asked Shyel.

At the same time, Rose and Zee raised their voices— "We'll tell you later!"

Dagon looked around the room, smirking like a hobbit with a full belly. "So. She's all bloody, near dead with a spear tru her, an she says 'save em.' I asks who? An she says 'babies!' Then she passes out. We dint knows if she dead or not. Tho' we knew what had ta be done."

"Bloody?" Joyal asked, "Near dead? Babies? What babies, what do you mean? Who did what?"

"Just listen boys, hold your questions till later," Thoran said.

"Plenny time fur questions, jest listen a bit. So, Zeck took young Zee to get her fixed up an I went ta go find da babies she was talking about," he said with a wink towards Thoran and Rose. "You see boys, ogres eat everythin, an they only strong an hungry. They don't have much up here," he said while tapping his head, "Get it? They stupid, but hunger makes 'em powerful. Very powerful! He paused and continued, "Me and da others—

"Others?" asked Yawnel, "Other elves?"

"Yeah, lots of us back then. Not so now."

"Did they eat your friends?" asked Grumel.

"Let him speak boys," Rose said, noticing a tear in Dagon's eye.

Dagon knew he didn't have to answer all their questions, so he chose which to answer. "I 'spect some are still around tho' I haven't seen any like me in a long tiem. Big battles back then. Those not killed ran an scattered, knowing we'd find each other somehow." Quietly the old elf said, "Thought we'd find each other, but none came lookin for me." He jumped up... "Me family have a special thing we do boys. Come outside and watch." He hobble-hopped out the door, everyone followed. "Stop here," he said, and everyone did. Hopping two more paces towards the woods, Dagon pointed his head upwards and let out a cough of fire. The boys were amazed. They were speechless.

"We from a long line of dragon-elves and yous better listen up now, else I'll burn ya bums," Dagon said with a sharp laugh. The elders joined him. The boys didn't see what was so funny.

"Do it again," asked Grumel and the others all said, "Yes!"

Dagon sighed and shook his head, "Sorry boys, hurts too much. Too old. Old days I fire tweny, turdy paces, all day long. Right, Toran?" Four of the boys chuckled.

"What so funny?" Dagon asked.

Shooting the boys a serious smirk, Rose knew the answer. Shaking her head, she said, "You said turdy, my friend. For some reason, the word 'turd' makes my *very mature* boys laugh." Every time she said the word 'turd', the boys giggled. Dagon smiled.

"Thirty? More like forty or fifty," Thoran said. "Boys, the dragon-elves were different than most. They could fly and make the fire-breath."

"You can fly?" six little boys barked out.

Dagon sighed, his eyes slightly twitched. "No, not any more." The boys' faces drooped a bit. "Got hurt long tiem ago an' lost part of a wing," he said while slightly turning. The boys watched, and were stunned as wings unfolded from Dagon's back. They could see one was cut— broken. "Okee, lets stop cuttin da cheese, we have lots ta talk about," the dragon-elf said.

Thoran added, "Let's all just sit in the garden, and let Dagon tell his story."

"How many others were in your family?" Alvis asked.

"Let him speak!" their father said, while giving Alvis a look.

"Okee, where was I? Oh. So Zee said, 'save the babies'. We took da spear out her, she fell ta sleep, an a pack of us went to da ogres caves ta find'm."

"Did the ogres have cottages?" asked Joyal.

"That's it!" Thoran slapped his knees, "The next one to open his mouth goes to his room. And then the next. And the next, and next, until it's just Dagon, Momma, Aunt Zee and me. So, who wants to leave first?" With wide eyes, seven sets of little hands clamped over their mouths; they obviously couldn't trust themselves.

Dagon paced slow and steady while he talked— "Okay, we had a good mind where ta start lookin, caves all over da place but a big one was up high-like, near a cliff and it's where we thunk da babes were. Dat cave's big inside, leading this way an that way. Like bugs, ogres and orcs live in dank, nasty places. We knew big ogres live there." Dagon stopped to bite his apple. He swallowed before he spoke again. "Some caves went far— to da grassy sea, some had rivers in' em, some just went down and down. Right down to dead places, where most of 'em lived." Dagon bit his apple again. "So a pack of us goes ta da big cave. We had a plan. We need ta kill somethin' ta feed 'em, take their minds, keep'm busy-like. It hurt ta do it, but we had ta kills a deer. When we got to da cave, we had to be careful. They's stupid, but they has good smell— an they eat everyting."

Dagon didn't talk fast. It was important to him to be clear; his words found a new home in seven sets of little ears. "Well, we flew till we got near da cliff from a back way. Stupid ogres couldn't go dat way. We snuck up. We got closer an we could hear babies cryin loud, cryin hard, like all through da land. We didn't have much tiem. Ya see, they eats anyting, but specially they like't eatin' people. An specially, specially, they like't little- uns. Babes were da softest an sweetest. After they eats all of da people around, they hunt fur anyting more. Everyting's in danger."

The boys sat motionless; the whole forest was quiet.

Dagon stared at the ground. He spoke quietly and slowly. "It had ta stop. We din't know how ta do it, but we hads ta stop 'em. But first, the spirits say we hads ta save those two," pointing at Rose and Thoran, who both slightly shivered. "Spirits wanted, so everyting bent on it." Rose, Thoran and Zee had never heard Dagon fully tell this story. As chance would have it, there was never any need. Their eyes became glassy. Thin tears escaped Zee's eyes.

"Spirits?" Alvis asked, "Like ghosts?"

"Yeah, sort of," Dagon said, "but a bit more like…uh, don't know da word. Ummm…let's see. They don't come to just anyone, they—"

"Why they come to you?" Grumel asked.

"Boys, that's enough," Thoran quietly said, knowing part of the answer, "Let him finish what he was saying."

"It's ok," Dagon said. He looked at Grumel, then the rest, and with a slight bob to his head he said, "Let's just say, and then we'll leave it for a bit, that way back… I was a King. And I was one of da chosen few that could speak ta them." Before anyone could respond, he said, "That's all I'll say about that right now." Again, everyone was quiet. His cadence quickened a bit, "Right, so eight of us went ta save ya, we sent one back ta tell da rest what we up ta, and ta get ready for more battle, so that left seven of us. It was sundown time, so's we had some dark on our side. We had good luck, they's just eaten, there were bones and bits all over da place. And you could smell blood and dead in da air.

"So they's kind of lazin around da mouth of da cave. They always look fur more. So we plan four of us ta fly inta da cave, find da babies an get out, quick-like. The others would draw away from da cave as many as they could. Da three takes da little deer and goes down da hill a bit, they make loud sounds, light a bush on fire an drop da little doe on a ground… then da gruntin starts comin. Us four was on da top point o' da hill looking down. As soon as our brothers make sounds, de beasts come about, start running at da noise," Dagon sighed, "Did they make *some* noise— an fire!" He stared at the ground and didn't say anything for seven clock ticks— nor did anyone else.

"Don't knows how many beasts in da cave; we didn't wait long. We left quick… us four swoop down inta da cave an da babies crying got louder, very much hurt our ears. We tired cause we flew really long tiems, but when we saw you two, hoooo did we make haste." Dagon stared at Rose and Thoran. He smiled. "Yous were dirty-like all over—an smelled of poo—but so beautiful." He paused, "Never saw anyting so pretty, so sad in me life. Yous were holding so tight on each other. So scared."

Zee started crying, quiet sobs…"I couldn't save you, I tried so hard." Thoran put his arms around both of his girls; the three stared at their boys, who in turn stared back. They all turned to Dagon.

Rose spoke quietly to the old dragon-elf, "Our family is…" she fumbled for words, "only because…of you."

Dagon smiled and spoke directly to Thoran and Rose, "You didn't know we was coming to save ya, when we grabbed ya, you thunk we was ta hurt ya more. Louder, louder screams came out yur mouths." He shivered. "Tis da only bad night dreams I ever still has. You must a thought we was gonna break you two up, cause even tho' you were babes," another pause, and slowly, "we couldn't get you apart. Oh, we tried, but we gave up. Yur cryin was mixed wit an anger. We didn't think ta bring a sack to put ya's in. I grabbed ya's up an it was hard flyin, you both were holding tight ta each other an squirming, an our wings kept wackin each other, as me brother wanted ta stay close. Well, we got ya's up in da air an we was quick leavin, but we sees ogres an a couple a scugs come runnin back screamin, 'Caaaaave, — don't let 'em get younglins!" He paused, "They had two of our friends. Da biggest ogre screamed, 'Drop 'em younglins or this'll be!' and he threw da body of our friend at us — his head were gone." Dagon paused and coughed a raspy breath. "Happened so quick… then me friend, Hurf turns an says, 'go— leave now! An' he turns ta fly at da ogres, screamin' his fire."

Dagon looked at Thoran. "I scream't 'we come back!'… He knew I wanted ta drop ya at da top o' da hill and come back ta fight! He scream't back, 'You save the little-uns, we'll help them,' pointing at our friends held by dem ogres. By then da ogres an orcs coming out from all over, throwing rocks at us."

Seven little mouths dangled open. The old dragon-elf continued, "We had ta pick our poison. We was gettin weaker an didn't have much time 'afore we has ta rest. Last thing I ermember was our friends breathin as much fire as they could, bobbin away from rocks, spittin fire, burnin anyting. Had ta keep da ogres fightin, keep most 'em from followin. Some tried ta follow, but we makes it over da cliff an was able ta get where they couldn't get us. You two were still screaming," he sighed deeply.

"Well, we find a spot out da way, rested an' stroked ya's a bit and talk't nice-like ta ya. Ya quieted down. You's were so tired."

Rose and Thoran, teary-eyed, held hands. It made them shiver thinking how close their family came to not being a family at all. Rose looked at her boys, then back to her husband... Why'd the spirits choose them... she wondered.

"Did the ogres have any weapons? Like axes or bows?" Achu asked. No one told him to be quiet.

"Only what they stole. An they made some spears. But they real good at throwin big rocks... throw 'em hard—far." Dagon paused and put his hand up to let everyone know not to talk. "Well, we only rest's a bit, we din't know what was in da woods. Ogres were pretty mad. Needed ta get ya safe. Knew our brother's probly dead, Hope't some come back, but none did. We flied ya back ta our nests, all were waiting. Our friends made such a fuss on ya." He paused and smiled. "You's quieted right down when you saw yur Zee, went fast asleep when we put ya on da soft ground next ta her."

Grumel interrupted. To his parents he asked, "What happened to your momma and papa?"

"Let's just listen to Dagon, Grummy," Thoran answered. "We'll talk more about this sometime." He knew the conversation could lead to too many questions, some he and Rose couldn't answer. Zee might be able to, but in his whole life, Thoran had never heard Zee speak about her and Rose's parents and what happened before he and Rose were rescued.

Dagon slowly walked while talking, "I ermember when ya woke," he said to Zee, "an' ya saw da babies next ta ya. So happy— right?"

Zee smiled at him. "Yes," and turning to her sister, "So happy. Right."

"Well, everyone knew what was happenin. I tells 'em what da good Spirits tells me, an' groundlins made talk wit other elves. They made talk with da dwarfs and some of da big fairies, an da plan was ta get you three through da forest an far, far away, across the Black River, farther than anyone knew about. We had ta gets you ta this side of da world. It'd be a long trek, and didn't know what we'd find, but we had ta get you far east in da Reach," Dagon said. "We didn't know how it was ta end in our homeland, we only knew da monsters were gettin stronger, and more of 'em, an they killed everyting or took'm as slaves." He stopped. "Killin's not a good thing, but either kill or be kilt. It's just da way it is with monsters." Dagon sighed… "Just couldn't' figure out where they all comin from." He was tired. He carried this tale with him for a long, long time, and as each word left his mouth, a bit of his spirit followed.

The boys were purely amazed at the story. Ayell thought he could actually see the air slightly shiver from Dagon's lips as words left his mouth, like a ripple in water after a pebble is thrown. Words travel, he thought—Dagon speaks so beautifully… will I speak someday?

"You should rest a spell," Rose said.

"Can't Rose, still much ta talk about— an I needs ta help ya make ready."

"For what?"Yawnel asked.

"For anyting boys," Dagon said. "Ya see, while yur ma an pa were being hidden an taken here," he said while opening his arms, "we battled em all. Ogres, orcs, nasty trolls, an some we didn't know what they were. I'm jumping da story a bits, and it's a long story an I need ta get ta important bits— but battles went on fur a long, long time.

Fights all over da place. Dis went on till da great fire battle, an most everything died, an we finally got their king, a huge beast of a thing who must a had some human in him, cause he had some smarts! When he got kill't dead tho', anyting left just scattered. But we got most of 'em. They got lots a us too. This was a long time ago, and far, far away."

They were silent, waiting for Dagon to speak when Alvis asked, "How far?"

"Where'd the rest go?" asked Achu.

The dragon-elf took a breath, "Don't know, underground maybe. Most that were fightin' got burned pretty bad, 'spect most died, some just crawled away, found holes in da ground an slunk in."

Out of the blue, like children sometimes do, Joyal asked, "Do ogres have mothers and fathers?"

Followed by Achu… "Are there ogre babies? Do they—"

"Boys!" their father interrupted, "Don't—"

"Is okay, Toran," Dagon jumped in, "no question is a bad 'un."

Rose looked at Zee, both looked at Thoran, they were happy to steer the conversation away from fighting ogres, but not to questions about baby monsters. Thoran spoke, "I know my friend, but these seven will question your tail off. We want to hear what *you* have to say. We hear each other all the time; it's your time to speak."

Cries of far-away hawks and gracklers made everyone look to the sky. Dagon started again. "Well—best I know, ogres are born frum a kind' a maggot that eats dead flesh of a hag-witch. Least some of 'em do."

"Witches?" five of the seven asked together.

Zee chimed in—"Okay, we can save those stories for another day."

"Yes… let's," added Rose. Dagon caught a glimpse from Rose; he sensed her apprehension about some of the talk. He nodded to her, an unspoken understanding.

"Oh please, we want to hear about this," Joyal said. One of the others added, "Yeah, we just want to—"

"Dead witches," three of the boys quietly chimed in, not looking for a response.

"Tell us about the fire-battle, Dagon," Joyal pleaded, with the other boys quickly adding "yeses" and "pleases."

"You'll find out about dat some day boys, not today tho," Dagon said, while nodding to Zee.

"How many days walk is it to the other sea Papa? To the other side… where you come from?" asked Grumel.

Thoran was happy to change the subject. He looked at Dagon, "Don't really know. Ninety, a hundred day walk?"

"Lot more'n that," Dagon answered. "I mostly flew it long time ago and it took me a long time. Dat trek is a slow one, needs ta always look out."

"How bout the witches?" Alvis asked, "You ever see a dead witch?"

"What's the biggest ogre you ever saw," Achu asked, ignoring Alvis' question.

"Just let him speak boys," their mother said, "you'll make him crazy with questions."

"Well, we can talk about witches later. There's some good ones, mostly real bad ones. Witches like to trick ya. Very smart. But I'll tell ya's someting 'bout ogres. Ogres eat a lot, an sleep a lot. Bigger da ogre, more food an sleep it needs. One tale has a giant of an ogre sleeping more'n turdy years 'afore wakin up. An it woke hungry! Lots a stories, you'll hear more. They's a tale of a beast with turdy-sevun eyes, never sleeps, da eyes take turns restin, always at least one eye open." Ayell, Shyel and Achu chuckled when Dagon said "turdy" instead of thirty.

"What's the biggest ogre you ever saw?" Achu asked again.

"Biggest one we ever kill't was a hugely beast, barely spoke a word but could rip a tree ten foot round, clear out da ground. It easy stood fifty paces tall, could swallow us down whole without chewin. Only saw one of 'em. Dang near took fifty of us ta kill'im. When them monsters start burnin', it gets 'em mad and they fight hard. But it went down. Kill't turdy of us too." The boys didn't laugh at that 'turdy'.

Concerned, Shyel blurted out, "But what do we have to get ready for?"

Dagon, already the center of attention, turned most serious. He looked at Thoran, then to Rose, then to Zee. "There's a story you need ta hear, probably should a told ya while back, but I didn't." He looked at the boys. "Might as well tell the whole mess of ya what I know."

Thoran, Rose and Zee looked at each other, concerned—anxious.

Dagon decided to speak slower, wanting to say his 'th's as clearly as possible. "Well... way, way before the time that the whole mess we was talkin about was, an I mean way, way back in time, before even the Time of The Ancients, The Good Mother's spirit came from above ta touch this special world." Grabbing a handful of dirt, kneading it, he said, "An make this ground that gave life to all. She came to make life happen." He paused and opened his arms.

"Life is magic. A little lightning here, a bit a water there, and things begin ta sprout."

"Where'd she come from?" Joyal asked. Rose, Thoran and Zee looked at Dagon and raised their eyebrows, wondering how he was going to answer that one.

Scratching his head, Dagon said, "Well, I can only tell ya what I was told. And when I was your age, I asked da same question ta my old one, an he tells me da Good Mother came from the lightening of the first star. I said 'like lightnin... from clouds?' He said no, lightening— as in letting-go of something. Like when a momma has a baby. So I asked... 'Where'd that first star came from?' He told me to be quiet, and just listen; I'll understand it better, by and by. I was mixed-up on it, but I let it go."

It was confusing to the boys and they just sat there, thinking about it. Before they could ask anything else, Dagon kept going— "So listen— as sure as ya like your momma's sweetbread, life happened. And with life, comes good and bad. Everyting has a part in nature's...

uh…what's da word…uh, like it's all kind a equal."

"Balance," Zee answered, "nature's *balance* of things?"

"Yes," Dagon said, "Ya can't know one without da other."

"But—

"Stop!" Thoran said to Alvis, then to his sons, "Let him speak," he said most seriously, nodding to Dagon. "Finish what you need to say." Thoran was concerned about the conversation; he was impatient, and Dagon knew it. So did the others; it was time for them to be quiet.

"Ok," Dagon said, " to the point." and taking a deep breath he said, "The story goes, in making all of life, Mother put it all down in two writings, one for da earth, one for da sky." Slowly he said, "…*The Scrolls of Harot*, she called 'em. In them scrolls was all her magic… her potions, her chants…her words and doings. How she made mountains rise, rain fall and stars shine, how the seas were filled, an' why rivers flow. How clouds float an' change colors. How lightning flies. All da songs of da forest trees. How elves an dragons came about, why ogres are here, how grimlers an chickens were borned. The colors, feel, the smell of everything…it's all in the Scrolls, so her story goes." Dagon paused and looked at the sky. "All high mysteries of nature are 'splained. The words in the scroll writings are most powerful." He looked around at the lot of them, "Tells how wizards make magic. And why human-kinds were made to be da most special, why they da chosen ones." He looked at Thoran and said, "The Scrolls—are real." Thoran looked at his old elven friend, confused.

"For her own reasons, our Good Mother hid them scrolls, her spirit telling only one from each of da high-beings da special cave where they's hidden. Trust and loyalty ta life was da Good Mother's first dream. So one human, one ogre, one dwarf, one elf, one fairy… one of every high-being was told the scrolls restin' place. And, as the tale goes, each of those beings she told became da first King or Queen of their kind.

"In the beginning, everything was good— no wars, no killing.

Ogres were part of good folk. Still stupid—but good. They were da biggest an strongest ones, theys moved stuff." He looked at Rose— "Then something bad happened."

Rose looked at Zee, then to Thoran, back to Dagon. "What?" she asked.

Dagon sighed. "It were da first human King, a man named Terron, da first being Mother ever trusted. He came unhappy, jealous. Wanted ta be big an' strong like ogres, magical like elves an fairies, an smarter than da dwarves. He wanted ta fly like birds, swim as fast as a whale an' spit lightning. He wanted the scrolls. He wanted dem all for himself an he wanted ta rule over all. He wanted them for all da wrong reasons. An evil grew…against the love of a Mother—a bad, ignorant, senseless evil, an enemy of good.

"So—as da tale goes, one dark an terrible, bad stormy night, King Terron snuck into da cave where the scrolls were hidden. He creep't through the tunnels like a scurve-rat until he came upon da spot— a small wooden door set inta a wall, covering a nook. Good Mother's mark on da door was simple—a small tree an a crescent moon above it. King Terron opened da door an picked up one of da scrolls; he began ta read. Then a bright light from behind scare's him. 'King Terron?' a sweet voice calls out. Snapped his head around an before him stood Therea, da oldest daughter of da goodly Elf King, Tromael. A charm hanging about her neck made a bright light."

Dagon sighed, and the old dragon-elf closed his eyes, then bowed his head. The boys thought he was tired, and maybe wanted to rest. But resting was the last thing on his mind. Dagon raised his head, and his eyes changed color. His hands lightly clasped as if in prayer. Staring at the sky, he began to speak slower, lighter. Sounding—different, a mesmerizing soft human voice… female sounding… "As they stared at one another,' he said, "the awkward, heavy stillness was broken by the stomping of her unicorn, Kylin. King Terron stared at the Princess and her colorful pet and knew not what to say."

The boys held their breath, slightly scared because Dagon's words were not his..."Therea spoke confused... 'I was... hunting...with friends...the storm... lost,' She slowly spoke, 'I, I feared the lightning,' her eyes darted between the King's face and what he held. Realizing what she stumbled upon— its importance, her eyes grew wide. 'Why do you hold that? she cried.

"Terron slowly said, 'It is as you think Princess. The Scrolls of Harot. I come to—"

'Those are not to be touched!' she screamed, Kylin stomped and whinnied his disapproval, 'So it is commanded to all,' she stepped towards him, 'those are never to be touched. You must put it away!'

"Terron tried to speak, 'Princess I only come to—

'No,' she screamed, 'the commandment is clear,' and she turned to run.

"King Terron grabbed at his waist and pulled a lance from its sheath. He threw it; his aim was pure. The Princess stiffened as the clean blade punctured the back of her head. Her last vision was said to be of her dear pet unicorn's teary eyes. Kylin stood shocked for only a moment, the same amount of time King Terron stood unmoved. The unicorn charged and jumped at the King who shifted hard, barely escaping the hooves of the fabled beast. Terron, still holding a scroll, rolled away and withdrew his sword. Kylin stole a quick glimpse of his dear Princess, Terron lunged and his sword found the pure heart of the princess's friend.

"Kylin, standing tall above the evil King, fought no more and bowed to death. King Terron withdrew his sword and as the wonderful beast fell, Terron sliced off the spirally white horn. Kylin's white blood splattered about him and the scroll. Scared the princess's friends would soon come looking for her, Terron devised a plan. He looked into the scroll and quietly memorized the first passages. He quickly put the scroll back, grabbed the unicorn's horn and ran."

Dagon sat still; tearing from eyes that have seen time in its infancy.

Thoran and his family were still. Thoran wanted to say something, but Dagon's tale was important, so he remained quiet. Dagon continued, still in the calm, soft female voice…"It wasn't long before the Princess and Kylin were found. The shock of their deaths spread like a disease. An angry search began over all the land, for clues to who or what could have committed the crime. Before long, King Terron came about with the unicorn's horn. He cried and pretended as he wept … 'at the mouth of the ogre's great cave, this was hidden in a tree,' then screaming, 'what say you, Bladen… King of the Ogres! Why did you do it? Why did the Princess and her magical pet die!'

"The Ogre King protested mightily, as did his subjects, but no good came of it. With a hard, stubborn tongue Terron accused the ogres and their King of his own crime. An angry mob of elves, men and dwarves captured the Ogre King and killed him— hung him from the mightiest of oaks in the land. The seeds of anger and mistrust were planted. They quickly boiled and grew. The trolls sided with the ogres, who were chased and killed. The ogres fought back, in turn killing former friends."

Dagon paused again, the colors in his eyes faded, he sounded like himself again…"Da Good Mother's dream of everlasting trust an peace was shattered. She began ta cry. Tears of anger, tears of sadness, an tears of pain gushed from her eyes. Her tears turned inta da greatest of floods that washed throughout da lands. When her crying stopped, oceans and rivers split mother from son, father from daughter, friend from friend an foe from foe. An all her creations were left ta fend for themselves.

"She hid da scrolls again. Though she separated them, telling no one or thing, except for inscribing *above* da spot where da scrolls were first hidden these words— *'Where da colors flow ta white, where da crying point ends bright, da strongest of hearts ta prevail.'* Ancient clues that seem more riddle than hints."

Dagon turned to Rose and said, "But da last thing da Good Mother wrote inta da wall of rock, *below* that spot where them scrolls were first hidden, da very last thing were da words…" and speaking slower, he said, "*If the seven fail in defending all, the hearts, the pillars, the love, will fall.*"

Rose looked at her husband and stood, clearly irritated. "That was a long-winded story," she said, unsympathetic. "And it's a grand tale of the…*world's* history," she lightly mocked, then to her sons she said, "But it's only a story." She angrily walked into the house.

Thoran breathed in sweet air and looked at his boys, who waited for Dagon to continue. Thoran walked up to the basket of apples, pulled one out and handed it to Dagon and smiled. "Are you trying to tell us that my boys are going to save the earth and the skies?" With mouths hanging open, the boys looked at Dagon.

"It's more'n a story my friend. Da spirits say it's the prophecy come true. They came ta me a long time ago an made me save yous. An' yur boys are the only 'seven' that's known." The boys looked back at their father.

Raising his voice, Thoran said, "That inscription can mean anything." The boys looked back to Dagon.

"I know so, Toran, but the day they was born, dat special, special day, spirits came back ta me. An told me ta go back an find ya, ta go back. That's what they told me. And that's what I did." The old dragon-elf looked at his friend, then at Zee. "I don't know," Dagon sighed.

"It doesn't make sense," Zee said.

"It does to me," Dagon calmly answered.

"What happened to the King…Terron?" Joyal asked.

Dagon looked at his dear friend's children, and to Thoran, to Zee, then the woods… "Well, he was found. He was found stuck right inta the ancient oak where da Ogre King was kill't an hung for a crime he didn't do. Terron was stuck ta that same tree, da unicorn's horn plunged inta his chest, inta his heart, through his back an' inta da tree." Dagon stopped and looked at the ground.

"Finish what you need to say," Thoran demanded, knowing that the story was not complete.

Dagon looked at his friend... "Legends have it a unicorn's horn cannot kill. Its magic is mostly unknown. The King had no breath an no blood came from his body. All were afraid ta touch Terron as he stood frozen, like he was holdin up da gigantic tree. Not knowing what ta do, da high beings that were left chose ta burn da tree, ta send it flaming into a darkness. But as da great tree burned, Terron did not. Its trunk was thick with orange flame, but that guilty King looked only like he was sleepin', stuck to da tree. An wit one last sound of anger, da land opened up an screamed, swallowing da ancient tree an Terron, down inta the bowels of da unknown."

They sat there silent, just a family and a dragon-elf.

"Why didn't Good Mother just destroy the scrolls? Why keep 'em?" Alvis asked.

"I asked da same thing," Dagon said, "an my old one told me that ta destroy da scrolls was ta destroy life itself, an that she couldn't do."

"This doesn't make sense," Zee said. "There's peace throughout. Every now and then a stray beast causes a stir, or something'll come out from the sea. But the Kings armies are strong, and nothing has come about for decades. And most of that stuff happened far, far away. Come now," she motioned to the boys while looking at Dagon, "Let's not put a scare into them. Let's have something to eat."

"I'm just saying da day da boys were born something happened," Dagon said, "an...

"And no more..." Rose interrupted while bringing a tray of drinks out. "No more on that for now," Rose said, both with anger and sadness. She handed drinks to Zee, Dagon and Thoran, and continued, "I don't want to talk about this anymore. We know it's time for them to learn how to defend themselves. That we'll do. Speak all you want to about the monsters of old; they'll probably never meet. But, no more fantasies about saving our world."

Thoran and Zee looked at Dagon, then to the boys. "We'll speak more about this later," Thoran said to Dagon.

"Well… we'll see," Dagon answered.

Alvis jumped in, "But we want——"

"No!" Rose said, "We'll not——"

"Something to drink," Alvis said, "that's all."

Rose looked at Thoran, they smirked at each other. "I'll go get more drinks," Rose said and went into the cottage.

They sat only for a few minutes before Zee abruptly stood and said, "Excuse me!"

She quickly went to the front door, grabbed the handle and screamed louder than she should have, "The door, Rose. The door is locked. Rose?"

Rose stuck her head out the window. "Oh? Is it locked? That's strange."

In a panic, Zee asked, "Please open it. Quickly." She said it in such a state, it grabbed the attention of the boys, Thoran and Dagon. Zee looked at them.

"I told you I'd *get* you," Rose said in a hard whisper, a bit overdramatic. Three ticks of silence. Zee knew right away what Rose meant. She remembered a day at the beach, decades earlier, when she played an innocent little trick on Rose and Thoran.

Frightened, Zee could only say, "No you didn't!"

"Yes, I did!" Rose answered with a hint of scorn. Zee gulped and looked at her nephews and at Dagon, who were confused.

"I, I…" Zee started to run towards the back.

"It's locked also," Rose said, comfortably resting her arms on the windowsill.

Zee looked at her sister, sweating. She turned one last time, to run, to hide, to save a last bit of dignity, but the fierce dragon wind would not be held back. From her mouth came the smallest of burps, followed by a tiny puff of yellowish gas that twirled and whirled, then took the form of a tiny dragon head. Zee grimaced with embarrassment. Great joy flew from the boy's mouths; all screamed different versions of "Hey", "Aha", "Wohoo."

Zee took another step, and another, louder burrrp, escaped, followed by another gassy serpent. Two misty serpenty heads twirled in the air against the background of their colorful woods. Rose and Thoran laughed hard. Dagon looked on, wide-eyed; he chuckled. Zee moved, said "Not again," and let go a loud, long burp, followed by a terrific twirling mist that took on a new shape: of a knight's head.

With delight, Rose said, "And a brave knight to slay the dragons!" Thoran whooped happily, three of the boys hollered, "I want to do that!" The others laughed hard. Grumel, Alvis and Yawnel grabbed at the cup they thought Zee drank from; their hands clashed and sent the cup flying, splashing it about.

"Nice one," Grumel said.

"You did it!" Yawnel screamed.

Clearly annoyed at the timing of her sister's revenge, Zee looked at everyone, then to her sister. "Nice example for the children." She stomped up to the front door and said, "Please open up!" Rose did and Zee ducked in. Everyone heard loud whispers; Rose laughed.

After being convinced that there was no more magic potion, the boys turned their attention back to Dagon, who didn't want the earlier conversation to just stop. As uncomfortable as it was, the boys needed to know of things. It was time to show them. "My promise was ta watch-over an help ya as best as I could. I have somethin' for da boys." Dagon whistled a loud, pointed single note that shot through the quiet forest. A quick rustling came through the treetops, a large grackler, flying strange, hovered above them in a clumsy fit. Everyone stared at it.

"What's wrong with it, why's it flying like that?" Rose asked.

"That's flying?" asked Thoran.

"It looks broken," Alvis said.

"It looks jerky," added Joyal.

"It's holdin something," Grumel said as Ayell shook his head in agreement.

"Yes it is, this bird is a special one," Dagon said. And on that note, the yellow and white chicken-like bird with a bald head dropped a sack and fluttered away thinking... I've been here before. Only last time, the grackler was covered in a gooey witch's potion. Dagon snatched the sack before it hit the ground. "Here boys," he said. He pulled out a book. A very worn book with a cover that looked thick and made of tree-bark. Something was left in the pouch, and only Rose noticed that Dagon hid the pouch behind a bench.

At first, the anxious boys thought it was The Scrolls of Harot. Dagon quickly said, "These are me wandering's as best as I could draw 'em. It's me journal. I starts da day after we rescued da babies. Tried ta draw as much as I could an did da best I could."

With mouths hung open, the boys hovered around Dagon. Delighted, and at the same time they shouted, "A book!"

"Careful, it's old an brittle," Dagon said trying to speak carefully. The boys looked at each other, then back to the book.

"An never, NEVER! let it leave you seven. It's got a little magic in it," he said while slightly winking, "Don't let anyone know you has it. Never! I need ya ta promise me. In da wrong hands this book can never be. You seven are da only hands ta have it. PROMISE!"—they jumped a bit.

"WE PROMISE!" they answered.

By this time, Rose, Thoran, and Zee had gathered around the boys. They said nothing.

Dagon held out his journal and fourteen little arms reached to meet it. They didn't fight over it. Ayell's hands found it first. He immediately sat on the ground, the others circled him and the journal was opened. On the first page was a drawing of three, clearly two babies and a young Aunt Zee. At the same time, Grumel, Joyal and

Achu said, "You have the same hair, Aunt Zee."

She beamed—"Not as red, just a bit more gray." Everyone smiled.

"Where'd you get a drawing pencil?" Shyel asked.

"Soft coal sticks," Dagon said, "they's all over da place."

The second page was a sketch of a large tree with many trunks and long odd shaped branches—and with huge leaves. The boys recognized the tree from their walk to the Dragon's Claw. "Hey, we saw that tree," Grumel and Yawnel said together.

"That kind a' tree is safe ta you if you ever need 'em. You'll see 'em, but da big one's far apart, scattered in da woods," Dagon said.

"Safe? What do you mean, How can they help, Dagon?" Thoran asked.

"They hollow inside, you can hide in 'em, Climb up high... ta see around. And you can eat everythin on 'em."

"Everything?" asked Achu.

"Everythin. Leaves, branches, bark. They mostly by da bushes with the sweet berries."

"We saw the berry bushes also!" Yawnel said.

"What kind of tree is it?" asked Alvis.

"Don't know. Me brothers used to call 'em dingle berry trees as there's small holes in da berries, an when wind blows through 'em, they make a dingling sound. You can call 'em what you want."

Joyal turned to a brother and smiled, "Dingle berry sounds good—we'll call 'em that."

Ayell turned a page; together the boys said, "Wooo."

"What's that?" Grumel asked while pointing. The sketch was of a creature drawn next to a tree. Its huge stick-like hands were outstretched; its arms were as long as the height of the tree. Big eyes. Big mouth. Big, pointy teeth, little body.

"Yeah, you has ta watch out for them in da deep woods," Dagon said, "I call 'em ash grabbers. See, they live in treetops, mostly ginkash trees; an they has long, long arms that kind a dangle down, lookin' like branches. Da hands stay on da ground. An when somethin' they wants comes by close enough, or right onta da hands, they GRAB IT!" he screamed, startling them. "They slowly swing up they arms an' bring what they caught up, up, up, right up ta dat big mouth in da tree."

Dagon nudged his way through the boys, stuck his hand at his journal and gently flipped a couple pages. "Here, look at these." The next pages were filled with beautiful little drawings of elves or fairies. "Those 'er me friends, drawn so's they can be ermembered. Look at 'em; keep 'em in yur minds. They'll come in yur dreams, they'll help ya'. You'll see." After many pages of his beautiful friends, came pages filled with monsters. Sketch after sketch of nasty ogres, orc, scugs, gobles and others— all with x's over them. Each page had at least a dozen X'd out sketches.

"These show how many you killed," Shyel said, matter-of-factly.

"Yeah, lots of 'em," Dagon said.

"Look at them all," said Achu.

In a low voice, Alvis added, "There's so many."

Page after page, many looked similar, though every now and then there were noticeably different ones. One page had a creature with a saw edged, bone-like bulge coming out of its forehead. One had a drawing of a two-headed beast. All of the sketched faces stared out through the pages. Dagon was very good at drawing eyes. Even large x's couldn't stifle their menacing look. Tapping his journal, Dagon said, "Dat was an easy one ta kill. Was a two-headed gork. See them gorks only has one big nose hole. Makes 'em breath funny. He was big, but one head wanted ta push, one wanted ta pull. A pull-me push-ya we called dat stupid one." Disgusted, Dagon said, "lots a weird 'ns met up wit over da years."

"What's a gork?" asked Shyel.

"Oh, dat's what I calls 'em. Gorlacks, gorks, orcs, scugs, it dun't matter—they all nasty."

They came to a drawing that made them each quietly shiver. "Is that an ogre?" Achu asked quietly.

They studied a full-page sketch of a monster that stood upright. It had an ogre-like face and sharp tusks, like a wild boar. Ayell noticed it wasn't X'd out; he furiously pointed to it and pretended to make an X.

"Dint kill 'im, don't know what it were. There's a couple of 'em, we tried tho', but they smart… fast." Dagon said while staring at it. Rose thought her friend was afraid.

"Where were they?" Thoran asked, startling Rose.

"Way out by where we called da Shadow Rivers. It's marked on a map somewhere in da journal," Dagon said, "Way, past secret forests that probably can't be found anymore." They flicked through more drawings of mountains, forests and colorful maps with arrows pointing this way and that, guiding eyes to all types of things.

"Are there baby ogres, with ogre families? Where do they come from?" asked Achu.

"We'll talk about that at a later time, boys." Rose said.

"Remember," Grumel said, "he said they come from witchy-maggots."

"Another time boys," Thoran said, ending that line of talk.

"Yeah, you'll be lookin thru da book for a long time, boys. Let's finish talking," Dagon said.

Rose interrupted, "You're tired Dagon. Let us watch-over a spell, while you rest."

"Thanks, but no sweet Rose. Okay boys lets get ta da jist a this."

Zee interrupted, "Dagon, should we four have a word first?" speaking about the adults.

Thoran answered, "No, not this time, Zee." He turned to his sons, "Boys, very soon boys, you'll be learning new things. Things having to do with weapons, fighting, defending yourselves and using the forest to help you."

"Quests of Mastery," Dagon added. Thoran shot Dagon a hard glance and said, "Let's keep it simple. We'll just call it training for now."

"Are we gonna learn magic?" Achu asked.

"Who we gonna be fighting, Papa?" asked Grumel.

"And where are you going to be?" added Joyal.

"We'll be right with you," answered Aunt Zee, "For a long time," she hoped, "Your ma and pa are just trying to say you're all getting older and it's just time to learn some new things." Zee's calm words made them feel better.

Thoran added, "Hopefully they'll never be any fighting, but we have to be prepared."

"Does prepared mean we might have to fight ogres or dragons?" Yawnel asked, as his brothers looked on with wide eyes. The children clasped their mother tightly. They eagerly waited for a calming response. "My beautiful boys," Rose softly said, "we'll be together for a long, long time. And nothing might ever happen. But if anything does, well, we face it together, as a family, as a *strong* family." The seven smiled again.

Quite loudly, Achu said, "The family that slays together— stays together!" His brothers shouted their agreement.

"So we have to learn things right now, Papa?" Alvis asked. The other boys looked around.

Dagon answered, "We just gonna talk today. But you has ta learn an' keep learnin. Keep yur mind open. Amazing things can happen. Never, ever close yur mind. You must understan— listenin is learnin. There's great power in silence and listening. Da strongest an' smartest get that way for they listen," he said while tapping his head with two pointy fingers. The boys were quiet. "Ta everything!" Dagon said loud enough to startle a smile from them. "You listen with yur ears and yur eyes." The boys noticed that Dagon's ears were wiggling. "Can any you make yur ears wiggle?" They quickly tried to mimic him, contorting their faces. Smiles turned to giggles. Dagon's ears flapped about and seven little faces bent and jerked around, trying in vain to flap their own ears.

"How bout this? Can you make yur nose do this?" The point of Dagon's nose started to wiggle back and forth; he really looked silly. The boy's giggles turned to laughs. The dragon-elf tried to stare at his nose; his eyes became crossed, making him look even sillier. The crossed eyes, coupled with the wiggling nose and flapping ears lasted only a minute before the old elf became dizzy and fell back, flat on his rump with a thump. At the moment of the thump, he let go a squeaky bottom-burp and at the same time, a deep burp came from his mouth followed by a short breath of fire that sent everyone into a fit of uncontrollable laughter. Even Dagon, mostly embarrassed, laughed in his own, strange, squawky way.

They calmed down and for the next few hours, they snacked, asked questions, got some answers, told stories and shared sketches, laughs and giggles. Dagon told them some of his whereabouts over the past thirty-odd years. His hands would open and close and his arms would wave as he excitedly described his travels through The Reach.

By mid-day, Rose and Zee put together another feast of frothy soup, bread and apples. Sadly, there was no more fish left from the prior day's fishing adventure, an adventure that now seemed very distant. The boys snuck away to play Grimmage.

While watching them play, Dagon grabbed the pouch he hid and brought out the last items in it. To the adults he said, "Tiem ta give ya's these." To Thoran, he handed a goblet, to Rose, a candleholder; both made of gold. To all three, Dagon whispered the importance of the goblet and the candleholder.

The boys' game was a short one. They came back, but Dagon wasn't finished talking to the parents. "Boys, I needs to tell yur parents something. Leave us alone...just for a bits." It was a suspicious request. The boys reluctantly went inside their cottage. Rose, Thoran and Zee also thought it strange.

"You have ta warn your King," Dagon said directly, "Someting's happening. Back in da West, and to the Center of da Reach. There's killing—deaths. Lots of 'em. Spirits tell me ta warn you; I'm telling ya ta warn the King. Let 'im send scouts out, ta da far parts, see if they can see anything. Find the wizards. I don't know what's happening, an' some can't be trusted, don't know which one's yet. It's tiem ta teach them how to defend themselves...the boys!" Dagon looked at Rose. "I know you don't want ta hear it, but you do as I ask."

"I'll go to the Council and *they'll* advise the King. I won't wait. I promise." Thoran looked at Rose and she nodded. Dagon's words were taken seriously.

"Maybe you should go to da King youself," Dagon said, "evil hides...you know that."

"I'll be careful," Thoran said, "I'll only trust those I know." Thoran put a hand on Dagon's shoulder and patted his friend. "I'll be careful," he said.

The boys came back, still suspect. "What're you talking about?" Shyel and Achu asked at the same time.

"Look up that tree," Dagon said while pointing to a large tree near the cottage. All eyes turned to look. A family of furry little monklings stood on a mid-way branch, they were watching Rose's family. Never had such beautiful little creatures been seen near their cottage. The boys were distracted, Rose and Thoran stole a quick loving peek at their smiling sons. It was out of the ordinary to see monklings so far from the coast. A pair of crystal hummingbirds buzzed near the colorful creatures. The monklings scattered, not to hide, only to get more attention. Everyone smiled. When the scattering stopped, the little tree creatures turned and waved to those on the ground. Only Ayell waved back, everyone else was being amused.

Quietly, so as not to scare them away, Dagon said, "Don't furget what I said about da book boys."

Looking at the monklings, the boys quietly said, "Yes sir."

When everyone brought their eyes back down to the spot where

Dagon stood, they blinked, glimpsing only his brief shadow, his light flashed out.

He was gone. Just like that.

Only Hours Later...

a storm rolled in. A whirling angry tempest bringing panic and confusion. Shutters smacked against the cottage and leafy branches knocked against the roof. While grieving the disappearance of Dagon, the whole family secured their homestead: animals needed corralling and gates were locked.

The family sealed themselves inside their cottage. Thereafter, the boys rested and talked in their room while dinner was being made.

A pounding came at the front door. Thoran opened it to find a wet and disheveled man. "Beg pardon, kind sir," he softly spoke while windy rain whipped behind him, "but the storm made it so I needed to find shelter." He dressed like a man of the pulpit. "My name is Pastor Pye, from the tiny Town of Tavernacle, and I'm hoping for a bit of dry patch until the storm passes. I'll be no trouble."

"Of course! Pastor, please," Thoran motioned him in. The boys heard the rap at the door and stood on the upstairs landing.

Without warning, a dart of a branch, twirling in the wind, flew true towards the front door and entered hard, the Pastor's back. The holy man tensed as pain shocked his body; he slumped, fell into the cottage and lay face down.

Rose and Zee screamed, "Boys, back in your room!" Thoran grabbed the Pastor, dragged him in, then jumped to the doorway with a hand tightly holding an axe; he looked to see if anyone was outside. It was obvious what happened. Debris within the fierce storm twirled and sliced about, as if they were weapons. Thoran closed the door right before other sharp, thick branches pounded the door.

"Papa?" four of the boys asked from behind the crack of their door.

"Back in your room!" Zee cried, then quieter, "Please, boys."

"Kind sir," the preacher whispered, while gently turning his head; blood flowed heavy from his wound; a trickle also came from his nose. "I have a child. Please…" he struggled, "tell her…I…" And he said no more.

"Oh, Thoran," Rose sadly sighed. Zee quickly gathered cloths and a pot for water. Rose cried, "We have to stop the bleeding."

Thoran looked at Rose and Zee. "The goblet!" he boldly said. "There's no time to waste. Get water." He ran to a drawer that held the goblet and pushed the cup at Zee. She held the water-pot. "Fill it!" he screamed. Zee overfilled the goblet. Thoran knelt by the preacher.

"Dagon said one drop to be mixed." Thoran pulled the wooden shard from the man's back; blood drained freely. Thoran stuck a finger in the stream of Pye's blood and held it over the goblet; a thick drop fell in.

Pastor Pye was firmly turned over and the goblet held over his mouth. Thoran poured only a light stream into Pye's mouth. No one noticed the Pastor swallow. In only one clock tick, his wounds began to steam.

The click of the boys' door opening startled Thoran, Rose and Zee. The three turned as one and screamed, "BOYS! DO NOT COME OUT OF THAT ROOM!" The door clicked shut. And when the three turned back to the pastor, it was over.

Pastor Pye's eyes opened and he stared at the smiling face of Rose. At first he thought it was the face of the Good Mother herself. "Welcome back, Pastor," she said. "That was some fall you took." Rose winked at her husband and sister. The pastor noticed Thoran calmly handing a beautiful, etched goblet to the redheaded girl, and she placed it on a high shelf. The preacher licked his moist lips.

The boys saw nothing, and the pastor didn't believe that he fell and hit his head. His rising spirit watched as a sweet liquid was poured on his mouth from a golden cup that now rested simply on a shelf. And as his spirit jumped back into his body, he saw his blood, smolder away.

From that point on, Pastor Pye would preach a tale… that sometimes what we think is divine intervention, is in fact a simple act of kindness. And being kind to others is a true gift to all.

Chapter Thirteen
Only Gone, Not Forgotten

The boys knew Dagon for only two days, but it seemed like he had always been there. And just like that he was gone. He was missed and they were sad.

Thoran knew he had to go to Laban to tell the council elders that a dragon-elf visited and spoke of monsters. But he, Rose and Zee wanted to distract their boys' sadness, so they decided to take them on a quick trip to a place the boys always wondered about—the mines where Thoran worked.

"Just a quick trip," Zee said. "Now is a good time." The boys were very excited when told. They knew their father was a carpenter. They would often see him work his craft. But what really had them curious was them knowing he worked, 'In the ground,' as their father would call it, digging for treasures.

So the boys woke before dawn one day and were told to get their bits together. Leaving before dawn, they went down the rarely used back path. After several hundred paces from their cottage, they stopped. Thoran and the boys looked around. Their cottage could not be seen. Old-growth trees and many older stumps scattered throughout the area watched them; stumps and trunks of trees felled from a much earlier time.

"Well... we made it safely," Thoran said. The boy's thought he was joking; they looked around.

"Whaaaaat?" Achu said.

"Where's the mines, Pa?" asked Alvis as Ayell looked on, his head slightly cocked.

"You're standing on them," Thoran said with a smirk. He grabbed a dead tree-trunk and pushed. Giving way with the crunch of dead leaves, the trunk was only a cover over a hole in the ground that was barely big enough for Papa to squeeze through. The boys expected a grander entrance, but a hole in the ground certainly piqued their curiosity.

"That's the mines?" asked Joyal.

"That's it!" Thoran exclaimed. "They're underneath us and scattered all throughout the land—tunnels and passageways, most you'll never even know are there."

"This is a special spot," Momma added, "No one else knows about it. This is the closest way in from our cottage," she said.

"I sometimes go to a spot that looks more like what you boys think a proper mine should look like—a great hole in a hill, like the ground is actually yawning—and I'll show you that someday. Tho' this chamber is our real treasure." Thoran stopped and pointed his hand at them— "You'll not come here on your own unless specifically asked, DO YOU UNDERSTAND?" The seven stared at him, a bit frightened, confused— "Yes sir," they said together, but they couldn't understand why they would want to come on their own.

"Come," Aunt Zee said, disgusted, "let's get this over with. I hate going down there. I don't know why you even wanted Rose and me to come with you."

"This will probably be the last time, my good sister, now that the boys are older. Come boys, follow me. Momma, can you go last and cover the hole?" Rose nodded.

A slightly rotten, bitter smell came from the hole. The boys peered in; a few rungs of a ladder could be seen, leading straight down into darkness. "Go slowly boys. I'll light a lantern. Hold onto the ladder." Thoran climbed down, he told Ayell to follow, then the others when Ayell's head was gone. "Be careful and don't step fast, or you'll step on someone's fingers." One by one they slowly stepped into the hole. Each looked down to Thoran's light, each grabbed at a bit of dark emptiness, slow step, slow step— little noses wincing at a musty smell. Each looked up—the hole got smaller and smaller, but was bright from the coming sunrise. Slow step. Slow step.

Their father's voice echoed around them, "Keep slowly boys, I'll let you know when I reach the bottom." The dusty wooden rungs were course and grainy. They wondered how far down they would go and hoped no bugs would crawl on their hands—especially spiders. Slow step. Step slowly.

"Ouch!" someone screamed, "Ouch!" "Hey!" "Ow, my fingers!" "Stop That!"

"Everyone step slowly...and be careful!" Thoran shouted.

Aunt Zee grumbled, "This is why I hate coming down here."

"I'm closing up," and abruptly Rose shut out the little light that had given the boys very little comfort.

All was quiet. "Papa? Mama?" Six boys urgently asked and one thought. The children clung to the ladder.

"No worries, men. Keep coming down slowly. I just reached the bottom. I'll get some light. You'll see." Thoran moved only a few steps from his spot, struck something, and a large torch ignited.

Light... good, good, the boys thought. Nasty place, Zee thought.

Thoran lit another, and another. A huge chamber came alive. Within minutes all were on firm ground. The boys were shocked at the space. The dirt walls had both thick and thin, cut roots sticking out from them, the dirt floor was dusty and hard, picks and other tools the boys didn't recognize were scattered about.

"Stay away from any flames boys," Thoran said.

"Stay together," Rose said, while grabbing a torch. Zee did the same.

"This is just a storage room," Papa said. "The special chamber is just through here."

He started walking. The boys watched their father walk up to an archway that was obviously chiseled away, strange markings were on the wall, but the boys took no notice. Thoran passed through the arch and lit another torch. A different glow seeped out of the archway, and as they entered, the boys saw why. The walls shimmered as thick streaks of golden dashes caught flickers from flames. The yellow veins pulsed as the torches caught a dash just the right way and soft rays of amber seemed to fly about. As far as the light allowed, the subtle golden beams waved at them.

"Is this gold?" asked Alvis.

"It is," his father answered.

"Where'd it come from? How'd you find it?" asked Joyal.

"Well... it's ours to watch over," Rose said.

"Watch over?" asked Alvis, "Why watch over? Who are we watching it for?"

"Did you find it, Papa? Isn't it just yours if you found it?" wondered Shyel.

"We were shown this chamber..." Thoran said, and before he continued—

"By who?" four of the seven asked.

"By some friends," Aunt Zee answered.

"Friends of Dagon?" Yawnel asked.

"Yes, boys. Friends of Dagon." Thoran looked at Rose. "Aunt Zee being one of them." The boys looked at their mother's sister.

"Dagon's lot showed me this chamber when we were brought here," Zee said, 'hurt dis treasure an it'll hurt yous,' Dagon said. 'Maybe even kills ya." Zee looked at her sister and Thoran—she smiled. "We use the gold sparingly— and we've only known happiness."

"Are we rich... like the King?" asked Shyel.

"Well, we don't look at it like that," said Thoran, "it's not really ours, and we only use what we need. The gold is not what is important in our lives."

"Our family, and helping those in need are what's important." Rose said. "We promised only to use it for good purposes. And if anyone else knew about this chamber, well, they would more than likely try to take it."

"And maybe even try to hurt us," Thoran said.

"Why?" asked Achu, "There's enough to share with the whole woodland."

"Because sometimes it brings out a bad side in people," their father answered.

"Why?" Alvis asked.

"Greed, boys," Aunt Zee said.

"Green?" asked Grumel, "Green what?"

"GREED, I said... taking more than you need," she answered. "Some greedy people are selfish, they do bad things."

"There are people that wouldn't use this for good purposes," Thoran said. "They wouldn't help others; they could hurt others. And as important— we made a promise. That's enough of a reason."

"You make us happy, our family, our cottage," Rose said. "We love our lives. We don't need to live in a castle."

"And we've rarely used what comes from this room," Zee said, "What your father earns from his wood-works is more than enough."

"All the happiness in the woodland is in our little cottage," Thoran paused, "and some day, in many years, we might only be here in spirit." He looked at his sons, "and you seven will be the keepers of this room. You must protect it, honor *it* and those who made our family possible. Working hard and being humble, that will bring you happiness. This room will not bring you happiness," he finished.

After a couple ticks of silence, Joyal said, "What if we use it only for good purposes? Like to buy books and stuff?"

"We'll talk more about this later. For now, just trust us. Never come back here, unless you're asked," Thoran said, "Both Dagon *and* us, want you to promise. So?" Together the boys said, "We promise."

"We probably couldn't find the hole again anyway," Shyel said.

"Why'd you show it to us?"

"Because you're getting older, and there are many new things you'll be learning."

"And Dagon wanted us to show it to you. So, you've seen it. Now let's go home," Zee said.

At home, Thoran gathered his bits for his trip to Laban. The council must be made aware of what Dagon said. The boys pleaded to go with him, but he decided to take the short trip alone. Thoran traveled lightly, but planned on coming back with full backpacks.

The boys studied Dagon's journal. Ayell was the first to notice a sketch on the last page, a sketch of their cottage and the tree with the monklings looking at them. He pointed at it and wondered... when did he sketch that? "When did he do that?" Joyal asked.

"I didn't see him do anything 'cept eat apples and talk," Alvis answered.

"Me neither," the remaining five said.

It would be sometime, before they would realize, Dagon sketched from his spirit-life.

Chapter Fourteen
Neighbors Never Known

Some days after Thoran returned from his trip to Laban, a trip where he told the Council what Dagon warned, a family named Sheef stopped by to visit as they were on their way to the friendly Town Of Tolk. They seemed to be a family of nine, with a mother, Jillain, a father, Trebor, their five children aged four to eleven, the mother's mother, and the mother's father. The children, four girls and one boy, all had names that began with the letter J—Jasmine, Juniper, Jinleen, and Joeen, the boy's name was Jarron. The mother was glowing and fat with child.

They seemed to be a family of nine, but in the prior year, twin infant girls died unexpectedly after their first month of life, so they should have been a family of eleven. Their mother couldn't stop thinking of their family as having eleven, with the eighth child on its way.

The Sheef's left their home near the sea coast, and were going to settle closer to Tolk. And on their trip west, they would visit the family with seven boys. The Sheef's knew about them, but had never visited. Trebor Sheef wanted to visit Thoran to thank him for a gift that Thoran didn't know he had ever given.

Many years ago, Thoran trusted the words of a stranger and gave him a sliver of gold. The stranger said the gold was to be used for medicine and food for his brother and family, all who were sick with fever. The brother and his wife were unable to work; the youngest children were near death. Thoran gifted the gold without any concern to its use by the stranger. It didn't matter if the gold was to be drunk, gambled or spent away. Thoran forgot about the gift.

Thoran and Rose treated each day as a gift, humbled by the magnificence of life itself. And possessions were only that. So if a sliver of gold made someone happy, for whatever it was put towards, then so be it.

Well, that stranger was Trebor Sheef's brother, and Trebor and his family *had* been very, very sick. And that sliver of gold saved their lives, and the Sheef's were forever grateful.

Trebor led his family through the trail that opened to the clearing in front of Thoran's cottage. Rose and Aunt Zee were in the front garden, Thoran and the boys were in the rear when they arrived. Momma and Zee turned to the noises coming from the main trail. Trebor greeted them loudly by saying, "Kind madam, my family humbly bids welcome to your beautiful garden."

Momma and Aunt Zee watched a large family, horses and carriages, unfold before them. Although surprised, they sensed no threat. Rose quickly saw the mother was with child and three of four little girls held hands. "My, my, my!" Zee happily said, "What a handsome family of princesses— and a prince."

The Sheef's all smiled. "Thank you muchly," the pregnant mother answered, and while rubbing her belly said, "tho' I myself am not feeling like their queen, more like an overblown yox."

"Well—you're the most beautiful yox I've ever laid eyes on," her husband added while tweaking her nose. Rose noticed the mother's slightly pointed nose was very, very cute.

Grumel came running out of the house, ready to ask a question, when the scene in his front garden stopped him in mid-stride and mid-thought. He was speechless.

None of the brothers had ever seen another child. The little girls before him were magically beautiful. A crush of emotions hit Grumel, all he could say was, "waaaaahhhh," and then he stopped, face flushed, looking silly. "Don't just stand there like a lummox," Aunt Zee said. "We have guests. Say hello!"

Grumel had never been called a lummox; he didn't even know the meaning of the word. None-the-less he meekly answered, "Hello."

The whole Sheef family said, "Hello!" back, the strength of their greeting made Grumel jump a bit, smile and blush.

"Welcome to our home," Rose said excitedly, "Grumel, go tell your father and brothers we have guests." While walking towards Jillain she added, "Come, in your condition you must be tired. Let's get you comfortable."

Grumel ran, screaming, "Hey, Pop...guys." He returned quickly, followed by the lot.

For the next half hour, greetings, names and handshakes were exchanged, awkward glances were made and children made smiles. Jarron Sheef was older and taller than the seven; he was suspicious of everyone. Four little girls befuddled seven little boys. Ayell quickly made the children at ease by bringing out a ball and tossing it at the youngest girl, who in turn tossed it back. A full-on game of catch began.

With eyes that quickly became wet, Trebor emotionally thanked Thoran. Though Thoran truly couldn't remember the gift he had given so many years before. Nor could Rose or Aunt Zee. But the intense gratitude of Trebor was moving; all the adults had moist eyes. Thoran thought— if this lovely family reckoned it important enough to travel such a distance to thank me, then I will humbly say, "You're very welcome."

The children watched their parents and wondered why all were hugging. It lasted but a moment, for they were much more interested in their new playmates. The two families mingled and played, a lunch of breads and fruits was shared, and nanny and granddad quietly shuffled about the grounds. A quick game of Grimmage was started, but not finished.

Rose and Thoran offered their new friends a place to rest for the night. The Sheef's appreciated the offer, but Trebor had their move well planned and they were to meet other friends to assist his family, so there was a schedule to keep. When it came time to leave, the families promised to keep in touch. The children were sad to part, but very happy to have met. Trebor again thanked Thoran, and they warmly embraced. As they hugged, Trebor whispered to Thoran, "I owe you my life."

Thoran whispered back, "I'll ask only for your friendship." And to that Trebor loudly said, "Done!" and he smiled while walking towards his small pack of horses.

Rose held Jillain's hand and wished her good speed on her journey. As they embraced, Rose whispered, "May the little girl or boy in you be healthy and strong." Jillain started to cry. "There, there, we'll surely see each other again," Rose assured her. But Jillain could only muster a weak, "Yes, I'm sure we will. Thank you, again," and quickly walked away. She didn't look back. It felt a curious goodbye, Rose thought.

It wasn't curious to Mrs. Sheef. She had to leave quickly. For if she stayed any longer, she might confess to her new, sweet friend Rose, a dark secret. That *she*, was a seventh daughter. And in her womb might be another seventh daughter. And a dangerous, possibly deadly decision had been made... that if their child were female, she would not be cast aside as all others had been. She would not be a slave to the blood-trolls. They would fight, they would run, and they would hide. They would seek the King's help, and they would sacrifice nanny and granddad if need be. They would do whatever necessary. They would save their child.

Their child would not become a hag-witch.

Chapter Fifteen

Weapons

Thoran had a dream, a terrible vision that woke him in the middle of the night. In a panic he said, "They'll need to fight." He didn't know if Rose was awake.

"I know," she sadly answered— she had the same dream. They both stayed awake, worrying and planning.

Thoran thought…special weapons for little men. Axes, bows, shepherd slings, lances. What else? A knife! How could I forget knives? And of course the strongest of swords. I'll go to Thundor and seek out the Kings' blade-smith—he'll forge blades of dragon-teeth and iron. What will they use when they study for their quests of mastery? He thought and brooded. Poisons? Herbs from the land? There are many of those. Purple ivy, brown berries… we'll do those last.

Rose clearly thought… they'd first have to learn to control their fear, to be smart, quick. Thoran pictured how they'd look, all dressed for battle. They'll carry sacks of rocks for their slings; they'll learn to sling-shoot anything. They can use their lances as walking sticks, their bow and arrows will be slung over their shoulders, their belts will hold a sword, an axe, a knife, and the sling.

Their children had to learn to fight, but the parents prayed they would never have to. They silently pleaded with the Good Mother to protect them. They begged the kind spirits to watch-over. What Dagon said… 'And the seven shall save all,' greatly worried them. It made no sense. Thoran remembered when they themselves began training. Rose and he were also seven years old and fortunately, they never had to defend themselves from ogres, trolls, orcs, or any other nasty monsters that were more than just stories in their world. He was shown a witch once and didn't make eye contact. Zee had a different story. Her father trained her, and she had killed monsters. But she never spoke about it.

Thoran missed Dagon. Dragon-elves are born of the forest and no human can match what they know about the mysteries of The Reach. On his last day, in a most serious tone, Dagon took Thoran aside and held his arm tightly—Thoran forgot how strong the dragon-elf was. Talking about his journal Dagon said, "Make 'em study hard, at night, in da mornings. Make'm draw they own if ya can also. It needs to be part of them. They needs ta use it. It be as good a weapon as any. Lots a answers be there. It's only for they eyes." So the boys would study the journal every day, however they wished.

All lessons would be paced and strict, as Rose, Zee and Thoran had been taught. Weapons were not toys. "You must understand," their father would say over and over and over, "that weapons—any weapon's first purpose is for protecting."

"But protecting might mean we have to hurt something," Alvis would reason.

"Yes, but your first concern always has to be for your own safety, not to cause hurt." Rose would also say to them over and over and over. And she'd constantly remind them that individually they are strong, but together they are stronger.

"When do we get swords?" Grumel asked, over and over.

And Thoran would always answer, "They're being made special, and you have enough other weapons to master first!"

They first concentrated on making weapons, using the forest for parts and fixings. For weeks and weeks, they chiseled ax, lance, and arrowheads from any rock they could find. They were taught that any rock or stone could be made into something. As could any twig or branch. Handles, arrows, darts, spear lengths, and slings, all were within their reach as long as the forest was nearby. Carving and whittling weapons was fun to the boys; it became a natural act. Many weeks were spent learning how to cut the strongest part of a tree for use as a bow. "The heart of a tree is always the strongest," Thoran taught. Holding blank wood, he'd caress it and show them how the heartwood is carved so the center of the bow is thicker than the mid-limb, and the mid-limb thicker than the tips. They'd spent hour upon hour learning the art of arrow carving. Thoran caressed pieces of wood as if they were alive… "Feathers work best for fletchings—the wings," he'd say, "though some types of leaves will work in a pinch." It wasn't long before the boys each had their own bow, each fitting their little hands perfectly. Stringing the bow with special string made from the ginkash tree took quite a bit of practice. But it was expertly taught and eagerly learned.

With bow in hand, Thoran would grab an arrow and pull back, while slowly saying— "The bow must be so strong as to give just enough to pull back the arrow without it breaking," softly he would finish, "and release." And with that the arrow would slice the air, gently hissing, leaving a wispy trail as it struck true a target—every target at which he aimed. The boys smiled when their father shot an arrow, even though they were frustrated, as mastering the bow would be the most difficult weapon to learn. For that reason, they would spend the most time with it.

Spears or lances were fun weapons. To watch them throw a lance, as if launching a javelin, and to see them use their little bodies to muster energy, was more a jester show than defensive battle training. For when a spear was launched, so were they. They always landed far from the beginning point of the throw.

They were disciplined to practice one type of weapon per day. Their only break came when Thoran traveled to Laban for bits and gubbins. Returning from those trips, the boys would bombard him with questions about the town, his travels, the Sheef family, and many other curiosities that children always ask about.

And Grumel would always ask, "When do we get our swords?" But Thoran was tired of repeating himself and stopped answering him.

As the months went on, they became more and more comfortable with their weapons. Targets were made and thrown at, shot and beaten. To aim true meant to breathe deeply and be calm, very difficult lessons for anxious little boys to learn. So they practiced. Accuracy was learned through the consistent use of smaller and smaller targets. When throwing axes, the seven would line up in various positions in a quarter-circle around a target. Papa taught them to always be aware of the position of others so as not to split open a brother's face, chest or leg. The same held true with bow and arrow, knife throwing — all weapons.

One day Yawnel had a grand idea…"Let's make an ogre!" The others quickly agreed. Impressed with the ingenuity, Zee offered to help. Large cloth bags were cut open and sewed together after filled with leaves, twigs, and other woodland bits. Arms and legs were made and secured by twine. Its head was also made of filled burlap and its face was painted to look like a monster from Dagon's journal. They named their ogre Terrible Timmy.

Timmy was the fiercest monster in all the land. He killed their King, made slaves of the children and ate their pies. Timmy attacked them frequently and needed to be hunted down and killed. Timmy attacked from trees, from behind bushes and sometimes from the cottage roof. After every attack, he would need a doctor, as he was quickly killed, and his head was usually chopped off. After a while, Timmy needed help from his brothers—Bonzo, Lucas and Patton— all enemies of mankind, all quickly shot, stabbed and killed.

Sometimes the boys were pitted against each other in hand to hand battles that always ended in draws, except when Ayell battled. Thoran saw an edge in Ayell. The six others seemed of similar strength, but Ayell's silence seemed to add to his sense of perception when attacked. Strength or awareness, Thoran couldn't tell, but Ayell was always one step ahead of his brothers. Cuts, bruises and scrapes happened every day. The boys were fascinated with blood, even when it was their own.

Every day without fail, they trained. In the rain, in the heat, in the cool mists, they trained. It was not a chore; it was how they had fun. The elders weren't trying to make it fun, it just happened that way. During their seventh year of life, their early training, they rarely hit targets. Tho' they became skilled at crafting weapons, quick in their running and expert tree climbers.

Throughout their eighth year, their aim greatly improved. Targets were hit more than half the time. And during this time, Thoran would wake them at night to begin training their senses. When dark, monsters and beasts had an advantage. In dark caves, ogres, trolls and dragons were comfortable. Warriors need to hear and smell differently in the dark. At night, the snap of a twig could mean death; the rustle of leaves could mean an attack was coming. "Control your fear," Rose would demand, "The dark is just another form of light," she would say.

By the time they were nine years old, Grumel stopped asking about swords, and they rarely missed any targets, be it day or night.

Chapter Sixteen
Their Tenth Birth-Date

A few days before their tenth birth-date, the boys said goodbye to their father as he left for a short trip to Laban. Supplies were needed and Thoran wanted to check on news from the council. He was more comfortable leaving for a short spell as the boys had trained hard and learned well. His fears lessened as they grew stronger and aimed truer with their weapons.

Each boy, except for Shyel, stood at forty-nine inches. Shyel was the tallest at forty-nine and one-half inches. They were short; and at almost one hundred pounds apiece, were thick and sturdy. Except for Ayell, each had a crop of brown hair that resembled a prickly, thangle-horned bush in color and style. Momma and Aunt Zee took turns cutting their hair every now and then, to keep it from overtaking their faces. "We don't want you hairier than our friend the hairy potter," Aunt Zee would laugh. The boys didn't care how their hair looked, rarely was a brush or comb used. Ayell's hair grew very faint and fine. In fact, he looked bald.

Their young hands were calloused; their arms and legs were thick with young muscles, muscles honed from daily training. Each boy was comfortable walking around with a belt to hold his axes and bits. Only ten years old, Rose thought...they carry themselves as if older. And they yearned to explore.

Collectively, the seven conspired a plan for a trip, possibly to Laban, possibly not. They thought they were old enough and more than competent, as growing children do. They just needed to convince their parents. So they planned. "Supplies," Alvis said proudly, "we can get the bits they need."

"Chicken feed, spices, cloth. We can get everything," said Joyal.

"We'll be helping them," added Shyel.

"They're not dumb," Grumel said. "They'll know what's up."

"They won't let us go alone," Shyel said, "but at least we might be able ta, ta, ta tAAACHOOOO!" Shyel stopped and they looked at him, a slight shniggle dripping from his left nostril, "ta explores a bit," he finished, trying to sound like Dagon but completely losing the effect because of the wet sneeze that hung in the air. His brothers shook their heads and semi-ignored him.

"Maybe we can go fishing again!" said Yawnel. Then as if answering himself, "Probably they won't let us go alone there either."

"Well, we have to try somethin', else we'll never leave the cottage," Grumel said.

"We need an adventure on our own," Joyal said, "something really exciting."

"I want to go to Laban," stated Shyel. "We're old enough to go."

"That's it," said Achu. "We're old enough to help more. They should let us help more. That should be our story."

"They're not going to let us go by ourselves," Grumel fretted. "All the talk about ogres and all. And still, only Dagon we've seen."

Yawnel said, "Let's go talk to Momma and Aunt Zee right away."

"Talk about what you little elves?" Rose startled them. She thought they looked guilty.

"Do we have a problem?" Zee asked, walking out from the cottage, carrying a bundle. Smirking, Rose said, "They're bored. They need adventure." She knew what they were talking about; she overheard them before.

"An adventure? Why isn't it enough to watch these lovely trees grow?" Zee said, pointing. They all smiled. "How about these flowers? Look at them; they're practically exploding with excitement." The boys stopped smiling; they realized she was making fun. "Where are your friends Timmy, Bonzo and… whoever the other one is?"

"Can we go to the Claw?" Shyel blurted out. The woodland went silent. Momma and Aunt Zee stared at him, then each other.

"By yourself? Did you hit your head? Ayell…" their mother asked. "Did you bonk your brother upside his noggin?"

Rose looked at Ayell; her silent child was not on her side. In fact, all seven boys were staring at her, pleading with their gazes. They knew this day would come, Rose wished Thoran were there. She had to tread lightly, she did not want a rebellion on her hands. Aunt Zee stepped in. "When Papa comes home, we'll discuss your next adventure." Their mood brightened considerably. "But not until he comes home!"

"This is a family discussion," Momma said, "and as a family we will decide. Tho' going to that lake by yourselves is not something I will vote for."

"We'll stay together, Momma," Alvis said, sounding every bit like a child.

"That's not the point," she said. "What happened to your father there was a mistake. I know that. Tho…" She stopped. She heard horses clomping—and snorting—then talking, coming from the woods, from the front path. The sounds became loud. Eighteen pairs of eyes shot glances at the woods, searching. Whatever it was, it was close and coming fast.

"In the house!" Rose commanded. They didn't listen. Instead, instinctively the boys formed a half circle around their mother and Aunt Zee. Three had their axes drawn; the others were only a clock tick behind with bows drawn and ready. A burst of pride filled Zee and Rose's thoughts.

Thoran and strangers emerged from the path. They were met with intent stares and weapons pointed at them, startling them. Even the horses were shocked for they stopped in mid-clomp. Thoran smiled. He thought if it had been dark, and he unseen, his boys would have let go their weapons at the sounds, and he probably would have been killed. Well done boys, he thought... but I'll have to be careful at night!

Rose whispered to her sons... "Say nothing about the journal."

The first sight of the seven little men sent a bolt of fear up Grimsdyke's spine, ending at his nose—it made him shiver, ever so slightly. It was a different feeling than his head pains. Only Ayell noticed that slight shake.

"Wohhhe...stay down men," Thoran barked.

"Papa!" they screamed.

Rose shot Thoran a quick, hard glance; he met her stare with a reassuring look. Extending his hand, Thoran gestured and said, "Rose, Zee, boys, please greet Council Master Grimsdyke and his companion, Maxwell."

The seven boys ran to their father while staring at the strangers. At first glance, the one assumed to be Maxwell just didn't look right to the boys. He was dirty and... scary. Grimsdyke was clean; he looked smart. But when he smiled, a sparkle came from his mouth, a sparkle from a tooth. A pointed tooth. A fang. A crimson fang. The sun, high above, bounced just the right way and caught a point in his mouth. His uneven smile unsettled the boys.

Slowly, elegantly, with a slight nod of his head, Grimsdyke said, "My, my, it is my pleasure." The men dismounted. Grimsdyke continued to speak, "Thoran told me about his family, but on first sight—well, the lot of you *are* something to behold." Grimsdyke studied them, one by one. He was taken by Rose's beauty and thought it would be a shame if she had to die. His eyes went to Zee and he froze, though only for a clock tick. He had trained his anger well. Her red hair, her green eyes, a flood of memories came back and he heard in his head an old hag-witch's cackle... 'an that little girl, the one with the green eyes and pretty red hair. She's alive I'm sure, an she told him to let you get eaten by these stupid things.' Grimsdyke remembered the pile of green ogre slime after Myrtle melted it. And Myrtle was right... "You're alive," the Council Master said.

"Sir?" Zee asked.

"I… I say it's good to meet you," Grimsdyke said. "Such a wonderful large family you are."

Maxwell had a slight dribble of spittle at the corner of his mouth. "Nice," was all he mumbled.

Slightly nervous, the boys curiously looked at the stranger's clothes. They tried not to look at his smile. Ayell looked a bit closer than his brothers when Grimsdyke smiled. Only he saw that the council master's left upper lip rose slightly higher than the right, and a sparkle again flew from his gum. Rose and Zee saw the ruby-red eyetooth and knew enough to look away so as not to be rude.

Grimsdyke's bald head was in stark contrast to Max's shaggy hair. His neatly trimmed beard was nothing like the dirty scrub on Max's face. Slightly taller than Rose, slightly smaller than Thoran, the Council Master wiped his forehead and studied his surroundings.

Max looked gritty, with worn, but not tattered clothing. He was taller than Thoran, not as broad in the shoulders. He stared mostly towards the ground, scritching bits of scraggly hair on his face. Fortunately, just moments before, Grimsdyke ordered Max to wipe the green and yellowed dried snot from his nose and facial hair. Thoran was silently thankful for that order, as he knew Rose and Zee were concerned about uninvited guests. And if they had seen Max before his quick cleaning, they would have been truly disgusted.

Nodding lightly, Rose spoke… "Welcome sirs, my name is Rose, this is my sister Grizelda. You're probably thirsty."

"Yes," Thoran said. "By chance, we *just* met on the trail. He's visiting around and came to advise us on the status of the scouting. I've asked them to stay until they're rested."

"Wonderful! We rarely get visitors and today does happen to be a celebration," Zee said.

"Yes, your father told me of your special day, boys," Grimsdyke smiled while thinking… could it really be…that witch was telling me the truth?

Max smiled and nodded. With a half-opened mouth, showing horrible teeth he said, "Haffy birfday boyths."

Grimsdyke shot his companion a quick, evil glance. Slowly, he said, "Yeeesss." Turning his gaze back to the boys, smiling, he said, "The happiest of days to you all. And if you ever happen to, or should I say, when you visit our town, a belated birthday gift will await you." The boys smiled and glanced at their mother. They welcomed Grimsdyke's comments; it was just what they were talking about.

Rose knew what was coming and spoke directly to Thoran. "After our visitors have left, the boys wish to discuss something with us." She turned to the boys, "But we have guests and we'll not discuss it now, as it is a family discussion." Thoran looked at them, perplexed.

"I pray we've not interrupted, Rose," Grimsdyke said, "I am sorry about our unscheduled visit." He tried not to look at Zee.

"Nonsense," Rose smiled. "We welcome your company. Our little men here seem to think they've outgrown their surroundings and we'll not bore you with our life's concerns. Do you have children sir?"

"No, I've never married," he answered and paused while thinking... If I did, I certainly wouldn't have any of these dirty children around. "My life's purpose has been serving the King and those within the Eastern Provinces."

"And a noble one at that," Thoran said, nodding. "Come, let's have a drink and some food."

"Life's purpose?" asked Joyal.

"I've devoted my life to the well-being of all those who live within our great lands, along our magical coast, my good man," Grimsdyke said with a smile. "The King has given me great responsibilities."

"Have you met the King?" asked Shyel.

"How many people are in Laban?" asked Achu while wiping his nose on his sleeve. "Is Thundor as grand as the stories we hear?"

"Please, use a cloth to wipe your nose," Zee said to her nephew.

Max smiled.

"Have you met other children sir?" asked Grumel, "We've only met a few."

Before Grimsdyke could answer anyone, his grubby companion spoke. "Lot'ths a younglins," Max slowly said.

Thoran, Rose and Zee looked at Max, their eyebrows crimped with concern. Grimsdyke sensed the parents' unease. He shot Max an angry look, "Go tend to the horses, Max. Sit with them to rest."

Max knew enough to take his leave. "Okay masther." The boys watched as Max grabbed the horse's reins and slowly walked them back towards the path they came from.

"Pretty as a painting," Grimsdyke said. "Your cottage— did you build it?" he asked Thoran. "I try to see as much of the woodland architecture as time allows. I must say I am impressed with your roof thatching. It looks most durable," admired Grimsdyke.

Proudly, Thoran said, "Sealed with my own special sap, never a drop of water, come take a look inside, sir."

The invite into the house was the true reason Grimsdyke was there. Although finding the girl with the green eyes was *the* most amazing surprise. He couldn't show his excitement, but he was so anxious he momentarily forgot that only minutes before, he had the stabbing head pains. He forgot about the anger he had carried around for decades. He was not honored to be the King's servant. He hated serving people. He only worked hard to achieve status of Council Master as it served a purpose to his end. Serving the people angered him; it always had. But he truly didn't think himself angry, even when he killed someone. He just thought it his fate to be that way.

Grimsdyke entered the cottage and immediately spied the goblet on the shelf and it all became clear to him. He saw the one named Zee die, but yet she lived. And how? Well—she drank from the goblet that was stolen from Myrtle by the dragon-elf that saved her. And this is where the dirty elf took her. Is that really it? Grimsdyke wondered why the witch didn't just come for it herself… she told me to go east. He didn't trust Myrtle… maybe it wasn't hers at all. Staring at the goblet he dreamed… how *can* a witch be killed. The candleholder meant nothing to him. It was the goblet that made him tingle. Stay calm, he said to himself. He needed to hold it, to feel it, to look for the mark. So as not to be obvious, his eyes drifted to the ceiling, "Simple, yet one of the most finely crafted structures I've seen," purposely commending its builder.

"Your compliments are appreciated," Thoran beamed, "I can't take all the credit, but we've kept it well."

"Perhaps one day we can do business," said the Council Master, "A bang-up carpenter is worth top pay."

"Well, I certainly have the helpers," Thoran chuckled, "Come sir, let's rest and eat."

Sensing a quick opening, Grimsdyke walked to the shelf and picked up the goblet. Hiding his true emotions, he lightly gasped as he found the mark— a simple crescent moon with a single tear dripping from its lower point. The weeping crescent, he thought. In his mind, he dreamed only of killing. "Beautiful piece— simple, yet elegant," he whispered.

Thoran walked up and put his hand out, expecting Grimsdyke to hand it back. "A gift from an old friend," Thoran said, "other than our family, the only treasure we have."

Grimsdyke studied Thoran, handed him back the goblet and thought… an old friend indeed! He decided not to ask any further questions.

Thoran, wanting to steer the conversation away from the goblet, said, "Come, I could use a drink."

"Cheers," answered Grimsdyke, they went back outside.

Shyel's curiosity got the better of him. Before his father and Grimsdyke sat down, he asked, "Did your scouts ever find the ogres?"

"Or orcs?" added Achu.

"Or the dark-elves?" said Joyal.

Grimsdyke respectfully glanced at Thoran, as if asking his permission to speak. "It's okay sir, we talk freely with the boys. They're old enough," Thoran said.

"I see," said Grimsdyke. "Well, in short, since your father's warning so many, many months ago, there's been no evidence of foul play." His eyebrows were raised and he smiled. "Our scouts have been nearly from coast to coast and have found many wonderful sights and very interesting creatures, but no massing of an ogre army; no killing fields of forest-lings or humans." Grimsdyke nodded at Thoran, "And thanks to your generosity, we've also taken advantage of this mission to update our maps of our *wonderful* Naturean Reach." Grimsdyke spoke with a bit of ridicule, then continued. "The scouts have been to the mountains, the deserts, to the Wells of Magog and to some of the central provinces and the West-Fields." Grimsdyke paused, "While not welcomed by all, the scouts even managed to visit three of the Seven Castles of Elberon."

"The castles? The actual castles?" Alvis asked.

"Were there any dragons?" asked Grumel.

"How bout Mullogs?" Yawnel wondered, "Any beasts with horns?"

"Boys let him speak," Rose said.

Grimsdyke smiled as he stared at Yawnel and thought... children really are only good for ogre food. "They also managed a visit to the black-jaw colony, those retched creatures are never happy to have visitors."

"What's black-jaw Papa?" asked Shyel and Joyal at the same time.

Thoran looked at Rose and Zee; he shrugged his shoulders as if to say... they might as well know.

"Black-jaw is a disease boys. It starts in the lower jaw. The teeth kind of..." he searched for the right word... "dissolve, er, melt and come apart, leaving horrid mouths and tongues that hang open. The poor people affected can't eat much, only soups. Then it spreads, to the brain, the neck, and chest. Most die from starvation. It turns people bad, they get sick and mean."

"Horrible creatures," Grimsdyke added.

"If someone gets the disease, they're forced to live apart from the rest. It's unfair and unjust, boys. I'd prefer not to call them creatures," Rose said, clearly unhappy with Grimsdyke's attitude. He ignored her concerns.

Alvis tried to add, "What if…"

Thoran stopped him, "Boys, let the Council Master finish. We can talk about this later."

"As I was saying," Grimsdyke continued, happy to try and appease the mother. "The scouts came across strange creatures, dangerous ones, odd people, old people, but no ogres. They met with sorcerers, found some witches and an assortment of elves and sprites…no ogres." He paused.

"Did they meet any dragon-elves?" four of the seven boys asked together.

"Boys!" Rose said, louder than she wanted. Then softer, "Please, let him finish."

Trying to not show his hatred, Grimsdyke smugly said, "I don't remember what they said about the dragon-elves. Well—I've come to put your minds at ease. With all due respect, I have concluded that your deceased friend's worries must have been mistaken. I have made my findings public at the last council meeting."

Ayell did not like Grimsdyke. The remaining six were disappointed in the scout's findings. Thoran, Rose and Zelda didn't know what to think. Dagon was never wrong, but they certainly couldn't disrespect the Council Master.

"Well that's good to know. We thank you for your time and efforts sir, for coming here to let us know," Thoran said.

Rose and Zee both added, "Yes we do."

"It's the least I could do. The council also convey their gratitude as the will and trust of the people is their utmost concern, and any potential threat brought to us must be handled for the people," he paused, and added, "and again, if it wasn't for your generosity, the trip would not have been possible."

As if sensing the coming questions, Thoran said, "Good! Well that is good news. Boys set your targets up and let's give Mr. Grimsdyke and his friend a showing of your skills."

"How were you generous Papa?" Joyal asked.

At that moment, Grimsdyke again wondered how Thoran was able to produce the bag of gold that partly paid for the scouts. Takes making a lot of tables and chairs to fill a bag of gold, he thought... he's found a vein of gold. I'll have to get that too. Stupid young-lings know nothing of their parent's wealth, nor of the real treasure that sits on their shelf... shame for them to die at so young an age.

"We helped pay for the scouting trip boys," their mother said. She slightly raised her voice, "And at this time, we will leave it at that." That was enough to end that conversation.

"Papa, we want to know more about the scouting trip," said Grumel.

Grimsdyke answered, "Then I suggest you come to Laban sometime. You can see the journals yourself. And if you come, a proper copy of the map shall be presented to you. Can you boys read?"

"Yes sir," all seven answered. Ayell answered 'yes' in his mind. The boys were excited. Rose didn't want to discuss the scouting anymore, so she said, "The point is that all is well and we should let our guests rest and have some food and drink."

"Yes indeed," Aunt Zee said, walking towards the cottage. "You sit and rest sister, I'll serve." Rose didn't resist. "Set your targets, boys. Show Mr. Grimsdyke what you've learned." The boys ran to get their bits, gubbins, and targets while the adults chatted.

Max watched everyone else have fun while he tended to the horses. Aunt Zee took a drink and a plate of bread and chicken to him. Zee's simple act of kindness touched him in a way he never felt before. Max was very afraid to say anything; he knew how evil the Council Master could be. He couldn't even bring himself to thank her. He looked at the Council Master with fear. In his whole life, no one had ever been nice to him. The Council Master took him in and fed him, but Max knew there was no kindness in Grimsdyke, only anger. Grimsdyke made him do bad things and Max was very sad, and very much afraid.

Sensing his shyness, softly, Zee said, "It's okay, you're quite welcome." Her hand brushed his arm. A tingly bolt of excitement coursed through him. She smiled, her green eyes twinkled and she walked back to the cottage. He would never forget that tingle and the image of her beautiful kind smile. It was the first spark of love he'd ever had.

The next few hours were spent snacking and watching. Grimsdyke and Max were quite amazed as the boys hit every target, from every position, with every weapon they had. Many times, Grimsdyke said, "My, my." Max said nothing.

Thoran was very proud of his boys. Rose wanted the visit to end; she was uncomfortable. They didn't overstay their welcome. Soon after they finished eating, Grimsdyke said it was time to go. It was at that point that a strange thing happened: a purple mantis-bug fluttered from a nearby tree and landed on the ground, in view of everybody and directly in front of the Council Master. He stepped on the bug hard, as if it tried to attack him. The boys gasped. They were shocked. So were their parents. "That's bad luck!" Shyel and Grumel screamed.

"Those are good bugs. It's bad luck to hurt 'em," Achu added.

"Yeah," Yawnel said, "not like twiglets, you can't eat them!"

Grimsdyke stammered, "I...uh..."

"Maybe he mistook it for a biting bug," Zee rescued the Council Master, although clearly not happy to do so; she gave Grimsdyke a stare that was not respectful.

"I, I did think it a biting bug," he answered, "and I am so sorry. Bug bites give me a rash and a fever. Certain bites can be fatal to me," he calmly lied. And slightly bowing to the boys he said, "I should be more careful, and I apologize if I offended you. Well, we must be off."

No one accepted his apology, and Max didn't like it that his master always killed bugs. Before leaving, awkward pleasantries were exchanged. Grimsdyke and his traveling companion Maxwell mounted their horses and lightly galloped away.

When out of view, Grimsdyke said, "Idiot. Understand Max, the parent-child bond is the strongest there is and—well, you have the look and sound of something that would boil and eat them... the children that is."

Lisping through his rotten teeth, Max asked, "Younglin sthoup?"

"Besides, I saw what I needed to see, but we must be careful. The father is enough of an adversary, but the boys also appear capable of defending themselves."

"Can I have the sisther, Masther?"

Grimsdyke looked at his simple servant and thought... is he smitten? "Maybe Max."

Max smiled. "When will us come back, Masther?"

"Soon Max, very soon." Grimsdyke knew his simple-minded companion could not understand the greatness of what just happened. Of the magic goblet and what it was. He himself wasn't even sure it was real—until he finally held it. Up to that point, Grimsdyke's quest only uncovered its tale...forged by alchemists of old and marked by the weeping crescent, simple water in it turns into a magic elixir, curing all diseases, making all pains go away. And legend has it that it holds a more powerful magic, unleashed only by a chosen one, a magic that can move mountains. Grimsdyke dreamed of having no more daggers of pain in his head. But Myrtle the witch screamed at him— 'YOU OWE ME SOMETHING!' His head pains were her fault. He wanted to kill her. For decades, he secretly searched and searched— not truly knowing where to look. And becoming Council Master—

well, that made it easier, because no one questioned someone of such high importance. "The Good Mother must have a special purpose for me," he said. Everything had come together. It all made sense. Fate now fully embraced him.

Angus remembered the holy man. "What was his name?" he asked aloud to himself. "Pye. That's right, Pastor Pye." He remembered the visit to Laban. And Pye's sermon: a story of a beautiful family's simple existence and extreme kindness. The pastor cried when he spoke of the wicked storm that nearly took his life, and how his spirit rose. And from above, he watched a wonderful man pour into his mouth a golden liquid from a beautiful golden goblet etched with a weeping crescent. He woke to what he dreamed was the Good Mother's smile, but what was really the face of an ordinary mother who said, 'Welcome back pastor, that was some fall you took.' The pastor spoke of divine intervention, but the lesson was one of kindness to others. For the mother had many children, but still treated the pastor as one of her own. That is the magic of kindness.

Grimsdyke heard only the words 'golden goblet, weeping crescent.' The Council Master invited the traveling pastor to his homestead where he killed him within minutes. No need for anyone else to hear his story, Grimsdyke thought. He was convinced... I am the chosen one. It all made sense. The goblet will be his. And finding the girl with the red hair and green eyes was his just rewards. Grimsdyke knew he deserved whatever he could take, from whomever he had to. And as fate would have it, Thoran came to town and said a dragon-elf had a warning— about ogres! And he would help pay for a scouting trip with large slivers of gold. They've all come to me... Grimsdyke thought.

"It will take many, many months, maybe years, to scout and search," Grimsdyke told Thoran.

"As long as we protect our good forest, time and price is irrelevant," Thoran answered.

"You're a good citizen. Come directly to me with any questions. I will see to this task personally. Trust only my words." And Thoran did. He had no reason not to be trusting. Grimsdyke took the gold and set forth a plan to search for ogres and monsters. But not to kill them, only to partner— to use them. And no one knew about it, especially not the King.

Clomping lightly along the path, savoring the moment and dreaming of treasure and of him ruling over all, to Max, Grimsdyke said, "Patience." He paused, "I need to keep watch over that family." He gasped, he had an idea. Smiling, he looked at his scruffy companion and said, "It's time to pay a visit to our dear old hag Myrtle."

Max knew Myrtle was a witch. He didn't want to visit her, but he had no choice.

Back at the cottage, when Grimsdyke and Max were out of view, Rose turned to Thoran and simply said, "How could Dagon be so wrong?"

Staring at the woods, Thoran simply answered, "I don't know. It doesn't matter. We'll be prepared."

Chapter Seventeen

Another Potion

Three days after their visit to the cottage with seven little boys, Grimsdyke and Max came upon a bridge. Thick, tattered ropes held wide, rotted planks together. The bridge spanned a massively long, dark crevice. A hole so deep, that not only could the bottom *not* be seen, but gray storm clouds hovered below the bridge, and partly covered where it led. Thin echoes of tiny crumbling rocks bounced throughout the abyss. It was not clear what lay on the other side. Few ever tried to cross, to pass over. The horses were not happy.

Grimsdyke kicked his steed to move, but the scared horse would only go at its own slow, reserved pace. Max's horse stayed close, close behind. Grimsdyke whispered, "No sudden movements Max. I've done this before." After a few quiet moments, both horses and riders were on the bridge; it began to sway, even though no winds blew. They went cautiously along the fog-covered, suspended path, dipping from side to side, as if off-balance. They moved slow and breathed hard. But not too hard, as both human and animal feared a cough, a snort or a twitch, would tip the balance to death's favor.

To Grimsdyke, the trip would be worthwhile.

The horses stepped *off* the bridge as carefully as they stepped on, and what lay before them gave no comfort. A craggy path went into a foggy forest of leafless trees. They lightly clomped on, into a tricky course that wound up, then down deeply into a gorge. The valley was shielded from the sun by colossal, overhanging ledges of rock and colorless brush. The air smelled burnt and dank, the mist was oily-thick and slick. Lifeless trees reached high into the sky and scrubby little bushes dropped black, sticky barbs. The few inhabitants of this land had no need of color, nor for sun.

They went to visit *her*—their old friend Myrtle. At one hundred ninety seven years old, she was close to dust. In her youth, she was strong enough to move mountains. Her powers lessened as age tired her out. Oh, she could still cause misery, she just couldn't cause as much.

Grimsdyke still thought he met her by pure chance when he was a child, but witches rarely meet by chance. And the only thing pure about a witch is her evil. She saved his life, and told him where she lived. "Come visits me sometime. I'll give yous whatever you want," she snickered, knowing full well that he would visit. The power of greed also has a might, all its own.

Myrtle's beast-pets smelled the horses, heard their clomping and became restless. Held captive in holes dug deep in the course ground, fresh horse-scent came through their grates. The closer the horses got, the hungrier her beasts became. Louder they growled. Through broken, rotted teeth and thin cracked lips, Myrtle's quiet command of, "Shut yer gobs," was obeyed.

Myrtle stood by what she called home; it was nothing more than bits of flat-wood and limbs, twined together to form a most decrepit structure. A few paces away stood a boiling cauldron set above a small fire. Max thought it was difficult to tell her saggy skin from her raggy clothes. He looked at her shack, and Max remembered the one, lonely, dirty room he once called home: it smelled, leaked, and was lifeless. He was much happier in the Council Master's barn.

A few paces from her shack, Grimsdyke stopped. He looked at Max, smirked and nodded. As they dismounted, groans echoed through the mist; moans of something in pain. Doesn't sound human...Grimsdyke thought. A cry... then the groaning stopped.

Myrtle giggled, "Isss dead."

Grimsdyke stared at the female thing in front of him.

"How does I look, council man?" she asked in a surprisingly feminine voice.

"How do you want to look, Myrtle?" he replied.

"Oh, to be a hunred again," she cackled and coughed. And spat— then cackled again, a raspy, dry sound that was *not* feminine. She shuffled to her bubbling kettle. Sticking out of its thick broth were some hairy tails and at least two or three bones. Eagerly escaping the cauldron were popping bubbles, each spitting a thin, rancid mist.

Max was getting hungry. Grimsdyke's head was throbbing.

"What brings ye here council man? Not only yer head pains I knows." At her kettle she stirred the pot with a colorful, moldy, wooden ladle. She reached in her pocket, brought out what looked to be a thick twig and threw it at Grimsdyke. "Here," she said, "smell this."

He caught it and thought… of course she knows my head aches. He looked at her and squinted. She nodded. Looks harmless enough… he thought, and brought it to his nose and sniffed. There was no scent. Within seconds he thought his head would explode. An uncontrollable sneeze followed, ending in a large stream of blue-gray snot that covered his boot. The sneeze startled the horses. His headache was gone. He wondered, did she just cure me?

Myrtle answered, "Just sumthin to keep it away fur a spell." She snickered and added, "you be cured when da maggots eat yur brain." She stuck her finger into the boiling cauldron to grab a bit of slime to taste.

Holding the twig-thing, Grimsdyke asked, "What is it?"

"Dried nose of a blood troll," she said. He was too happy to be disgusted.

Very quietly, stirring her swill, Myrtle babbled words— strange words. Then she spoke, "I haven't seen the baby in long time," she moaned, "straaaangeling's came out the ground afore'. Tried to eat me. I cook em up," and she tapped the kettle with the ladle.

Grimsdyke looked at her, thinking…this very well might be her last hex. "Myrtle?" he asked slowly. She looked at him. Just above a whisper he asked, "Can you conjure up a spell and turn my friend here into a cute little puppy?"

"A puppy," she said slowly, lovingly. "So sweet. So tender."

Max looked at Grimsdyke, confused. He asked, "Masther?"

"A puppy!" Grimsdyke barked, "Can you still conjure!"

She looked at Grimsdyke. Angrily, she stuck her hand into the boiling cauldron and pulled out the head of a small creature, its flesh mostly boiled off its skull. She threw the head towards Grimsdyke, purposefully missing him, aiming at his horse while screaming "BEALTA DOMONDO, CAALLLENDINNN"

The boiled head struck the horse; it whinnied in panic. Myrtle screamed and a bright flashing mist erupted, surrounding the poor creature. The mist quickly settled, and in place of a majestic animal stood a headless horse. After two clock ticks, the legs carrying the headless trunk buckled and the massive torso fell to the ground with a loud, dead thud.

Grimsdyke was mistaken. She still had power.

"Oops," she cackled, "I tried ta makes it inta a beautiful unicorn. Musta' forgot ta add salt." She laughed so hard at her own joke she made herself gag, choke and throw-up. She did this while holding onto the kettle.

Grimsdyke and Max stood there, one angry, one very frightened.

In a loud whisper she said, "Can I conjure! Paaah," she swiped her hand at nothing. "Why you want ta turn him inta a dog?" she asked.

Containing his anger, Grimsdyke said, "You killed my horse."

Myrtle looked at him, grayish throw-up dripped from her hairy chin. She smirked and grabbed a bone out of the kettle and threw it while whispering.

The headless horse was again struck, again there was a bright mist. When the mist lifted, the horse had its head back. It lay there, dazed and confused. After a few clock ticks, it jumped up and stood—still too afraid to run.

Myrtle sat down where she had just thrown up—"I asks ya why you want him ta be a dog?"

"Let's just say I'm trying to repay my debt to you. And I need his help," he answered while pointing to Max. "It has to do with the goblet," Grimsdyke said.

With a dull look on her face, the witch stared at him. Then she smirked. "Need to rest," she whispered.

"A puppy," Grimsdyke said, throwing a small sack of gold at her.

She let it drop at her feet. Stupid maggot, she thought. Thinks I want gold. "Tired," was all she said, then she passed out.

In a feeble voice, Max asked, "Masther, what's going on?"

Grimsdyke took Max's shoulder, "You will go back to the cottage— as a puppy. You will stay with them for two full moons. After the second full moon, I will come for you. When you see me, you run away and we'll meet up on the trail back home. While you're with them, you will watch them. Look for treasure Max. Look for gold. You can have everything you want if you find their gold. Do you understand Max?" he asked.

"A puppy?" Max asked.

Grinning, Grimsdyke answered, "Everyone loves a puppy, Max."

"What if they don't?" Max asked.

"They will. You just act nice to them and they'll be nice to you. After all, they're a very nice family."

Max thought about it for a moment. "Can I sthill have the nice lady masther? The one called Zee?"

Grimsdyke sighed and stared at the sleeping witch. She was curled in a fetal position on a bed of twigs and throw-up. "Sure Max. Anything you want." Looking at the hag, Grimsdyke realized how tired he was. After grabbing his bedroll, he found a patch of ground that wasn't too moldy and damp. He sat, and then lay down. Max quietly also found a patch. "We'll take a little nap until *that* wakes up," Grimsdyke said, pointing at Myrtle.

"It won't hurt me, will it, sir?"

"Don't worry, you'll be fine. Haven't I always treated you fairly Max? Mostly. Right?"

Max didn't answer; he just stared at the ground. After a few minutes, both fell asleep. When their eyes closed, Myrtle's opened. She stared at them as they slept. Stupid maggots, she thought. Greedy spit. The perfect tools for makin misery. She hobbled around them. Simple, stupid thing…she thought of Max…a dog's too good for him. She walked up to Max and gently plucked one hair from his head. He scratched at the spot of the plucking. She whispered, "Tis a dog I makes ya then…baby black shuck you be…devil hound."

She looked at the Council Master and thought…lets take 'nother for safekeeping. She plucked one of his hairs. He scratched and she put his hair in her pocket. Scuttling up to her brewing kettle, she dropped Max's hair in— it sizzled when it hit the brew. From her other pocket she pulled out a small stone vile filled with a brown, gooey sauce. She plopped a few drops in her brew, then quickly hobbled to her hut while whispering and grunting and stepped inside. She popped out, holding a small, wriggling grimler by the tail. Her other arm was wrapped around some small urns. She threw the squealing little animal in her pot, plopped in a few more drops of vile goo, picked up her favorite ladle and started to mix. She stirred and stared at Max while chanting:

"To black shucks heart, I stir thee swill,
ever the howl, ever the mongrel,
blood of canine, howl to trill,
sweet and tender, mongrel howl,
bones and heart, bones and heart,
blood red stare, black the hair."

Myrtle stared into the kettle. Whispered and stirred, stirred and whispered. After a bit she screamed, "GET UP BOY!" while kicking

Max. Both men jumped.

Confused, Max looked around, then at Grimsdyke.

"Masther?" Max asked.

"Come here, he can't grants a wish," she cackled.

"Go on Max, it's ok," Grimsdyke said quietly, hoping, if he kept calm, Max would be calm.

Back at her kettle, she stirred, "Times wastin, maggots."

"Come," Grimsdyke grabbed Max's arm and lead him to the kettle. They slowly walked up to Myrtle and her ladle full of her brew.

"Drink," she held it out.

Max could not remember a time when he was so hungry. He also could not remember ever being so scared. So scared, that he peed himself. He could not bring himself to drink.

"Drink it, Max. I promise no harm will come to you," Grimsdyke lied. Max closed his eyes.

Myrtle brought the ladle to his mouth, "Stops breathin' through yur nose an open up!" she said. And he did. She put the ladle to his mouth and tipped its contents in. The potion ran down his chin. He couldn't swallow.

Angrily, Grimsdyke put one hand over Max's mouth and with the other, grabbed the hair on the back of his head. With clenched teeth, Grimsdyke sneered, "The quicker you do it, the easier it will be," and he pulled hard on Max's hair.

Max swallowed. The pain started right away. He couldn't hear anything except a loud throb that beat at his brain. He stopped seeing. Everything became foggy. A gray mist seeped out of his pores. Myrtle was unimpressed; she hobbled away.

Grimsdyke watched—impressed. His companion, once larger than himself, quickly shook, convulsed, and shriveled inward. A fog surrounded Max and the slightest of cracking sounds came from his body. Max's clothes became sizes and sizes too large; he seemed to disappear. Grimsdyke couldn't see curly hairs growing under loosening clothes, Max's nose sprouting into a snout or his hands and feet as they shrunk into paws. He also didn't see Max grow a tail. When the fog dried up, all that remained was a pile of Max's clothes, with a punching bulge to one side.

Max was a puppy. A little, black, confused dog that shook with fear; still with horrible teeth. He squirmed out of his clothing, clothes that were now seventy sizes too big, and looked down at what were once calloused hands, now his two front paws. He cried, but his cries sounded like little canine whimpers. Looking straight ahead, Max saw two huge legs. Following the legs up, he saw the immense shape of Grimsdyke. He cry-barked again, *"Master?"* he barked, *"I don't like this!"*

Grimsdyke looked at Max with disgust. The only sounds Max could now make were mongrel whimpers, howls and barks.

Back at her kettle Myrtle said, "Don't lets him grows up. He might be all tender-like lookin now, but in a few months, he grow quick. Big and nasty he'll be. An watch out when the moon is fat! Blood red is what he'll see."

"How do I turn him back?" Grimsdyke asked while looking at the shaking, little dog. "After the second full moon forthcoming, I'll need him back," he stated.

She laughed. "Yea—sure you does council *man*. Maybe ee jest won't want you back," she cackled. Grimsdyke looked at her, puzzled. "Here," she threw him a vile, "makes him eat this. Be back goods as new."

With a nod of his head Grimsdyke said, "A pleasure, Myrtle." He pocketed the vile, grabbed a sack from his horse, picked up Max the puppy, and shoved him inside.

Max started to howl-cry... *"What's going on Master?"*

To Grimsdyke, Max only made pathetic, dog whimpers. "SHUT UP," Grimsdyke yelled at the sack.

Max howled louder..."*Please, please let me out master!"* It was dark. He couldn't move.

Grimsdyke knew he couldn't take the howling for too long, so he took out his knife and cut a slit in the sack, reached his hand in and pulled out Max's head. "There, now be quiet." He secured the sack and mounted his horse. A horse that was still dazed after having a dream about losing its head.

Max was more comfortable with his head sticking out of the sack. He became very tired and soon passed out.

With Max's horse in tow, the Council Master headed back towards the bridge. The horses were happy…they were leaving. The bridge was better than the witch. Glancing back, Grimsdyke saw Myrtle stirring the kettle, staring at him. They both thought the same thing— ugly old maggot! She screamed out, "YOU OWE ME SOMETHING, IF YA DON'T HELP, THEN I DON'T NEED YA."

A flood of memories came back. Grimsdyke remembered Myrtle melting the ogre that was going to eat him. He didn't want her to have his goblet.

Horrible Teeth

Almost three days later, Grimsdyke stopped the horses. They were close to Rose's cottage. He dismounted, pulled out his knife and slit the bottom of the sack. Max tumbled to the ground with a quiet thud. He sadly looked at his master and whined, *"I don't want to be a puppy. I want to be me again. Please."* Max knew he smelled of poo.

To Grimsdyke, Max was just a whimpering little mutt. He was tired of hearing dog cries. He pointed… "Just up the path is their cottage. They'll feed you and take care of you. Be nice to them and they'll be nice to you." Grimsdyke paused, bent down, grabbed Max by the scruff of his neck and lifted him. Their noses touched, their eyes met. "Do you know what I'm saying Max. Do you understand?"

Max understood and shook his head. He barked and barked— *"I do, I do master, but I'm afraid. I want to be me again."* It was all barking to Grimsdyke, but he knew Max understood.

"The moon will be full soon. Then it will shrink. Right after it gets full the second time, I will come for you. Until then, you will watch," Grimsdyke tapped Max's head. "Remember what you see. Look for gold. Look for treasure. If they take you anywhere, remember where they take you. If they hide anything, watch them. Do you understand?"

Max barked, *"Yes!"*

Grimsdyke was satisfied; he stared at his dog-friend. "I think you're smarter being a dog, Max. Too bad Myrtle couldn't do something with those nasty teeth of yours."

Max howled, *"You will come back for me, won't you master?"*

Grimsdyke pointed and said, "The cottage is that way. Follow the path. It will lead you to them." He paused, clapped his hands and shouted, "Go!"

Max started to walk and thought... boy does it feel good to walk... and the sun was more than good, it was—really good.

"And Max..." his master said. Max stopped and turned around, expecting a kind word. "If you mess this up," Grimsdyke smiled, pulled the vile out of his pocket and shook it, "You'll stay a mangy mutt for the rest of your life." He mounted his horse and while slowly clomping away, he finished with... "Or I'll just kill you." Then louder, "IF YOU DON'T HELP, THEN I DON'T NEED YA."

Max watched his master go. He wanted to make Grimsdyke proud. Max turned and started bouncing up the path to the cottage. It wasn't long before he heard voices. One particular voice made him feel—happy, a feeling he wasn't used to. The cottage popped in front of him. Max saw Aunt Zee before she saw him; he didn't know what to do. He stopped and stared at her. After a few clock ticks, Zee sensed something watching, she turned. At first she didn't know what to make of him. They both just stared at each other, their heads slightly tilted.

"Well, well. What have we here?" Zee said, "Come here little one."

He didn't waste any time. He sprinted at her, stopping just short of her able to pet him. Max was very hungry and smelled something cooking.

Up close she saw he wasn't the prettiest of animals. And he looked dirty. "You are a mangy looking thing aren't ya," she said.

Max didn't know what mangy meant, but he was called it often. He knew it wasn't a good word.

"Big paws you have." She studied him. Loudly she said, "Rose, Thoran, you'd better come look at this." The cottage was small. Everyone heard her. The boys were there in an instant. Although they had never seen one, they knew what it was. "A PUPPY!" six boys screamed and one thought. Thoran poked his head out of a window and said, "A dog?"

Rose came out the front door, looked at Max and also said, "Well, well. What do we have here? And where did it come from?"

Thoran walked out the front door and again said, "A dog?"

The family formed a circle around him. Max wondered what they would do with him. So he whimpered. And he whined, *"If I'm nice to you, will you be nice to me? He said you'll be nice to me!"* The family heard only a puppy's short barks and whimpering.

"He's scared," said Zee.

"I aaammmm," howled Max.

"Maybe he's hungry," said Shyel.

"Or thirsty," Grumel and Alvis said together.

"I am, I am," Max barked and barked. *"I'm really hungry and master has only given me a little drink of dirty water and— oh please just a little drink and something to eat, I'll be nice to you if you're nice to me."* They stared at Max.

"Noisy little thing." Thoran said. He walked up and placed his hand in front of Max's face to allow him to sniff his scent. Having no canine instincts, Max just stared at his hand. "Strange," Thoran said, "dogs always sniff to pick up scents. It's in their nature to sniff."

"Look at his teeth," Rose said. "He might be sick. A diseased animal can not stay here." That scared Max. Instincts or not, he quickly knew enough to sniff Thoran's hand. Then he licked it. I might be dumb, but I'm not stupid, Max thought... What would a dog do? Be a dog.

"That's more like it," Papa said, "just scared aren't ya boy?"

"Other than his teeth, he looks healthy," Zee said.

Excited, Max barked, *"I'm not sick. I feel fine. I'm just hungry and scared. I'll be nice to all of you."* And starting with Zee, Max went to each family member, gave them a sniff, a lick, and a happy howl, amusing them.

"Something about him, isn't there?" Zee said.

"Can he stay?" asked Joyal. They first stared at Thoran, and all eyes moved to Rose.

Thoran said, "I don't know. It's strange. Where'd he come from? All this time here and we've never seen a stray dog. A puppy has a mother and a father. Am I right?"

"Please, Papa. He's alone," pleaded Achu.

"He could just be lost," said Shyel.

"Maybe his mom and pop are hurt!" said Grumel.

Max whimpered, *"Please, please. I'll be nice to you."*

Thoran again said, "I just don't know."

Rose gave the final word. "He can stay as long as he's a good dog."

"I will, I will be," Max barked, still excited. All the boys barked with excitement.

The adults thought it strange; the puppy seemed to answer Rose's last comment. And his teeth. Something about them looked familiar.

Nonetheless, that day, Max became part of their family.

Chapter Eighteen
Sweet Smells

Trebor Sheef and his beautiful 3 year-old daughter, Flower, sat high up inside the ancient tree as it burned. He closed his eyes and smiled, remembering years ago, how his wife glowed as all women did when with child. Women radiate and bloom as the softest of scents, the scent of a child, makes way from their body. And he thought of that wonderful family with seven brave little men. He remembered that particular fun day, as it was the last day of happiness he could remember.

On that day, Trebor couldn't imagine that grandma would soon lose half of her false teeth, and while stubbornly searching the woodland, would fall down and break her leg, hobbling her.

On that day, Trebor couldn't imagine that a flying spider would soon bite his middle daughter, and that her unknown allergy to the bug would make her too weak to walk.

On that day, Trebor couldn't imagine that the blood-trolls had already woken to the smell of a seventh of a seventh. But they had, and they followed.

On that day, while his family rested in a thicket, he couldn't foresee the early birth of his baby, and that they would have to fight for her life. The trolls came while a sweet mother wailed; first from birthing her child, next from the panic of attack. Her agonizing cries woke one of the ancient tree-folk, the Borrais, from his long slumber. The mighty oak-being helped as best as he could, shielding the baby and helping the family fight and run. And fight they did. But the trolls drove them deeper and deeper into the forest. And one by one the family fell: first the mothers as they were the weakest, next the children, then the grandfather. And the trolls chased, cut and burned.

In an ancient redwood, Trebor hid with his little angel. But now, it too burned. Shrieking its sorrow and bellowing with anger, through flames the mighty tree cursed at vicious little monsters that jumped from the ground. In the hollow of the great tree, Trebor cradled his little girl and sobbed… "I'm so, so sorry my love. You will always be our little flower. Mommy and Daddy love you so… forever and ever."

Flower watched with horror as the blood-trolls reached for her. She was the most difficult seventh to find.

Chapter Nineteen
A Dog?

Their dog needed a name, but they just couldn't agree on one. They tried on many, but none fit. As darkness fell on his third night with them, Rose called to her boys… "Come in boys, lest the gobles try to eat you in the pitch-black night." As soon as she said it, the boys knew his name. Max liked it also, but it took him a long time to remember they were speaking to him when they called out… "Come here Pitch."

Thoran made a great doghouse for him. Max, or Pitch, didn't like sleeping outside, but it was comfortable and clean. They gave him a blanket and food and water; he ate what they ate.

On his seventh night with his new family, all were asleep and Pitch listened to the woodland sounds. Crickets and cicadas argued with each other. Gracklers and owls planned their attacks. Four-winged bats fluttered after their favorite food, four-eyed flying spiders. The moon was bright. It wasn't quite fat yet—one more day, maybe two. Grimsdyke's words were still fresh in his mind… "After the second full moon, I will come for you. Look and watch." So far Pitch saw nothing, but he sure was enjoying himself. The boys played with him all the time. And Aunt Zee and Momma fed him all the time. Thoran scared him, but was friendly.

When the first full moon came, Pitch stared at it thinking he'd never seen a red moon. But it wasn't the moon that was red— it was his eyes. The moon got fat, an anger boiled in him and his eyes turned red. Myrtle turned him into what the witches call a black shuck. A dog of the devil. His stomach made noises…boy I'm hungry, he thought. They weren't hunger pains—they were anger throbs. So he went into the woods to find some meat. Even though it was dark, the fat moon lit up the woods, and he could see just fine. When the fat moon was gone, so was the anger.

After three weeks, Max the puppy doubled in size. He was nearly two thirds of a yard long and at twenty-two pounds, weighed more than a stone and a half. He thought to himself… I'll be nice to them 'cause they're so nice to me. I like being a puppy. Maybe the master will let me stay with them for a bit.

After a month, Pitch forgot about looking for gold or any treasure. He only thought about keeping the boys and the grownups happy, because they were being so, so nice to him. The adults watched Pitch for any sign of trouble or disease. Other than his teeth, he seemed a healthy specimen. But they noticed that he was growing quickly, and they knew old tales of viscous, black shucks spawned from evil. They just couldn't imagine that their cute little puppy was a devil's pet. So Pitch was watched. Fortunately, he seemed every bit as simple an animal as their donkey or chickens. Except he did have the curious ability to bark, howl or yelp when questioned or talked at, as if he were answering whoever spoke, and that amused the whole family.

By the seventh week of his stay, Pitch was a yard long and weighed over two stone. He learned to be much more like a proper dog. So much, that when a bird flew by, he'd bark at it. If a stick was thrown, he needed to chase it. Not had to, as if he was playing the part of a dog, but actually needed to chase it.

One day he followed a squirrel deep into the woods, not realizing how very far from the cottage he was. The squirrel scurried away, but Pitch wasn't afraid as his strong sense of smell brought him straight home. To Pitch, each member of his family had their own special scent. Momma and Aunt Zee smelled the sweetest. The boys always smelled like sweaty dirt. The chickens always smelled like, well, chickens.

The day the second fat moon started was a particularly good day. It was September and the weather was just starting to cool down. Crisp, sweet air filled the woods and deep colors jumped about the trees, leaves and ground. That day, everyone was up early. The whole family went for a walk. They played in caves and Papa showed them some shiny rocks that they picked at with tools. Funny... Pitch thought... I don't remember them bringing tools. *"Ho,"* he barked, *"is that a bird!?"* And off he went, out of the mouth of a cave.

That day, they played in the forest all day. After, they went home and made a grand feast. At sundown, everyone was tired. Ayell filled Pitch's water bowl and brought it to Pitch's little house. The other boys followed, and together they petted, patted and scrunched him while saying, "Good night Pitch, good night boy, good boy." Pitch replied with enthusiastic barks and thumped down, he too was tired. He would have liked his belly rubbed, but the boys were on their way to bed. It never dawned on Pitch that Ayell didn't speak. In Pitch's mind, Ayell spoke as much as everyone else. He understood Ayell's eyes.

As the second full moon rose, Max's eyes changed from ash gray to blood red. He stared at its fatness, watching bats and bugs flit through its bright light. The bats made him angry. If I could fly... he thought... I would kill them and eat them.

Pitch stared at the fat red moon and didn't fall asleep until he couldn't see it any longer.

Meanwhile...

the only regret Shniggles ever had was that he shouldn't have made that one large kettle the young witch asked him to bake. It happened a long time ago. He was a young, headstrong man and didn't know she was a witch until it was too late. But he used the clay she gave him, mixed with the bits she threw at him to burn in the kiln. Stanley didn't know the clay was made from bones, both human and animal. And the bits—well, he couldn't fully remember, but now thought it was dried hair. After the large kettle came out of his kiln, it was so heavy he dropped it. If it were a normal kettle, it would have just smashed into seventy pieces. But that kettle was not normal. It fell and landed with a thud, sitting upright, inviting something to be thrown in. And as he went to pick it up, Myrtle appeared in a blink, surprising him by saying, "Tis okay my good Stan, you done well."

He looked at her and should have been scared, but felt only guilt. "I got's it," she said, "You go back and get yurself somethin' ta eat."

He couldn't move. She brushed against him; her hot scent burned his nose. She grabbed the kettle with one hand, lifted it and easily walked away. In the other hand she had a small bag of gold chips. She threw the bag up high, he watched it float above him and drop, landing at his feet. He looked at the bag and then to her—she was gone.

Stanley Shniggleton picked up his first payment of gold and threw it into the fire of his kiln.

Chapter Twenty

The Master Returns

Grimsdyke made his way through the forest. He was excited, but most of his thoughts were interrupted by throbbing head-pains, searing aches that were sharp and becoming more frequent. He sniffed the dried blood-troll's nose every few hours or so. After each sniff, he would sneeze out the vilest looking matter that he was sure included pieces of his brain. And there was now blood coming out of his nose. But oh—there was such a relief after each sneeze.

He thought...surely Max would have seen something by now, it's been nearly two full months. Grimsdyke dreamed about the goblet, fantasized about gold and treasure. "Will I be immortal?" he asked himself. He knew the goblet would not be his on this trip, but it would be by the next one. Smiling, he dreamed... It will be a shame to kill all of them. Perhaps sweet Rose would come if she thought I will spare the others lives. A plan had been going through his diseased mind for a long, long time... they'll probably have to die...I will not take any chances. When the time is right, my secrets will be released.

Pitch smelled the Council Master long before the clomping of his horse was heard. *"I know that smell,"* he barked and barked, *"I know who that is."* Pitch had forgotten everything his old master had asked him to look for. Max remembered nothing of why he was turned into a puppy, but he knew Grimsdyke's scent.

"What's the matter, boy?" asked Grumel, "You smell something?"

"Come here, Pitch," said Alvis.

"I do, I do," yelped Max, *"it's him, it's him. He's coming back for me."* he barked with excitement. *"My master's come back!"* Then it dawned on

him. In a low, frightened howl he growled, *"He's coming back for me."*

"What's that dog yapping about?" asked Aunt Zee.

"He smells something," Achu said smiling, "probably an ogre."

"Maybe a dragon, with knives for teeth," said Yawnel, with outstretched arms.

Answering them, Pitch barked, *"It's not an ogre, it's the Master. I don't want to go back. I want to stay."* His jaws quivered, he howled louder, *"I don't want to go back!"*

"Easy boy," Shyel said.

"I can't go!" Pitch angrily barked and paced.

"Something's got him upset," said Shyel.

Everyone started to look around for the culprit. Except for simple echoes of chirping insects and birds, the woodland was calm. Grimsdyke's scent got stronger, Pitch's plea cut through the quiet. *"NO, NO, NO, NO,"* he barked as he ran around. He dashed here, he dashed there, ran in circles. He ran to the house. He ran to the path where he knew the master would be coming. Back to Grumel. Back to the path. Back to Ayell.

"PAPA, MOMMA," Alvis screamed.

Rose and Thoran rushed out of the cottage, "What's all the barking about?" they asked together.

They heard a horse clomping. Thoran snatched his ax from his belt and started walking towards the path, saying loudly, "Everyone—in back of me." Thoran stared hard and stood watch. He was the front line. Pitch ran to his side, barking at the woods... *"Send him away. Tell him to go back."*

Papa glared at Pitch. The dog exhibited strange behavior. Their eyes locked and Pitch pleaded with Thoran while barking, *"Please, please send him home,"* then louder, *"I DON'T WANT TO GO BACK YET!"*

"Easy boy," Thoran patted him. "Everything's fine. Easy. Easy," he said while stroking him. Pitch calmed down.

When he saw Grimsdyke, he barked like a dog possessed by goblins.

Grimsdyke heard the barking some distance from the cottage. "Still making all that noise, eh Max?" he said to no one, "I'm sure they'll be grateful to get rid of you." He clomped out of the path and saw all of them. Again, like the first time he had seen them, a shiver of fear shot up his spine and ended at his nose. His head pounded with pain. He was impressed at how much Max had grown and thought…what a racket he's making. Grimsdyke fiddled with the vile of antidote in his pocket, thinking his simple-minded friend would soon be back.

Their eyes met, and before Grimsdyke could greet the family, Pitch howled loud, *"NOOOOOOO, I DON'T WANT TO GO!"* The howl made Grimsdyke's horse buck.

Grimsdyke hollered, "STAY DOWN STEED, STAY, STAY." He tried to meet Max's eyes, to will him to shut up, but Pitch only howled at the top of his canine lungs.

All were perplexed at Pitch's bizarre reaction.

"KILL HIM!" Pitch barked furiously—loud and angry, sounds they'd never heard from an animal. *"KILL HIM NOW!"* he barked hard while on his haunches.

The horse whinnied, panicked and threw the Council Master— he landed with a hard thud on his duff. Everyone except the dog was speechless for a few clock ticks. Pitch, crouching low to the ground, clenched his teeth and growled, *"I'm not goin."* It was a growl so deep Thoran felt it in his feet. Max was just about to pounce on his old master when at the top of her lungs Aunt Zee screamed, "Staaaaaaaaaaap!" Pitch stopped growling. Everyone stared at Zee.

"Council Master, I beg your forgiveness," Thoran said, horrified, while running to his aid. Rose followed, Pitch started growling again.

"BOYS! Take that dog away. MAKE HASTE!" Thoran screamed. "Rose, please help." The boys surrounded their dog and bullied him away while the animal yowled and grunted. Grimsdyke—shocked, in pain and furious, held his composure. His anger was stronger than his pains. He hoped he had no broken bones. Thoran tried to help

Grimsdyke up. "I don't know why he acted that way sir, perhaps the horse scared him. My deepest apologies sir. Please let me…"

"Stop," Grimsdyke interrupted, "I'm winded, but hopefully not broken." He looked where Pitch was dragged away. "Dogs are stupid animals." Grimsdyke wondered…why did he act that way? Was his simple mind broken by the witches spell? Getting up gently, standing, his legs wobbled, he needed Thoran's help. "That little black beast should be punished," Grimsdyke said, and thinking… he will be!

"Please sir," Rose offered, "it's better for you to rest inside, to lay flat. You'll not have to see that dog again while you're here."

"No, I'm fine, perhaps just a drink of water," the Council Master asked. A thought came to him; he remembered what Myrtle the hagwitch said… 'maybe he wont's want you back.' Her sick laugh filled his twisted mind. Could that be? He wondered…could that simpleton prefer a dog's life? Did that old hag trick him up? This could be a problem. I can't believe he'd prefer a dog's life. Maybe he's seen the gold and wants to keep it for himself. "Could that be?" Grimsdyke asked himself aloud.

Rose looked at Thoran and asked, "Sir, please. Come inside."

Grimsdyke ignored her. He was angry with himself for not foreseeing this. He knew more than anyone that no one can ever be trusted, not even simpletons like Max. Then something dawned on him. He laughed. Rose, Zee and Thoran watched him with grave concern. They noticed a trickle of blood coming from his ear. Grimsdyke laughed again and thought… it just doesn't matter! He laughed out loud and stared at the ground.

"Go get him something to drink," Thoran asked Zee.

Grimsdyke continued staring at nothing. Smiling, he thought… when my army is complete I'll take hostage of the whole lot. It won't take much torture for them to talk. When they see those little ones hanging by their feet over a boiling kettle, they'll beg to tell me anything. He laughed at the simplicity of this, and of his silliness of not thinking of it sooner. He laughed loudly. His thoughts screamed at him...and my army will eat those who get in the way... we'll rip this forest apart branch by branch. I'll kill them all if they don't talk. I'll find the treasure.

Rose and Thoran looked at each other, then at Grimsdyke. At the same time they asked, "Sir?"

Grimsdyke's head shook back and forth. He smiled at his black thoughts; he dreamed of darkness. Swirling corpses filled his world. And gold. His desires for the goblet and treasure would not end there. He now saw the King in a pool of blood. Again, he laughed aloud. Thoran touched the Council Master's shoulder..."Sir?" he tentatively asked.

And that idiot can stay a dog, Grimsdyke thought... I'll kill them all and watch those stupid ogres eat them, one at a time. Maybe I'll let them watch each other being eaten. Grimsdyke's smile widened, then he passed out. A trickle of blood came out of his nose and right ear.

"Get him inside," Thoran snapped.

"The goblet?" Rose asked.

"Perhaps," Thoran answered. Alvis, Joyal and Achu came out from the back of the house to survey the situation.

"Papa? Is everything ok?" one asked.

"All is well," said Rose. "The Council Master took a nasty spill and needs to rest." They brought him inside. Grimsdyke stirred a little, mumbling something that sounded like... "Eat Max." The elders stared at each other. Everything happened so fast they didn't realize the Council Master came alone.

Knowing Grimsdyke was inside the cottage, Shyel brought Pitch back to the front yard, to the spot where moments earlier he caused so much commotion. Louder than he wanted to, Pitch barked..."*Is he gone? Is he dead?*"

Grimsdyke's eyes shot open. For a moment he was confused and wondered... is this my parlor? In front of him was the goblet of his dreams…am I dreaming? Max's barking brought him back to reality and he knew it was time to go. He sat up quickly, surprising Rose and Zelda.

"Sir, please sit and rest, you've only just laid down," Zee pleaded.

Grimsdyke coughed to clear his throat, then said, "No, I feel fine. I must be going back. I thank you for your kindness."

Thoran asked, "Sir? Please, you should stay and rest."

Not wanting to waste time, Grimsdyke said, "Many thanks again, however, I really must be getting back. My purpose in coming was to personally invite your family to the King's Festival… it's to be held in the village square in six weeks time." Thoran, Rose and Zee were deeply embarrassed. The Council Master came all the way out there for such a fine purpose, and their dog almost killed him.

"Again, our humblest of apologizes sir," Rose said.

Thoran added, "Is there anything we can do to make your trip back more pleasant? If it comforts you, I can travel with you. In fact, I insist on it. Rose, help me…

"No," Grimsdyke interrupted, "Thoran, I'll be fine." He paused but didn't miss an opportunity… "Though a donation to the council for, *civic* purposes is always welcome."

Thoran was more than happy to make a donation… "It's the least we can do," he gladly said, then went to a small cupboard, opened it and retrieved a small sack of gold chips.

Grimsdyke's eyebrows slightly arched. He thought to himself… not a bad day's pay. He smiled at Thoran and slightly nodded his head. "Good, then it's all set. Your family will attend the festival and I am still in one piece," he said while patting his rump. They nervously chuckled. Grimsdyke quickly walked to the door and opened it. He stepped outside, surprising Max, who was within an arms length of him. Max froze, their eyes met, Rose lightly gasped. Without fear, Grimsdyke said, "I'm leaving. Have a good life—dog."

Pitch was bark-less…wha… he thought… are you really leaving

me here? Grimsdyke brushed by close enough to wap Pitch's nose; his scent burned Pitch's nostrils. Zee and Rose looked at each other, perplexed. They thought... strange thing to say to the dog.

Joyal added, "We're very sorry for our dog, Pitch, sir. We hope that when we visit we can still look at your maps." Thoran smiled at his son's sincerity.

"Is that what you call him?"

"Yes sir, 'cause he's pitch-black," Achu added while smiling.

Grimsdyke looked at his old companion. "Pitch," he mocked. He turned back to the boy, "No need for your sorrow young man. Your parents will tell you all about the grand festival your family will hopefully attend. It will be a most special day." Even more special for me...he thought, because by then most of you will be dead and I will have my treasure. Grimsdyke smiled and nodded to Achu. The boys heard the word 'festival' and mumbled, excitedly.

"Now where's my mostly trusty steed?" Grimsdyke asked. The horse stood quietly by the edge of the path. He walked over and mounted him. Rose, Zee and Thoran followed.

"Again, please accept our apology sir," Rose said, still quite upset.

And Grimsdyke thought... I might not kill her. Though I'm sure she'll wish she were dead when this all gets sorted out. He answered, "Again, your apology is most accepted... tho' not necessary." He smiled, "Until the festival."

"The festival!" six boys cheered and everyone smiled.

Pitch barked... *"The festival."*

Grimsdyke gave him a quick, hard, angry look and said, "Don't bring that." Pitch bowed his head slightly. An uncomfortable silence hung about for a bit. Grimsdyke steered his horse to the path. Seething with anger, he maintained a fake smile as he slowly clomped away.

Before he was gone, Aunt Zee had one last question... "Oh sir?" she yelled.

Grimsdyke stopped, turned, and raised his eyebrows instead of asking...Yes?

"Where is your companion—Maxwell was it?"

Pitch heard his old name, his ears perked up; he stared at his old master. Again their eyes met.

"Oh... poor Max," Grimsdyke said slowly, "He proved to be most untrustworthy. He badly hurt some local children and the council imprisoned him in a far-away dungeon. He'll never hurt anyone again." He smiled at Pitch, turned his horse and clomped away.

The adults looked at each other. "Well, he was quite unsettling to look at," Rose said.

Pitch sadly thought... Why'd the master have to say that? I never hurt children. He looked at his family and in a low voice howled, *"I'll be nice to you if you're nice to me."* He walked to his doghouse, crept in and sat. He wasn't in the mood to play.

As Grimsdyke clomped away, to no one he spoke, "I'll let them enjoy a few more days of their family—and that stupid dog."

Thoran, Rose and Zee watched the Council Master clomp away, talking to himself.

A Decision Was Made

After Grimsdyke left, the adults sat around the table; the boys had gone to sleep. Pitch slept outside. And when he slept, he snored. Max thunderously snored as a boy. It was a trait that followed him into manhood. And, as it were, into dog-hood. "I didn't know dogs could snore that loud," Rose said, "and he's only a puppy! How loud will he be when he's full grown?"

"Loud enough to shake the moon," Thoran laughed.

"He's growing quickly," Rose said.

"Almost too quickly," added Zee.

The three glanced at each other. Something bothered each of them about Pitch. Although only a puppy, he gained size and weight seemingly by the day. "What if he's a black shuck?" Zee asked, "A death-hound?"

"Those are just old wonder-tales. Can't be true. But it doesn't make sense how he came here either," Thoran said, "I'll have to ask Shniggleton if there are any families around with dogs. He'd know. He's taken his cart full of bits and gubbins to everyone around."

"Well, he's only shown love and loyalty. Maybe he thought the Council Master's horse was a threat, maybe he was protecting the boys," Zee said.

"We do want that," Rose said.

"He'll grow bigger—much bigger. He'll be scary if confronted," Thoran said.

"I'm okay with that, too," Zee said, "as long as he's on our side." They listened to their dog's snoring; it echoed through the quiet woodland and was followed by some chirping, clicking and a sound they couldn't quite place.

"So the boys think they're old enough for an adventure on their own," Thoran said.

The sisters glanced at each other, and then back to Thoran. "So they think," answered Rose.

"Well, perhaps they are—a short one," Zee wondered.

"No more than a couple hours away," Rose insisted, knowing the time really has come for the boys to spread their wings a bit.

After a deep breath, Thoran said, "I'm thinking of a trek to Grumblers Hill. At their pace, they can get an early start, a couple hours for them to get there, a couple hours playing there, then a couple hours walk back. It's not that far. It's a straight walk along the back path. We'll point out a position of the sun that'll be their mark when to return. If they don't dawdle, they can be there in less than two hours."

A surprisingly well thought out adventure, Rose thought. Quick, easy, and it should satisfy their urge to explore. "I want them to take the goblet and the candle holder," she said.

Thoran said, "I understand the goblet, tho' I can't see the reasoning for the candle holder, my love."

"I don't know," she answered, "I just think they should stay together."

"I agree. They should also take the journal," Zee added, "it's not only about their learning a bit of independence, it's also about responsibilities. And they should write about their adventure."

"Okay," Thoran said, "but we're entrusting them with things that if in the wrong hands, or lost, might lead to horrible consequences." He paused. "Tho I must admit, we truly don't know the purpose those gifts will ultimately serve. That goblet has sat on that shelf for so long, I think it's taken root," he chuckled.

They sat and listened to their dog snoring.

"Fine," Rose said, "we'll discuss it with them in the morning."

"Pitch will obviously go with them," Aunt Zee added.

"Obviously," Rose and Thoran said.

They went to bed, but rested uneasily. They would let the boys go out on their own for the first time. When *is* the right time they wondered? Maybe we should follow them? Together, the seven are strong, they're smart and fast. But the mother worried…they're only children.

Chapter Twenty-one

It's Time

Grimsdyke knew it was time. Time to take what is rightfully mine, he thought…and everything must seem as normal. First, all civic matters must be attended to. The King would want to know how the festival plans were going. Grimsdyke will send word with a messenger to the towering castle built into the Cliffs of Mauleron. He'd also have to visit and grovel to the Thundorians, who he especially hated. Pompous maggots, he thought.

The King's Festivals are the most special of holidays. They're where the King shows his loyalty to the people. All work is stopped in all towns and villages during the weeklong celebrations. There are two festivals: one in the spring, where the end of the cold months are celebrated, and one in the fall where villages and cities rejoice in the bounty of the prosperous warm months. The festivals are grand times for everyone to mingle and have fun. All townsfolk are honored to volunteer as the King shares the wealth, supplying all foodstuffs, drink and gifts for all— no expense is spared.

Grimsdyke himself appoints committees that oversea and plan entire festivals in all the provinces. Except in Thundor—they plan their own celebration. Decorations on every building, wondrous fireworks displays, puppet shows, mock battles, jugglers and jesters walking about—"Oh what a festival it's to be," village children sing with glee.

"And I hate it," Grimsdyke said aloud, to no one. He always had, especially the traditional carving of the first roast beast. Every year, Grimsdyke would watch the King stab the giant fork into the first seventy-odd pound of spit-cooked meat, and he would dream it is he holding the knife, and the King being carved. This will be the last time he'd have to put on a wonderful show he thought. He's waited long enough. From a nook out of view, he looked on at his little Village of Laban. The town-folks happiness made him cringe. He watched and thought…I detest these people. I've done everything for them and not one ounce of gold or gratitude has anyone ever given me. His brain hurt. He sniffed the dried troll's nose and calmly sneezed a river of blue green shniggles to the ground— a common occurrence for him.

He watched mothers and fathers, sons and daughters go in and out of the shops that line the town square. They came out of the bread-smiths with loaves, out of the cobblers with boots, and out of the barber with less hair. The clang of the blacksmith beat at his brain. The smell from the fishmonger stuck in his throat. And the shop he hated most was the most colorful in town—Skajellyfetti's Confections. There, pastries, candies and yummies of all sorts were made, each marked with a funny shaped S—the mark of its maker. Grimsdyke stared at the children coming out of the confectionary. Smirking, he thought… they'll all be food for my army.

An unmistakable laugh followed a man who came out of the Harvey-House, a local pub. The laugh came from a person the Council Master especially loathed, Shniggleton, that beastly potter. Grimsdyke thought….I hope that man just rots. Always happy, helping everyone. He's like an animal and should be treated like one. Grimsdyke dreamed of what life could be like… how grand it must be to live in a castle. Servants would cater to my every need. I'll sleep on the finest of linens, and the sweetest of foods will be brought to me. He closed his eyes and dreamed, dreamed of sitting on a throne with fair maidens at his side, sipping the golden goblet. Its elixir will make me the strongest, the wisest, the most handsome. Slaves will build monuments of my likeness.

A trickle of blood dripped from his ear; he wiped at it thinking it a mosquito… "All for my taking," he said aloud. And at that precise moment, Grimsdyke's last bit of sanity rode that small stream of blood out of his ear. The kingdom would be his. Blood will be spilled. The King would be killed. "His death is necessary. He can't be a slave," Grimsdyke said, not realizing anyone was listening. A small child and her mother were passing by and overheard him, but thought they were mistaken.

In a small, sweet voice the child startled Grimsdyke by asking, "Sir?"

He stared at the child with a look of hatred. The mother looked at Grimsdyke. She knew that stare—it was the same gaze of hatred her husband gave the sweet child before he abandoned his family in an angry fit, blaming the innocent little one for his own misfortune. He called it misfortune, but it was simply the father's own laziness. The stare made the girl's mother angry and frightened at the same time.

A few clock ticks of silence. "Yes, what is it?" Grimsdyke demanded, clearly irritated. His tone frightened the little one; she held her mother's hand tightly.

"You're bleeding," the mother said.

Grimsdyke stood and walked away.

The mother grabbed the child and also walked away, to the council chamber to report that the Council Master has been injured in some way.

Grimsdyke went into the woods to a hidden cave. To a cave that held secrets.

A cave filled with his monsters.

Twenty-Two
They'll Not Sleep

The day the boys were told of their upcoming adventure was the happiest day they could remember. That day, they woke and all went as usual. After a hearty breakfast, they practiced the shepherd sling. Pitch enjoyed these practices as he retrieved the rocks that were flung far. He treated them as if they were balls of yarn, only harder. Arrows and lances were not as much fun to retrieve, as he often broke them. His horrible looking teeth were very strong. So strong that he sometimes broke small rocks without any damage to them. Their dog amazed them; he seemed to grow before their very eyes.

On that mid-day, the boys were called inside. The smell of butter-tarts hit them as they went in. Pitch barked with excitement, *"Me first, me first."*

"Down boy," Thoran said, mildly irritated.

Achu first noticed the goblet, the candleholder, and Dagon's journal on the table. Grumel noticed the butter-tarts, then the goblet and the candleholder. "What're they doin' down Momma?" Achu asked.

Ayell picked up the goblet and studied it. None of the boys had ever held it. They never had much interest in it. Showing the markings to Yawnel, then passing it to him, Yawnel showed and passed it to Joyal, Joyal to Achu, Achu to Alvis, Alvis to Grumel. Grumel dropped it, picked it up and passed it to Shyel who gave it back to Ayell. The goblet was inscribed with strange objects. A crescent, the boys knew was the moon, the sun, trees, little people, strange animals— all etched into a woodland scene.

"These were given to us by Dagon. He said he rescued them too," Rose said.

Stroking the goblet, Aunt Zee said, "They're very special."

"Why?" asked Yawnel.

Alvis picked up the candleholder—"They're gold, ain't they," he said excitedly.

"That they are, tho' that's not their magic," Thoran said.

"Magic?" four of them asked.

"Sit boys," their mother said, "eat and we'll talk. We have some exciting things to talk about."

Pitch barked..."*Me too, me too.*" And he sat. They all looked at him. Again, everyone thought that he was a very smart dog; he listened very well.

While their mother handed out the sweet butter-tarts, their father spoke... "Boys, the golden goblet, as Dagon explained to us, is an ancient object of healing."

"Like a doctor healing?" asked Joyal.

"Yes but more powerful." Pitch looked at the goblet and remembered something. He remembered his master saying something about a goblet, something about it being important. It's very pretty, he thought.

Achu asked, "What're these marks momma? This looks like a moon with a drop of water."

Rose put her hand out. Ayell handed her the goblet. Running her hand over its smooth surface, the etched markings slightly tickling her hard fingertips, she looked at Thoran. "Well, we don't know what all the marks are."

"But that's a crescent moon," said Thoran, "and that's a drop of blood coming from its point...it's a weeping crescent," he added then stopped, waiting for a reaction. But there was none, only stares—he continued... "One of its powers is to heal. If someone is injured, and death is near, you put a single drop of the hurt person's blood in the goblet, mix it with simple water, drink it, and death will not come."

"Did you ever use it?" asked Joyal.

The elders looked at each other. "Only once," Zee said, "we used it to save the life of a holy man that was injured. And it saved his life."

"I remember that day," Grumel said.

"That was Dagon's last day," Joyal added. "An you guys really screamed at us!"

"Well," Rose remembered, "everything happened pretty fast that day. It was a wicked storm."

"Anyway," Thoran continued, "there's other magic in the goblet. We just won't know about it until the time is right. Dagon didn't tell us much, just what he thought we needed to know. It doesn't make much sense, but we trusted him with our lives, so we didn't question his reasons."

"What about them scrolls?" Joyal asked, "Should we look out for them?"

"Don't you worry about them," Rose said while looking at Thoran, "They're of no concern to you."

"Still doesn't make much sense," Shyel said.

"You can say that again," Grumel added.

"Still doesn't make much sense," Shyel said again. Grumel backhanded his brother's arm. Shyel hit Grumel back, pushing him into Ayell who pushed back, sending Grumel into Achu who hit Joyal who...

"Stop!" Zee said, "We're being serious here." They stopped, but looked at each other suspiciously. "When I was a youngster, like you seven, I drank from the goblet." Those words made the boys pause and look at their aunt. She looked away. "I don't remember doing so. I do remember an ogre's spear sticking from my neck. I knew it cut my soul and I remember the sweet taste of lightning dust that our father— your grandfather, gave me." Grandfather was a word never used, and rarely thought about by the boys. They had questions, but their aunt continued... "And I remember being with the pack of dragon-elves, and waking to find you two sleeping next to me." Zee looked at Rose, then Thoran. "I remember naming you," and she smiled. "I never asked, but I hope you like your name." Thoran smiled.

Zee said, "I died, Dagon saved us, and the goblet brought me back to life." All were quiet.

"Dagon last said a soul can only be saved one time with the magic of the goblet," Thoran said, "so it must only be used in the most dire of circumstances."

Alvis asked, "Why're we talking about th, th,th th aaaaa..." and Grumel stuck his finger under Alvis's nose, stopping the coming blast.

"Thanks Grummy," Alvis said.

"No problem."

And without warning, "AAAAaaaschooooo!"— Ayell sneezed all over the back of Grumel's head.

"You got shniggles on your head," Shyel pointed, smiling.

"Eewww, that's nasty," Yawnel added.

"Momma!" Grumel cried while quickly wiping at the back of his boogered head and looking at Ayell... "Why'd you do that?" Smiling, Ayell could only throw his arms up. He couldn't say, "I'm sorry."

Aunt Zee threw a cloth to Grumel. "There's nothing there. Wipe your head... now listen up—all of you!"

Thoran spoke. "Boys... your mother, Aunt Zee and I have come to an agreement."

"An agreement? What kind of agreement?" Joyal asked.

The adults looked at each other. With raised eyebrows, Rose motioned to Thoran to tell them. "We agree that you're old enough for a short adventure on your own."

It dawned on the boys quickly. "To Laban?" three of them shouted while the others screamed, "Ahhaahhh," and laughed.

"Not to Laban," Rose said, taking them down a notch.

"But we will let you go by yourselves to Grumblers Hill," their father said. They couldn't contain their excitement. They slapped each other, wrestled, and congratulated themselves as only siblings could.

Aunt Zee chimed in— "We're talking about..." The boys got louder; they paid no attention to their aunt. So she shouted... "WE'RE TALKING ABOUT THE GOBLET. IT'S GOING WITH YOU!" They stopped in mid-stream, staring at each other.

Their mother continued. "The goblet and the candle holder are going with you. Listen why. And sit back down," she demanded. "You must listen carefully." She paused. "The goblet is going with you. If anything happens to any one of you, you must quickly use it like we discussed."

"You mean put a drop of blood and water in it?" asked Yawnel.

"An mix it and drink it?" finished Alvis.

Together the adults said, "Yes."

"Why the candleholder?" asked Joyal.

"Is it magic?" Grumel questioned.

"Yes," Aunt Zee said, "we can show you that magic at sundown."

"Why sundown?" wondered Achu.

Rose held the goblet and softly said, "For only in the dark, when held to the heart, will its light brightly shine." All stared at her. Thoran, fully in love with his wife, had a soft smile. "That's how Dagon explained it to us." Rose held it to her heart, "For the true of heart, to battle the dark, for any reason, this light will shine. The two objects must stay together."

"Do we put a candle in it?" asked Shyel.

"That's its magic son," Papa said. "No candle is needed. It glows with brightness all its own."

The boys sat silenced and stared at both objects. Their excitement, their wonder was tempered with apprehension. "Well, what happens if something bad happens to one of you, if we have these and they're not here?" Shyel asked.

Aunt Zee rubbed the backs of Ayell and Alvis, Rose patted Grumel and Joyal, Thoran patted Shyel, Achu, and Yawnel. "Don't you worry," Thoran said. "You won't be that long and nothing will happen to us. To any of us. You'll go on a little adventure, have a wagon full of fun, and come back hungrier than a black-jagged dragon."

Zee picked up the journal, opened it to one of the last pages that was blank and said, "I'll write down what we've told you about the goblet and candle holder. Dagon said there will always be a blank page for you to add your thoughts— or anything you want. Show us some of the sights you find on your adventure. We want to see what you see through your words and drawings. Anything you want to write down. Dagon will be very happy for you to add to the journal. It's your journal now."

"We could all go together," said Achu. Ayell nodded his head, agreeing.

Joyal added, "We could just go on a family outing."

"If that pleases you boys, then we will," said their mother. "Though we have chosen a simple trip that shouldn't take you long, and if started early, you can be back by mid-day."

More silence. "Well, no decision has to be made today," Aunt Zee said. "The choice is yours. It's important for you to know that we trust you. And we know that all of you are skilled and smart enough."

"And old enough," added Thoran.

"To take a little trip on your own." finished Rose. More silence.

"When can we go?" asked Grumel.

"Whenever you want," Thoran said. "But it needs a bit of planning. We were thinking in a couple of days."

Pitch sat quietly through the whole conversation. It was time for him to bark something. *"I'm going,"* he yowled. They all looked at him.

As if answering Pitch, Rose said, "You're going too!"

And to that Pitch barked… *"Good!"*

Twenty-Three

The Screaming Cave

Some cave openings look like giant open mouths, screaming from the land. Or humongous yawning peaks, tired from their long years of working. Grimsdyke slowly entered his cave, focused on a task. Usually the smell nauseated him, but he didn't notice it. He stepped on bits of bones and squished double-tailed maggots that fed on scraps of bloody, crusty skin. Tiny crunching echoes followed his steps. Those that were hidden in large dark crevices heard the echoes.

"It'll soon be time," Grimsdyke said. "One, maybe two, days."

The darkness moved. In a gargled, gruff voice, the largest ogre spoke... "Hungree." The others grunted in agreement. There were seven stashed in the cave: four ogres and three orcs. The ogres were fatter, the orcs were lanky and thin creatures. One ogre was huge, at nearly nine feet tall. The six others were slightly larger in size than Grimsdyke. All were partly covered with wraps made from the skins of whatever they killed. Their own skin was stained dark from dirt and blood, both fresh and crusty old. Mixed with the dirt and blood were hairs, also from whatever they killed. "Meat gone," an orc grunted.

The Council Master looked around and saw the deer skulls. "Four?" he shouted. "You've been hunting!" he said, disgusted. "If you were seen, the King would have the full army scouting," he scowled. "They would catch you, cut your heads off and burn the lot of you." Grimsdyke had to be careful not to stir up too much anger in the stupid creatures. Their simple minds combined with their always-hungry belly's could turn them quickly against him. Human meat was their favorite, especially younglings. But they'd eat any human in a pinch. Actually, they'd eat anything in a pinch. The smell of dead in the cave was thick. Grimsdyke's head ached, he felt nauseous. "UNGRY," a different one screamed.

They stared at Grimsdyke with hunger in their eyes. They needed to feed. "I'll be back with food," Grimsdyke said, "man food…before nightfall." He quickly left the cave and knew what had to be done. And he knew who could die and not be missed.

There are unfortunate souls that rest in a shed in back of a church. The shed's only use is for the purpose of housing the few that have come upon bad luck. With the promise and payment of a gold chip for assistance, one was easily lured. The one coming for dinner that day was named Finnegan Ortleib. Grimsdyke waved a sliver of gold; Mr. Ortleib was only too happy to follow.

To Finny, as his friend called him, the rancid smell in the cave was overpowering. "I thought you said we're going to a silver mine?" a nervous Mr. Ortleib asked.

"And I call it beggar's tomb…" answered the Council Master with a smile and a laugh.

Ten paces into the cave, Finnegan knew he would never see his family again. The action was as quick as watching a spider feed. Turning to run, he was met by the belly of a beast. Finny looked up, could barely focus on or comprehend the sight. He thought…Whaaaat? It didn't matter, for a giant hand grabbed his face and lifted. His feet left the ground. As his head ripped from his body, the last thing Finnegan said was… "Where's my shoes?"

To Grimsdyke, the sound of a head being ripped off reminded him of loud POPS from dried trees that burned in a fire. As heads offer the least meat, it was thrown to the side. Later, if the ogre was still hungry for a snack, Finny's skull would be smashed for its brain. When finished rolling, Finnegan's head lay there and watched his body being eaten, his eyebrows still raised in shock, his mouth wide open in an ever-silent scream.

The feed lasted for about seven minutes. Grimsdyke watched. He was pleased it didn't take long. Grabbing and pulling, the arms and legs were ripped from the torso with slight sucking sounds. The body itself was hacked at with crude axes; the clothes were torn off and thrown about. Each creature quickly had a piece of Mr. Ortleib. Flesh and bone met gnarled black and rotting teeth.

Grimsdyke walked over to Finny's clothes and hunted for his last chip of gold. Fishing it out of a pocket, Grimsdyke said, "I'll hold onto this for you." He turned to the ogres. "Soon we'll go to a house with lots of food— all yours to take."

"Younglins?" a snarly orc asked, blood still dripping from its hands and teeth.

"Lots of them," Grimsdyke said.

"Good," the largest ogre said, "we sleep... an' go."

Grimsdyke thought about it for a few clock ticks, and then said, "Sure— why not."

They slept and slept. After one day, Grimsdyke tried to wake them, but they wouldn't move. After two days, they still wouldn't budge. By the third day, a frustrated Grimsdyke woke the monsters by bringing a calf into the cave. The noisy young cow cried, the beasts woke— and ate their snack. "Make it quick. It's time to go," he said.

His plan was to travel with his band of not so merry pranksters through the thick of the woods. Near to, but not on, the ancient main road from Laban. He hoped to make it to the cottage in two days. His diseased, cunning brain knew he had to be careful not to be seen. Their hunger drives them, he knew. They'll eat whatever they can kill. Can't waste any time. His biggest challenge was taming the untamed. So he'd bribe them with their favorite food...children. They would bring along sacks of rocks and rope. Rocks are the preferred weapons for ogres. And rope— well, rope always comes in handy. In preparation of a kill, ogres spend lots of time gathering rocks that comfortably fit their hands. "When we get there, we'll wait until it's dark, then attack.

I want them alive until I get some answers. Then, do as you want with them."

"Kill 'nuff ta eat, rest we take," an orc said.

"Girl one's mine!" the largest ogre demanded.

"ONE, female is yours. The second is mine—I'll show you which one," Grimsdyke said. He knew it was tricky trying to reason with the simple, dumb beasts. But they can easily be lied to; their stupidity usually leads to their downfall. "There's another cottage with more younglins I'll take you to," he lied. "So one female is mine," he said.

They grunted in agreement.

Grimsdyke's head started to ache. He knew it's the witch's fault his brain hurt. He didn't realize that a small stream of blood came out of his ear. The ogres smelled that small stream of blood; blood makes their belly's tingle.

"There's a dog I also want killed."

"Dogs meat good," a grinning ogre said.

"Really?—I wouldn't have guessed," Grimsdyke lightly mocked. His companions weren't smart enough to be offended. They left the cave and walked in silence for many hours. They didn't realize that reddish gray storm clouds followed them from the west.

Twenty-Four

The Adventure Begins

The day of the boys' adventure, they woke early and made sure everyone else did too. The morning started crisply, the full breath of the sun's heat was hours away. Pitch woke when the boys woke. Excited, he darted around, woofing in quick hard barks, *"Lets go, lets go, lets go."* Everything was packed the day prior except for the sacks of food. Momma filled seven little sacks with nuts, bread, apples and honey. Papa checked their weapon belts. It was decided they would walk and not ride the ponies. Not that they needed the exercise; the boys were fit. But rather, exploring was much easier while walking. Each had a water pouch and three of the boys would carry an extra. Each also had a lance to be used as a walking stick.

Aunt Zee made sure the goblet, the candleholder, and Dagon's journal were wrapped and in a sack. "Who shall be in charge of this?" she asked, holding up the sack with the treasures.

"We'll take turns," said Grumel reaching for the sack.

As dawn arrived, blue gray haze crawled through the brush and pushed away the dark of the prior night. Excited, the boys chattered about the great adventure about to unfold. What creatures they hoped to see, what oddities they hoped to meet.

"Stay straight on the path," Thoran demanded, "under no circumstances are you to wander beyond the sight of the path, do you understand?"

"Yes papa," all said, Ayell shook his head.

"This is important to remember boys," Rose added, "If you get lost, even the smallest of animals, beasts or bugs could do great harm."

"And remember not to touch any strange plants. No berry picking, no matter how sweet they smell," Zee added.

"And if you come across any strangers, strange beasts, or anything that makes your stomach twinge, uneasy-like, you draw your weapons as one— quickly," their father added.

The boys responded with a triumphant "Yes sir!" Ayell saluted and smiled.

Pitch, barking with authority added, "*We won't get lost, I promise, I can smell the cottage from a long way. Bye bye. Lets go!*" and off he ran.

Smiling, Rose said, "He seems the most excited."

"Remember boys," their father calmly said, "have fun, but keep a careful eye."

"Come, give us a hug, my little men." The boys hugged their mother.

"Remember the sun's position," Thoran instructed pointing to the sky, "When you see it in front of you, it's time to come home."

"We remember, Papa," said Joyal.

"We'll be back before you knows it," said Alvis.

They walked to the rear of the cottage. A fuller sun started to peak through the trees; a very faint rumble of thunder came from the distance. Maybe some rain later, Rose thought. She looked to the sky and around…blue-green sky, no clouds. They hadn't talked about bad weather… how could we forget about the weather? "If a storm rolls in without warning you must make your way back home. Rain won't hurt you. Tho' the lightning can," Rose said. "We haven't talked about the weather, Papa."

"No, we'll just have to leave that to chance today. Doesn't smell like rain," He looked at them, "Just trust your feelings and your instincts boys. If bad weather does roll in, turn around and come right back home. There'll be plenty of adventures in the future for you." Thoran looked at his boys, nodding with a proud smile. The entrance to the back path was overgrown. The boys huddled at its beginning.

Momma looked at her sons, "We love you very much. We want you to have a special day, one you'll remember forever. One that will be only the beginning— the start of many, many adventures." Thoran and Aunt Zee smiled, nodding in agreement.

The boys spoke at once, but were heard separately by their parents. "We love you too."

"We'll come back soon with a grand tale. We'll take care of the goblet and the candle holder," Joyal added as Ayell stood by, shaking his head.

"And we promise not to do anything too silly," said Alvis.

"We trust you, and know that you'll watch out for each other," Papa said. "Now off you go!" And into the woods they went.

Watching them go, the parents resisted the temptation to go with them. Their children were going away for the first time; it's only natural to feel a pang of irrational fear, a silly fear that they would never see their little ones again. They whispered a little prayer for their little men. When the boys were out of sight, Rose and Thoran walked back to the cottage. Rose gently cried.

Zee stayed outside, looking into the woods. Above the cottage the sky was blue—mostly. A low, low thunder rumbled in the far distance. Glancing up, she noticed some soft whitish-gray clouds rolling in from the west. She had a flashback—of devil-hawks battling dragon-elves, tossing heads from beak to beak. She fought an impulse to follow her nephews.

Glancing back while moving forward, they watched their parents, their home, and their world become blocked by a web of branches and trees. In back of them, the sun crawled up the sky. Pitch took off at first chance. "Pitch, ho, Pitch, come here boy!" screamed Grumel.

"Let him run," said Shyel. "He's as excited as us." The forest air smelled woodsy and fresh. Sounds that were new to them vibrated through the air. They watched colorful bugs flit and flutter, feathery birds and unseen creatures rustle and tussle about. They heard calls of angry gracklers and grunts of happy grimlers in the distance. At least that's what they thought they heard.

"I say we move fast, and maybe go a bit further." Achu said, "Maybe to the Claw!"

"Let's see how long it takes us to get to the hill first," Joyal added.

"They'd be *really* mad if they found out," said Yawnel.

Shyel coughed, "Then they just don't find out. It's only us. They'd never know."

Ayell shook his head in agreement.

"We'll decide at the hill," Alvis said.

"I'm hungry," said Joyal.

"Me too," Grumel added.

"We just left," said Achu, "let's walk a bit."

"The first big clearing we come to, we'll stop. I think there's one a bit ahead. I remember it from our trip to the Claw," said Alvis.

"That seems like such a long time ago," said Yawnel.

"Remember Papa's scream when that poison slug bit him?" Shyel blurted out.

"It was," said Shyel, "it's been nearly four years!"

"I try not to think about that," confessed Grumel.

"He would have died if Dagon didn't pop up," said Shyel.

Clapping his hands to get attention, Ayell shook his head as if saying "NO!"

"You're right, we would have saved him somehow," said Alvis.

"Just remember," Achu said in a deep voice, clearly trying to imitate their father, "Don't do anything foolish or the hoblins and ogres will eat your face off." They all laughed.

Trying to imitate Aunt Zee, Grumel added, "An' make sure you wipe your bum else a groundling will crawl in and make a nest!" They laughed, because it was a very poor imitation.

"And don't...," Joyal paused, "don't...," he forgot what he wanted to say. His brothers looked at him as if he were dopey, and burst out laughing. They chanted in silly voices, "Don't, don't, don't," laughing and walking into the woodland.

Pitch ran back, barking loud, *"All clear ahead!"* He playfully bumped into all the boys and ran into the woods, staying within their view. Silly talk, quiet spells and happy thoughts happened for the next hour. They scrutinized their surroundings, looking for things that could be heard rummaging in the leaves and scuttling about the trees and shrubs. Individually, they were a bit nervous, a bit scared even. But the group gave them comfort. They forgot about being hungry, as the forest kept them busy. They tried to whistle. And like their first attempt, many years ago, all they did was spit and drool. Pitch would run ahead, stop, sniff and scavenge about, keeping their seven scents strong in his nose. At the first small clearing, they sat and had a quick feast. They studied Dagon's journal, amazed that there was always something new in it. Some new face of a beast—some new beautiful elven friend. The goblet and candleholder were left in the sack.

"Look at the teeth on this one," Joyal said while pointing to a beast whose teeth were half the size of its face.

"He said some day we might meet one of these," Shyel said pointing to a one-eyed scug, or maybe it was an orc, with tusks, "That's crazy—right?" he asked anyone.

Achu stood up. "If we do, then I'll do this—" and he drew an arrow from his sling, quickly set it and pulled back. He aimed at a knot, high up in a tree, pretending it was a monster's single eye. He let go and they watched the arrow fizz through the air, hitting just below the knot, sticking in the tree with a sharp THTUNK!

"Well, you hit its nose," said Grumel, who by that point had his own arrow aimed at the knot. He let go and his arrow stuck hard just above the knot.

"Forehead...maybe hit its brain," said Alvis. Quickly, the rest of them had arrows out and one at a time they shot. Only Ayell's arrow sliced through and hit dead center in the eye. A lower *thtunk* sound was heard as his arrow struck the tree inside. When finished, six arrows were stuck just around the knot.

"Well, that orc had only one eye. One good shot to the eye. The rest of our arrows hit the face," Grumel pointed out, "It'll definitely leave some marks."

"C'mon, let's get going," someone said. The clouds, far away, colored four shades of gray, started to thicken and swirl. Pitch again ran ahead barking, *"I'll make sure all is clear."*

Far, far away an old hag-witch stirred her evil slop, smiling, knowing that one of the four shades of gray in her boiling kettle was darkened by blood. She looked to the sky...the swirls in her kettle matched the swirls in the clouds.

Twenty-Five

Traveling with Monsters

They made better time than he expected, they didn't stop to rest, didn't stop to eat. Grimsdyke, on his horse, watched the beasts move through the forest with the ease of most animals. By human standards, they were stupid. In their world, he thought... maybe they're kings. He watched them sniff the air. Grimsdyke wondered how they could defend themselves if attacked by say, devil-hawks or a black dragon. Or would they just run? He pondered... hard to believe these are the same creatures storied to be great warriors in old tales of ancient battles. It's all about food to them. They perk up only when they're on the kill. Well, we'll soon find out what they're made of. They don't talk, they just grunt at each other every now and then. Grimsdyke quietly asked himself— "What could they possibly say to each other?"

They were getting close to Thoran's cottage. It wasn't yet mid-day. If he wanted to attack at dusk, he would have to wait in the woods or travel much slower than their current pace. Looking up, he first noticed odd-shaped storm clouds at their backs. The sun hid behind the clouds; its colorful sunbeams tried to fight through dull, puffy swirls of gray. The clouds were winning. He thought... if a storm rolls in, we could attack earlier. "Just maybe," he said aloud.

One of the ogres looked up and said, "Cloud demons smell like."

"Rubbish," Grimsdyke said. He knew the superstitions of storm-demons and cloud monsters, riding down upon lightning bolts, throwing icy daggers of poison and fire. He thought... unless it can be held or seen, like proper magic, it's all, "Rubbish," he said again.

"Hungry," a scug said, "tired." The others grunted in agreement.

"Let's sit and rest. Soon you will feed," The Council Master said. They stopped in their tracks, sat down hard on scrubby, brush-covered ground and the ogres quickly fell into a deep snooze. Grimsdyke dismounted and walked a short distance from his companions to a small clearing.

He sat down and thought—I can't let them eat my horse. Then he looked at the creatures and thought—I can't let them eat me!

Twenty-Six

The Adventure Continues

The boys were getting close to Grumblers Hill. They had been traveling for some time. The sun was still in back of them, though dark clouds did come to battle in the blue sky. Colorful sunbeams tried to shoot through the clouds—some were successful. They hoped the sun and her beams would defeat the clouds. The forest was alive with sights, sounds and smells. They were having fun and hoped they would make it to the hill before a storm forced them to turn back. Pitch led the way, walking in pace with them and acting as their leader. He barked, *"Follow me guys!"*

"We're getting close, aren't we?" asked Shyel.

"Can anyone hear anything yet?" asked Joyal. All were quiet, listening for a rumble.

Pitch looked around and yowled, *"I only hear thunder."*

"We'll feel it in our feet first, remember?" said Alvis.

"That's right," said Alvis, "can anyone feel anything?"

Pitch sniffed the ground, sniffed the air, and sniffed the bushes. His eyes darted around. They all heard a rumbling and thought they felt something. "Is that it? Or is it thunder?" asked Grumel.

Joyal said, "I remember seeing the hill and then Papa asked us if we felt it. I think we just heard thunder. Let's keep walking. Storm looks like it's trying to ruin our trip."

Everyone, including Pitch, looked to the sky. They hoped the hill was close; they had to at least stake their flag on it before having to hike home. They prayed the storm would hold off. Momma, Papa, and Aunt Zee were surely watching the sky, and they wouldn't be surprised if their father came running out of the path behind them shouting, "Come boys, storm's coming, let's make haste back to the cottage!" They really hoped this wouldn't happen. It was important for them to prove they could take care of themselves.

Pitch barked while running ahead of them, *"Come on, move faster!"* They quickened their pace.

Back at the cottage, Rose, Thoran and Aunt Zee knew the boys had to be getting close to the hill. They feared a storm was inevitable. It wasn't the rain they worried about, as much as it was lightning, which always brought anxiety. Some types of lightning were good, as Aunt Zee would say. Yet old tales of storm-demons and lightening-devils, silly as they may seem, still brought out fears. And a dark tale of the ancient City of Nee, burnt to the ground by streams of red lightning was known as fact. Rose didn't remember telling the boys about those old stories, so the boys wouldn't be worried. But she, Zee and Thoran knew. "I should take off after them," Thoran said.

They studied the sky. There were still patches of blue and beacons of sunlight mixed in with the darker, more ominous clouds. It was just about midday. "Lets give it a little more time," Zee said. "My heart agrees with you, tho' my brain says just a little bit more."

"I don't see any lightning. That makes me feel a little better," Momma added. "The bad storms have early lightning veins crossing the sky."

"A little longer, then I'll go to meet them," Papa said. Looking at each other, the three nodded in agreement.

After their nap...

Grimsdyke commanded, "Lets go, it's time." The ogres sat up and were groggy. Surveying their surroundings, they first noticed the agitated dark clouds high above had closed in on them. The scent from the trickle of blood coming from Grimsdyke's ear caught their attention. The largest ogre said, "We eat human today." It wasn't a question.

With his head pounding, Grimsdyke sniffed the dried blood-trolls nose and snorted out the biggest glob of blue green snot he had to date. It landed near an ogre who looked at it, as did the others. With a slight swiping motion, it dipped one of its four fingers and scooped up the shniggle. The whole of the snot stuck to its finger. Bringing the finger to its mouth, it puckered, sucked and the booger disappeared. It didn't chew. The monsters turned. They glared at Grimsdyke. A bolt of fear, one the Council Master had only felt two times before, shot up his spine and ended at his nose. At least he didn't have a headache.

The biggest ogre stood up and said, "We go. It's time. I smell 'em."

Meanwhile...

Joyal said, "I still can't tell if we're coming to the hill. Is that thunder in the ground? I feel something." Ayell shook his head up and down. Pitch sniffed the air. There was no more blue sky above them; any hint of a clean sky seemed very, very far away, but they really couldn't tell. They only knew the sun was gone.

"If a storm comes quick-like upon us, we'll have to go back as fast as we can," said Achu. "Momma will be worried and I'm sure Papa is on the way."

Alvis added, "And we'll be allowed to come again. They won't cheat us out of our only adventure."

No one said it, but they all thought at the same time... maybe we should just come back another day. A far off, loud thunder-rumble filled the air. It didn't come from the ground, but it got their attention. There was no lightning, and that was good. The boys didn't admit it, but the lack of a warm sun high above frightened them a bit. Grumel and Shyel noticed leaves on the farthest tops of the trees fluttered fast. The winds tickled branches. They were very happy to have Pitch with them. They moved a bit faster. Achu and Yawnel were just about to say, 'maybe we should go back', when the seven saw it— the huge tree with huge leaves that their father pointed out to them. "We're here!" four or five of them screamed.

Pitch barked, "*Where? Where?*"

"The tree! It's right after that tree!" cried Shyel, pointing. He ran; they ran. The sky darkened. As they ran past the massive tree with humungous leaves, their prize— Grumblers Hill came into view.

"Doesn't feel like it's been years since we were last here," Achu said.

"Stop!" said Grumel. They stopped, bumping into each other as they did.

"Listen—ah, feel the ground, I mean," said Alvis. They could all feel it—they smiled. Every now and then. A rumble, or a thunk in the ground. They all thought… we're here and Papa will be very proud when we get back. Pitch barked. No words tied to it, just a bark. A slight misty drizzle started to fall from the sky.

Back inside the cottage, three adults were busy doing nothing. They were just biding their time. He probably shouldn't wait much longer, Rose thought. "There's no more sun, Thoran. You should go after the boys," she stated.

"I have the same thought," said Zee. "We'll let them go again. They shouldn't get caught in a bad storm. Maybe we should all go to meet them." They considered this for a few clock ticks.

"No, you two stay here. I'll go. I'll take the horse. I shouldn't be too long." Thoran quickly started to gather bits for the trip to meet his boys. Outside, a light drizzle started to thicken. In the distance there was some thunder, thunder from clouds that had minds of their own.

Twenty-Seven

Rain, Rain, Go Away

Grimsdyke knew it would rain harder. He thought… there is no more sun and I am tired of waiting. In a loud whisper he said, "Stay down. And don't speak—your voices are too loud." He added that last statement because ogres can't whisper. They're just too stupid, he thought. The beasts stared at him with a curious type of anger.

The chimney of Thoran's cottage could be seen from their vantage point in the woods. Grimsdyke left his horse tied to a tree, many paces back. In a hurried, high-pitched whisper he spoke— "You will follow me. You will lie in the woods where I tell you. Quiet." He paused. "We'll be close to the house. When you hear me scream the word 'attack,' we will go after them. Try not to kill them— except the dog. Kill him whenever. I want to capture them— all of them. We'll tie them up. When you throw your rocks, aim for their legs and bodies. Hitting their heads will surely kill them—especially the little ones. They might not come out of the house. You must listen to me, and I promise you the younglins, all of them."

"And a girl," a snarly scug said, too loudly.

"Will you shut up," Grimsdyke hissed. They listened.

"Follow me and…," he stopped to listen. Quietly he finished, "Just do as I say and you will be very happy." The rain fell harder. Clouds fought in the sky. Darker, black clouds beat upon grayish, blue clouds. Although only mid-day, it seemed as if it were dusk. Grimsdyke, cautiously and with purpose, crept through the brush. He smelled a fire burning— something lovely was cooking.

The beasts followed quietly. "You," Grimsdyke pointed at an ogre, "stay here until you hear me." He crept, they followed, and he said that to each of them. When finished, the seven, ugly, hungry and curious beasts were scattered in the woods around the front of the cottage. Each beast had a sack of rocks and crude axes.

Grimsdyke stood alone at the edge of the woods, close to the front clearing of the cottage. He stared at the simple thatched dwelling. He couldn't foretell how this battle would take shape; he only took comfort in knowing how it would end. If need be... he thought, I will kill them all. I'll be happy just to have the goblet. Tho' he craved so much more.

All was in place. They were all in the cottage. Maybe I should just burn it down...he thought. "Do not change your plan," he whispered to no one. "Burn it down? Why would I do that?" The pain came back into his head. "Shut up, you fool," he again said aloud to himself. "*Is* this the easiest way?"— still speaking to no one.

"Greatness does not come with ease," something said to him. The Council Master swung his head around. No one—nothing. He spied the largest ogre staring at him through the trees. "Nor does it come without sacrifice," something again said. And again, Grimsdyke looked around and into the woods— nothing. He wondered... could there actually be ancient spirits shadowing me? I will make them proud. The rain fell harder.

Grimsdyke stepped out of the woods and into the clearing in front of the cottage.

At that precise moment, a gigantic, cracking bolt of lightning exploded from the sky, hitting the ground with a force so fierce it could only be described as the Good Mother herself pounding the land in anger. On its tail, a fantastic barrage of thunder wasted no time shaking the air. The sleeping donkey and ponies awoke, braying loudly, frightened and anguished. Thoran's horse, unafraid of storms, whinnied in anger. It smelled trouble coming.

Thoran, Rose, and Zelda came running out of the cottage. Rose screamed, "Go now and—" They stopped. Grimsdyke stood not thirty paces in front of them, his head slightly cocked, a crooked smile on his face. He looked a completely different person from the one who visited not that long ago. His hair was longer, wet and unkempt. He looked—dangerous. An intense glare came from his eyes, a stare that could only be described as— evil.

Thoran first noticed a bow slung over Grimsdyke's shoulder. Aunt Zee wondered…was that blood coming out of his ear? It was a scene that made no sense. Something was terribly wrong. Shivers of anxiety awoke in Thoran's belly.

From deep in his throat, the Council Master simply said, "Rose." Thoran couldn't hear what he said. Rose shuddered as her eyes met Grimsdyke's.

Thoran's hand went to his axe. He turned to the girls and spoke quietly, "Go inside, arm yourselves." Thoran, Rose and Zee were numb, but not frozen with fear. Confusion was not an option. The boys were their only concern and their anger quickly boiled. Their thinking needed to be clear. The two women dashed inside to a closet near the door that held only weapons—bows, arrows, and spears. They knew that if they ever had to use them, something or someone was going to die. Their eyes filled with tears. Rose cried—"We must go find the boys, now!" They went outside.

Thoran spoke loudly—"What brings you here on such a stormy day sir? You have startled us!" The rain dropped steady and hard.

Grimsdyke, seeing the girls armed thought…smart. "Always prepared, aren't you." Did I say that out loud? He hoped not. He also thought—where are the children? He walked slowly towards them and spoke softly, though loud enough to be heard. "Thoran, Rose. There's no need to be startled."

"Please stay where you are, sir. I beg you not come closer!" Thoran implored.

"Where are the children? It's too early for them to be sleeping,"

Grimsdyke questioned, "How come…

Half screaming, Rose said, "Our children are of no concern to you sir, please state your business!" The parents and Zee glanced at each other, sensing that Grimsdyke knew not where their boys were—yet. And the rain fell harder— the forest grew darker.

The Council Master stepped closer. "My business? My business?" He paused, "Welllllll, I only came to give you an update on the King's festival." Muddy little streams ran down his face. He paused again, thought, and proudly said, "Aaand to let you know that the council would like to show their appreciation for your generosity by awarding you a scroll. May I come in? I have traveled very far in this horrid weather."

Thoran wondered…where is his horse? Rose wondered… where is his sack? Zee was positive blood was coming out of Grimsdyke's ear. "Are you bleeding sir? Hurt in some way?" Zee loudly questioned. Thunder rumbled above the treetops.

Grimsdyke was getting impatient. "No, just wet and hungry. Where's that bloody mongrel?" he asked, slowly creeping towards them.

"Please, come no closer!" screamed Aunt Zee. Something felt very, very wrong. The horses in the backyard clomped and made a right fuss. The air didn't smell right. Even through a beating rain that sounded like a distant waterfall, a foul smell hung about.

The Council Master became angrier. His head pounded with a fierce ache. He reached in his pocket for the dried troll's nose and couldn't find it, and that really angered him. "Don't come closer?" he asked. "Curses—well, then I will keep this simple," he paused. "Maybe we can do this with little bloodshed." That last statement he thought he kept in his head— but he said it out loud.

Rose, Thoran and Zee instantly thought… Bloodshed? Did he say bloodshed? Thoran gripped his axe tighter.

Where are the boys? Grimsdyke thought…And that stupid mutt?

Another thought quickly occurred to him... Maybe, just maybe, they would hand me everything I want. That would be the simplest plan yet. No bloodshed? Could that be? He remembered the ogres in the woods. They're hungry. Oh well, let's get this over with. "The goblet Thoran. I want the goblet!" Grimsdyke said.

For a moment they just stood. No words. One tick, one tock, the rain kept time.

"Why did you say bloodshed Grimsdyke?" Thoran yelled, "Why would you use those words? Answer me!" Grimsdyke asking about the goblet wasn't Thoran's concern.

Grimsdyke wondered... did I say bloodshed aloud? He couldn't remember. "Speak," he commanded himself— "Uh—poor choice of words sir, I assure you that...," and a curious silence fell over the woodland as the rain stopped. A silence that happened so quickly, the Council Master's voice seemed very loud as it echoed. The raindrops just— quit, but dewy drips fell softly onto leaves, the trees, to the ground.

The slightest sound of rustling came from the woods. Stupid beasts, Grimsdyke thought... or maybe it's the boys.

Rose and Zee prayed... please, stay away boys.

And through the rainy, misty, duskiness, Thoran spotted it. It took a moment for his eyes to adjust. He blinked. He extended his neck ever so slightly, thinking his focus must be mistaken. Thoughts raced through his head as he comprehended what was staring back at him. It was an ogre. An **ogre**!— his mind screamed. How could this be? Why is it here? His instincts took over. His hand, already tightly holding his axe, quickly rose and with a swift two-step charge he let it fly. It cut through the thick, wet air. The sharp hatchet made swishing sounds as blade turned handle over blade over handle. His aim was true— the blade met that ogre's forehead with a mighty THWUNK! Its head split open, the axe firmly stuck in its brain. Its body went limp before it felt pain.

It happened so quick, the girls at first thought his target was Grimsdyke. When the axe passed him and landed in the beast's head, they let out a gasp and a shriek... it all seemed a dream.

Grimsdyke didn't fully see what had happened, but it didn't matter. "The goblet, Thoran, don't be foolish," he screamed, "you'll only get them mad."

Them! Thoran's mind raced, breathing hard he said, "There's more." He looked at his wife, "I love you more than life itself. There's more. They must die. Use their stupidity against them. We can't go after the boys yet. We must kill all of them. Remember the hidden weapons."

"The boys," Rose said, tears streaming down her cheeks.

"We must kill them all," Thoran said. Thoran sensed it wouldn't help, but he had to say, "You can have the goblet. There's no need for..." And with Thoran still talking, Grimsdyke screamed as loud as he could, "ATTACK! ATTACK!"

Thoran screamed, "GRIMSDYKE, NO!" And from the forest came their rustling, and the rustling came from all sides.

Zee spoke quickly, "You two, into the woods. I'll fight from the inside." As that last word left her mouth, a small boulder crashed into the cottage next to her followed by two more.

"Follow me Rose," and while grabbing arrows, the couple ran towards the dense woods near the house. Zee ducked inside and latched the door.

Grimsdyke, thinking he'd be attacked, ran and was able to crouch near a large rock, partially shielding himself. But Thoran did not chase him. He and Rose needed the cover of their woods. Rose and Thoran jumped into the thick woods and blended into the foliage, praying the attackers were scattered. Grimsdyke, a bit confused, lost sight of them. The rain slapped harder, overtaking rustling sounds in the woods. The parents' sharp eyes looked for monsters. Their keen ears listened for twigs snapping. Their forest would help them. Grimsdyke screamed at the ogres and orcs, "There's two in the woods. The others are in the house. Younglings in the house!" That got the beasts' attention; they came from the woods to meet their dinner.

Rose quickly said to her husband, "You are the spirit in my soul. The boys are safe for now. I feel it. We must kill these monsters." They kissed for one clock tick, stared deep into each other's eyes for one more clock tick and split up. At the same time they both said, "Use their stupidity. We must kill them!"

Back at Grumblers Hill...

Pitch barked with pure happiness, *"We're here, we're here."* Though he really didn't know where they exactly were; he had never heard of Bumblers' Hill. But, he was running up and down the path as if he knew exactly where he was. The rain was a bit heavier, though not heavy enough to cause the boys alarm. The skies darkened a bit more and the woodland sounds were muffled. The seven little men stood on the path at the foot of the rumbling hill.

"We have to be careful of poison and biting plants. Remember what Papa said," Alvis reminded them. After he said that, the seven felt slightly nervous. They could now really feel it. Every four or five clock ticks. A low rumble-thump that tickled their feet. They took their sacks off and piled them together.

"Maybe we can find a cave that'll take us to the rumble," Achu said excitedly.

"If we had more time," said Grumel.

"Yeah, if it rains any harder, we'll be pretty sloppy," said Joyal.

"And Papa's probably right behind us," Shyel added.

"Hey! Look at the size of those dingle berries," Yawnel laughed while pointing to the biggest dingle berry bush they'd ever seen.

"There's another one," said Shyel, pointing to another bush.

Ayell ran to the closest bush and plucked a berry off.

"Don't eat it, it might only look like a dingle, but might turn ya into something ugly," Alvis said.

Ayell studied the large, soft purple berry that took up nearly his whole hand. He sniffed it, smiled and did what needed to be done. He threw it at Alvis. As it squarely hit Alvis in the forehead, it exploded, covering Alvis's face with bits of its purple-red meat. Its purple skin stuck in his hair. Alvis was mad. The other six were not.

"Hey look, yur right. It turned ya into an ugly purple bogie," Grumel said, laughing. They all laughed. And quickly, *they* knew what had to be done. The seven scattered to nearby bushes to arm themselves with the soft, large and tasty dingle berries. As quickly as they could pick them, they threw them. And within only a few clock ticks after the first one was thrown, a full-scale dingle war was happening.

Pitch furiously barked with happiness as he dodged the incoming fury of dingle bombs being thrown about. As they were very good marksman, their aim was mostly true and all were hit quickly and covered with berry slop. They stayed close to the path, darting in and out of the edges of the woodland using trees as shields, grabbing ammunition, throwing, screaming, ducking, and battling. The soft rain allowed them to wipe their eyes clean, though their clothes were getting gooey and sticky.

And without warning, a gigantic, cracking bolt of lightning exploded from the sky, hitting the ground with a force so fierce it could only be described as the Good Mother herself pounding the land in anger. On its tail, a fantastic barrage of thunder wasted no time shaking the air.

"Let's put the flag up and go home," Grumel quickly said. And as quickly, the others said, "Okay." The boys didn't tell their parents that they made a flag with their names on it to be placed on the top of the hill. Ayell went to the sack that contained not only their flag, but also the goblet, and slung it on his back. He reached back, grabbed the flag and held it up for all to see. Joyal grabbed a large stick to be used as a flagpole. With some twine, he fastened the flag to the pole. The rain dropped harder. The sky darkened. The boys were ready to briskly walk home.

"Who's gonna put the flag up?" asked Achu.

Pitch barked, *"Me, me, me. Oh please let me carry the stick,"* and he tried prying it from Joyal.

"Hey stop that," complained Joyal, pulling it back from the dog.

"Here, you do it— and be quick," Joyal said, forcing the flag into Ayell's hands.

Ayell looked mad at Joyal and shook his head to say no, but his brothers pushed him into the woods saying, "Yes be quick, be quick about it." Pitch grabbed onto Ayell's shirt, clenched his jowls tight and pulled him while barking, *"Come on, come on, let's go. Let's go."*

Scowling, Ayell-the-brave grabbed the flag. And with his trusty dog, he stomped through the brush to the top of the hill. With his sack slung over his shoulder and the flag in one hand, he grabbed his axe in the other and started slashing through the brush on his way to their claim. Pitch was quickly ahead of him, bouncing up and down, yelping, *"Over here, I'm over here."*

Still scowling, Ayell looked back at his brothers and plotted ways to get even with them. I'll get 'em while they sleepin', he thought... I'll put worms in their shoes! Better yet— worms in their britches. He smiled, plotted his plan and plodded to their claim. Pitch reached the summit first. But it really wasn't much of a peak. It was more like a big bulge in the woods, though it was higher than the ground around. Pitch sat down, and as if he were royalty; he stuck his nose as high as he could in the air and howled, *"This is our mountain!"* Ayell quickly joined Pitch. Ok, let's do this, he thought.

Pitch barked, *"Here, here, put the stick in here."*

From the trail, his brothers became impatient. "Come on, claim our land," yelled Grumel. They wanted to get home. They were wet, dirty and getting tired of this adventure. They missed their cottage and wanted Momma's fired chicken.

"Give it a mighty stick in the ground—so's it don't fall down," screamed Yawnel.

Ayell looked at them and shook the flag as if to say, 'if you want to do it so badly, then you do it!' They all knew Ayell was angry. That was part of their fun. With two hands, Ayell held the flag over his head, Pitch barked a loud approval, and with the mightiest of stabs, Ayell stuck that pole as deep in the ground as he could and twisted it to make sure it stuck mighty and strong.

But it wasn't only dirt that the pole stuck in. The flagpole went deep into the eye of a great beast. A monster that had been sleeping for a long, long time. Sleeping for so long, that mounds of fallen leaves covered it— blanketed it, like a cozy quilt. And mixed with rain, a bit of bird poop, and time, the leaves became soft soil. Maybe the gigantic jolt of lightning had something to do with it, maybe not. But at that moment, a giant awoke. And it was in pain. And angry...

Twenty-Eight

Back at the Cottage...

Zee charged upstairs and climbed through a window in the roof. The window opened to a ledge that spanned half the length of the cottage. Thoran decorated the ledge so it looked as if it were a nice feature of the roof. Though in fact, it was a well-thought out battle perch where the entire woods surrounding the cottage could be seen. The perch ran to the chimney. In the chimney was a cubbyhole where weapons were hidden. From the perch, Zee watched six monsters lumber out of the woods— they seemed confused. Stupid, she thought— they'll all be dead soon.

Crouched by a boulder, Grimsdyke screamed and waved his finger, then pointed, "You three get them in the woods. You three, in the cottage, capture the younglins and the other one." Grimsdyke prayed the beasts would listen, as most couldn't even count. Again he wondered... why weren't children screaming?

"Hungry!" one of the orcs screamed back.

"You capture them first, then eat!" Grimsdyke screamed, louder. The beasts tried to follow his orders. Zee had her bow in hand with an arrow pulled back. She let it fly.

Unseen, Rose also let fly an arrow. Well hidden, Thoran had thrown an ax.

Zee hit an ogre in the neck; Rose's arrow hit one in the eye, sticking in its socket, just barely missing its brain. Papa's ax hit another in the ear, splitting and sticking into its skull but alas, not puncturing its brain. The three wounded beasts screamed first in agony, then in anger. The other three stopped and stared, they watched blood splurt out of their friends' wounds. The rain continued, thin and hard.

"Go! Move!" Grimsdyke screamed. He spied the sister on the roof. Puzzled, he again thought…why aren't the boys fighting? Where's that mutt? They're hiding. "On the roof!" he screamed.

The attackers tried to scatter, tried to retreat, and to attack, but they knew not where to go. For the most part, the ogres just ran into each other, their erratic movements kept sharp arrows from hitting them. "Throw rocks, attack them!" Grimsdyke screamed, now knowing full well their stupidity left *him* vulnerable. The uninjured ogres grabbed rocks and threw at the cottage.

The ogre with the ax in its ear pulled at the hatchet with a grunt. It wobbled and was dizzy with pain, as were the other two stuck ogres. One tried pulling the arrow out of its eye, but that made the pain worse. The other pulled the arrow out of its neck, and that made its head pound with pain as its blood flowed more freely. The one shot in the eye reached for a rock. It looked up, right as Zee pulled back and let another arrow fly, and with its good eye, watched the arrow grow larger in size, landing smack dab where Zee aimed. Darkness swallowed it. That second arrow hit its brain—deep enough to make its legs and arms stop working. It fell to the ground with a thump and blood flowed from its eyes. It could only listen to the soft sounds of drips and arrows whizzing while it felt blood pulse out of its head.

Zee thought…two dead, five to go.

Gripped with fear, the remaining ogres wildly threw rocks into the woods and at the roof. They could smell the humans. The largest ogre was also the smartest; it suddenly realized it would not capture the humans as the Council Master wanted. Instead, it would kill the humans, including the Grimsdyke, and eat for days. They might be stupid, but the beasts do have basic survival skills. It only took watching their companion, twitching on the ground and bleeding from its eyes for them to realize they were truly in battle. These humans had speeding arrows, sharp and narrow, flying through the air. The largest ogre ran to the cottage. An arrow sliced its right ear in half; it grabbed its head, roared and ducked.

Curses! Rose thought… just missed!

Another arrow hit the neck of the beast earlier wounded by Thoran's ax. The same beast turned and screamed in pain and its forehead was met with another of Thoran's hatchets. A fountain of blood sprayed far enough to hit the Council Master, who had grown silent, watching the speed of the battle. With a perfectly good axe protruding from its forehead, that scug fell to the ground—face first, further splitting its head.

"That's three dead," Zee screamed, "the rest will die soon."

Hidden, Thoran screamed loud and quick, "I'm up in a tree Rose, as soon as I get a clear shot, I'll call out!" The four remaining attackers stopped and looked up and around for the voices of the humans. Three ogres were still not wounded.

"Get into that house!" Grimsdyke screamed while boldly running towards the cottage. As the word 'house' left his mouth, he was hit in the shoulder with an arrow marked for him by Aunt Zee. She screamed, "One more to your head you foul thing and your beasts will eat YOU!"

Grimsdyke fell to the ground; in pain, but not mortally wounded. The arrowhead went clean through him and stuck out his back. The feathered fletching on the shaft's end tickled his chin as he looked at his wound. He stayed on the ground. He needed to think for a couple of clock ticks.

Rocks were again being thrown haphazardly at a fast clip by the beasts, thrown at the roof, at the woods and into the trees. Erratically thrown rocks could be *very* dangerous.

Zee took cover behind the chimney.

A flat-faced orc ran into the woods. Smell human…it thought. It glimpsed Rose's hair. Its adrenaline jumped— her over there! Excited, it quickly grabbed a rock and threw.

Rose heard the orc enter the woods, but she was aiming an arrow at an ogre near her cottage. She let it fly. Her brain screamed in crisis…Stay away from MY home! Her aim was true. She instinctively ducked from a flying rock, but her attacker's aim was true enough. It smashed into her neck; she yelped in pain and fell to the ground. Zee and Thoran heard Rose's yelp.

The orc ran towards its female prey and was met head on by her mate. Thoran's anger was quick and strong. He smashed an ax hard into the beast's forehead, cleanly cracking its skin, its skull, its brain. Thoran swiftly yanked the ax out. Knowing the animal was dead, a husband turned before his prey hit the ground and ran to his beloved. "Kill them," Rose pleaded, before Thoran reached her. She needed him to hear those words. She knew he would not leave her, but he had to.

Thoran couldn't speak. He saw the deep gash on his wife's neck and ripped off his sleeve to bandage her wound. He had never seen her wounded, as there was never a need to fight. They knew they *could* fight, Dagon's friends made sure of that. It was just never necessary. Now his wife was bleeding from the neck, her sister was on their roof fighting for her life, and his seven boys could come back any second. For the first time in his life, he was confused. What action should he take? Love sometimes did that to you.

Rose knew he couldn't stay with her. "Go kill them. I'll be fine," she said while starting to tend to her wound. With clenched teeth she said, "Turn it to anger and kill them!"

Thoran turned and ran. He thought…be smart. But he couldn't get the picture of his wounded wife out of his mind. Stopping abruptly just before the edge of the clearing, he threw a fourth ax that landed square in the chest of the scug that Rose earlier hit with an arrow. It did not puncture the beast's heart as Thoran had hoped, though its scream indicated a good hit, none-the-less. The beast stared at the ax protruding from its chest, and just before it went to pull it out, Zee's next arrow sliced through the air and spot-on struck the top of its head, landing deep into its brain. Its head shot up. It stared at its nearest companion and simply said, "Hungry," as a fountain of blood spurt from the top of its head. Its knees buckled, and it dropped to the ground. The companion ogre was trying to pull an arrow from its cheek.

Two remaining ogres stopped again to watch a counter-part die. The smell of blood was strong and usually made them hungry. But not this time. They were fighting for their ugly lives.

By Zee's count, there were two beasts alive: a big ogre and an orc with an arrow in its cheek. She knew the Council Master was wounded, but not dead. She screamed, "YOU'LL ROT IN THE DUNGEON! WE'LL MAKE SURE OF THAT!" Zee knew her sister was wounded. After Rose's last cry, she watched Thoran's axe come flying out of the woods, hitting a beast. That was her signal to aim true to its brain. Her footing was solid on the battle perch. She was confident the beasts would die, and Grimsdyke would be brought to justice. Brought to justice for an act that made *no* sense, whatsoever. Why... she thought, why?

As Grimsdyke lay on the ground, the steady rain couldn't cool the nervous jolts of fear coursing through his spine. By his count, only two beasts were left. He realized *he* very well might die. He thought...I am so very tired. He heard Zee scream at him. Then, a calm, face-less voice whispered, "Patience master, patience." It was a voice that gave him confidence. He knew his own fighting skills were weak. He believed his own lies when he thought— strategy is my strength! I will be patient. Fate will show me the way. He had a knife in his belt. He had a bow. He reached back to grab it and crawled. He screamed, "BREAK THE DOOR DOWN!"

The orc with an arrow in its cheek threw rocks at the girl human on the roof. The largest ogre, mostly unharmed, sought shelter. It wildly and stupidly pounded at the cottage's doorframe, one of the strongest parts of the house. It stopped when the butt end of a hatchet crashed into its head.

One more half turn, Thoran thought—and its brains would have spilled out.

The ogre rubbed its head and scowled.

On the roof, Zee slightly and lightly sidestepped a large rock that zipped past her head. Tho' in that one slight side step, the tiniest patch of green moss in a vast forest of a hundred shades of green, a small speck of moldy softness, was under her foot. It betrayed her. She slipped and went off the perch. Aunt Zee slid down the roof; she couldn't grab the covering that sheltered their family for so many years. Frantically, she grabbed at the thatchy roof. She went over its side. For one brief moment she caught the roof's edge, stopping her fall. She hung over the side, swinging like a pendulum and desperately tried to right herself.

"GET HER," Grimsdyke screamed. The two beasts didn't miss a beat, and Grimsdyke thought it time to ignore all pains and aim an arrow.

Thoran, hidden by the forest's edge, watched in horror at what quickly unfolded. Rose was able to make her way to him and her soft cry of, "No," made Thoran hesitate for only a clock tick.

The largest ogre was tall enough to grab at Zee as she hung. While it reached, an axe flew out of the woods landing clean in its forearm. A whizzing arrow grazed its other ear. Rose cursed herself; her aim should have been true. Her mind cried…she needs me!

The large ogre recoiled, screamed in anger and turned to spot the culprit. Grimsdyke studied the woods intently. He saw Rose aiming an arrow at him. He set his own bow in place. "Damn the pain," he said. Rose and Grimsdyke let their arrows fly. Both missed their mark.

Zee fell. She hit the ground hard, her left leg twisted, shattered, and her left foot pointed the wrong way. Do not pass out, do not pass out… she screamed in her thoughts.

The Council Master screamed, "GRAB HER, DON'T YOU DARE KILL HER YET."

The smaller orc was first upon her, grabbing her by the head. It turned to the ogre and said, "In woods kill 'em, less theys kill us." As it spoke, an arrow thunked hard into the cottage. The ogre quickly turned, picked up rocks that fell out of their sacks, and started to heave.

"NEVER YOU MIND ME, ROSE, THORAN, NEVER MIND ME. INTO THE WOODS YOU GO," Zee screamed.

The Council Master stayed still. He hoped that Thoran and Rose were intent only to save their sister. The intense pain in his shoulder barely masked the pain in his brain. He reached in his pocket for the dried blood-trolls nose.

In a hushed cry and lightly sobbing, Rose begged, "Why is this happening? Why? I can't leave her, Thoran. They have her, they have her and she's hurt."

Holding his wife, he answered, "The boys, Rose, we have to think of our sons."

"I LOVE YOU, TELL THAT TO THE BOYS, I LOVE YOU," Zee screamed.

The rain had nearly stopped again. The largest ogre heard Rose and Thoran whisper—it smelled their fear. Aiming, with its might it quickly let fly a rock. Into the brush that rock went. Again, a direct hit was not needed. It hit enough of Thoran's knee to shatter it. Thoran gasped in pain and fell backward. Rose let out a stifled scream and went to her husband's aid.

Grimsdyke had been aiming another bow. When Rose moved, he let his arrow fly. It hit sweet Rose in the back shoulder. She cried out a yelp that made Thoran and Zee scream, "NOooooooooo!" The misty drizzle muffled Rose's light sobs. Thoran tried to stand, but his shattered knee would not allow it, so he crawled.

Clenching her teeth, Rose said, "We must try to reason with him. He wants only the goblet."

"We can't wait for the boys to come back with it," Thoran said.

"We need to steer them from the cottage. The ogres will kill the boys. There's more of those monsters somewhere. I now feel it. And if they know of younglins, they will not stop until they have them. We need to get them away from the cottage."

"STOP, PLEASE STOP," Zelda sobbed loud as she was held about the neck.

"WHY DO YOU DO THIS TO OUR FAMILY WHO HAS ONLY BEEN KIND TO YOU?" Thoran screamed. "SURELY, THE GOBLET CAN'T BE AS IMPORTANT AS OUR LIVES. I IMPLORE YOU, SIR. PLEASE STOP. ANYTHING YOU WANT WE'LL GIVE YOU. THE GOBLET WILL BE YOURS. YOU HAVE MY PROMISE. PLEASE STOP!"

"COME OUT AND DROP YOUR WEAPONS," screamed Grimsdyke.

"YOU WILL GET NOTHING IF WE ARE HARMED. LET US COME OUT AND TALK. THIS SENSLESS BATTLE IS YOURS," screamed Thoran. "WE ONLY WISH YOU TO LEAVE. YOU WILL GET WHAT YOU WANT."

After a few ticks of silence, with the soft cadence of light raindrops filling the air, Grimsdyke calmly said, "Come out then." Grimsdyke felt more confident than he ever had. He knew the goblet would be his. It was just inside the cottage. And now he also wanted sweet Rose. In a civilized tone he said, "We will do you no more harm. NO MORE ATTACK," he screamed at the monsters he brought. The two remaining beasts looked at Grimsdyke.

Defeated, but mentally planning, Thoran said, "We have no choice at this point, Rose. You're wounded—*we're* wounded." Gritting his teeth he said, "We need to get them away from our cottage."

"Oh Thoran, how can this be happening? Why is this happening, where are the boys? What's happened? This all happened so quick, we..."

"I don't know why or how, but Dagon didn't see it coming. And us?

We need to believe they're taking care of each other. And I *do* believe that. Our boys are strong. We can't let these monsters sit here and pick them off. Follow my lead. We need to convince Grimsdyke to leave." Then softly he said, "Help me walk, my love."

"WE ARE COMING OUT," Thoran said confidently. "WE ARE WOUNDED AND WILL COME OUT SLOWLY."

Grimsdyke shouted back, "NO TRICKS SIR. ELSE MY COMPANION WILL RIP YOUR SISTER'S HEAD CLEAN OFF."

A husband and wife hobbled out of the woods. "No tricks," was all Thoran could say. For the second time that day Rose's eyes met Grimsdyke's. Only this time, it was he who shuddered. Not from fear, but from the intensified pain in his shoulder and his brain. Rose and Thoran stared at the smaller beast that held Zee, then at the huge ogre, both drooling with hunger. Even in the rain, their drooling was obvious. They looked at Zee— she looked back. Thoran winked at her. She tried to smile. They could see she was in pain; her skin was pale. Rose helped her hobbled husband to a bench in the front yard.

For a few clock ticks, Grimsdyke actually felt sorry for them, even doubting his actions. His throbbing shoulder had an arrow sticking through it. The pounding in his head brought on by a driving, diseased rage made him angrily say, "Let us go inside and dry off."

Abruptly, Thoran said, "The goblet is not here."

Grimsdyke turned and looked at him, puzzled. His mouth slightly opened.

"The boys are training, with a friend sir. They have taken the goblet. You obviously know of its powers. We let them take it in case they get hurt in some way."

"Not here?" he paused. "NOT HERE," Grimsdyke screamed at Thoran.

"We—"

"STOP." Grimsdyke shrieked. He stared at Thoran, at Rose, at Zee. He didn't believe Thoran. Calmer, he said, "Let us go inside, out of these harsh elements." The Council Master walked to the front door; it was still locked. To Thoran he said, "The key?"

Thoran looked at his wife, she shook her head. "You attacked us— we didn't think to carry one."

Grimsdyke looked at the large ogre— only moments before it was pounding at the frame. "Hit the door HERE!" he scolded, while smacking the door's center. With one large swing, the ogre pounded its thick forearm at the door center. It smashed inward. The ogre stomped into the cottage. Grimsdyke staggered towards the door while saying, "Inside."

The orc holding Zee tried to drag her. She screamed in agony. Together, Rose and Thoran pleaded, "Stop!"

Smelling the rancid breath and stank of her captor, Zee perked up. She was able to grab a rock. With a burst of energy and a mighty swing, she smashed the rock into the orc's one large nostril, properly cracking its skull inward; its greenish, sulfur-smelling blood flew about. The orc dropped her, staggered backward and fell on its bum. It quickly jumped back up and wobbled on its feet. In a garbled voice, the ogre mumbled, "Kill you," and tried to lunge at Zee, but fell back down.

Grimsdyke screamed, "STOP you idiot. She can't walk. Just leave her for the time being." He turned to Thoran and said, "Inside." He walked into the cottage.

Rose said, "I'm not leaving her," and hobbled to her sister. Inside the cottage, loud rustling about and crashes could be heard as the large ogre searched for food.

Turning around in the doorway, Grimsdyke said, "You bring her in then."

Rose cradled Zee as best as she could. She whispered to her, "Stay strong. I need to get you inside, where it's dry. It's going to hurt."

Zee could only weakly answer, "I know."

"This is madness, sir." Thoran said while grabbing a piece of wood to use as a crutch. He walked towards his wife to help with Zee. ' makes no sense. Why couldn't—"

"Stop it!" Grimsdyke bristled, spying the empty shelf where goblet—*his* goblet, last stood. "It's a bit late for this. Just shut up let me think."

In great pain, Thoran and Rose were able to help drag Zee their cottage and onto a love seat near the entrance. They both down hard on a bench.

The large ogre was pounding at cupboards and making a ri mess. It found sweetbread and other bits to eat. Although still or mid-day, it seemed much later. Stumbling up to the door, the bea with its face smashed-in held onto the doorframe to steady itself. stayed there as if it were guarding the entrance.

Could they be telling the truth? Grimsdyke asked himself, hi mind racing, his thoughts straying.

Thoran spoke, "We need doctors. Infections set quickly. YOU need a doctor."

"DON'T TELL ME WHAT I NEED," Grimsdyke shrieked. Though he knew infections *did* set quickly and typically meant death.

"There is no reason for any of this. Your actions have no defense," stated Thoran.

"WHERE ARE THEY?" Grimsdyke impatiently bellowed, ignoring Thoran's comments.

Rose asked, "Please sir, I beg you— let me take her to a bed for comfort. I can also tend your wound."

Grimsdyke looked at Rose and only said, "Shut up," and then, "Where are they?"

"We don't know," groaned Zee.

The bloodied orc at the door wanted revenge. "I kill her," it said.

"WHERE ARE THEY?" Grimsdyke impatiently asked.

"WE DON'T KNOW," Zee roared back.

"That, my good sister, won't do," Grimsdyke said.

"Ungry," the large ogre mumbled.

Rose prayed her sweet boys would stay away from their home.

Thoran answered, "What she means sir, is that we brought the boys to a friend just two days ago—a friend who is an expert woodsman. You know how we've trained the boys. We thought it time for them to learn to live off the land. They're—"

"Who?" Grimsdyke asked, "What is your friend's name?"

"Sheef—Trebor Sheef," Thoran lied quickly, in a strong voice.

Grimsdyke never heard of a family named Sheef. He thought he knew most that lived in Laban. "Are they in Laban?" he asked.

"Not in Laban proper, just outside, near the Elden Ridge. That's where they are training. We are to meet back with them in three days time at the Tree of the River Wanderer. They could be anywhere in the mountains," Thoran said.

The Council Master studied all of them and rubbed his aching head. His shoulder throbbed. He did need a doctor; he needed the arrow taken out of his shoulder. The boys weren't there, that was obvious. The goblet wasn't there. He caught them by surprise. There was no way they could have foreseen him coming, and they probably were telling the truth.

"Fine," he calmly said. He looked at the bleeding orc and the large ogre, "Tie him up."

"Please, there's no need for that," Rose sobbed.

In a weak voice, eyes closing, Zee said, "Leave them be."

"TIE HIM UP," Grimsdyke shouted, "There's rope in the sacks." The largest ogre, happily chomping on bits of sweetbread, stopped chewing. Ogres don't like to stop eating. It grumbled and fumbled through its sack for rope. The other beast—wounded and dazed, slumped in the doorway, suddenly, and violently shuddered, shivered, stiffened, and fell face first on the ground. It twitched, and gurgling sounds came out of its smashed-in face; at least it fell to the outside of the cottage. Grimsdyke sighed. "Just as well," he said watching it lay there, with only its fingers lightly trembling.

The remaining ogre watched his last companion die. It stared back at the Council Master, then at the others. The thought of killing all the humans, just to be done with them, quickly crossed its mind. "Him first," Grimsdyke said, double pointing at Thoran. The ogre obeyed. As stupid as these beasts were, they somehow could tie a simple, strong knot. "Then her," he said pointing to Rose. "I don't really want to harm you," Grimsdyke said to Rose.

"There's no need to harm any of us," Rose responded.

After Rose and Thoran were tied, the ogre walked to Zee. Grimsdyke said, "Not her, she's not going anywhere. Don't waste the rope." The ogre stopped and stared at Grimsdyke. Slowly, Grimsdyke said, "Now for the real moment of truth, my friends." He walked around the parlor, went to Rose and stared directly into her eyes, quietly asking, "Is your husband telling me the truth, my love?" The hair on Thoran's neck straightened when the word "love" left Grimsdyke's lips.

Rose glared at him. With tears in her eyes she quietly answered, "He always has, sir."

Grimsdyke studied Rose's eyes, looked at her brow, and looked to see how her lip trembled. "Maybe," he said. He stood and walked to the ogre. He looked up at it and asked, "Are you hungry?"

The ogre smiled. From the corner of its rotten mouth, a drip of drool dropped to the wooden floor, "Ungry, yes, ungry."

Fear, anxiety, confusion, and anger, the waves of emotions were thick in their thoughts. Thoran and Rose pleaded at the same time, "Please sir, we're begging." Thoran appealed, "Sir, anything we have will be yours." Rose added, "Anything sir, please, please, no more harm."

Zee, slumped on the floor, was barely able to comprehend anything. Numb from the pain of having her femurs and hips shattered, she stared and calmly said, "Our love is forever, my little Rose." She smiled. Thoughts of her life flashed in her mind. She remembered the day the boys were born. "Our little elves," she daydreamed. She turned her stare and spoke to the Council Master. "Your pain will last forever. Your regrets will hurt you more. Your soul will bake, you'll not be forgiven." She still smiled.

Grimsdyke looked at Zee and said, "I was there the day you spoke with lightning. I saw that dragon-elf save you. He didn't save me." He mocked, "The *little* girl with green eyes and red hair. You told him not to save me, but I *was* saved." Zee looked at him. She couldn't understand what he was saying, but she clearly remembered the lightning dust. "Greatness does not come without sacrifice." He turned to the ogre and said, "Start with her legs."

It was upon her quickly. As it flipped her and grabbed the right leg, Zee let out a simple deep breath. Though she didn't scream, she still smiled. Rose and Thoran pleaded, "No, no, no…please." Thoran cried—"I'll give you gold."

It bit down, snapped its head back and tore out a chunk of Zee's right thigh. Grimsdyke quickly said, "STOP!" The ogre gave Grimsdyke a puzzled, very angry look while it chewed on sweet thigh meat; it did not want to stop.

Sobbing, Rose and Thoran clutched each other. Thoran again pleaded, "Please, please sir, I beg you to stop."

Grimsdyke walked to Zee, grabbed her by the hair, and pointed her face at her family. Clenching his teeth he scowled— "Is your husband telling me the truth, MY LOVE."

They stared into the eyes of their sister. Her eyes were full—of life and of joy. She stared back, smiled and loud enough for all to hear she said, "I'll watch over." Zee closed her eyes and dreamed of her father's last words to her… 'eat the dust, call to them—they will come', and of their mother's… 'babies have special magic.' She dreamed of the night the boys were born, the crickets and cicadas sang a rare and beautiful tune. And she remembered how Ayell made a deep bottom burp that sent them into a fit of laughter.

Rose screamed at Grimsdyke, "HE ALWAYS HAS."

Grimsdyke dropped Zee's hair, turned to the ogre and simply said, "Have at her." He walked away, and speaking to Rose and Thoran he said, "I don't trust you." He paused and pointed at the shelf where the goblet once stood saying, "First, take her head and put it on that shelf."

As Rose and Thoran pleaded, the ogre wasted no time. It had the taste of human blood in its rotten mouth. Its thick, scabby forearm was under her jaw, the other arm was wrapped around her chest. In one swift hard movement, it yanked upward and Aunt Zee's head popped off her torso with a slurping crunch. The ogre let her lifeless body fall to the floor, grabbed Zee's head by its hair, stumbled to the shelf and placed her head on it, face side out. It wouldn't have eaten the head anyway; there's not much meat on a human's head. And the brains aren't very sweet. Aunt Zee's last expression was one of serenity—closed eyes with a smile. That was how she left her world; she arrived in the spirit world smiling.

Their pleading ended, Rose and Thoran could only blink, while breathing hard. It all happened so quickly, it made no sense. Everything seemed so—dreamlike.

Back at Zee's body, the ogre grabbed and dragged her to another part of the room to feed. "Take that outside," Grimsdyke said. The ogre obliged. It would rather eat in peace anyway. Grimsdyke sat down at the dining table. "We'll leave for Laban as soon as that's done eating." He tapped a finger on the table. "I agree with you Thoran. I need a doctor."

"Why—why have you done this?" Thoran sobbed. "We would have given you anything."

The Council Master looked at them, smiled and sighed. "I will have what all great rulers have had throughout eternity." He paused, "My will shall be law." He sighed again. "And sacrifices must be made. What you have is only the first of many pieces that I need for my very important puzzle. Your sons will have the option to show their loyalty to me. I will keep you both alive for that reason. I need the goblet. *Not* having it isn't an option."

Thoran and Rose knew that Grimsdyke had lost his mind. "We would have given it to you," Thoran sighed.

"Or you might have killed me," Grimsdyke responded. "*That*, also isn't an option." He stood up. "If your boys are where you say they are, then I will find them. I don't expect them to give up the goblet without your blessing—I don't trust them either. I have no intention of killing children," he lied. "I'm hoping to reunite you with your children. Your family still might be of use to me. Everyone's loyalty will then be tested."

"You're no longer a good liar," Rose said.

"No, you're wrong. I'm a very good liar," he replied, "What I'm not good at, is the truth."

Twenty-Nine

The Hill Came Alive

A lvis remembered Dagon saying a long time ago... "Da big-uns can sleep for twenny, maybe turdy years." He remembered that because the word 'turdy' made them laugh.

It took a few moments to register, but register it did. A giant was awake. And the drowsy stupid, gargantuan beast was in pain—and angry—and hungry—and thirsty... all at once.

With Pitch by his side, Ayell held onto the flagpole and looked down at a hole that opened up. And out of that hole came a loud, dismal, gagging moan. Then a booming cough, sending a fountain of dirt into the air; the hill they were on moved. No one could scream yet. It all happened too quickly. The giant ogre sat up. Ayell, Pitch and decades of woodland growth that covered the monster, flew off its face, shoulders and chest, landing in its giant lap with soft thuds. It shook its head to clear its face and head. Its one good eye opened, the other couldn't as it had a flagpole sticking out of it. It sat there woozy and befuddled, smacking its dry and dirty lips. A steady rain fell, and what moisture hit its lips, the beast thought was good.

The six brothers on the path blinked, they tried to comprehend what was happening. Before them sat an ogre; and the half they saw was larger than their cottage—much larger. They recognized its face from Dagon's journal. They now knew what made Grumblers Hill rumble. They watched their brother and their dog get thrown from its face and at that point, they couldn't tell where they landed.

The ogre grabbed and yanked the pole out of its eye and howled in pain. It let out a series of coughs, each shaking the air and leaves of nearby trees. In its lap, brush and branches rustled and Pitch's head popped out. Pitch looked up and saw a sight that made no sense. High above him was the face of a dirty, nasty giant. Without knowing it, he growled deeply. Then barked loudly, *"GO AWAY!"* The ogre looked down and saw a dog and a tiny human foot sticking out of the brush in its lap. It wiped its eyes and cocked its head. The little foot's toes wiggled. Up popped the head of a younglin. In a deep, muffled type of voice, the ogre said, "Foooood."

Pitch started to bark furiously at Ayell, *"Run, run, run, run, as fast as you can!"* But before Ayell could run, the giant picked Ayell up by his tiny legs and lifted the tasty morsel to its waiting crusty mouth. Pitch vaulted himself, scream-barking, *"Nooooooo!"* He bit and clung to the ogre's hand, chomping as hard as he could. Ayell hung upside down, he couldn't scream. He couldn't do much except squirm like a worm. Staring at the monster, for a moment he thought he was in a nightmare; he prayed he was in a nightmare. But he wasn't.

The pain the beast felt in its hand was not enough to make it drop its food. With the other hand, it grabbed the little dog and pulled him off. Only Pitch's head now stuck out of the ogre's cupped hand. Pitch furiously swung his head back and forth, snapping his jaws, biting at air. Ayell still hung upside down by his feet.

The six brothers watched in horror and reacted. All screamed at the top of their lungs and as one, "DROP HIM, LET HIM GO, HEY, DROP HIM, LET HIM GO!" Their voices carried strong.

The giant ogre turned and saw a pack of younglins. It had one simple thought… FOOD. The ogre threw Pitch into its mouth and swallowed him whole. It then threw Ayell into its mouth and tried to bite down, but only succeeded in biting its own tongue. Not having anything to drink in decades, the ogre tasted its own blood. It was moist and sweet. Although in pain, it felt the little human scratch at its tongue. It threw its head back to swallow, little Ayell flew to the back of its disgusting, fetid mouth and was in fact, swallowed.

In complete darkness, Pitch howled, Ayell silently screamed and they slid down a giant ogre's throat. Bumping this way, thumping that, tumbling head over feet, feet over face, they fell. The slimy throat-cave they were in smelled. Pitch snagged himself on something, Ayell bumped into him and was able to grab hold, but Pitch's hold didn't last and again they fell. The fall lasted forever in their minds, and when they landed in a shallow pool of what can only be described as smelly ogre belly slop, they could only breathe in short gasps, surrounded by the blackest of black. Ayell thought... this is a serious black.

Outside the ogre, the six brothers were in attack mode.

The ogre rolled and slowly stood to its full height to feed on the others. It towered above all except the largest of trees. Although its legs wobbled, it was anxious to get its body moving.

The boys sized up their adversary. "It's got to be fifty, sixty paces tall!" Shyel screamed. It was covered in some sort of animal skin, and Alvis wondered how big the animal must have been for its hide to cover the giant. Without thinking, Grumel, Alvis, and Joyal had axes out and with their mightiest of throws, they let them fly. Almost at the same time, Shyel, Achu, and Yawnel had their bows out with arrows pulled back and they too let them fly. Their aim was true.

The giant had barely stood and turned to catch its food when it was met with the first barrage. Two little axes in the forehead, one in its undamaged eye, one arrow in the flag-poled eye, one arrow in the now damaged eye and one arrow in the nose. The giant was not only instantly blinded, but its head was lightly split open and blood gushed out. Surprised by the attack, it fell backward.

Inside the ogre, Ayell and Pitch were thrown about. The stench should have been unbearable, but it truly was the least of their worries. Pitch whimpered, *"I'm afraid, I'm really afraid, what do we do? What do we do?"* Ayell clutched his sack for comfort. He couldn't even tell Pitch to come to him. There are many types of reasons to be scared in life, and at ten years old, most types of worry are simple. But the type of scared from being eaten alive can't be described. Ayell heard his mother's voice, softly saying, 'For only in the dark when held to the heart will its light shine.' He looked around for her and thought... she'll save me. How he longed for her hug.

The sack started to glow. And it felt warm. He forgot he had the candleholder and the goblet. He reached into the sack and pulled out the glowing candleholder. The light was bright, warm, not hot. He brought it to his chest; he felt his mother's touch. The stomach of the ogre lit up and it wasn't a pretty sight. Pitch barked, *"Light! Light's good!"* He stopped. He growled low and deep. Creatures that could only be described as large maggots were attached about the whitish-brown stomach wall. Maggots that were the length of Ayell's arm, had no eyes, only mouths, and with large jagged teeth. They were angry maggots. Ayell didn't remember seeing those in Dagon's book. He grabbed his axe. If they attacked, he would fight— or he would die. And he didn't want to die. Pitch knew a fight was coming. Ayell began to furiously chop at the stomach wall closest to him, determined to cut whatever path he could out of the beast that ate him. Following his master's lead, Pitch lunged at the stomach wall himself, biting and digging with his paws. Blood and ogre bits flew about them. They were getting used to the smell.

The giant sat, in shock and in pain. The brothers scattered to gain better vantage points for another attack. They again took aim with their weapons.

As the ogre lifted a hand to pull the little weapons from its face and head, an excruciating pain welled up from its innards. It clutched its gut and grunted in anguish. And while clutching its stomach, another barrage came from the six. This time, one ax hit its nose, two spears went deep into a cheek, two arrows cut through the other cheek and a last arrow somehow went right up a nostril. Never having been in such pain, the giant didn't know what to do. Something inside was causing it great pain. That dog? "Kill you,"— it screamed while grabbing whatever it could to throw at the six little humans.

The boys got showered with a storm of dirt, branches and squashed dingle berries, but they weren't injured. They jumped up and readied to attack again.

The wounded ogre was not happy. It didn't want to fight. It instinctively wanted to eat. It would find food that doesn't fight back. It decided to run and made to get up again.

Every time the giant moved, Pitch and Ayell were thrown about. Ayell knew his brothers wouldn't run, they would fight. They would try to help him and Pitch. He just hoped they too wouldn't come sliding down the monster's throat. Every chance he had, with one hand he chopped and attacked the stomach wall, while clutching the candleholder to his chest with the other. Pitch growled, clawed, bit and spat out chunks of ogre stomach.

With a mighty swipe, Ayell's hatchet broke through the stomach wall—a high-pitched hissing sound filled the air. Another ax swipe and the opening widened. When the hole was large enough, Ayell held the candleholder out like a lantern. The light did not go out. At the bottom of a giant belly, a boy and his dog peeked their heads through an ogre's stomach and looked up. Ayell knew he was looking into the guts and bits of a giant's chest. It looked like a huge cave. When their eyes adjusted, in the distant part of the 'cave', they saw what looked like a giant wishbone with thick ribs extending from it. The ribs extended and covered where he and Pitch were. Usually, wishbones are special. Ayell remembered that every wishbone, in every chicken ever eaten by them, was saved and dried. And when a good deed was done, Papa, Momma or Aunt Zee would grab one, wrap their little pinky finger around it and offer it to whoever did the good deed by saying, "Wish simple, wish kind." Loads and loads of the angry maggots clung about the ribs.

While being amazed at the wishbone, it dawned on Ayell that a thump bump sound was coming from—somewhere. He looked around. And Pitch let out a scream, a terrible howl of pain. Ayell jumped and whirled to his friend. A maggot latched onto Pitch's back. The leech that almost killed their father flashed through Ayell's mind. He prayed the maggots weren't poisonous. He ached for his father; he knew there was only one way to see him again. With a mighty swing Ayell swiped along Pitch's back and sliced the maggot in two— still wriggling, it fell. White bubbles came from the maggot's deadhead that stayed attached to Pitch's back.

With all his might, Ayell screamed, "STAY STRONG BOY." It came out only as a whisper. But it was a loud whisper, loud enough for Pitch to hear and Pitch beamed with excitement, hearing the first words from his silent friend.

"I will, I will!" Pitch barked back. And to show his strength, he jumped outside the stomach and grabbed onto the lowest rib. The dead maggot's head fell off his back.

Ayell looked up and squinted— he saw something. At the top of the wishbone was a chunk of something, and that chunk was moving. It was orange and blue with yellowy-white cracks. Back and forth and forth and back, it throbbed. *It* was making the deep thump bump sound of Grumblers Hill. His eyes focused. Ayell saw that it was the monster's heart, and he knew exactly what must be done.

Grunting and breathing heavily as its anxiety grew, the giant ogre stood and quickly tried to move its legs to run. But they had not moved for many, many years. Running was not possible yet. However, it was able to lunge one stride, and one stride of a seventy-foot tall ogre covered quite a bit of ground.

The six brothers were quick to continue their attack. Spears, axes and arrows again flew through the air. All hit various points on the back of the beast's head and neck and again, the ogre screamed in great pain. The giant stumbled, and grabbed onto a small tree to balance. With a mighty pull, it ripped the tree out of the ground and tossed it back. With blind luck, the tree flew and only hit other trees, with branches and limbs crashing about all over. The forest animals: grimlers, grackens, bumblers and jowlers, they and all others screamed their displeasure at the disruption of their quiet forest. Even the griblics, the rarest of the fairy animals, showed themselves to whistle and shriek in anger.

But sounds meant nothing. The six boys were hit with some part of a flying tree. Again, they were not seriously injured, but they were thrown off stride and the ogre was able to take another great stomp away. Two more stomps and the giant would be out of their range. The six knew the ogre must be killed. They saw their brother get eaten but they couldn't leave him. They would not run away. They would not go home without him. It didn't need to be spoken; they could not face their sweet mother and strong father as only six. And for that, the ogre must be killed and sliced open. It didn't need to be discussed; they ran at it while they readied to attack.

Inside the beast, there was great turmoil. As the ogre tried to flee its tormentors, Ayell held onto the stomach walls and Pitch desperately held onto a rib. Stomach slime and nasty ogre slop sloshed about. Ayell knew time was running out. Angry maggots flew all over, and as they flew, they would snap their jagged-toothed, bloody mouths trying hard to latch onto Ayell or Pitch. When the giant suddenly stopped, Ayell flew out of the stomach, through the air and grabbed onto the same rib as Pitch. It's now or never, Ayell thought. While clutching the candleholder in one hand, he wrapped that same arm around the ogre's rib and quickly steadied himself. With his other hand he held his ax, took one practice aim and let fly his weapon. Its aim was true, hitting a rib, shattering it, but unable to meet the heart. But there was a clearer path to the beating muscle. With barely a thought, he pulled an arrow from the holster and reached for his bow, but it wasn't to be found. Fuddlesticks! he screamed in silence, throwing the arrow anyway. It landed well short of the heart. My knife! My knife! He reached down. He felt the soothing handle of it and quickly pulled it from its sheath. With a quick aim, he let it fly. The blade flew straight but slightly missed its mark, striking hard into a rib. Ayell silently gasped, searched for other weapons, and screamed, "Where's my spear? Where's my bow?" even though no voice came from his throat.

Panicked, time moved too quickly. Ayell's mind raced. He looked at his friend and cried out, "I'm sorry, sorry, I love you." It was barely a whisper, but his dear friend understood. Pitch set his feet and with an angry growl, he lunged up and found a rib. He growled again, jumped and found another rib. Another loud growl— another rib. Another growl, a thrusting jump, another rib. Ayell watched Pitch growl, jump and climb ribs like climbing a ladder. He missed once and his back legs found no rib, though his front paws and strong jaws did. He easily righted himself. Pitch did this seven more times. The ribs got shorter and shorter, and he was near the point of the wishbone, close enough to the pumping heart to smell its musty odor. He looked down at Ayell. Pounding his chest, tears streaming down his face, Ayell mutely screamed "KILL IT, KILL THE HEART!"

Pitch knew what had to be done. He dove with all his might at the ogre's heart. But he couldn't see all that well, and something that Pitch thought was part of the heart, wasn't. Something was wrapped around it. And that something quickly uncoiled. Before Pitch's eyes could adjust, before he could react, one head of a serpenty-thing snapped quickly and bit into his leg. Pitch cried and was barely able to hold onto a bit of shattered rib. He then saw a second snake-thing, which was eating a maggot, turn and stare at him. The second one opened its mouth. Three large fangs glinted from the light of Ayell's candle, and it lunged to help its companion. Pitch prayed there was no third head. He wondered…is it two heads or two snakes? Although he was in the most pain he had ever known, Pitch violently bit into the snake-head attached to his leg, chomping down, crushing the snake's skull. Splinters of bone pierced the roof of Pitch's mouth. Pitch shook the serpent head with hard, angry shakes, ripping the head off while the serpent's fangs were pulled out of his leg. The severed head was thrown into the innards of the giant ogre. During Pitch's battle, Ayell climbed ribs to help his friend.

When the first snake-head was killed, the second head stopped its attack in mid-air, the pain of losing its twin so great, so bewildering, that anger was replaced with deep confusion. The confusion lasted only a clock tick. It spat a hiss of seething hatred and stabbed at Pitch's face with its large saber-like fangs, timing its attack to inflict a quick death. But Pitch wanted life more. And that special desire quickened his response so that his canine choppers met the snake's fangs, closing on two of the three, snapping them to pieces, as if he were chomping on icicles. The serpent recoiled. Its body twisting, its head off-balance. It melted into the darkness beyond the ribs. Ayell furiously climbed.

Pitch was so close to the heart, he could smell its foul breeze with every beat. A fleeting thought, of him—Max, killing Grimsdyke flashed in his mind. Then he, Pitch, barked loud, *"I WILL KILL YOU FOR MY FRIENDS."* and he lunged at the heart. With his teeth, face and front legs, he met the beating muscle. It engulfed and swallowed him. Pitch burst through the muscle while ripping and shredding it. To Ayell, Pitch looked as though he were swimming in the heart. Pitch clawed, bit, clawed and ripped, blood and chunks flew about. Ayell was nearer to his friend. He watched every move of Pitch's battle while climbing and he was now splattered by bits a' blood and ogre heart. A quick glance to his left and Ayell found the axe he last threw wedged on a rib. He grabbed it. He closed in enough to help Pitch and was about to swing hard when the heart stopped thump bumping. Just like that.

And when it stopped, the ogre died. And for one moment, the monster's black spirit hovered, as if it had a choice of where to go. Then its darkness was sucked into the ground.

The six brothers knew nothing of what was happening on the inside of the giant ogre. They launched another attack when suddenly, the giant clenched its chest and let out a deep, long groan of pain; one last great rumble, quieting all sounds in the woodland.

The massive brute stiffened and grabbed onto a tree for its last gasp at life. Lifting its head to the sky, letting the soft, misty rain fall on its face, the giant opened its mouth. It was very thirsty. As life flickered out its eyes, it said, "Rain," and died while standing up. Its fat knees wobbled, its thick shoulders, neck and head rocked. The ogre fell backward with a weighty force that sent most everything not rooted in the ground, including six little men, up into the air and back down with a THUNK!

Pitch and Ayell were thrown hard as if they had fallen from a high tree. Fortunately, the ogre's innards were soft, as were the maggots that softened their landing. The candle still shone brightly. The giant's rib cage loomed above them. They were thrown back where they started, near the ogre's stomach. They looked at each other and blinked, knowing they had killed a giant. There was no more heart thumping. They remembered the maggots, and Ayell jumped up. But the maggots weren't attacking—there was no squirming about. Just like that, they were dead.

Outside the giant, six brothers did not feel the happiness warriors usually experienced with the slaying of a beast. "How can we tell Momma?" Alvis asked. They had lost their brother. A giant was heroically slain, but there was no pride in it. Somehow, they now had to dig into the mountain of a beast and get the bodies of their brother and their dog.

Pitch's wounds were deep; Ayell had to get him out of the monster...quick! Still clutching the candleholder and the sack with the goblet and the journal, Ayell thought... this'll be something to add to our journal. Ayell smiled at his friend, Pitch could only manage a whimper in agreement. Having been bitten by maggots and a snake, the bleeding was worse than Ayell could even see. Ayell searched for a way out of the ogre. It dawned on him... same way we got in. He decided they would cut into the throat and crawl out the of the ogre's mouth. Ayell stroked Pitch's head and mouthed the word—"home."

Trying not to waste time, the six sad brothers climbed onto the belly of the dead ogre, reasoning Ayell and Pitch would be in its stomach. They picked a point that looked like where the stomach would be, and reluctantly, but without hesitation, they got to work. The ogre's skin was thick, and to cut through it required their full strength. With each heavy, hacking ax-swing and stab, hissing blood flew, sprayed and splurted about. They would never forget the death-stink that came from the gut.

Ayell could only guess where the throat was. He reasoned that the point of the wishbone must be the center of the beast—at least that's the way it was on the chickens Momma made. The throat has to be near that point...he thought. He gently prodded Pitch to follow him. They slogged through muck and dead maggots. The ribs above them became smaller and smaller, as did the space that surrounded them. They passed the ogre's shredded heart and had to start crawling. Pitch looked around for the second serpenty-thing. A rounded slimy wall blocked their path, they could crawl no more. It must be the throat... Ayell prayed. Looking back, he noticed the rounded wall went further down than where he could see. With a mighty hack of his ax, the pipe split open, and a burst of fresher air hit them in the face. Ayell sliced, opened it wider and excitedly mouthed, "Let's go!"

Pitch knew he was badly wounded. The pains from these bites felt different from other pains he had during his life. A poisonous bite has a different feel than say, a knife stab. The wounded muscle itself feels— sick. Diseased. Not just achy. And the heavy sickness was spreading through his body. He was very scared and couldn't tell his friend how much he loved him. He prayed he would see the other six boys one last time. He knew he was dying.

They climbed into the giant's throat and crawled. Ayell held the candleholder in front of him. Most would have been claustrophobic inside a tight space with slimy, rounded walls, but the draw of seeing your mother and father again excited their senses. A boy and his dog squirmed their way through a tunnel. Fortunately, the giant died with his mouth open. It wasn't too long before Ayell saw a dull gray light, a subdued brightness from outside the beast's mouth. He crawled a bit further, smelled fresher air, and smiled when a sweet, little mist touched his face. Pitch's spirit also jumped. He too smelled the fresh outside and freedom. Ayell crawled onto the ogre's teeth and turned to help his wounded friend, as it was difficult to navigate. Pitch looked at his silent friend, too tired to muster even the slightest of happy howls, but not too numb to howl when the second snake-head darted out from the tunnel and bit down on him with broken teeth. The snake pulled on Pitch's back legs while Ayell pulled Pitch's front paws. It was a last tug of war with a creature that lived within a creature. Pitch had no more tug in him. He gave up; he passed out. But Ayell became angrier. Jumping back into the ogre's mouth, Ayell punched at one albino eye of the snake, grabbed it and quickly snapped it out of its socket. The snake let go of Pitch and before it could do anything else, Ayell plunged the candleholder he still held, deep into its empty eye socket. With a sizzle and fizz, the light from the candleholder went out; sparks flew from the snake's eye. The serpent shook hard, coiled, twisted and made one last feeble lunge at Ayell, landing just short of the child's face. The snake's mouth opened and it hissed a last breath.

A wisp of smoke came from its throat. Pitch was barely breathing. Ayell pulled out the candleholder, shoved it in his sack, hoisted his friend over his shoulder and climbed out of the ogre, once and for all. Standing on the ogre's teeth with a dog and a satchel flung over his shoulders, Ayell was not a proud conqueror—his friend needed help.

And there they were, his beautiful brothers— stabbing and attacking the belly of the giant ogre. Maybe they wanted to make sure it's dead, Ayell thought. Until that moment, Ayell couldn't comprehend the true size of the ogre. And everything happened so quickly. But now he saw what they killed. And he was truly amazed. He climbed down the hairy chin of the ogre and staggered to his brothers.

Other than grunts, the six boys did not talk as they went about their task. They were lost in their thoughts. The ogre skin was tough, but the muscle seemed tougher. Staring down at the giant pool of blood they were making, they didn't lift their heads. A part of them had died and they were doing all they could to hold onto their emotions. Wishing they never came on the journey, they couldn't imagine the reaction of bringing the bodies' home to their cottage and placing them in front of their parents and Aunt Zee. They were numb with sadness. Grumel was the first to cry. The rest followed. They cut into the beast while sobbing. They didn't notice Ayell had softly laid Pitch down and joined them. The rain had stopped.

Joyal was staring down, taking a breath when Ayell put an arm around him for comfort. Ayell patted his brother and pointed to Pitch. Still looking down, Joyal took Ayell's sleeve to wipe his running nose. "Thanks," he said while wiping at a long, clear shniggle but not looking at the sleeve's owner. Ayell vigorously shook his head up and down, his way of saying, 'you're welcome.' Still patting his brother, he pointed at their dog while stomping a foot.

Then came the sneeze. It happened so quickly and with such force, that Joyal flew backward, landing on his bum. He looked up whilst sitting and saw his dopey, beautiful brother trying to shake the booger off the sleeve he just used.

"HEY! HEY! HEY! It's him. It's you!" Joyal screamed.

Snapping their heads to attention, they gasped as one at the sight of Ayell. Elated barks of "Ho, Hey, Ayell," were screamed. They dropped their weapons and attacked their not-dead brother with hugs and pats and more hugs. After a brief, happy hug-fest reunion, Shyel said, "You stink!"

Joyal said, "I wiped a shniggle on you."

Yawnel asked, "Where's Pitch?" Ayell double-pointed and they all saw Pitch lying near them, one leg slightly twitched. They ran to their dog. Pitch was lying on his side, bleeding badly. The commotion barely woke Pitch from his painful stupor. He heard his friends and wanted to see them one last time. Raising his head only the slightest bit, his tail wagged once. He mustered a weak bark to say, *"Hi."*

"We thought you were dead," Shyel said. Ayell quickly cocked his back as if to answer, "So did I."

"Are those bites?" asked Alvis. "We need to get him home. We need to wrap those bites to stop the bleeding!"

"What're we gonna wrap him with?" asked Grumel. "The sacks!" He started to empty his, as did the others, except Ayell. He stroked Pitch's head, mouthing, "Good boy, good boy." They fumbled with cut pieces of sack and prayed they could stop Pitch's bleeding. The bandages were rough, but they worked. They needed to get home and quickly, Pitch was barely breathing. The boys were afraid for him to go to sleep. "Be strong, boy," said Achu.

Pitch just stared; he couldn't whimper any longer. He wanted to scream that he loved them. And he loved the mom, the pop and especially Zee. Pitch wanted to thank them. He now knew he would die, but Ayell was safe. He closed his eyes. Grumel cried, "The goblet! The goblet!"

"Yes, the goblet," said the others. Pitch half opened one eye.

Ayell fumbled through his sack and grabbed the golden goblet and unwrapped it.

"Do ya think it'll work on a dog?" asked Joyal.

"We have ta try," said Achu.

"How much water, ya' think? How much blood?" asked Joyal.

"Don't know, but Momma said one drop of blood," Grumel answered. They filled the goblet halfway up with water from a jug.

"Now just be still boy, we need just a little of 'ya," said Alvis. Ayell held the goblet. The others unwrapped one of Pitch's wounds to expose bleeding.

"You do it," said Grumel.

"YOU do it," said Alvis.

Ayell shoved his brothers out the way and gently touched a wound. Pitch's blood covered his finger. Holding his finger above the goblet, all watched as a single drop fell, landing smack in the center with a slight plop! They fully expected some bubble and fizzle, tho' nothing happened.

"Now what?" asked Yawnel.

"Make him drink it." And with those words, Ayell placed his hand under his friend's head and gently lifted, while bringing the goblet closer. Shyel softly said, "Drink it boy." A thought passed quickly in Pitch's mind... he remembered the Council Master forcing him to drink the potion that turned him into a dog, and the bad pain that came from that brew. But this was different. These were his friends. They loved him. So, when the water was poured into his mouth, he painfully swallowed. It slid down his throat and there was no pain. It was sweet and cool. He closed his eyes.

Then came the bubble and fizzles. The blood around Pitch's wounds crackled, sizzled, and popped. A light mist rose from each wound and covered each bite. A slight wind brushed across them. The mists cleared, and bare patches of skin were left, where just moments before, bloody gouges had been. Little black hairs sprouted from the bare skin. And magically, before their eyes, the wounds healed. "Amazing," Shyel said.

After only a few minutes, his mind still thinking that he should be in pain, Pitch barked loudly. *"IT'S GONE?"* He jumped up, barking, *"It's gone, it's gone, it's gone."* Tail wagging, howling, and running in circles, he jumped on whoever was the closest, pushed off and jumped on another. They hugged and patted him. Alvis, Grumel, and Achu asked, "How ya feelin boy?"

"Hungry" Pitch barked, *"Yes, I'm hungry."*

"You're right," said Joyal, "it's time to get leave and tell Momma and Papa about this!" He pointed at the dead, smelly giant underfoot, that for a moment, they had forgotten about.

"No," Pitch barked irritated, *"I said I was hungry."*

"Okee dokee, let's go home. We have a lot to tell Momma and Papa about," said Grumel.

Pitch again tried to explain, barking, *"I said, I mean, I haven't eaten... Oh never mind."* And he bounded away, looking for a lower spot than the high belly of the dead ogre to jump down. Pitch ran to the shoulder, down a limp arm and jumped off its hand. He sniffed the air for anything that smelled like food, but the ogre stench was still strong. The seven boys followed the lead of Pitch and made their way off the dormant beast. They gathered their bits to begin their trip back home. Small droplets of rain began falling and the sky was still overcast, but not as dark as it was before their battle with the ogre started. They took a few steps and turned back for a last look at the dead giant. The boys all thought about what had just happened. Grumblers Hill tried to eat them. They would bring their father back. Everyone would want to see the giant. And boy, was it going to stink soon.

"We killed that," said Yawnel. He turned to Ayell, "That thing ate you."

"An' you made it out," added Alvis. They all looked at Ayell and smiled. Ayell shook his head. Someday, he thought, he'll write about it, but not now. Right then he just wanted to go home, as they all did. Pitch gave a quick howl—*"Let's go."* He hopped off down the path, but not out of sight.

"Let's get out'a here," Shyel said. Little bursts of sunlight shot through the clouds. The rain still came in small drops. They were late leaving to go home, but they were together, and alive. They knew they wouldn't get in trouble.

The woodland was again quiet, save for the distant sounds of grimlers, bumblers and gracklers voicing their approval of the slaying of a beast. Even the rare, frog-like, fairy griblics whistled an approving, melodic tune. The hill rumbled no more.

Thirty

Goodbye My Sister

Grimsdyke didn't allow Zee to be covered. So perched on a shelf Rose's sweet sister, or rather her head, watched with a chilling, serene look on her face.

In a pained daze, Rose cut the point off the arrow that stuck through Grimsdyke's shoulder. She took little pleasure in hearing his gasp when she pulled the shaft from his wound. The ogre held a rock to Thoran's head. Rose tended to Grimsdyke's wounds. Grimsdyke then allowed her to tend to her own and Thoran's wounds a bit. Why? They didn't know; he just did. He said he wanted their family "reunited," but she didn't believe him. Grimsdyke was impressed, for despite her pain, Rose moved with grace and efficiency. But it was fear that drove her. Mentally, Rose and Thoran were in a pure panic; their boys could come back at anytime. They should have been back already. Time, which their family usually savored and embraced, was now feared. They needed to get Grimsdyke away from their cottage—they couldn't let the boys be ambushed.

"What say we make our way back to civilization? Yes? Let's try to find your children." Grimsdyke said to all, and turning to the well-fed ogre, "You'll have to go to the cave for a bit. Tie her back up." The ogre grunted. It didn't care. It was not hungry—yet. It wanted to get moving. Grimsdyke added, "We'll try to go straight through, back to Laban. I want my own bed."

Under protest, the ogre tugged at nooses, placed around Rose and Thoran's necks. The beast was the master. The ogre picked up the husband and wife and easily slung them over its shoulders as if they were sacks of rocks. So deep was their sorrow, the mother and father were numb from sadness. The pain from their broken bones or wounds paled in comparison to their grief. They knew that by the grace of The Good Mother, if the boys could find them, they would be rescued. They needed to get away from the cottage— the boys couldn't help them if they themselves were ambushed. The goblet was the only thing keeping them alive—it could save them. The insanity of what had happened to them defied any logic.

Thoran was tied tightly, he couldn't move; there was nothing he could do. Thoughts of failing his family swirled around his head. His mind cried—this can't be how our lives will end! Weak and weary, he hoped for a miracle. Why isn't he watching-over, he wondered... where is Dagon?

To the ogre, Grimsdyke said, "Same way we came my good... uh... thing. To my trusty horse." The large beast started walking towards the woods. "Wait!" Grimsdyke said. He thought for a moment. "Let's make this a bit easier on us. Come, let's go to the back." The ogre followed Grimsdyke to the rear of the cottage. There, in a small corral were seven small and one large horse, standing at majestic, agitated attention, along the fence closest to the cottage. The ogres' stench, from the dead and the one alive, had been swimming though their nostrils for some time. The horses had nervously watched bits of the earlier battle. They smelled the sickly odor of a predator, heard screaming, and were on their guard. At the sight of the large beast carrying their friends, agitation turned to panic. Donkey, the most forgotten member of their family, crouched in a dark corner of the barn, unseen, and happy to be that way.

Grimsdyke said, "Let's see if I can ride the big one. We'll take a small one for you to eat later. But let's be quick." The ogre dropped the couple. Rose and Thoran landed with a painful thunk. As the beast lumbered up to the coral, Thoran's horse neighed angrily and lifted itself high on its hindquarters. It punched and pawed at the air with its forelegs and came down hard on the fence, easily crushing it, creating a breach. It whinnied a call to the smaller horses. Heeding the cue, the little horses ran to the opening their friend created, leaping over the broken beams, running to freedom.

For its size, the ogre was swift. Surprised when the big horse jumped up and came down, crushing the fence, it staggered back a bit. But when the small horses started to escape, the ogre's feeding instincts took over—it sprang at them. It had no rocks to throw. The big horse snorted loud, cursed at the beast, and rose back up on its hind legs. At its height, its head was barely above the large ogre. Thoran's horse was afraid of the ogre, but it was a protector. The horse came down hard and charging, its back legs kicking up a small dust storm. Little horses scattered into the woods. Shyel's horse, the last to flee the opening, screamed in fear as the ogre lunged and grabbed its hind legs. Caught, the little one's fear quickly turned to a quiet submission. Thoran's horse clomped hard and jumped towards the attacker. It landed strong on the ogre's back. Its force knocked the ogre about and the little horse broke free. Shyel's horse didn't look back as it ran towards the woods.

"A rope!" Grimsdyke screamed, throwing one to the ogre in hopes it could subdue the large, angry horse. But Thoran's horse had keen eyes, was wise and would not be tied. It feared the ogre, but the strength of love for his family drove it to fight. Wake up, Thoran, wake up and kill these things…the horse thought in its own way.

The ogre grabbed the horse around its broad neck and tried to wrap the rope around, but that was not going to happen. The steed shook violently. The ogre held tight. Thoran's loyal horse watched it's last little horse-friend blend into the woods. The ogre overpowered the horse and squeezed, cracking its thick neck. Thoran's friend fell to the ground.

Grimsdyke walked towards the horse that lay twitching on the ground, quietly saying, "Loyal to the end—a good quality. Shame it's now wasted," he paused. To the ogre he said, "Gather what you want, but let's be quick." The ogre didn't care. It didn't want to weigh itself down any more than need be. If it really wanted to, the humans would be eaten, including the Grimsdyke. The monster picked up Rose and Thoran, who were so numb, they could only stare. It walked towards the front woods, turned to Grimsdyke and said, "Come." The Grimsdyke followed.

Rose caught one last glimpse through the cottage's front door. Softly she said, "Goodbye my sister, my love, my friend."

"I'm so sorry," Thoran meekly wept, also catching that last glimpse, "So sorry…" he passed out from the pain.

Grimsdyke thought—somehow I will get those little rats and the goblet. Disgusted, he said, "Let's go." Grimsdyke walked. The ogre was slightly ahead of him. Thoran and Rose were slung over its back. They disappeared into the woods.

Meanwhile, on the path home, the boys didn't know they had just slain one of the largest ogres that had ever lived. The sun couldn't be seen, not in the sky, nor through the trees. They knew they were late and fully expected their father and mother—and probably Aunt Zee, to meet them on the path home. They also didn't know how cruel fate sometimes can be. Just barely due south of them, their parents were being taken hostage. And the off-and-on-again, misty rain made the air heavy—a heavy air, that squashed their parents' scent. For if there were no raindrops falling, Pitch's keen sense of smell would have made his nose tingle with Rose's sweet aroma. They couldn't, and didn't, know how close they were to their parents.

His Steady Steed…

smelled the ogre first. Then it smelled Grimsdyke. The ogre smelled the horse before the horse was seen. The horse was happy to see its owner, as it had been tied to a tree for some time and was afraid no one was coming back. It was *not* happy to see the ogre, but seeing Grimsdyke gave it comfort. It brayed an approval. Grimsdyke pet its forelock. "There's my trusty friend," he said. "Finally, a smart beast. Come let's go home."

The ogre pointed its large, swine-like snout in the air, sniffed, snorted and said, "Dead ogre." To it, the smell of the quickly rotting giant that the boys killed was strong. Grimsdyke paid no attention. He wasn't about to stop for anything. His head throbbed. He forgot about the pain while battling and kidnapping, but now his brain pounded. He began to not think straight— not that he ever had. Reaching into his pocket, he grabbed the gift from his old friend Myrtle, the piece of dried blood-troll and sniffed. Its power was waning. He wasn't able to fully sneeze out his pain; his anger grew. He needed more beasts. He wanted an army. He wondered if he should visit the witch. "She's too far away," he said out loud, speaking to no one. It wasn't that the witch's medicine stopped working; it was that the disease had completely turned his brain black.

The ogre looked at him and grunted.

Grimsdyke dreamed of sipping yellow tea and resting in his own bed. He fantasized of killing the King. Tired and dirty, he had first decided to keep Thoran, Rose, and the beast in his cave while he mended for a day or so. Mayhaps I'll keep her somewhere else, he thought... stupid ogre will get hungry and eat her—that won't do. "Him, I don't care about." Did I say that out loud? Grimsdyke wondered...maybe I do need him. The Council Master needed to re-think his plan. He knew he had been stupid, wasting time, energy and resources.

"Need to rest," Grimsdyke said, "need to get home." He mounted his horse. The ogre grunted. It could do with a bit of moving faster. After all, its stride was equal to three of a humans and it was bored waiting for the Grimsdyke to catch up. Slung over the ogre's back, Thoran and Rose were still passed out.

Thirty-One

Something Smelled
Very, Very Wrong

The boys' pace slowed. They knew they were getting close to home, and they were very, very tired. The rain stopped, but the air was still wet and heavy. The whole woodland seemed muffled. Only the simplest sounds of water dripping from cupped leaves, plipping and plopping on branches from trees, could be heard. Pitch smelled something— and it wasn't good. He howled, *"Something's bad, very bad, bad smells."*

"We know boy," said Joyal, "just a little longer and..."

"NOOOO," Pitch howled, *"there's bad, bad smells!"* and he took off. He needed to get to the cottage before the boys did, to see what the problem was. And he knew there was a problem, because he smelled death. He knew that smell all too well.

Behind him he heard the boys screaming, "Hey Pitch, come back, we can't run that fast. HEY, COME BACK! We're right behind you. Hey wait, hey, wait. Wait....wait."

Pitch ran hard. As he got closer, he smelled many scents. He smelled his old master. He smelled Momma and Papa. He smelled the giant ogre they just killed— the biting stink of dead. It made his hairs stand on end. He panicked while thinking... why can I smell that dead ogre? It's too very far away. Why? Oh please, I'm scared. Something's wrong. I smell it. Oh please, I hope I'm wrong. The cottage's roof came in view through the forest. He barked while running to get their attention, *"HEY, HEY, MOMMA? PAPA? ZEE?"* Nothing— something was very, very wrong.

As Pitch burst into the front clearing, the sight made his legs wobble and his heart flutter. He saw a dead ogre with one of Papa's axes in its head. Another one was one off to the side with arrows in its eyes. There was another, and another. The front door was smashed in. Pitch swallowed. He forgot to breath for a clock tick. These monsters were really dead. He barked, *"MOMMA, PAPA?"* And again. *"MOMMA, PAPA?"* He couldn't move—he was numb. Why didn't they come, why?

It was clear that a fight took place. A terrible, terrible fight. There were dead beasts all over the place. Grimsdyke's stink was heavy in the air, and deep within Pitch's body, a rage boiled. He growled, *"He did this!"* As loud as he could, he barked, *"MOMMA, PAPA, ZEE."* He ran into the cottage. The chaos of the battle followed him; he didn't realize he stepped in dried pools of blood and muck. The strong stank of death made his eyes burn. He thought—the boys'll be back soon. They'll be…he stopped breathing. Pitch saw Aunt Zee's head perched on the shelf. His heart missed a beat. He sucked in a short gasp of dead air. His legs shook and slowly buckled, forcing him to sink to the floor— in shock. He stared and didn't realize how heavy the tears were that quickly flowed out of him. What? he thought… why? Pitch then remembered the reason Grimsdyke turned him into a dog. He hadn't thought about it for a long, long time. But it came back… that ugly man wanted to hurt my friends. He wanted the goblet— he killed her. Pitch stared at the head of the first person that was ever kind to him, thinking—she looks like she's sleeping, she's beautiful, she looks peaceful. Confused, he lightly stepped around the parlor— all this blood. Pitch wanted to start cleaning up, but he had no hands.

A thought screamed in his head— THE BOYS! THEY'LL BE BACK! GOT TO WARN THEM! He looked at his Aunt Zee while running out of the house. He stopped and lightly woofed, *"Where's Momma? Where's Papa?"* He smelled their scent, still barking… *"They're not dead. I don't think they're dead. They're not dead! They have to be alive!"*

Pitch ran and ran. The boys were now close. He smelled them. He barked, *"They're not dead."* The boys will be very scared when they see Aunt Zee. He needs to warn them somehow. As their dog ran up to them, they could tell something was wrong. He wasn't barking happy and excited. He whimpered, whined and howled.

"He looks like he's crying," Joyal noticed, "his eyes are really wet."

"What's the matter boy?" asked Joyal… "Yeah, what's wrong," added Alvis.

Ayell sensed the panic in Pitch and grabbed him by the face, staring at him. Pitch was crying. Ayell had seen this look on the dog not that long ago. Pitch was as scared now, as he was when they were inside the belly of the giant ogre.

In short, hard barks, Pitch cried, *"They're not dead! We need to find them. I can smell them if we go look."*

"Sumthin's wrong," said Grumel, very concerned.

Ayell took off to the cottage. The others also took off towards their home. Pitch ran after them.

"We need to go look for them," barked Pitch. *"They're not dead. We need to go find them!"*

"It's okay boy," said Joyal, running and panting, "We'll be home real quick."

His boys couldn't understand him. For the first time, Pitch wished he weren't a dog. He briefly thought of finding the witch to turn him back to Max. He wondered if he could help them more if he were a man again. He ran past the boys, barking his warnings, but they weren't listening.

When the boys burst out of the forest at the clearing in front of their cottage, they stopped— bumped into each other. They grunted. The sight confused them—the smell hit them. They saw a dead ogre, and another dead ogre. The door was smashed open. Purple and white butterflies flew around the flowerpots near the door—one flew into the cottage.

Pitch whimpered, *"Boys, they're not dead. I don't think Momma and Papa are dead."*

All seven thought—why aren't they running up to us? Why? Momma? Papa? Why aren't you running up to us? Aunt Zee? Where are you?

Very, very bad things had happened. Their forest was still, very quiet. Only a few animal sounds could be heard, muffled in the distance. The hazy sun above started its journey to set. No momma running to hug them, no excited papa asking how their adventure went, no Aunt Zee wondering if they had eaten. The seven walked slowly up to their home, not prepared for the emotional battle twisting in their bodies. There was nothing Pitch could say. He watched his seven friends stare at the dead beasts with arrows and axes sticking mostly out of their heads... so many monsters. At first they didn't notice the nits, flies, maggots, colorful beetles, and shrub-bugs eating quickly decaying flesh. But as they focused, the movement on each dead beast's flesh disgusted and scared them. A fear hit them, much deeper than what they felt battling the giant ogre.

At the front of the cottage, they stared at the door. A dead orc was face down, almost blocking the door.

"We weren't gone that long," Yawnel softly spoke.

"MOMMA? PAPA?" screamed Alvis, Joyal, Shyel, and Achu.

"AUNT ZEE?" screamed Grumel and Yawnel.

Low and whiny, Pitch yowled. *"They're not here. They're not dead. We need to go find them."*

They weren't paying attention to their dog right now, and their dog knew it. Looking around, the realization of the havoc that took place barely sunk in, but the after-battle was clear. They were confused, helpless, afraid little boys feeling very alone, very small and very sad. The day was not bright, but their eyes squinted, as if in pain. A tired haze crept into their heads, the likes of which they had never felt before.

With little strength left in his voice and praying for a response, Alvis asked, "Ma? Pa?"

They started their walk inside. Pitch jumped in front of them, whimpering, *"Please, it's very bad, we need to go find them, don't go in there, not yet, your parents aren't dead."*

"He saw something in the house. That's why he's sad," Achu said.

Ayell brushed Pitch aside and went first through the door, followed by the others. Pitch whimpered in the background. As they entered their cottage, many eyes were first drawn to the mess. The blood, the bits and pieces of home scattered and smashed all over. Their heads drifted slightly up. Their many eyes focused on the shelf where Aunt Zee was. The serene look, a resting smile on her gentle face, all together they stared and thought… she's just sleeping, that's all.

Their emotions joined into a dreamlike confusion. Ever so slightly, all seven started to shake. Speechless, with grief, anguish, fear, and shock, they stared. The look on her face was not one of pain, but that gave them no comfort. They stared, their eyebrows only slightly arched, their mouths only slightly opened. They were afraid to look around, afraid to see two more heads. For they knew, seeing two more heads with closed eyes would make them scream a scream that would never end.

But look around they must. So slowly, seven pairs of weary, teary eyes looked about their once beautiful home. They expected more horrible sights—not prepared for it, just expecting. But in that room, there was nothing to make them scream. Again, they were drawn to and glanced at their dead aunt. They didn't wonder where the rest of her body was. In shock, they didn't grasp the thought that the goblet might help—they were too overwhelmed. But the goblet wouldn't have helped, as their special Aunt Zee, the person who taught them how to catch glow-bugs and lightning flies, had already drunk from it— a long, long time ago.

"We need to check the other rooms," Achu and Yawnel

cried together.

Pitch was frustrated, sad, and angry. He howled, *"They're not dead. I'm sure of it, they're not here. We need to go find them."*

"Ma... Pa...," Joyal meekly said.

"Why would someone do this?" sobbed Achu.

"Something's more like it," Grumel said, pained and disgusted. "Where'd all these ogres come from?"

"Could they all a been sleeping. Did we wake'm up, like the giant?" Alvis desperately asked, while praying the answer was no.

"That don't make sense—nothin does," Joyal wheeped.

"There's lots of 'em here," Shyel said, just above a whisper. "They killed a lot of them."

"Poor Aunt Zee," Achu said, teary eyed. "Where do ya think they are?"

"Where could they have gone?" Joyal added.

"He took them!" barked Pitch, *"They're not dead, he took them!"* The boys looked at their dog.

"You know somethin' boy?" asked Grumel.

In short, hard barks Pitch answered, *"Yes, Yes, let's go, follow me."* and he ran out the front door still barking...*"Come on, let's go, come on!"*

"How could he know? He was with us," Achu asked. They paused for only a clock tick and looked around their home. Ayell patted his own nose, jumped up and down, pointed at Pitch, and patted his own nose again.

"He smells them," Shyel said surprised, then shouted, "HE CAN SMELL THEM. WE HAVE TO GO. FOLLOW HIM."

Pitch heard them. He was outside and excitedly barked, *"YES, YES I CAN SMELL THEM. LET'S GO,"* and he ran into the woods, sniffing low branches and leaves that had the scent of Rose and Thoran. The boys wanted to move, they just couldn't... not yet. A combination of sadness and adrenaline coursed through their little bodies. Their tired legs could only shuffle about. Shyel said what none of the others wanted to say—"We can't leave her like that." They knew what had to be done.

Moving quickly, Achu, Yawnel, and Shyel went outside and came back with their father's short ladder. Ayell grabbed it from his brothers, placed the ladder where it would be most useful and climbed. Pitch, now watching from the doorway, knew what they were doing. He remained quiet. "Here, put her on this," Grumel said, holding out a platter—the same platter their mother put a whole fired-chicken on for the prior night's dinner. By placing, not grabbing his palms and fingers about the side of her head, Ayell gently lifted his Aunt Zee, carefully stepped down and rested her head on the platter.

"We have to bury her," Grumel solemnly said as the others shook their heads in agreement. In their back yard, they saw more of the battle—the horse's pen was busted, their father's strong horse was dead, their seven little horses were gone. Again, they had no words. They brought their aunt to a patch of garden where purple beans were grown. Purple beans were her favorite garden plant. She never said why. The ground was soft and the burial was quick, as only a small hole had to be dug.

Pitch quietly watched the whole funeral. Nothing was said during the saddest task they ever had to perform. Standing by her grave for only a few clock ticks, Pitch broke the silence. He barked, *"It's time to go, we need to go help Momma and Papa."* The boys were very, very tired at this point. Pitch's barks brought a sound from within the stable, and from the darkness came out the snout of the most forgotten one of their family—their donkey. Hearing friendly voices again, he thought it safe, so he stopped hiding.

Joyal softly asked, "Should we clean up anything? I feel kind a bad. It's a mess."

"We need to get going as quick as possible," Achu said.

"I'm so tired, maybe just a quick nap?" asked Yawnel.

They were exhausted, and they knew they had to get going, but they were so very tired. Tired from the excitement of leaving early in the day, tired from battling and defeating a giant, tired from coming back to a shattered world. "Ok," said Alvis, "we'll put it to a vote…

"*NO!*" Pitch interrupted, he barked, "*No vote, we need to get going, now!*" For one quick moment, Pitch thought of just running, of going to find them himself. But he couldn't leave his boys—they needed him, and he needed them. They must stay together, so he would do whatever they agreed upon. Darkness would be upon them soon.

Confused, the seven little boys were lost in thoughts… What're we gonna do? Where we gonna sleep? Which way did they go? What if Pitch is wrong? He's only a dog. Where's our horses? We could move so much quicker if we had 'em. Momma wouldn't be happy us leavin the place a mess. What if we don't find them?

"All that say we leave now, raise their hands," said Alvis. Fourteen hands quickly reached for the sky, one loud bark made the vote unanimous.

"Ok, first we need to put a couple things in order, and then we leave. We'll each bring a bed sheet and we'll just have to sleep when we can't go no more." Yawnel said, "I can hear Papa saying, 'You need your rest, boys. A tired body can't be strong.'"

"But we need to get moving," Joyal added. "The horses must've run away. Maybe we can find 'em. We'd sure move quicker." Everyone, including Pitch, nodded in agreement. It didn't seem odd to the boys that Pitch nodded in perfect time with them.

Grumel spoke, "Can't worry about the horses now, we just have to get on."

"Let's at least close up the door and gather some bits," said Shyel. "We'll take whatever we can hold without taking too much heavy stuff… weapons, flint rock, food."

"You should jump into the bathing hole real quick, Ayell," Alvis said, a bit disgusted, "You really stink!"

The others agreed, so that was what Ayell did. He ran to their room, looked around for what he prayed would not be the last time, and grabbed some clean clothes. Their window was wide open. It was never open—Ayell stared at it for few a clock ticks, wondered why it was open, shook his head, and ran downstairs and out the back door. Outside, Ayell carefully stepped to the bathing hole while staring at two dead ogres slumped on the ground near a side of the cottage. Axes and arrows stuck out of their heads and faces. They took Momma and Papa, Ayell thought, why?

Pitch heard his friend in the back and went to him. Ayell stroked Pitch's head and mouthed, "Good boy." Pitch licked his hand, just like a real dog. After a quick scrub, Ayell went inside motioning for Pitch to follow. Pitch sat down outside in defiance and barked, *"I'll stay out here."* Ayell nodded and went inside where his brothers were packing, gathering and cleaning up a bit.

"We should load up the donkey," said Joyal. "We'll put stuff in sacks."

"But we can move faster without the donkey," Shyel said. Ayell shook his head in disagreement or agreement, nobody knew.

"Okay, we'll take him. He'll just have to keep up," said Alvis.

An orc, slumped dead in their front doorway, was reluctantly and painstakingly dragged out of the way. They blocked the front door with their dining room table as best as they could and nailed it shut. They didn't touch any of the other dead ogres. Pitch was outside, darting between the front and the back, keeping watch. The blood on the floor was not cleaned. The inside was only quickly straightened out. The boys knew that darkness would soon join them. They still agonized over whether or not they should go or rest a bit—they were so very tired. But they needed to get going, every minute could be crucial and the vote had been cast.

Grabbing a clean pouch, while his brothers filled up the last of their sacks, Ayell grabbed the dirty sack with the journal and the goblet, pulled both treasures out and put them on a table.

Instantly, the book flew open to the end pages with a WHAP! The boys quickly surrounded the table— they realized there were new entries. On the left side was a wonderful scene—a drawing of Aunt Zee, in a half crouch with her arms outstretched holding the seven of them. Her eyes twinkled—she was smiling, as were they.

The right hand page was blank, though something appeared to have bled through from the following page. Alvis turned the page and revealed a rough sketch of a large ogre carrying, on quick glance, something over its back. In the background was the outline of another man, though they couldn't recognize who it was. As the boys studied the sketch more closely, they realized the ogre held two people. And one had flowing, *squiggly* hair...a girl! They gasped. It had to be their parents.

"That ogre stole them. C'mon we got to get moving," Alvis said.

"Yea, no more wastin time," finished Grumel. The boys studied the drawing. Luckily, pain was not sketched on their parent's faces.

Shyel recognized the cape on the person in the background, "I, I think that's that Council guy."

They didn't realize Pitch had come back into the cottage. He barked loudly, *"IT'S HIM, IT IS HIM,"* and deeper he growl-barked, *"He stole them and he killed our Zee. He killed her, we have to go after them, c'mon,"* and he ran to the door.

"Dagon's doing these drawings. He's trying to help us!" said Achu.

"How come he didn't tell us about the ogres? How come he didn't warn us somehow?" asked Joyal. "Aunt Zee's dead. HE could have saved her."

"Don't know and don't matter," Alvis answered, "maybe he's just doing the best he can. Don't matter none. We need to go find Ma and Pa."

"Why'd hc do this? What's he want?" Grumel angrily asked.

Alvis again answered, "Agin, it don't matter none. We need to find them and we need to get going."

"We should go right to the King," said Achu. They all looked at him. Joyal said that was a great idea, but first they had to hunt down the ogre that stole their parents, hoping their mother and father were not that far ahead.

Packed sacks with weapons, food stuffs and water pouches were slung over their, and the donkey's back. Ayell held the sack with the goblet, the journal and the candleholder. They each grabbed some chips of gold held in a jar hidden in a cabinet, just in case. They were not acting or thinking like little boys who celebrated their tenth birth date only a few weeks prior. They were not crafting a fort from branches to defend from a pretend ogre. They were forced to mature at an unnatural pace, at a young age, as children at war must. The happiness, the exhilaration of an earlier triumph, battled their soul-searing sorrow of extreme loss. Because deep down, they knew sadness will not save their parents. They were afraid. And fear had a might, all its own.

Achu asked himself... will we laugh again? Alvis and Ayell felt guilty about being hungry. Joyal wondered how could he ever truly be happy again?

The boys were going to Laban. They weren't going with grand plans of having a grand time at the King's festival. They were going to save the lives of their mother and father. And they would kill anything and anyone that got in their way.

Pitch would lead the way, and he would not stop until he found Grimsdyke. He looked up; the moon was blotchy and fatter than the prior day. He growled low and woofed deep. It was not at its fattest, and his eyes were not yet red. With every breath—every exhale, he thought of his old master. Pitch knew...I won't wait. I will kill him quickly. And I will kill anything or anyone that tries to stop me.

Thirty-Two

The Coven

Myrtle knew the time is coming. The only master will rise. And he'll need an army. And an army need not only be of the living. That's where she could help. To be sure, there are those that can wake dead bodies and use them as their own. The dead feel no pain—they only have thirst. They will fight and kill for those who help satisfy that thirst that can't be quenched. And the spirits of those dead bodies are never happy when their decaying flesh, if there's any left, is taken from the land.

She couldn't do it alone, because an army is of many bodies, and she could only summon dead one at a time. Ancient and tired, she just couldn't work like she could in the old days. "Dat's okay," she said to herself while hobbling and mumbling around her shack… "I'll finds me a coven." She was well aware that a proper coven doesn't need to be only of witches. Warlocks and evil shamins'll do just fine. "An there's 'nuff a dem around," she laughed.

Myrtle walked outside and up to one of her holes. Held behind bars, in a hole in the ground, she questioned an animal that hadn't spoke human words for decades. "I don't trust that maggot Grimsdyke, do you?" Her pet just stared at her, no grunting, and no sounds. "Ee forgot why's I let him live, I should a let dem ogres eat 'em, ee should a had me goblet back. Mayhaps ee found it, an he gonna try to keep it himself? Ya think. Stupid maggot he is." From her pocket, she pulled the single hair of his she plucked from his head the last time he visited her. She twirled it between two crusty fingers. "Mayhaps we go find him, eh…puppy? What say you?"

Her pet stirred and growl-barked… *"You let me eat him? I can find him."*

She lightly laughed — a dry, simple cackle. "Eat 'im? Mayhaps I will." She untied the chain that held the gate. Her dire-wolf jumped out and shook its shaggy shoulders. The others, still captive, heard their brother and howled. The one she set free, in another life, was named Fagan. It looked at the witch who kept it captive for decades. "Don't do anything stupid," she said while slowly moving her hand to its nose, twirling Grimsdyke's hair.

The wolf's mouth trembled, its tongue lapped its upper lip. "Take a good sniff," she said.

The dire-wolf did. It growl-barked again… *"Follow me."*

And she did.

Thirty-Three

Heavy Little Hearts

Weighed down with sacks of food and weapons, they started. Heavy little hearts also carried the burden of deep hope—that they could save their parents. The sun was beginning to set—the woodland was calm. Physically, they just couldn't move fast; they were so very tired. But they did the best they could—as they always did.

They stayed on the main path, even though Pitch smelled that his old master and the monsters with him had strayed into the woods. But he didn't worry, because he still caught their parent's scent.

After a spell, it became dark and the boys couldn't go on any longer. Pitch looked at them. They had to rest. With tears in his eyes, Alvis said, "I can't move any more. My legs and arms hurt." Reluctantly, the others agreed.

"Lets just rest right here, just for a bit," said Yawnel.

"Okay, only for a bit, then we'll get up and move faster," Grumel said.

"We can make better time when we get up," added Joyal. "We'll wake and run to find them."

"Okay, it's agreed. But whoever wakes first," demanded Shyel, "wake everyone else." Everyone agreed.

Pitch knew that he wouldn't sleep—couldn't sleep. He wasn't tired. He lightly howled, *"I'll watch-over... you rest,"* and he walked away from them.

They unraveled their bed-rolls, laid them on the damp ground, and slumped down, close enough to touch each other with only a slight move of either hand. Curling into fetal positions, they quickly fell into a dreamless sleep.

They were being watched by something other than Pitch. A bat hung above them. Pitch heard the bat make the quietest of licking sounds and thought... I hate bats. He didn't want to, but he too, fell into a dreamless sleep.

Thirty-Four

Do Not Eat Him

A little more than a day after they destroyed a family, Grimsdyke and his large ogre stood at the mouth of the cave he affectionately called 'beggars' tomb'. A rancid, biting smell preceded the cave opening. A smell so bad, so thick, even flies weren't enticed. A smell so terrible, it woke Thoran and Rose.

Grimsdyke dismounted and walked into the cave, motioning for the beast to bring his prisoners. To Thoran he spoke, "This will be your home, only for a short spell, my friend. I'll take Rose to my cottage and have the doctor tend to our wounds. Sorry we all can't go back, but I fear the potential of being found would be too great." Grimsdyke walked up to Thoran and shoved a water pouch to his mouth and poured. "Drink," Grimsdyke calmly said, as if talking to a true friend. Most of the water streamed down Thoran's chin. At the large ogre he commanded, "Tie him up over there. And be gentle with her."

Their thoughts were clouded, but Thoran and Rose knew they were to be separated. In a low, weak voice Thoran begged, "Please sir, do not harm her."

Rose quickly added, "Please sir, let him go."

"No," said Thoran to his wife.

And quickly speaking to her husband, Rose softly said, "Take a horse. Go find the boys and the goblet. Bring it back and give it to him."

Grimsdyke interrupted, "That—won't do my dear." He paused, slowly continuing, "You see, your husband has to stay here. Oh I'm sure he'd come back with the goblet, but he would also kill me when he came back."

Thoran tried to speak, "Sir…

"PLEASE STOP, THORAN," Grimsdyke screamed, then calmer, "We'll not waste any more time. Tie him up. We'll come back for you shortly." Grimsdyke walked towards the cave opening. He grabbed the rope that held Rose and pulled her to follow.

"Please sir…" Thoran started but stopped, forgetting what he wanted to ask.

"Ungry," the large ogre simply said, "Now."

"Do not eat him," Grimsdyke commanded, as if talking to a child, "I will bring you something shortly—do you understand? We need him alive," although Grimsdyke really didn't know why. "In fact, I will send someone here shortly… *That* person can be eaten. Do you understand—the next human that comes into the cave can be eaten."

It asked, "Even you?"

Grimsdyke squinted at the ogre, waved his hand and scowled. "Just wait for the next human that's not me."

The ogre looked at Grimsdyke and actually smiled.

The Council Master was feeling much better. Perhaps the adrenaline coursing through his body kept the pain at bay, perhaps he was just getting used to the pain. Trickles of blood came out of his ear, but it didn't matter. He was thinking clearly, if only temporarily. Going over a plan in his head, he reasoned he would take sweet Rose home, let the doctor tend to them, then figure out how to get the goblet.

With no finesse, the ogre tied Thoran to a rock formation jutting out of the center of the cave. It's strange… ogres can barely count to two, but they can tie very strong knots. It watched the Council Master walk away with the female. It stared at Thoran and even before the Grimsdyke left, it knew that some of the male would have to be eaten. Not all of him—just an arm, maybe a leg. It didn't matter to the ogre if the male lived. The Council Master cared, but the ogre was losing what little interest it had with the whole situation. It might just have to eat the whole male, then leave to find more of its kind. Rests a bits... the dimwitted creature thought. So it sat down, and quickly fell asleep. So did Thoran.

At His Homestead...

Grimsdyke tied his horse to a hitch-post in his rear garden and pulled Rose off, catching her before she thumped to the ground. "We'll rest, get cleaned a bit and you'll see, you'll feel much better."

In a hushed whisper, Rose only said, "No."

He really needed a wash. Before fetching the doctor, he knew he had to look the part of the respected Council Master. Staring at himself in a mirror, Grimsdyke thought...I wouldn't invite me over for tea. He admired Rose—she was the type of person that always looked good. His bed looked wonderful and he thought a little nap would be so nice. Then he'd fetch the doctor. His head hurt, but he seemed to be getting used to the pounding, and he forgot to try the dried blood-troll's nose. His body ached so much that his fingernails throbbed. He set down a blanket, plopped Rose on the floor and tied her to his bedpost. Then he gave her a pillow—a wonderful attempt to make her comfortable. She was barely conscious.

Lying on his bed, he planned how many vagrants or blackjaws it would take to find the seven little rats. He would have to get them quickly. He'd leave first thing in the morning... in mid thought, he fell into a deep sleep.

With little strength, Rose tried to escape. But her depressed, tired, and lonely body couldn't fight; there was just too much pain. She was tied very tightly to his bed. After a short spell, she also fell into a deep sleep. She dreamed. In her dream, the spirits were not happy with her. A ghostly vision of Dagon, wings bright with fire, hovered above her. The dragon-elf held her sweet sister's head by the hair and bobbed it up and down while screaming, "SHE JEST WANTS TA

SAY G'BYE ME SWEETS." And he drooled. No, wait… that wasn't him drooling— it was Zelda's bloody spit flying out of her mouth as she hollered, "TELL ME BOYS WE'LL SEES THEM SOON! WILL YOU TELL THEM THAT? WILL YOU? PROMISE US YOU WILL. PROMISE? PROMISE?" And louder, "PROMISE!"

Unable to wake, but able to answer, Rose cried while clutching a pillow… "I promise, I promise, I promise…"

Grimsdyke didn't hear Rose sob while he slept. His mind was in a darker place, as it had been his whole life.

Thirty-Five

Time Wasted

Their donkey woke all of them up with a braying sneeze. They slept much longer then they wanted. Joyal called out, "We're late. C'mon we have to go!"

Pitch woke hard and angry; angry for sleeping at all, let alone sleeping for so long. He barked, *"Wake up, wake up, wake up!"* All jumped to attention and fumbled about, even the donkey. Early morning sunbeams cut and sparkled through the trees. Silky, milky mists floated about the leaves. Ayell saw that high above, the soft clouds formed a vision of steps leading to the heavens—he looked around for other cloud shapes. All around, anxious sounds of bumblers and grimlers playing and fighting could be heard. It should have been one of the most beautiful mornings they had ever seen. But its beauty was lost that day. Although sleep had given them strength, their bodies twitched with anxiety. And they were very, *very* angry that they'd slept too long. Pitch again barked loudly, *"WE MUST GO. NOW!"* And he began the lead.

They listened to the forest sounds, the waking grackens, griblics, jowlers and other forest-lings. They wondered if Aunt Zee watched them from the clouds. They wondered if their parents were alive... they had to believe they were. Pitch would pick up their scent. They would have to go to the King soon and ask his help, but the Council could not be trusted. Their father always spoke very highly of the King. He spoke highly of the Council Master too, but something went wrong there. Pitch tried to warn them the last time Grimsdyke visited. That's why he went crazy, the boys realized. "We'll move as fast as we can," said Shyel.

"And then we'll go faster," Grumel added.

All said as one, "Lets go!"

Pitch darted away from them and quickly returned. *"This way,"* he barked. *"They're this way!"* Pitch found the scent and it was now time to find their parents. Alive——or dead.

Thirty-Six

The Beast Would Feed

Grimsdyke woke ravenous. At the foot of his bed was his prisoner. She's the perfect wife, he thought. Pretty, smart, strong...all the qualities of a fine mate. "Are you awake, my dear?"

She was; she just didn't want to answer him. The sleep had done her good. She needed to think, to be strong. She had to believe that all was not lost.

He knew she was awake. He sensed her slightly stirring. He wondered what it would be like to kiss her. "Never mind. You'll speak soon enough." Grimsdyke wanted the doctor, for himself and her, and he needed to feed the beast in the cave. It would be best to keep Thoran for a bit, he thought. I hope that stupid ogre didn't eat him already. He decided to pay a vagrant to go to the cave. He'd say he lost something there and needed it returned. And he'd pay a sliver of gold, with more to come when the item was returned— much more. And the beast would feed.

He made sure Rose was secure to the bed, and gave himself a quick wash and a rough shave to at least look presentable. He'd let her wash later. Before leaving, Grimsdyke leaned close to Rose's ear. While looking at her, his hands fumbled to find hers. When they touched, a frigid bolt shot through her hands, up her arms, ending at her eyes that were filled with tears. She gasped as his hands tightened around hers.

It was at that point that he could feel a ring on her finger; a ring that he never noticed before. He looked down and was struck by its beautiful simplicity. It was a ruby cut to look like a rose of four petals, secured to a simple loop of gold. It nearly cut him as he tightened his grip. He paused and thought of all that had happened over the past few days. He slowly whispered, "I'll be back shortly with the doctor's helper. You've never met him, have you? No, I think not. He's new in town, he won't know who you are. Your husband he might recognize, but not you. I'm telling him you're a gypsy that I've taken to. Someone to tend to my home. He will help you. Any tricks and I will kill him in front of you. Then I will kill your husband, and you will watch the ogre eat him. Then I *will* find your boys and bring them to the other beasts I have, and you will watch those monsters fight over the right to eat your children. And they will be eaten one by one. Please don't make me do that to your family." He moved so his face was in line with hers; their eyes met. "There's still no need to speak, but you will be a good girl. Am I right?"

A single tear crawled out of the corner of her left eye. With both of her eyes closed, he had his answer. He smiled and walked away while saying, "I'll bring you something to eat. Don't...do anything you'll regret."

Once in Laban proper, he wasted no time surveying the festival preparations. Nobody paid much attention to him while he checked on things. To the villagers, nothing seemed out of place. He asked about the decorations and was satisfied. He asked about the baked goods— again satisfied. He pretended to be pleased. Truth be told, he cared about none of it. He probably wouldn't even be there for the festivities. For all he cared, the King could hang in the courtyard—he hoped he would. He walked on, to the back of the church where the vagrants gathered.

With one sliver of gold, and the promise of more if the task was done quickly, he found someone willing to go to the cave. Her name was Ruth Fagash. He wanted to know her name, as he thought the least he could do was thank her by name before sending her to her death.

"Go quickly, young Ruth," he fibbed, as she was not young, "For upon your return a handsome reward awaits." She hobbled a bit, so there was less of a chance of her running away whence she realized her predicament. And she had a few extra stones in her rump, so she should be good and tired when she entered the cave. Tho' she *was* able to hobble at a brisk pace.

His lie was that he dropped or lost a key while he was hunting and that it might be in an old cave that he rested in. The key was to a safe that contained bags of silver slivers needed for the festival. She didn't question Grimsdyke. For a chip or a coin, Ruth would do anything. Grimsdyke told her the location of the cave. She knew the general whereabouts of the old hole, having lived in Laban her whole life, and convinced him she could get there quickly. She hobbled away from him and went into the woods.

Through the bustling town, heads only slightly turned at the sight of Grimsdyke. He went to the doctor's cottage. If the doctor became suspicious, Grimsdyke was fully prepared to kill him. But he was hoping that wouldn't come to pass. Fortunately, the doctor's apprentice, Mr. Tuff was in. He would also kill the apprentice if need be. But Tuff hardly asked any questions. He believed Grimsdyke's lie, that he and the gypsy fell off their horse and landed on sharp arrows. In Grimsdyke's cottage, Tuff tended to their wounds, wounds that had very little early infection, a testament to Rose's nursing, the Council Master thought.

"Your wounds were not that bad. You both should rest and sip this tea," Tuff said, handing over a package of herbs. He then scratched his chin and slowly said, "Curious."

"What's curious?" Grimsdyke asked, while slowly walking towards a cabinet holding his sharpest blades.

Tuff looked into Rose's eyes. She stared back with a vacant, simple-minded look. "No expressions. Almost as if she's a mute. Can you speak my dear?"

Rose closed her eyes and whispered, "I'm a gypsy."

Very good, Grimsdyke thought.

"Hmmmmm," the doctor said, "anyway—I'm off to see to a pitchfork in the bum of a mule. A doctor's work is never done." He smiled and turned to Grimsdyke. "I hear all preparations are almost complete for the festival. It'll be a grand time," and he walked to the door.

"The grandest of times will be had by all," Grimsdyke said, reaching into his pocket, retrieving three chips of gold. He handed them to the apprentice.

"Why, I thank you, sir."

"No, it is I who should thank you. The pains are nearly gone."

"Well—you'll be sore for sure, but the infection should be minimal. Please visit if you or your house girl needs attention. Drink the tea. It will help." Grimsdyke watched the doctor leave his house and walk the path leading back to town.

He walked back into his room. Rose was lying down. "Rest, my dear, we both need it. Then we'll go tend to your husband."

In a hushed voice, she said, "You still can't tell the truth."

He looked at her and decided not to say anything. He actually considered himself a very good liar.

Thirty-Seven

The Cave

The boys moved through the forest, sometimes with grace, sometimes awkwardly. Their donkey kept pace. There wasn't much
talk—they didn't acknowledge the new terrain. Normally, a new path
would excite their senses. A trove of wonderful sights would be studied, grabbed and held tightly. But so much had happened in such a
short time that their little minds could only drift... a giant awoke,
ate Ayell, they fought to save him. They had to bury Aunt Zee's head.
Where are their mother and father?

Pitch darted in and out of the woods, jumping ahead of them on
the path and coming back from different directions. *His* mind wasn't
drifting. He was thinking as clearly as he ever had. His only quest was
to find Momma and Papa. He smelled their scent, though it sometimes
became faint. It didn't matter—he knew they were going towards
town.

"You still smell them boy?" Grumel asked.

In excited yelps, Pitch answered, *"Yes, yes I do!"*

"He really does smell 'em," added Alvis.

"I DO, I DO, THEY'RE THIS WAY," he barked, and ran slightly ahead,
stopping and pointing his right front paw up, an action that left the
boys speechless and staring at each other.

"Is he pointing?" Joyal asked.

"Yes," Pitch barked and darted off. Excited and only slightly
confused, the boys moved a little quicker. They believed their dog
would lead them to their parents.

"Ok, we need to think on this a little," Shyel said as they continued to briskly walk.

"He's gonna hide them, ain't he?" asked Joyal.

"He wants something, "added Achu, "that's why he took em."

"Let's look in the journal again. Maybe there's something new in it," said Alvis.

They stopped. Ayell was quick to get the tattered journal out of the sack. He turned to the last page. "Nuthin," said Grumel.

They continued on, realizing the new forest they were in was certainly beautiful. Through openings between glistening leaves, they spotted far-away peaks.

"He wants the gold!" blurted Yawnel. "In the mines. It's the only thing he could want. Remember. Papa warned us."

"That's right," Shyel agreed, "that makes the most sense."

"Why'd they have to kill Aunt Zee?" wondered Joyal. "And where'd he find them ogres?"

"A couple of 'em were scugs. Remember the one big nose hole?" added Grumel.

"This is what they were talking about. This is why they trained us. We have to kill any monster as quick as possible as soon as we spot one," Shyel said. Ayell furiously shook his head in approval. Pitch added his sharp barks— *"Yes, Yes, we do!"*

"Dagon knew something was coming," said Achu. "That's why he came back after all those years."

Scared, Pitch whined, *"I can't smell them!"* and he took off into the woods.

"PITCH," the boys screamed.

They turned, Pitch thought. He stopped and pointed his nose in the air, taking in a deep sniff. Nothing. He kept running and hopping to see over the brush. He caught a faint whiff of them. He turned and ran. Their scent became stronger. They went this way? He jumped at the woods in a different direction. Why'd they turn? It dawned on him—*"The cave!"* he barked loud. He turned and ran back to his boys barking, *"The cave, the cave, he's taking them to the cave!"*

Pitch had forgotten, but now he well remembered the cave. In his former life, and many years ago, the Council Master punished him for drinking too much frothy mead and tied him to a rock deep in the cave. He was left there for two days. Picked at by giant bats, bitten over and over again by horned spiders— Max's simple mind swore allegiance to the Council Master to secure his release. Pitch dreamed…the Council Master. Master. I used to call him that. His only desire now was to kill the Council Master. When he saw him again, he knew that he would lunge and sink his teeth deep in his chest. Pitch would find and stop Grimsdyke's heart. Lost in thought, Pitch burst out of the woods, stopping in front of the boys in position as if to pounce.

All were quiet for only a few clock ticks. "What's the matter boy?" asked Grumel.

"The cave," Pitch growled, *"this way, they went this way,"* and he bounded back into the woods.

"Hey, come back," somebody yelled.

Pitch turned and saw no one was following. So he went back. In front of them again, he barked, *"This way,"* and he turned towards the woods. *"They went this way,"* he barked.

"Do you know where they are, boy? Can you smell them?" asked Shyel.

"He has to, he's barking all crazy-like," added Alvis. Pitch stopped, and again pointed in a direction. All the boys stared at him.

Joyal crouched down and put his hand on their dog's back. He asked Pitch, "Do you want us to follow you, Pitch?"

With a resounding bark, Pitch answered, *"YES!"*

"He wants us to go a different way," Yawnel said, "They changed direction, and he wants us to follow." Ayell readily agreed. They rarely talked to the donkey, but Grumel turned towards it and asked, "Donkey, we're going faster. Can you keep up?"

They expected the donkey to be as confident as their dog. He wasn't, and as usual, there was no response. "He'll just have to follow if he can," said Achu.

All agreed. With Yawnel's final command to Pitch of, "Lead the way to Momma and Papa," they veered off the path and went into the woods, leaving their donkey behind.

Thirty-Eight

Just a Little More

Thoran snored loudly and woke himself up from a deep sleep. His mind was fresher. He quickly noticed two things. One: the sun was fading and all light would soon go with it. The second was that the rope wrapped around him rested on a slightly jagged edge of rock close to his right shoulder. And when he moved, it rubbed against the rock's edge. With each movement of his shoulder, he could see thin strands of rope pop, as they were cut.

He watched the sleeping ogre heavily grunt, snore and drool. Studying it, he was disgusted at its sight, disgusted at its festering grayish skin, disgusted at what oozed from its open sores. Cursed thing…Thoran thought hard… more to curse would be that foul Council Master. After all, this stupid beast only follows its stomach. Grimsdyke's greed has caused a wound so deep, it can never be filled. I *must* get out of this.

Bolts of anger overcame Thoran's pangs of guilt and hurt. He moved his shoulder—the rope gave way ever so slightly. Though give it did. Just a little more, he thought. With quicker movements, more strands were cut. A ray of hope quickly followed each strand cut. Move, cut, move, cut, move, cut, move, and cut. And snap! He lightly gasped—a wrap broke and his shoulder moved. It was nearly free… Hope!

The beast stirred, though only slightly. More grunts, then it snored again.

Quietly, Thoran shifted his weight and was able to maneuver another wrap to the jagged edge. Move, cut, move, cut, move, cut, move, and cut… Hope! He continued. A second snap! The second wrap was undone, now both shoulders were set free. He held his breath, let it out slowly, and breathed in again, still slowly. With quiet back and forth shimmies between the shoulders, the ropes became loose. His arms could move! Adrenaline pumped through his heart. He thought more clearly than he had in what seemed like a long, long, time. While his beastly captor slept, he lifted his arms up and out of the wraps.

As Thoran shimmied the wraps down his waist towards his feet, he brushed against his shattered, swollen knee. The pain nearly blinded him, though no sound escaped his mouth. His anguish only came out as silent tears. He mustn't make a sound.

Breathing deep and slow, he set himself free and looked around for something to use as a crutch. But nothing was available, and he knew he would have to crawl as quietly as possible to his freedom— to his family. To his family that he had let down. His brain screamed— No feeling sorry for yourself... MOVE! He couldn't forget about the pain. He just wouldn't let it stop him. While putting all weight on his good knee, he dragged his other leg and moved.

The cave floor was grimy with bits of rock, earth, bugs and what looked like dead bits of something. He moved quietly and slowly. He only stared down at where his hands were going. He chose not to look back at the ogre. He had no time to waste. Every clock tick mattered. And he couldn't waste any more, so he moved. When he did look up he was surprised to see the cave opening in front of him. Beyond the opening were beautiful, thick trees with leaves that slightly glimmered with fading sunlight. And with each sparkle, a brief, confused emotional charge shot through his heart, a strong heart that remembered feelings of love, anger, happiness and sadness. No feeling sorry for yourself... MOVE! his brain again screamed. He didn't stop moving. Smooth gusts of sweet air, freshened his senses. Every inch closer to the opening added to his hope. A weapon, he thought... I need a weapon. His eyes opened wider in search for something— anything. Rocks would do little against the ogre. He needed something sharp. He kept moving, passing through the cave opening, leaving that lair. Seeing the open forest he prayed…if I make it to the woods, I can hide. He moved faster.

When the beast stepped on his dragging leg, Thoran didn't hear his own blood-curling scream echo throughout the forest. A scream so deafening, it silenced all the animals and insects for moments. It carried far into the woodland.

The blinding pain sent Thoran into a deep sleep. He was still screaming as he passed out.

I'm Going Back

While scurrying through the woods and talking to herself, Ruth Fagash heard that terrible scream. It stopped her quick hobbles and she said aloud to no one, "I'm going back." She didn't know exactly where the cave was, only that it was close-by and she didn't want to get any closer to *whatever* made that whoever, scream.

She turned back, even quicker than she had been going. Another sound stopped her— a loud bark that sounded angry, though she wasn't exactly sure. But whatever it was, it sounded big. She heard voices and dropped to the ground. She wondered if the jumbled voices could be what made the screamer scream. She could tell they were excited. Stumbling into a thicket, she hid herself and waited to see if the voices came closer. Peering through the brushy forest, she was confused by what her eyes focused upon, only a short distance from her. Her eyesight was keen, but the sun was fading, and she thought she was watching a group of people— short people scuttling about through the woods. And ahead of them was a dog. A dark, shaggy dog that bounced and barked. I think they're short, she thought… oh, never mind, they're moving away from me. "They don't look like elves or wood trolls," she said aloud.

The dog stopped sharp, turned his snout, and stared directly at her. She froze. One of the short people said something like, "What hear fitch?"

That dog heard me. Are they children? she asked herself. For a few clock ticks, everything stopped. The dog turned, barked and bounced away. The short people, still excited, said, "Let's go," and followed.

She didn't wait. She knew the Council Master would be concerned for her safety and would appreciate her coming back safely, even if she didn't complete the task. It was getting dark, and the woods were no place for a young, tasty woman to be in the dark, she thought. Adrenaline made her hobble turn into a trot.

They Followed Pitch...

through the thick woods, each stride taken with gusto, Pitch's excitement gave them optimism. Their donkey was keeping up with them just fine. They weren't waiting for him. They just kept an eye towards their backs and noticed he was always there. Every now and then, Pitch would disappear for a spell. The boys would scream for him, he would bark back, then come cutting through the woods. Pitch was noisy. His grunts and groans always came before his bouncy shag was seen. They hadn't stopped since sun-up, and except for a quick pee break, no time was lost. They traveled fast and only Pitch knew they were close to the outskirts of Laban.

Pitch was convinced that Momma and Papa were at the cave. He couldn't run too fast ahead of them. He didn't want to lose the boys.

Thoran's scream cut through all other forest sounds.

The boys knew it was a loud yell, as its echo beat the air hard through them. It gave them goose dimples, stopping them, making them gasp. They heard a cry like that before... a long, long time ago when a poison slug tried to kill their father. Only this scream was worse—more agony, more pain. And the boys knew it was their father. It was a cry for help. Breathing hard, they looked at each other for only a clock tick, then ran hard, dodging through the woods, jumping over fallen trees. Adrenaline pumped through their veins. They ran like arrows seeking a target. They were in full battle mentality. As they ran, Pitch stopped suddenly and looked in the distance towards his right.

"What'd ya hear Pitch?" Achu and Grumel asked at the same time.

Pitch smelled another human, but not the ones he sought. Leave it, he thought. He growl-barked and bounced away forward, knowing the cave would jump out at them shortly.

"Let's go," six of the seven said out loud with a purpose. Ayell's eyes were focused far into the woods, in the direction Pitch ran.

Something Else Heard That Scream

In the far, far distance, Seena's beast-pets also heard Thoran's scream. It woke them—it angered them. And when they got angry, *she* got angry. Because those loud, nasty beasts rarely shut up once they got going. They answered Thoran's echoing scream with garbled, loud howls that cut back through the forest. The witch angrily filled her ears with dirt and leaves, quickly grabbed from the ground. She ran at them screaming, "Shut yer gobs, ya bloody mess a' fur," and while running she grabbed what looked like a wad of paper from a pocket and threw it at them. Before it reached the beasts, it blew up in mid-air—exploding into a yellowy-white stink cloud that burned the eyes and noses of her pets, shutting them up. But they were hungry and wouldn't stay quiet for long. Thoran's scream lingered in their minds.

The sound of screaming usually meant prey to the pets, and Seena could only tolerate their screaming and crying if she was making it happen. She opened the thick wooden gates covering their hole and simply said, "Go... kill's em. Jest make sure ya's brings me back some bits ta stew, Aye." It didn't matter who or what they killed, as long as they shut up and brought something back.

Out of the hole came deep, gruff, sounding growls. Then two shaggy-winged beasts blasted out, seeking only Thoran's echo in the distance. A hunting they will go. Seena picked at flaky scabs on her chin, swatted at fleas and clivets that pranced about her face, and started to pick dirt out of her ears. All had quieted down.

She was confident that her pets, after they killed and fed, would bring at least two half eaten corpses of younglins back for her witchy stew.

Not Waiting

The ogre was surprised to wake and find the male human gone. It quickly saw him crawling at the cave opening and realized the human couldn't run and would be easy to catch. Its stomach also made a decision that it was not waiting to feed. It might not eat all of him, as he was a big human, but it would feed now. It walked slowly and followed. The human didn't hear it. When it stepped on his leg, the human let out the loudest scream it had ever heard, so loud that it hurt its ears. The human fell asleep. It was glad the human was quiet.

The ogre plunked down next to Thoran, grabbed his leg, lifted and thought... not too meaty. It ripped at Thoran's pants exposing his leg and bit down on his tough calf.

Thoran's eyes fluttered open. He could barely focus. There was tugging and pulling at his left leg. He saw what was happening, but couldn't feel any pain. He humbly watched the ogre eat him. His right leg still felt strong, tho' most of it was gone, and he couldn't move. He knew death would win this battle. He was bleeding badly, and there was no fight left in him. As his teary eyes fluttered into a soft darkness, he could only think... Good Mother, please take care of them... let my family live. He again passed out.

The ogre knew the male woke up, but it didn't matter. It looked at him again, and he was sleeping. Blood dripped from the corner of the ogre's mouth as it chewed.

Thoran flinched, but didn't wake— couldn't wake.

While staring around the pretty green forest, the ogre ate. When finished, it thought it would leave the Council Master and go find more of its kind. It was tired of the Grimsdyke and his orders.

Thirty-Nine

Who Could Be Knocking?

Grimsdyke wasn't a light sleeper. When Ruth Fagash frantically knocked at his door, he was startled awake and angrily whispered in a low voice, "Who-oo could be knocking?" He jerked the front door open and was very, very surprised to see her. Rose heard the knocking, and like her husband, she woke and was thinking more clearly.

Out of breath, sweaty and smelling of stale smoke, Ruth spoke quickly before Grimsdyke could—"Beg pardon sir, but I was so near the cave ands heard an awful scream. It so scared me, ands you see I can't likely defend myself as I used to," she panted, "I figured I can go back at sunup, maybe stay here the night, make ya a nice tea. Yous can wake us up as early as you see fit."

"Well...my, my. That was a quick trip," he calmly said. Grimsdyke's first thought was that the stupid ogre was feeding. He didn't send her quickly enough. Ultimately, no harm was done, he thought.

"Then I saw a bunch of little mens runnin with a dog through the woods, ands I got more scared. I thought they heard me, but they ran opposite to me. I comes back real quick."

Grimsdyke's breath stopped. His heart thudded, a bolt of anxious adrenaline shot down his neck. He stared at the mess of a woman. Did he hear her correctly? "Did you say a group of little men? And a dog? Wha... what color dog?"

"Well, it getting a bit dark, but t'was a dark dog I think, I think it black sir," she answered.

With closed teeth, he made a low, very quiet grumble, as if clearing his throat. He asked, "How many... little men?"

"Dunno sir, a bunch. Maybe five or six."

His mind raced, his thoughts shot from ear to ear. If Thoran had a breath left, he would tell the boys to rescue their mother, to not waste a valuable second. They would come at him with a vengeance. Grimsdyke recalled the day he and Max met them; he remembered well their skills. Max would help them. Grimsdyke was impressed at their speed in coming to find their parents. He forgot about the parent's lie about the boys training with a relative. He must move quickly. There was no time to defend himself. He needed the scurvy woman gone.

Calmly, to Ruth he said, "Thank you, my dear. You did well, tomorrow is fine... no reason to put yourself in harms way. Here's something for your time and efforts," he reached into his pocket but found it empty. "Silly me, come here for a sliver," and he motioned for her to follow. She stepped in a few paces. The door remained opened. She politely noticed the simple décor. Grimsdyke walked to a small desk and opened a drawer, grabbed what he needed and stepped back towards her.

"Your home is quite cozy, sir," she said, a bit seductively, "mayhaps we can...

"Why thank you, I find it so," he interrupted. And as he lunged at her neck with the knife pulled from the desk, he simply added, "Tho' it is a bit drafty in the colder months."

Ruth Fagash was so surprised at the speed with which she was struck, she didn't realize that blood gushed from her neck. He pushed her slightly out of the way to close the door. She turned, stumbled just a bit, and watched. Puzzled, she asked, "Sir?" A swoon of light-headed air hit her. She fell to the floor. Grimsdyke said nothing.

Rose heard commotion. She sensed something was happening. She tried harder to un-wrangle herself, but her ropes were too tight.

Grimsdyke rushed into the room commanding, "We're leaving!" and went to a closet, grabbed a case and threw bits into it.

Rose snapped out of her stupor… "Why? What's happened?"

He looked at her and realized she had some strength back. He didn't like it one bit. He screamed, "Nothing that concerns you, as long as you do as you're told. If you even want to entertain the slightest chance of seeing your family again, you'll do as you're told."

He's afraid, she thought… he wants to run. A voice shouted in her head…slow him down! Rose yelled as loudly and sharply as she could and started to thrash about. Her wail took him by surprise. Its shrillness pierced his brain, sending a devastating bolt of pain through his head. Without thinking, Grimsdyke, dropped his case, ran at her and let fly his fist, square into her jaw, and screamed, "Shut your mangy gob!"

Rose was hit unconscious. Grimsdyke looked at her. His brain in pain, but scheming. He grunted in approval and grabbed her hand. He pulled her ring off and said, "Sorry my dear, but it's for the good of us all." He ran to the front door where Ms. Fagash had just finished bleeding to death. He angrily grabbed Ruth's hand, shoved Rose's ring on a finger, said, "I now pronounce you…" laughed, and then threw Ruth's cold, crusty hand down.

Planning his action, Grimsdyke ran outside to his small stable, grabbed his two horses and led them to his back porch, quickly tying them to a post. He hurried back into his cottage. Fate was now fully coming into play…the sick man thought as he mumbled incoherently. He opened the trap door to his cellarium, or his 'special cellar,' as he fondly referred to it, and hurried down the dusty wooden steps to the rarely visited chambers, his pantry of the dead. He wondered which corpse he should bring up to keep Ruth company. The dead resting below his dwelling weren't kept for any particular reason at the time of their respective demise. But now one would have a grand purpose.

"Let's see," he said to no one that could hear, "I think Master Cline will do." He grabbed the mummified body of Basilton Cline, one of the chamber's oldest inhabitants. Mr. Cline, a tailor, had a pocketful of gold slivers the Council Master wanted. He was duly killed for them, many years ago. Grimsdyke easily lifted the stiff-as-a-board corpse. His body is much lighter now then when I threw him down here, he thought while grabbing Mr. Cline around the chest. A breath of musty dust escaped through a decades old grimace, startling Grimsdyke. He brought the old, dead man up from his cellar, placed him next to Ruth, more to the inside of the cottage and said, "Bazey, meet Ruth. Ruth, meet Basilton— you two make a lovely couple."

With piercing pains in his brain, Grimsdyke ran and grabbed his prized Rose, hoisted her over his shoulder and carried her outside. He slung her over a horse. She landed with a grunt as her belly met the horse's back. After grabbing a rope and tying her hands across the horse's underbelly to her feet, he ran back into his house. Fear drove him to act with haste and efficiency. He grabbed whatever belongings he could, careful not to forget his gold. He would travel light and buy anything he truly needed.

His earlier plans changed. He had no fear of leaving his home and Laban quicker than anticipated. To no one listening, he ranted as he ran about…"Battle plans change. Success depends on the ability to adapt…, and I will adapt. I will wake that which has been waiting." He knew the next time he came back to Laban, whenever that may be, he would come with an army—an army that would obey and destroy anything in its path. First, he must kill those seven little animals borne of his sweet prize. He would not attend the King's festival… "But I will preside over the King's funeral," he whispered. Happy and anxious, his last trip inside his cottage wasn't melancholy. He was excited. Before visiting Ruth Fagash and Mr. Cline again, he grabbed a jug of lamp oil. Grabbing Ruth's hand, the one he put Rose's ring on, he purposely positioned it so it barely stuck outside the front door frame. He wanted the first person that came upon the cottage to see that hand sticking out the front door. In a low monotone voice he spoke, "Now for the warmth, my love." Some lamp oil was emptied on Ruth's face, the remainder poured over Mr. Cline and onto the wood floor.

After one last look around, Grimsdyke walked to his fireplace, grabbed a flint-rock and holding the flint-rock against the wall, he eagerly stepped back to the dead by his front door. Sparks on the wall followed his trek. Standing above Ruth and Bazey, Grimsdyke threw the rock hard at the floor. A spark flew, flames engulfed his guests, and he only watched for a few clock ticks as clothes and flesh first darkened, then burned. The smell of burning hair and flesh wasn't as rancid as he would have thought. "I'm hungry," he said, as he turned to walk out the back door.

In only a matter of seconds, the front of the dwelling and two corpses burned. Grimsdyke was lost in his fantasy.... smoke will soon fill the house— it'll drift out the windows. The seven little maggots could come at anytime. The townsfolk will see smoke. They'll panic to find where it's coming from. Eventually, they'll see it's coming from my cottage. They will run over to make sure I am okay. Isn't that nice of them? Too late. Someone will find the charred remains of a woman— or at least her hand. They'll find Baz.... or should I say... me, the poor Council Master. He smiled. It was perfect... the boys will make it here, I'm sure of it. I hope it's soon. Someone will hopefully notice the ring on the charred body. The boys will be very sad as they look upon the burned remains of who they have to believe is their mother. 'It's her ring,' they'll say. When they find the other body, they'll reason a great battle ensued and their mother put up a brave fight. A fight where she died, and she took me with her. Good for Mom. No comfort in it, though. After uttering some disbelief, the townsfolk will curse me... they will say it serves me right to burn... but, oh that poor, poor woman. And I will be well on my way to building my army. And Rose will be my new bride.

Grimsdyke tied the reins of the horse carrying Rose to the saddle of his horse. After mounting his, he gave it a soft kick. The second horse was not happy. She was afraid that the sweet smelling girl tied on her was uncomfortable in such a strange position, so she tried to clomp gently.

He would travel to the lands where nightmares are not only in dreams; to secret forests where monsters hide...and wait. To feed. To hurt. Where dying is only a luxury, as it ends pain. Into the lands layered so thick with old growths that anything can hide.

He looked back one last time at his smoldering cottage. He wanted to get away quickly, so Grimsdyke kicked his horse hard. The second horse followed, but was sad, as the girl on her would not be comfortable.

Forty

Their Aim Was True

Their donkey, well behind them, had the stamina, fortitude, keen sense of smell, and a rare bond of family to carry on until he found them. He had to. Because he couldn't express how very scared he was or how he had grown to love the boys and the family with the black dog. Donkey didn't understand what was going on; he just knew he didn't want to be alone in the woods.

Pitch ran at full speed. The boys were only steps behind. All navigated the forest as scared deer would. Nine pair of little legs moved back and forth as fast as a muzzy's wings. Pitch's stride was the longest. When he burst through the thicket surrounding the cave, he thought his normally keen eyes were playing a trick on him. Waning sunrays shone through the trees, blinding his view of the feeding ogre. He could only partly see Thoran, who seemed to float upside down. Pitch focused.

The boys burst through the thicket and saw that a horrible scene was taking place. There was no time to gasp, though they did say "Papa" together in low, hushed voices. By that time, their father's right leg was eaten up to the upper thigh and most of his left leg was gone.

The ogre turned to the sounds that came from the woods and was very surprised to see a large group of younglins and a dog appear. It sat there, confused and chewing, wondering what to do. It could only think...stand up. So while holding a partly eaten human, it stood.

Alvis, Grumel, Yawnel, and Ayell had arrows drawn and were already taking aim. Joyal, Shyel and Achu had axes out, also taking aim. All seven let fly their weapons, which raced from their hands, seeking a prize—the ogre's head. Their aim was true.

Points and blades struck about its face and crown. Arrows pierced through eyes, skin and bone, axes split its head open, exposing a throbbing brain. The beast's hands sprung open, dropping its human meal. Stumbling backward in pain and surprise, the monster fell down backward while clutching its face.

Fearful and confused, the boys ran to their father. Pitch took no chances. He lunged at the ogre, growling and angry. The nearly dead ogre put up no fight as Pitch ripped its neck.

Their actions were tight and clear. The boys surrounded their father and cradled him. Ayell fished through the sack, grabbing at the goblet as Achu, Grumel and Joyal shouted, "The goblet!" Thoran's blood ran thickly out of him, onto his boys, onto the ground. He didn't move.

Not knowing if it would work, unsure if death stopped the goblet's magic or even if their father was dead, a water jug was drawn and the goblet filled. Thoran quietly coughed up spits of blood. He wasn't dead. "Only one drop," someone said as many little hands, each covered in their father's blood, moved towards the golden cup. Grumel's hand wound up first over the goblet, his pinky finger hovered above the opening and a single drop plopped in. A simple film of blood spread on the water's surface, then disappeared.

The boys had to gently lift their father's head and pull on his chin to open his mouth. They poured water from the goblet. Without realizing what he was doing, Thoran drank. His eyelids were closed, but his eyes twitched behind them. The power of the goblet coursed through his body, carrying along a fast moving river of blood.

Fourteen pair of eyes widened…amazed. They watched a miracle. The blood from his eaten legs stopped spurting, Blood surrounding Thoran's mouth fizzled; a mist seeped out. He gasped and coughed. Clean air entered his lungs. His whole self twitched and shook. Then came the sizzle. The ends of what were left of his legs bubbled and fizzed. Faint popping and crunchy snapping sounds filled young ears. A yellowish, creamy steam oozed from Thoran's stumps. Then his legs... *his legs!* They sprouted right before their eyes, rolling out as if a red carpet was being laid for a queen. Thoran's eyes opened. He awoke, watching his life spring back.

"My boys," he whispered, and sobbed. "My boys." He grabbed his sons and pulled them close, "My beautiful boys!" he cried. His legs and feet were back, his wounds healed. Flexing his fingers and toes, their strength quickly returned. Again, his boys rescued him. They beat back death as it tried to eat him. Although he should have been, he was not exhausted. Although his belly was empty, he was not hungry. He was angry!

"Wh.. wh... where's Momma, Papa?" asked Shyel, Achu and Joyal. "What happened?"

"What happened, Papa?" asked Grumel, as Ayell shook his head.

Thoran jumped up, startling them. "HE has her. That Council Master. It's all his doing," he said through clenched teeth, "We must go find her." Pitch barked his approval.

"Where is she?" they all asked together.

"I don't know. We'll start in Laban... at his house...in the town," Thoran said while surveying the area for clues as to the direction in which they would go. "Did you bring water?"

Pitch chimed in, *"This way,"* he barked while turning to run, *"Town's this way."* He started to run. The boys instinctively followed. Thoran hesitated for a clock tick.

Achu said, "He led us right to you Papa. He'll take us to Momma. He smells real good."

Thoran smiled. It was the first time in what seemed like an eternity that he could smile and not feel too guilty. "Okay, first my shoes." He ran a few steps towards the cave and picked up his shoes. "That my boys, is an ogre. Well done for killing it."

The seven boys quickly looked at each other. Yawnel spoke, "We've seen bigger." Thoran looked at them, confused. Grumel added, "We'll tell you on the way. Let's go."

Joyal screamed, "Lead the way boy," and off they ran to rescue Rose.

Their donkey, still well behind, didn't know where they were, but heard a scream in the distance. So that was the direction he decided to go.

Forty-One

Something Burned

While breaking down his table of wares in the village square, Stanley Shniggleton smelled smoke. It was a strange odor — part burnt wood, part burnt something else, a smell he couldn't quite place. He looked to the sky for smoke, for a source. Others meandering through the town also caught a whiff. A little girl, the same one the Council Master scared a few weeks back, spotted the dark plumes. "Smoke!" she screamed in a sweet, little voice that carried quite well. She pointed to the sky.

"Who lives that way?" someone asked.

"Jimson the joiner," somebody answered.

"And Ballzier the baker," somebody else said.

"The Council Master also lives out that way," added Shniggleton.

"Something's wrong," said the mother of the little girl.

In a sweet voice, the little girl asked, "What Mama?" plainly sensing concern on the adult's faces.

"Something's wrong." Her mother lightly screamed, and nervously smiled at her little one. She turned to the gathering crowd. "Mr. Snoot, I think you should gather as many men as you can— see where that smoke's coming from."

"Gotcha, Bertha," Snoot answered, then shouted, "Sound the bell!" The town center quickly bustled. Warning bells were placed in various locations in most towns. Sometimes there was a fire from a lantern being lit at dusk. Sometimes horses escaped and needed catching. And sometimes, though most couldn't remember the last time, bells were rung when a beast or thing from the deep forest or mountains needed to be hunted and killed. The townsfolk usually tried to keep that quiet from the children. A group of seventeen men and women quickly gathered up shovels and picks and hustled towards the smoke.

Meanwhile, Thoran, his boys, Pitch, and a donkey, also headed towards the smoke. They too smelled it and the course back to Laban put the smoke directly in front of them. In quick steps, they pushed through the woods. Thoran was utterly amazed when the boys told him of their battle with the giant ogre, especially the part when Ayell was eaten. "We'll sit around a fire one day… you'll tell us what it was like being in the belly of a beast," he said to his first-born. Thoran was sad when he spoke of the tragic battle at their cottage that took their sweet Aunt Zee's life. And he was again proud when his sons told him of her burial. "You've grown so…you're all so.…" He stopped—his eyes became moist. Stop, his mind raced…there's no time for sadness. "We'll find your mother, and we will bring her home," he confidently exclaimed to his sons.

Pitch barked, *"Let's go!"* and ran. He knew the search for Momma would begin at Grimsdyke's house. Pitch sniffed his nasty scent. They were getting closer. The Council Master traveled this way, Pitch thought. In his former life, all of Grimsdyke's secret hiding places were burned into Pitch's brain—the special 'places.' Max mostly feared the cave, because going there or to the 'special room' in the basement, always meant death was coming to someone. Pitch also knew where gold was hidden. The smoke made him uneasy; its strong smell confused all other scents in the air. And there was something else mixed in that smelly smoke, something really bad.

Pitch didn't smell Seena's pets until they flew out of the forest, landing smack-dab in front of them, barely ten paces away, smelling of rot. Shaking their shaggy hides while they crouched on their haunches, their chests heaved as they sucked in air. From their agitated black lips, they bared rows of dark teeth. From their throats came the most viscous sounds the boys ever heard.

The creatures thought… let our prey hear how hungry we are— let them see what will be eating them.

Like towers they loomed, two—things: one black, the other gray, the likes of which were not drawn in Dagon's journal. The boys thought they looked like deformed, shaggy horses with bat-like wings. Tho' their heads were more dog-like and their mouths were filled with teeth shaped like broken arrowheads. Joyal, Achu, Grumel and Alvis wondered at the same time… are they dragons?

At quick glance, Thoran thought the monsters before them looked like Pitch, but older, much larger, and they could fly! But they screamed piercing, garbled shrieks; sounding nothing like a dog. They stood still for only a clock tick before attacking their food.

Pitch froze for only that same clock tick. When they moved, he howled a warning, trying to intimidate. But his voice was no match. Seena's pets stood fully five times his size and their sounds were five times as menacing. Never the less, Pitch attacked.

The gray beast lunged and snapped its mouth at Pitch, but missed. Its face hit the ground with a thud! Pitch was much more nimble.

The black one half flew, half hopped as it lurched and bit at the largest, meatiest human—Thoran. Its front hoof-paws landed on Thoran's newer feet, tripping him, but not pinning him down. It tried to bite him. Thoran ducked at the last second. He fell backward and landed on his rump. He smelled the creature's breath and was hit with a broken tip of a splintered tooth that flew out of the black one's mouth. The boys had weapons at the ready and aimed, the action was quick. They had to be careful.

Thoran was off balance and tried to get a good grip on his axe.

Pitch ran under the belly of the gray one, forcing it to turn awkwardly. Achu threw an axe that only skimmed it. "Drat!" he screamed. The others had arms cocked with axes or arrows pulled, ready to fly.

The black one had a clearer path to bite Thoran. It swung it's head, it's large, dark mouth aimed for Thoran's face. Thoran thrust his axe upward into the monster's red sloppy mouth. It tried to close, but Thoran's blade cut through the roof of the mouth, stopping the angry gob from fully chomping down on his hand. It's teeth only touched lightly on Thoran's wrist. A full chomp would have easily taken the hand. An opening was all Thoran needed. He pulled his hand back as if burned. Four of his fingers cut themselves on the monsters lower jaw, his fingers bled and stung, but they were whole.

The black one growled in pain, lifted its neck, opened its mouth and violently shook its face trying to dislodge the axe. Like a crab, Thoran scampered backward.

Pitch bit hard on the hind leg of the gray beast. It screamed a pained, angry howl and kicked its hindquarter out, sending Pitch flying into the brush. The boys let their weapons fly, tho' all aimed only at Pitch's battle. Two axes and three arrows hit about the gray one's mid section. One axe and one arrow missed. The shag and skin of Seena's beasts were thick. Weapons found their mark but couldn't penetrate deeply enough to fully rupture innards. But they did cause great wounds. The gray monster buckled and turned to the younglins.

Thoran screamed, "THE EYES, ARROWS TO THE EYES!"

Pitch furiously barked, *"I'LL KILL YOU. STAY AWAY FROM THEM!"* He bolted back, jumping at the gray creature.

The boys had arrows drawn. Ayell and Shyel slid arrows towards Thoran. He was able to grab them. The black one jumped straight up as if shot from a canon. It was able to hover like a bird. With a last mighty shake of its head, it sent the axe in its mouth flying, then dove from the sky, aiming at the group of younglins. It wanted to kill them and be done with the battle.

The boys let fly their arrows. Four of seven hit directly into the eyes of the gray one. It shuddered and let out an unearthly scream while Pitch landed hard on it's shaggy back. Pitch drove his teeth into the neck. Blood cried from the gray ones' eyes.

The boys were grouped too closely. The black pet swooped down hard at them, crashing into and scattering them like leaves tossed about a strong wind. The shaggy attacker stumbled on landing, but quickly regained footing. Inches away from it was a youngling. It bit down hard, lifted, shook and threw. Shyel passed out, his leg severed from his body and swallowed whole, and he crashed to the ground. The black one was also close to Grumel. It looked at him, hop-flew, then pounced, landing on Grumel with a thud, pinning him down with claws and weight. It triumphantly howled as it had prey. It glanced at its badly wounded sister beast and opened its mouth to bite off Grumel's head.

Thoran screamed... "Nooooo," and with axes in each hand, let them fly. The blades swished through the air, ends over blades. They landed hard, one lodging deep in its neck, the other sliced through a wing and into its back. The black one growled and turned, its wings instinctively trying to flap in defense. It tried to rise up, forgetting its pinned down prey.

Grumel, was scared and surprised. Scared because everything moved so quickly, surprised that in his hand, he held an axe. Where'd this come from? he thought, not realizing it had been in his hand for some time. He swiped hard at a shaggy leg, cutting it deep. Thick blood sprayed out as the beast jumped back surprised by its wounds.

Thoran screamed..."AYELL, ALVIS... TO SHYEL WITH THE GOBLET. OTHERS ATTACK!" The others had their arrows drawn. Ayell and Alvis raced to their fallen brother.

Grumel, shaken from the attack, quickly regained his composure, rolled and swiped again, but the black one was just out of reach. Thoran raced to the nearest boy and grabbed a knife and axe from the boys belt.

The gray one, blinded with blood gushing from its eyes, weakened with each clock tick and stumbled about. Pitch clung to its back, his teeth deeply embedded in its neck. Its knees buckled. It howled sad, long, deep breaths and thunked to the ground with Pitch still latched onto its neck.

Hearing his sister's sad cry, the black one hesitated a clock tick. It was the same howl of hurt she made when the old hag-witch turned them into ghastly animals, decades and decades ago. Stopping to give a quick look-see, he saw her on the ground with a small dog biting at her neck. He knew his sister would be dead soon. Panicked, he decided to beat his wings like never before. He wanted to run away. He didn't want to play with this food anymore. He beat his wings once, but a painful tug on his tail stopped his ascent to freedom.

Donkey had burst through the forest and jumped up to attack the tail, chomping down on it with a fury no one knew he had. Donkey had just caught up to them. He briefly watched from the forest and knew the boys would feed him, but not until these ugly— things were gone. One was nearly dead, the other would be soon. He would help kill them, and his family would feed him.

As the black one turned to see what had its tail, it was met with a barrage of arrows, a knife and an axe, all hitting about its face and neck. They aimed pure: Joyal, Grumel, Achu and Yawnel's arrows were dead shots to the eyes. Thoran's knife and axe hit its neck. Grumel's arrow went in the deepest, its point nearly coming out the other side of the creature's head. It dropped to the ground hard and made another painful, sad howl. His sister did not hear it—she was already dead. Donkey let go. The black one's last thought was... witch *will* be mad.

Shyel had already sipped from the goblet, his stump bubbled and fizzed. His family ran to him. Shyel smiled as he watched his body heal itself. Like his father, he grew a new leg and thought... this is the greatest thing ever!

Donkey walked up to the group and nudged Pitch. The boys patted him. Thoran said, "And you, our fine mule. Our mighty ass! You just might have saved our lives." A quick pause, then louder he commanded, "Come up Shyel. Boys, we have to keep moving." He looked at the dead, but twitching beasts and shook his head. "Your mother needs us. Which way, Pitch?"

The smell of smoke was strong. Pitch barked, *"This way,"* and off he ran. His family followed.

Again, donkey was left to follow them. He was so sure they would have fed him.

Forty-Two

A Witch Is Hungry

Seena waited, confident her gray and black pets would soon be back. "Hope the dumb maggits din't eat everthing and go ta sleep," she said. "Stupit people turn inta stupit pets," she muttered to herself while looking around for firewood. Fresh meat was a treat, and she fancied some that night. The last time she let them hunt, the gray one came back with half a young boy, who was good, because it was the upper half, and she fancied the ribs best. She would often follow them, posing as a bat and watch them do the dirty work of killing. "Don't wants to get me hands dirty...cause I'm a lady, I am," she'd squeal and cackle while grinning and twitching. She didn't go with them that night, as the human that screamed earlier, she thought, was just about dead, and all she wanted was a nice meal. But Thoran's scream was really just a call to battle. "Soon they's come back. Shunt be too long afore they's bring me supper." She walked to her boiling cauldron. She knew they would come back. They gave up trying to escape long ago. She always found them. And she always tortured them, to the point that loyalty wasn't a question anymore. It had been a long, long time since she thought the only way they wouldn't come back was if they were dead, so she stoked her flame and waited for her pets.

While the witch waited, the boys, their father, a dog, and even a donkey, moved faster. The sound of a ruckus made Thoran and his sons prepare for another battle, but the scene that greeted them was a group of townsfolk using shovels to throw dirt and sand on a cottage partly engulfed in flames. Pitch barked loudly. He knew the cottage. *"It's his, it's his!"*

Thoran and the boys saw Shniggles in the mix of townsfolk helping, but Thoran looked for only one man. As they ran to those trying to extinguish flames, they passed a charred body under a blanket. Pitch stopped at the blanket and sniffed, long and deep. The scents confused him. The fire raged. Pitch barked loud and hard, *"It might not be her! It might not be Momma,"* but Thoran and the boys weren't paying him any mind. Pitch knew though, that the body under the blanket was not Grimsdyke's—it was too small.

Panicked, Thoran screamed, "Where is the Council Master? Where is Grimsdyke? I beseech you! Does anyone..."

"Thoran? My friend?" Shniggles interrupted, confused at seeing the lot of them. Within crackling flames he answered, "This is his cottage. We fear the worst for him, as has happened to that poor soul," he said, and pointed at remains under a blanket.

Pitch stood next to the blanket, barking. Shniggleton continued talking, but Thoran walked away from him. His heart sank at the sight of the blanket. It covered someone. As one, the boys thought... why is Pitch barking? A hard thought hit them and their little minds cried... no, no, no! Please, no.

Sensing their concern, Pitch calmed his barking, and in short, rational barks he said, *"I don't think it's her, it might not be her."* But it didn't matter. His family was focused on something else.

Thoran and the boys surrounded the blanket. Thoran slowly grabbed a corner and started to pull. He uncovered a face—a blistered and black, crispy charred face that barely resembled a skeleton. The shoulders and body were as crisp as the face. There were no clothes left. The charred hand of Ruth Fagash was exposed. And Rose's ring, a ring that never left her hand, reflected the bright twinkling flames that occupied all others. Thoran dropped to his knees. He grabbed the hand in both of his, as if in prayer, bent forward and cradled it to his cheek.

He began to cry. The boys also saw the ring, and they began to cry. They fell to their knees, placing hands on the blanket. "The goblet!" Thoran said, trying to sound strong, "give me the g…g… goblet."

Sadness and confusion quickly turned into action, Ayell fished it out of his sack. The other boys bumped into each other. Some of the townsfolk looked from the fire towards the family. Achu grabbed a water sack and held it out while Ayell moved it towards him. With excited anticipation of another miracle, water was poured into the goblet.

"One drop of blood," Thoran wished for, holding her charred hand, "Please. Just one."

No blood could be drawn. The fire had eaten all moisture from the body. "Please. Please, Good Mother, bring her back to us," he cried while gently squeezing a lifeless hand, trying to coax one single drop of blood. The boys closed their eyes and prayed, prayed for one drop of blood. Whispering "Please, please, please," Thoran held her hand, bringing it to his cheek. He cried a whisper, "I'm so sorry my love. I'm so, so sorry. I'll watch over them, until my last breath. I'm so sorry. I love you." Papa gently laid his arms over the blanketed body and wept. His boys closed their eyes and as one, they thought about butter tarts and Momma's fired chicken.

Pitch shoved his snout in the air and breathed in deep, the deepest he had ever sniffed. He smelled something. He moved slightly towards the woods and sniffed again. So many smells, he thought… but there's something. He closed his eyes and sniffed deep and long. That's Momma! I can smell her! He ran into the woods. That's her! He looked into the woods, closed his eyes again and sniffed hard. He didn't see the drifting, floaty ember fluttering towards him. Pitch sucked that red hot floaty up into his nose. The pain was sharp and quick. He yelped loud.

"Pitch!" Yawnel, Grumel and Achu said sharply, "Shhhhhhhh."

Pitch shook his head, trying to clear the pain. He thought… her scent… I think that was her scent. But he only had pain. He sniffed, but the pain made him teary eyed. He smelled nothing. He only felt pain. Pitch noticed the faint outline of the full moon coming into view, and it scared him. He didn't know what to do. He paced and whined, *"I don't think that's her... under the blanket. We must go look for her."* He looked at his family thinking... I need to go. Should I leave them? I can move fast. I can't smell now, but maybe, just maybe, I did smell her. He ran to see if he could pick up her scent, but his nose just wasn't working right. The moon, Pitch thought. The moon is bad—it's fat! He whined one last time, *"I'm going to find Momma. I love you."* Needing to get away, he ran. Ayell, Grumel and Achu noticed he ran, but didn't call after him— they were too sad.

Some of the townsfolk noticed goings-on behind them and wondered why the little ones and the man were crying around the blanketed corpse. Shniggles and some others, including the proper town doctor, walked up behind the crying family. Concerned, Shniggles asked, "What's happened?"

Slowly looking up, in teary, broken voices, Shyel and Alvis said, "This is Momma."

Stan gasped. He was confused. He knew Rose from his visits to their cottage, but she rarely, if at all, traveled to Laban. Most folk had never seen her. Same with their Aunt Zee. They were the kindest folk he'd ever met. His trips out of Laban always included a visit to their cottage. "How can that be? It can't be." he said with tears forming. He looked at the doctor "I don't..."

"My apprentice said he treated Grimsdyke and a gypsy here." The doctor added, "He treated some wounds earlier. Are you sure?"

Thoran jumped up— "HE DID THIS!" the doctor and the potter stumbled back. "HE DID THIS," Thoran screamed while pointing at the burning house— "HE DESTROYED MY FAMILY!" His screams overtook the crackles and pops of the burning house. Everyone stopped in their tracks and turned to hear. Tears streamed out of his mouth making it look like he was spitting. He shook a finger at the cottage, "YOU LET THAT HOUSE BURN. YOU LET THAT HOUSE BURN TO THE GROUND. HAVE YOU FOUND HIM? HAVE YOU FOUND THAT MONSTER?"

Shniggleton pleaded, "Thoran my friend, please, what happened? We don't understand."

"THAT'S MY WIFE, THEIR MOTHER UNDER THE BLANKET. HE KILLED HER," he screamed while pointing to his boys surrounding the corpse. Then, with less anger, "Her ring still sparkles...my sweet Rose," he sobbed. "He killed for a piece of gold. We would have given it to him. We would have given it to him." The boys watched their father, tears streaming down their cheeks. Shniggles bent down and stared at the corpse's hand, squinting every time Rose's ring twinkled a flame's reflection. Thoran turned to the small crowd of firefighters, "Have you found him?"

A townsman spoke, "We've found no one else, sir. Tho' we've not been able to get inside yet...sir." The same man continued after a pause, "I know you to be an honorable man," he pointed. "Are you saying that poor soul is your wife? And her death caused by the Council Master?"

Achu spoke, "He killed our Aunt Zee! We buried her head."

"And he brought ogres!" Grumel angrily added, the crowd gasped and murmured.

"And orcs and scugs!" said Shyel followed by more gasps and louder murmurs.

"Have you proof?" someone asked.

Stomping towards the crowd, pointing at the corpse, Thoran screamed, "DO YOU NEED MORE PROOF THAN MY WIFE'S CHARRED BODY?" Spittle flew from his mouth, "THERE'S DEAD OGRES AT MY HOME! YOU DOUBT OUR..."

"No, No, No," the potter quickly answered. He put both hands to Thoran's chest, "We've no doubts, just confused, but no doubts." Murmurs grew louder in the background. Low voices asked, "Why...? How...? Where are...?"

"There's a cave outside town, we just killed an ogre that held Papa prisoner," said Yawnel.

"There are many caves," a townsmen said, "which one?"

"I don't know," Thoran said, defeated.

"Then we'll search them all," someone screamed. A rustling noise came from the woods. Anxious eyes turned. Fists clenched. Then, donkey came trotting out of the woods. Everyone looked at him curiously, then turned back to Thoran.

Another townsman spoke loudly, "We must go to the King! We must find Grimsdyke and let justice take hold. And I quote... 'Any and all heinous acts against humankind shall promptly be rewarded with like kind act and or death!'

Another voice, "We must bring the body of the ogre to him—as proof!"

"Just its head'll do!" someone screamed. The crowd, clustered in small groups, gained strength in numbers and outrage. Their murmurs grew. They spoke amongst themselves. Someone asked, "What if there's more? They could be coming to attack right now."

A tired Thoran spoke, "I don't think that's the case... at least not yet," he paused. "He came to us at our cottage with what I believe was his full arsenal. If there were more, they would be here. Remember, they're stupid creatures."

"Smart enough to get away with murder," someone in the crowd yelled.

"HE, was fiendish enough to destroy my family," said Thoran, clearly speaking about Grimsdyke. "He must be found." Voices of fear, anger and sadness murmured throughout the air. Grimsdyke's cottage crackled and popped as it burned.

"Another body!" someone shouted. All heads snapped to watch two firefighters carry out another crispy body. The crowd settled down. Stilled by those words, even the crackling fire eased down.

Thoran and his boys became the focus of attention. The fire became irrelevant. Everyone assumed it was the body of the Council Master being carried. A search party would not be needed. So much of what was happening made no sense to anyone. More town folk came to help, and new gasps of shock and confusion followed.

A plan hatched from a diseased mind worked wickedly well.

Holding each other's hands, Thoran and his boys surrounded the remains of one they thought was their sweet mother. They cried. The boys didn't know what to say. Their father couldn't say anything, not at that moment.

The burnt body of one thought to be Grimsdyke was laid on the ground and not covered. Townsfolk surrounded it trying to catch any resemblance of the Council Master. No one thought to check the teeth for his crimson fang. It had to be him. Who else could it be? It looked the right height— burnt to a crisp though.

Meanwhile, Pitch ran through the woods, jumping over brush, dodging branches, trying desperately to catch Rose's scent. The moon was becoming full. He wasn't aware his eyes had turned red.

Grimsdyke's cottage burned. All attempts to put its flames out stopped. The townsfolk now gathered in support of the grieving family. A small group took it upon themselves to go to the King. Another group made arrangements to help care for a broken family. Thoran reached for his boys. His heart was heavy; his thoughts were dark. "We need to take your mother home," he sobbed. "I am so sorry." The boys, too exhausted to cry anymore, circled their father and held him. They didn't know what to say. Their own pangs of guilt—emotions they never had, tore at their hearts. If they had not gone on their selfish quest to Grumblers Hill, they could have helped. What lay before them should have never happened.

The female corpse was carefully wrapped in soft cotton blankets and lovingly placed on a cart. That night, Thoran and his sons stayed in the local inn. They brought her corpse inside. She had a room to herself. In a candle-lit room, Thoran stayed with a corpse, the boys stayed in one large room on feather mattresses laid on the floor. The father slept not one wink. Seven little boys slept without one dream.

Pitch Finds Her

His sense of smell was off, but the bright fat moon helped his eyes see clearly. He ran as fast as he could, hoping his smell would be back soon. And when it comes back, he thought… I will be close to finding her. I will find her. I have to. She has a special scent. First, I will kill Grimsdyke. That will be easy, he thought.

His eyes blazed red. His anger grew stronger with every deep breath. He ran fast. He knew parts of this forest. Even in the dark the trees looked familiar, and that gave him comfort. Master's going west. Pitch thought… had to go this way… to the places he used to talk about. Wish I would have listened more. He had to be aware of the ash-grabbers, for they feed at night. He didn't want to have to fight off the long, long arms of the treetop monsters that grab prey and bring it up to a waiting mouth with sharp teeth. Chomp. Stop it! He thought… none of that talk here.

A smell hit his nose hard, his favorite smell—Momma's fired chicken! Relieved, he thought… I can smell again! In an instant, Pitch became ravenously hungry. He couldn't remember the last time he had eaten, let alone something so delicious and yummy. Thinking… she has to be cooking for him. He made her cook. I will kill him and then I'll save her and eat. She will be so happy to see me, and I will be happy to eat…I mean see her. And I will bring her home and our family will be together. While thinking, he ran. The smell got stronger. In the distant woods, he saw a flicker of light. A fire! His brain screamed… it's her! He ran faster, knowing that he would go slower as he got closer to them… I will be careful, but first I get closer. His eyes were focused on the flicker of light that grew larger as he ran. Just a little more…

he thought. And then I'll…

He yelped loudly when the ground gave way to nothing, and he fell. It only took a few clock ticks for Pitch to thump down hard on the bottom of a hole. For a quick moment he thought he was back in the belly of the giant ogre. All was dark until he looked up and saw the fat moon staring at him. It covered nearly the entire hole's opening. Why's it so big? The hole wasn't wide, but it was deep. He jumped at the side of the wall, trying to claw and climb while frantically whining, *"No no no no no, please no, not now."*

Quickly came the crunching sounds of something walking on twigs and old, dead leaves. Then a grunt followed by a cackle; a raspy hard, mocking laugh. Pitch gasped—his heart skipped a beat. She walked up to the trap mumbling, "Yous killt'em… yes ya did. I seen 'em, an now ya's comin with." Pitch couldn't hear what was said, but his hair quickly stood on end. He was scared—confused. He growled when a silhouette interrupted the bright moon. It was holding something, a club, or a branch.

She screamed at him, "YOU'S KILL'T 'EM. MY PET'S. AN NOW YUR COMING WITH… FOREVER!" Her club flamed up at its top—a bright reddish glow lit her face. Pitch saw it wasn't Myrtle, the one who turned him into a dog. This was a different witch.

He saw her eyes. She saw his.

"Blazin' red eyes…aaaaaa, black shuck, devil's hound… ehhh. Don't know where's ya from, but yer mine now." Seena threw the flaming club down the hole. Pitch sidestepped it. The hole lit up. She fumbled in her shawl and pulled something out, a pouch. Laughing, she threw it down the hole. Right before the pouch sparkled, flamed up, and blew out, leaving a sickly sour smelling mist— she said, "I'll git yer friends later."

When Pitch woke up—many hours later, he was chained about the neck and legs. He still smelled the sickly sour mist.

Forty-Three

After the Fire

At sunup the next day, Laban woke to a slow, somber melody played by the King's trumpeters. The tune— 'A King Mourns,' was not played often, though when it was, the town mourned as one. Darkness stained the bright fabric of those once-calm lands, and with darkness comes fear. And in darkness, death can hide.

There was much to do. The King was made aware of all that had happened. The startling presence of ogres meant plans not used in many, many decades had to be dusted off. All the King's horses and all the King's men, would sharpen their blades to battle again. The festival would be put on hold. There was no choice in the matter. Scouting parties were organized, guards were posted, and messengers were sent to all other towns and cities. A special council meeting was to be convened, to choose a temporary Council Master until a new one could be appointed. A group of soldiers was sent to dispose of the giant the boys had killed. The plan was for them to dig a moat around the beast, separating it from the forest, then to burn it. A group of townsfolk, including more soldiers, gathered to help Thoran and his family return to their cottage. Based on what Thoran and the boys told them, there was quite a mess at their home—and friends help. A family shouldn't have to worry about such things while they mourn.

The boys and their father woke to sun sparkles through crystal clear windows and heard for the first time the King's somber tune. Ayell stared at a sunbeam filled with dancing dusties… the tiniest bits of bits, his mother would say. It's only been a few days without her, but her children mourned so deeply, they had to remind themselves to breathe. Before the tune ended, they were ready to make their way back home.

Thoran, at his window, looked at the sun-filled square of Laban and thought…it's not as warm as I remember. Will our sun ever warm me again, my love? He watched his dear friend Shniggles walk about town, and behind him there followed his wagon, all loaded with clay. Ready to make pots, my friend? The kindly potter stopped and dumped his load, then looked directly at Thoran. Standing many paces apart, both stared at one another. Stanley Shniggleton lost his wife years prior, and Thoran remember consoling his friend with soft advice, words that now seemed hollow.

Thoran had a plan. He would ride a horse and tow the wagon carrying his wife. He would ask friends for ponies to carry his sons and would pay them when they got to the cottage. "There's much they'll have to learn, my love," Thoran said aloud to his silent partner.

When the seven brave boys and their father walked out of the front door of the local inn, they were greeted by a group of kindly folk, led by Stanley Shniggleton. It was a serious group, armed with shovels, tools, and other bits, all loaded on carts. The men had banded together. They realized what had to be done with the monsters' corpses at Thoran's cottage. "No family should have to go it alone in the face of such sadness," said Sara Hedgepog, a local pie maker. They would travel with this family and help them, as only a community of good souls could. And Thoran was grateful.

A small group of men on horses went ahead at a quicker pace to survey the scene and to get a start on the messy task at hand. The rest, some with cart and horse, some on horse only, left Laban, their hearts heavy with sadness. They would let Thoran and his boys lead the way, moving at their own pace. Donkey was last in that family line. The path they took would take them directly to the cottage, not past the giant ogre the boys had killed.

There was very little stopping and little talking. The boys just didn't know what to say—to their father, to each other, to themselves. Thoran only stared ahead.

Some townsfolk tried to make small talk… "The frosty mists will be here soon, how were your grapes this year? Have you set your traps yet?"—meaningless questions meant only to break the silence. The day was somber, the weather beautiful. There wasn't any need to say much. Quiet was okay. The forest creatures chirped, squawked, gawked and screamed without any regard to the travelers. As the dark air filtered in, they lit torches and lanterns and traveled through the night.

When the broken family returned home, the lead group of men had already dragged decaying ogre corpses into a clearing and were burning them. None of that group had ever seen ogres and monsters. Arrows and axes protruded from eyes, chests and heads. The air was filled with a rotted smell. There was still one corpse in the forest that Thoran had to point out when he arrived.

"Let their rot end here," said Luke William, son of the town smithy. Thoran had known young Luke since his birth, built his crib in fact. Luke, like the rest of the townsfolk, still tried to grasp the magnitude of all that happened. The story that circulated throughout the land was that Council Master Grimsdyke wanted Thoran's gold. So he banded monsters together to kidnap Thoran and his wife. The children would be food. Oh, they put up a fight, they did, but in the end, two family members were gone. And Grimsdyke died a coward's death and couldn't be hanged for his crimes. It still made no sense, but then again, pure evil never does.

"I fear we've not seen the last of these beasts," Shniggles said to anyone, but not expecting a response.

The townsfolk helped clean up the mess in and about the cottage. Walls and floors were scrubbed clean. Doors and windows were mended. Plates and cutlery were put back in their place.

On the first night back, Thoran quietly brought a blanket and pillow into the boy's room and laid down on their floor. His sons grabbed their blankets and pillows off their cozy beds and placed them next to their papa, close enough to touch him. Pitch had not returned, and there was pain from his absence. The boys continually asked, "Where could he have gone?"

Thoran tried to console them, "I don't know boys. He's dealing with sadness in his own way."

"We haven't seen him… not since the fire," Joyal said.

"I thought he was with us when we left. I don't remember him leaving," Achu said. No one remembered him leaving.

"We have to stay here now," their father said, "Momma would want you all to be strong. If it's meant to be, Pitch will find us. He's strong and he loves you."

Shyel said the last thing that night. "Papa?" he asked.

"Yes?"

"I think we should make one big bed tomorrow." Everyone smiled—the boys quickly fell into a dreamless sleep. Thoran slept in bits and fits.

After two days, the townsfolk thought it was time to leave. Thoran's family needed to grieve by themselves. At the goodbye, Shniggles was the first to speak. "Boys," he said quietly, and glanced at Thoran and back to them. "Your loss is deeper than any of us can know," he sighed, "and we can only share a sliver of your pain." He walked up to Thoran and put his hand on his shoulder. Their eyes met. "You have friends." He turned back to the boys and smiled.

"Thank you," Thoran said. He turned to the other townsfolk, and louder said, "Thank you all." He paused. "We'll be mourning our loss for the rest of our lives." He turned back to his sons, "And we know what Momma and Aunt Zee would say." Another pause.

Shyel feebly asked, "What would they say, Papa? I don't know what she would say. I can't remember what she would say," he sobbed, as did all of Rose's sons.

Thoran looked at his children; all had the same scared, sad and very tired look on their faces. He said loud, "They would say be strong." He paused and held back his own tears. Then softer... "and *she* would say how she loves you. She would not want this to hold down your wings. We both want all of you to be full of life, able and only happy." Thoran looked at the sky then back at his boys. "We have a long life together. And I need you," he frowned. "I'm only strong with you boys." Thoran tired himself out with the brief speech. He walked slowly and slumped down on a bench near the cottage. His boys circled him.

"We promise only to be sad, Papa, never defeated," Achu said, and the others agreed.

"We promise to make them proud of us," added Grumel.

"We promise to help, and not disobey you... as much as we can," said Alvis.

"We promise to learn all things they spoke of us learnin," said Joyal.

"We promise not to hurt anyone or anything unless it tries to hurt us," added Yawnel.

"We promise to love the woods like they did," said Shyel.

They all looked at Ayell, and he looked back at them. He clenched his fists and raised them in the air, angry and with tears in his eyes. His brothers finished his thought by screaming, "And we will be strong!"

The townsfolk watched an amazing family start to come to terms with grief. It was time to leave. There was nothing left to clean. "Some friends will come every week or so, to check up," said Shniggles. "We'll keep you informed of the King's decisions, anything we find out. We'll not trouble you while you mourn." And again he said, "You have friends." Shniggles walked to the horses, and motioned for the townsfolk to follow.

"You're always welcome," Thoran answered, "Please come whenever you'd like," he said to all.

"May peace be with you and your family." They patted the boy's shoulders and heads as they left. Some mumbled further condolences. With heavy hearts, Thoran and the boys watched them leave. After the last clomp of the last horse, the sad family just wandered about their garden. "What do we do now?" asked Joyal.

"Let's build something," said Shyel.

Startled, Grumel said, "We haven't looked at the journal! Ayell! The journal!"

No one had thought about it for some time. Ayell fished it out of a sack and everyone eagerly gathered around to see if there was anything new. Thoran joined them, but cautioned, "Boys we don't know what the journal will show us."

"Dagon wouldn't scare us with Momma," Yawnel said, "the picture he drew of Aunt Zee is beautiful." The cover was opened, and although there was no wind, the pages flipped fast by themselves, past monsters, past dragon-elves, past strange plants and trees, stopping on the picture of Aunt Zee, looking at peace with her family. The second to the last page had a new drawing on it. Scratched out roughly, almost finished, there was a scene showing the boys and Pitch atop the giant ogre they killed.

"Woah...was that really how big that thing was?" their father asked.

"It picked Ayell up like a dingle-berry and popped him in its mouth," Yawnel said as Ayell shook his head up and down. "An' it swallowed Pitch without chewing." Thoran shook his head in disbelief.

On the last page there was an unfinished drawing of a horse. It was a bit confusing—it really didn't show them anything. Thoran wanted no more confusion..."Put it away sons, we'll look at it again tomorrow," he said. Thoran looked at his boys. They stared at him. Ayell looked lost. Stroking his first-born's shoulder, he said, "Don't worry, Ayell," he turned, "or any of you for that matter. I miss him too, and I pray Pitch will come back. Tho if he doesn't, there's a reason. We have no control over what happens... sometimes." He paused—a thought quickly angered him, the Council Master's face entered his mind. Forcing the anger away, he said, "Okay boys, before we turn in, we must prepare— follow me."

Curious, they followed their father as he walked to a nearby large tree, where stashed away in a fake hole were weapons. Lots of weapons. "I don't think they will, tho' if any monsters do come back, we will always be prepared. Grab a handful, boys." Everyone grabbed weapons. Thoran showed the boys that almost every tree surrounding their cottage had hollowed out sections filled with axes, arrows, knives and some bows. Each hollowed cavity had a bark cover to hide it. The boys never suspected and were amazed at how many weapons surrounded their cottage. After the last battle—the *only* battle—some trees were empty and needed to be re-stocked. After they finished, Thoran said, "Lets go inside."

Forty-Four

Rose's Dream

She had no idea how many days they'd been traveling nor did she have any idea where they were. On some days it rained, clouding what little sense of time she had. She asked herself many, many times...Have I counted six nights, or seven moons?

Earlier in their lives, she and Thoran had traveled the woodlands, taking in all the sights and sounds, visiting other villages, learning as much as they could. The land she traveled with Grimsdyke was unfamiliar. It could only mean she was in an area avoided by most. It was thick with darker growth. The trees seemed—suspicious, rather than the majestic, comfortable ones she lived amongst. She felt no connection with these woods. She barely sensed connection to life itself. She wondered...is my family dead... can that be? Can that really be? Is this just a dream? But she knew it wasn't, for the dream had lasted.

Grimsdyke hit her. He would scream at her—"SHUT UP." even though she talked little. Sometimes he'd hold his head and cry. He was taking her somewhere. He would talk about a place unseen, but he talked to no one and answered unasked questions. The sick man sometimes just made sounds— delirious laughs, pained grunts, and idiotic snorts.

She slept a lot, and in her dream-worlds, she was always at home...

Zee was cleaning something, Thoran was cutting wood for something... under piercing sunlight, she bathed her boys in the cool waters of their bathing hole.

"Stop Ma, you already cleaned my ears," Shyel barked.

"I got soap in my eyes,"Grumel complained.

"I got soap in my mouth,"Ayell foamed.

"I got soap in my nose,"Alvis added.

But she never slept long, especially when Grimsdyke was in pain. His angry rambling always woke her up. He last woke her by mumbling, "Whens I get there, they'll come to me." He said that a lot, Rose thought. And like most everything he said, it made no sense. But some things he said scared her greatly, though she didn't believe they could be accomplished.

"Kill the King?" she laughed, "You're daft...impossible!"

Slow and steady he'd reply, "Nothing... is impossible my dear. With an army of those that hunger for human flesh, helped by those that have been shunned by the handsome, pretty human-kinds, the King will bow to my demands." He bowed— "And when he bends his knee to me," Grimsdyke snapped his head up, "I will take his head off."

Still hunched over the horse, Rose mocked him, "You'll not get away with it."

He walked over to her, grabbed a handful of her dirty hair and lifted her head while screaming, "I HAVE ALREADY GOTTEN AWAY WITH YOU, MY DEAR." His breath stank, his crimson fang stood out, and she could see a stream of blood trickling down his ear. She chose not to taunt him anymore. She groveled, and simply said, "Sorry," then closed her eyes. His face still haunted her mind.

They carried on; Grimsdyke mumbling words, and making no sense. Rose thought that he was actually chanting. He intensely stared into the woods—seeking, saying, "Show yourself," over and over. Then more chants, strange chants, and every now and then— "I can feel you, I can feed you," he'd say.

Rose searched her fading memory for clues, wondering where he could be taking her. What tale had Shuran, the wood-sprite, told them in the past that could help her? A shock of despair hit her heart... I can't picture Ayell's face. Her eyes shut tightly, her lips pouted, her forehead crinkled with sadness—she thought hard. Grumel's smile and Achu's nose. Shyel's round eyes. My first-born—where is his face? And my Zee. My sweet, dear, brave sister. It ate her? Rose shook and began to sweat uncontrollably. Her breathing hurt. She felt her heart would soon explode.

"Beautiful," was what Grimsdyke said, loud enough to stop her thoughts. She knew it wasn't meant for her. She looked up. Great snapping and crunching sounds filled her ears. And the forest moved.

There it grew. From within those dark woods, towering red oaks groaned, then bloated, turning into bulging pillars that guarded an entrance—a great arched doorway made of thickly-veined wood. Rose let out the quietest of gasps as stout arms— massive tree limbs with thick leaves moved, crunched and crackled, locking together to form looming walls with quoins, and turrets with more arches. Ashes, birches and pines, the trees and land shifted, the cracked lightning sounds grew louder still. And high up, humungous knotholes swelled into dark windows. Empty windows where Rose sensed something was watching her.

It stayed hidden within the dense forest, but now it showed itself. Rose watched it grow. Her thoughts drifted back to her little men building little forts out of branches, limbs, leaves and mud. As her little ones grew older, their forts became little castles, with little turrets. It looks like what they built…only massive, she simply thought. And a sinister reality now smacked at her. At the same time Grimsdyke said its name, she remembered the tale, and her heart sank even further. "Ghastenblood's Keep—The Black Asylum of Death," he sneered at her.

"It can't be. It's just a fairy-tale," she cried. "This is just a dream!" She thrashed about, trying to wake up, not fully realizing that her reality was her worst nightmare. Ghastenblood's Castle was the most dreadful of the ancient torture chambers. Built by the black wizards and witches of old, it showed itself when it needed to feed.

The sad horse she was tied to whinnied and stomped, scared at his passenger's thrashing and of the heavy crashing and crunching sounds that surrounded and engulfed them. It was also confused as to its next move. The hidden castle grew before their eyes.

"No dream, my dear," he laughed loudly as he walked up to her and stared hard into her eyes. Speaking even louder, enough to be heard over the thrashing and cracking behind him— "You see my love, I have a story for you." He plunked himself on the ground, smiled at her and louder began… "A long time ago, a lovely family gave gold to a man they trusted," he waved a hand to himself. "Gave gold for a trip to see if there were monsters. Gave gold to help others. And that man took the gold and went looking for monsters. And he found them. But he didn't tell the King, as the lovely family had thought." He sneered…"It wasn't the King's business. Didn't tell anyone in fact— because the monsters were for him. But he also found something else." He laughed hard, swung his head around to admire the ghastly castle as it grew, then back at Rose. "He found something being kept prisoner. Something dark that was very happy to be set free. Something that told me how to find THAT!" And he pointed at the castle, "And showed *me* how to protect myself in THAT!" He laughed again, stood and cupped her face in his dirty hands and said, "Welcome to your new home." As Grimsdyke spoke, the door to the castle swung open with a broken scream, and he whispered… *"May the darkest of the dark, eat the spirits of the pure, soon to be fed, soon to be bled."*

"No," she cried, "I beg and beg of you, please…"

"I could make you… happy Rose," he said. "Please. Be my wife."

She stopped breathing and looked at him, "Are you serious?"

"This can be yours," he said, while sweeping his arms. "Say the word, and they'll do your bidding." Rose saw what she had sensed was watching from within the hidden walls. She had never seen creatures of the kind that started coming out of the door and that crawled from the windows. At first glance, they could have been related to the dragon-elves, but with more arms or legs, almost spider-like. But no dragon-elf stared as these creatures stared. Dragon-elves had— eyes. The creatures that came towards her had only hazy, black circles in deep sockets. Rose thought they were buttons and wondered if they could actually see. She prayed they wouldn't touch her. "We could make you happy," he said again. "You could be my queen."

She couldn't control herself— she spat at him.

He didn't control himself— he clobbered her.

When she woke up, the first thing she sensed was the floor squirming beneath her. Before her eyes adjusted to the dim light, the smell of rot hit her nose. Rose knew she was in the dungeon of Ghastenblood's Keep.

Forty-Five

A Sad Cottage

One hour turned into one day. One day into one week. One week into many. There was no normal in their home. There was just a cloudy sense of slogging through the slow clock ticks of each minute. Clean what had already been cleaned, shuffle what had already been shuffled. It at least *felt* like something was being accomplished. The boys played as best as they could, and they continued training. They talked about moving closer to where the boys would go to school. It should have been a time of excitement. Rose and Zee so wanted the boys to walk the grand halls of schools on The Islands of Learning, and the boys still wanted to go, but they could not be away from their father, and he would not be far from them. And because all schools were far away from their cottage, Thoran would have to move to stay close to them.

He hadn't had a full night's rest since they returned from Laban. He just went through the motions of sleeping. But one night, he finally fell into a deep, deep sleep. And he dreamed. And what he dreamed made him wake with a scream… "THE RING." He jumped out of bed, with wide eyes he panted, "The ring!" He grabbed a lantern, lit it, and shouted at his sons… "Boys… BOYS! Wake up— quickly."

From the other room came tired voices. "Papa?" They asked, "What's the matter?"

Panicked, he burst into their room saying, "Her ring! It wasn't on the right finger. IT WASN'T ON THE RIGHT FINGER. IT'S NOT HER."

"What?" Three or four of them asked, groggily. All sat up and began to climb out of bed.

Thoran calmed down, tho' only a bit, and paced, "I *should* have known, but didn't. The ring was on the wrong finger. Her ring was on that dead body. It was on the wrong finger!" He turned to his boys— "Your mother's alive! SHE'S ALIVE." He turned and ran out the door, mumbling—excited. "I should have known. I should have felt it." Out of the room, down the stairway, into the parlor... "How could I be such an ass?" Still talking to no one in particular, "I am so sorry my love. So much wasted time, so much— I will make it right. We must leave. At once!"

Together, and to one another, the boys said over and over, "She's alive? She's alive." They quickly got dressed and followed their father downstairs as he talked to himself, saying, "...must leave, must go at once."

Grumel asked loud, "What are we doing Papa?"

Thoran stopped and turned to his sons, "We need to dig up that corpse. Right now. Then we're going to get your mother." His fists were clenched, "Everyone get dressed!" the boys looked at each other. They were already dressed.

Thoran talked to himself, "...shovels and weapons... must pack food, weapons." The boys had so many questions, but they asked none, because they saw their father was in full action.

Dawn was close. Cool, misty dark still filled the woods. Clenching an axe, Papa lit lanterns and mumbled, "Grab sacks, weapons and stuff." He stopped and thought... if I rush, they will rush. He knew strategy must be his strength, otherwise there would be disaster. Outside and looking around at the darkness, he thought... monsters hid in that darkness not long ago—could any still be there? He truly didn't know. He sensed that something was watching. But thinking it only his imagination, he took a deep breath and said, "Boys, we need to prepare." They waited on his words. "I've been... confused, and you can't be afraid to tell me to stop and explain anything I am doing. Or, if you think I'm doing anything wrong, you tell me. Scream at me if that's what you have to do to get me to listen. The seven of you have earned that. I'm your father, but you've earned the right to answers." All were quiet.

"Why are we digging up Momma's body, Papa?" asked Achu.

"It's not her. I'm going to take the ring off that corpse, and we're going to find her."

"How do you know it's not her?" Alvis asked, "Maybe she put it on a different finger for some reason."

"No," he answered, "she wouldn't do that. I'm positive. When we married, we looked in each other's eyes and promised we'd *never* take these rings off." He lifted his hand to show his right hand ring finger. "She wore that ring on this same finger. That ring has never left your mother's finger," a quick pause, "and she also has a swelling in her knuckle...the ring wouldn't come off. *He* ripped it off her hand. He wanted to throw us off his trail." Thoran frowned as he realized how painful it must have been to get the ring off his wife's finger.

"So Grimsdyke is still alive too?" Yawnel asked. Thoran thought about it for a clock tick.

"Yes. He must be."

"So he also killed someone else? To make everyone think it was him that got burnt?" His sons realized it before he did. And it was a terrible, but uplifting realization.

"We can't waste time. Let's gather our bits," their father said.

"And Pitch smelled her." Everyone stopped for a moment. "He knew she wasn't dead," Alvis said. "We wouldn't listen to him, so he ran after her." Ayell shook his head in agreement. Thoran sighed and felt ashamed and angry at the same time.

"Let's get some shovels," Joyal barked.

"Something happened to him," Achu added, "or he'd be back with Momma. Something happened."

"Can't deal with that now— let's get moving," Thoran said.

They dug up the corpse of Ruth Fagash. Maggots, earthworms and bugs made cozy homes amongst her wrappings. It wasn't necessary to unwrap all of her, just her right hand. Thoran grabbed the ring. Ruth's charred, bony finger snapped off with the ring attached. The boys watched their father stick his pinky finger through the ring to pop out a remnant of Ruth's finger. Then, in his fingers, he rolled the ring clean, kissed it, and put it in his pocket. He grabbed the corpse and held it upright. "When I hold your mother, her eyes would stare at my nose. This body is shorter than hers." Tearfully he said, "I should have realized that right away."

"It's okay Pa," said Joyal.

"You did your best. Momma knows that," added Achu.

"Besides, we're going to get her and bring her home," Grumel said.

He looked at his boys. "Yes," he said. "Yes we are. I don't know where she is, but she is alive. We'll go quickly to the King. And we're going to bring her home. Let's go inside, finish packing and prepare the horses. "While they were inside, a loud, cracking branch was heard outside; then a barrage of hard thumps pummeled their roof. Some hit the ground. Terrifying jolts coursed through Thoran and the boys. Not again, Thoran thought... he's come back for the goblet. They sprang into action. Most of their weapons were outside. "Grab what you can, boys. Take the knives. We need to get outside. Remember about the weapons."

"I'm scared Papa," six of them said.

"Scared is okay. I'm scared. He wants the goblet. Where's the goblet?" Thoran asked. Ayell fumbled it out of a sack and gave it to his father. "Stay away from the windows. Grab your bows...or whatever you can." He felt trapped inside the cottage. He needed to get the boys outside, but first he had to try to give the monster what he wanted. "Stay here and only come out when I say," Thoran said.

Grumel and Shyel begged him, "Don't go out there Papa. Don't leave us."

"Throw it outside, but don't leave us," Alvis pleaded.

Thoran looked at his boys. Everyone was quiet.

"Maybe it was just a branch or somethin'. Maybe it was nothing," Achu said. A thump on their roof startled them.

Thoran quickly opened the door and screamed, "I will give you what you want Grimsdyke. Here it is. Take it! Where is my wife? You can have all the gold I own. Just tell me where she is." Thoran looked hard into the front garden. Dawn was just touching the treetops. What he saw confused him. Scattered about the ground were balls of some sort.

From behind him, one of the boys said, "Those are apples."

"Apples?" Thoran asked. One was close to their front door.

"Funny looking ones," Yawnel said, "There's something on it. It's… wet or something. What do ya think—"

"Blood," was the quick answer coming from outside, startling them, making them jump back a step into the house. But the boys had heard that word before, said the exact same way. Their excitement grew quickly. "It's Dagon, Dagon!" three of them screeched while all seven went to push past Thoran. Concerned, he held them back with, "Whoa…stop. Wait."

"It's him, Pop. He's back!" Shyel said.

"Wait. Stay." Thoran walked out the front door and yelled, "Show yourself."

From up on the roof, a dragon-elf said, "Don't…don't, shoot. Very, very stupid I am. So, so sorry. Tried not ta scare ya, but I has ta drop me nuts and bag o' apples and make a racket. So, so sorry ta scare's ya. Me—"

"Hold it," Thoran said, looking up to see what was on his roof. It wasn't Dagon. On his roof was a younger dragon-elf. Thoran tried to speak but the dragon-elf continued.

"Well, I gets here late, late last night, I'm sittin up in da tree," he said, pointing up. "Dint wants ta scare ya's, but a big bat comes at me.

I jump and drop me bits an—"

"Where'd the blood come from?" Yawnel asked. The boys were making their way out the cottage.

"Who are you?" asked Shyel.

"Yes, come down from there. And who are you?" Thoran asked, obviously relieved.

"Yeah, well... I'm Zeck. I been lookin for ya. Found ya an was watchin ya's. Was gonna wait till daybreak. Din't want ta scare ya." From his shoulders and back, soft wings sprouted and flapped once. He floated up, then glided down, landing near Thoran. The boys were impressed.

"So, so sorry for scaring ya'. We need ta talk. I need help."

"Help? Help. You need help?" Thoran asked angrily, "We need help!"

Zeck's wings dropped back. His eyes crinkled, concerned, "Why?" What's happened?"

"Do you know where Momma is?" Grumel added.

Zeck, concerned and shocked said, "Sweet Rose? What do you mean?" He was shaken. "Oh no. No, no, no."

"We were attacked," Thoran said.

"By ogres— and monsters," Grumel added.

"How do you know Momma?" Alvis asked.

"They killed Aunt Zee and took Momma," Shyel barked.

Zeck let out a cry and stepped back saying over and over, "Oh no."

"But she's alive, and we're going to rescue her," Alvis said triumphantly while the others shook their heads.

"Da goblet," Zeck asked. "Did they take da goblet?"

Thoran couldn't believe it. "The goblet?" he screamed shaking the goblet at Zeck. "They killed Zee and stole Rose trying to get this! I would have given it to them."

"NO," Zeck shouted back, with a bit of fire-spittle flying out his mouth. "I, I'm sorry, but you were trusted with da goblet for a reason."

Even after saving his and his son's life, Thoran cared little for the piece of gold. He stomped up to Zeck, still shaking it... "I know of its healing powers, but healing wouldn't be needed if I had given it to him—there would have been no blood shed." He turned his back on the dragon-elf. To his boys, louder he said, "None of this should have happened. None of it!" Turning back to Zeck while squeezing the goblet, his anger boiled. "This is cursed. I wish it never were given to us." Thoran threw the golden object on the ground and withdrew his axe. He thrust his hand up. Zeck cried in the background, fearful. With a quick, hard lunge, Thoran struck true and through the goblet's thin neck. A blinding, golden blast of light escaped from the goblet's wound, shooting about them all, sending them back hard on their rumps. The blast quickly faded. They sat on the ground, breathing hard, confused.

"Why?" Zeck cried, "Why would you destroy da very thing that could save you?" Thoran couldn't answer. He only stared at the sky.

"Look!" Shyel blurted out, "Look at the goblet!"

The goblet lay broken on the ground, its base severed from its neck. But something was inside the stem of only two inches long. Ayell ran to the goblet and picked up the two pieces. A piece of paper was up inside the stem, and as Ayell pulled on the paper, it came out. First two inches, then impossibly three, then four, magically five, six...he kept pulling and it kept coming until its end popped out. Hidden in the two-inch stem was a scroll that was at least one foot long. All watched this bit of magic. All were quiet. Zeck walked up to Ayell and gently put his hand out, respectfully asking to hold the scroll. Whispering, Zeck said, "This is what they were talking about."

Thoran turned to their new friend, "Who?"

"Spirits. Maybe Dagon's—maybe not. Don't really know. But they came in me dream and said fate will show itself to me." He started to unroll the scroll.

Grumel stammered, "Is that...,are you saying that's the..."

"The Scrolls of Harot? No," Zeck quickly answered. He unrolled the scroll to its end. It was folded. He unfolded once, twice, then a third time. Everyone saw what it was.

"A map!" the boys said, shocked. Zeck turned it and showed it to them, but wouldn't let them touch it. On it were bold colors, scratch-pen drawings and spidery script words scattered about. There were strange numbers, and at the base of a large, roughly drawn mountain, there was one large heptagon with a strange marking in the middle. Clearly, it was the point where the map led. It was a marking that Zeck recognized immediately.

"What's it to?" Yawnel asked.

Impatient, Thoran asked, "Is that where Rose is?"

Zeck sighed, "No— it's not." He looked hard at Thoran and said, "But it's where a most important weapon is hidden. Something that can help us find her."

Thoran sensed what was to be asked of him. "We can't waste time looking for a map, we're going to find Rose. That map means nothing to us," Thoran said.

"It means everything to everyone," Zeck shouted a bit. "I can't keep you from looking for her, an I'll help as much as I can." He held the map up and pointed at the marking where the map led. "But this is where I must go. This can *help* you." Zeck turned to the boys, "And I can't do it alone." He turned back to Thoran. "I was there da night Dagon saved you's. This is all part of it. I now know where da map leads to. It makes sense ta me now. Hidden long time ago, it's being sought by the most evil…an' it's our duty ta make sure that doesn't happen."

"Our duty? Not *my* duty. *My* duty is to my wife, and she lives. I didn't ask for this. Dagon never said anything about a map. The goblet was a gift. And *it* has hurt us." Angrily Thoran asked, "What is it?"

"Da Glass of Ioua," Zeck answered. "A tablet of glass made from bits an gubbins of da ancient's: Wizards; priests; magicians; elves; dwarves.

An' men! Their wands, scepters, potions… all kinds of magical tools. Melted together in da fiery Pits of Pythin. Da glass is one of da most magical things there is. You can see things in it. An it can talk…and tell you things. It was hidden centuries ago, for in da wrong hands it is the most dangerous."

"It's like a magic mirror," Achu beamed.

"Yes," Zeck said.

Still angry, Thoran said, "We're wasting time."

"Than we must get going to find da mirror. With that we can find her. But the spirits came to me. Actually to ME! And told me that evil seeks da mirror, and all could be lost. For if evil finds it, then the evil can get to the Scrolls of Harot, and if that happens—" Zeck paused and looked at his new companions. "Then all is lost, and everything you know will be gone, either eaten or enslaved—for eternity."

Thoran shook his head and clenched his fists. There were too many burdens— too much to ask: of him, of his children.

"The evil that seeks the scrolls has but one purpose." Zeck somberly said. "To have…" he searched for a word. "Uh…command. Dominion! Over Mother Earth and all Celestial Empires."

The boys thought about Zeck's last, bleak words. They understood what he said, but couldn't accept their magnitude. It seemed too much. It just made no sense. Surely all the King's horses, and all the King's men, could handle the ogres and monsters again.

"We're going to save our mother," Joyal said.

"Then we'll help you save your… magic mirror, or whatever it is." Alvis finished.

"You should come with us, to the King. His armies will help," Joyal said.

"All are needed, but you seven are needed now." Zeck knew of the prophecy of the *seven,* all dragon elves did. He paced and pointed to the spot on the map again, "We need to be here." Thoran grabbed the map out of Zeck's hand and looked at it.

"These lands are well outside of the Reach! *Across* the Frosted Northerns?" His fingers traveled on the scroll. "Past the Yawning Caves?" he asked loud. "No one has traveled that far. It'll take months to get there, if you get there at all. I can't take my boys out there. And no one knows what's out there. It'll take too long."

Zeck grabbed the map back then started walking in circles, complaining, "You're wrong—what's *out there* is the mirror. And we have to get it first or destroy what's trying to get it." He continued to pace and spoke lower, more to himself— "This is bad. Was hoping ta come here and just watch-over. Thought we had more time." He looked at Thoran. "So, so sorry about Rose and Zee." Zeck remembered Zee fondly and smiled. "It was me brought da goblet to her lips, so many years ago."

"You saved Aunt Zee?" Shyel asked.

"Dagon did most of the saving. We all just helped," Zeck said. "Okay. Need ta get goin. I needs ta fly off for a bit, but I'll be back."

"Wait a minute," Thoran said, "We need your help."

"I know Thoran," Zeck said. "This wasn't planned. But because of Rose, we need ta get there quicker. I need ta meet with..." He paused, "With somethin."

Thoran looked at the energetic dragon-elf and was confused. "I'm not leaving my boys."

Zeck scratched his chin, "That's why we need to get to da mirror. You head west. I'll find ya, and we'll fly here," he said while pointing at the mountain on the map.

"So you know how to get the magic mirror?" Alvis asked.

"Not yet," Zeck said, "but we has ta trust that we'll find that out when we get there."

Thoran grabbed the shoulders of the dragon-elf and held him tight. He looked into Zeck's eyes. "I'm putting my trust...our lives, in your hands." He paused. "I do need your help. I've heard of that looking glass. That...mirror. So, we will do what you ask." He turned to his boys.

"We'll head west and wait for him to come back to us." Turning back to Zeck, he said, "Go. Find your friends. For every second a mother is not with her children, a piece of happiness is lost. She *is* alive— I feel it. We need to get to her. Make haste, my friend."

Zeck smiled, "Take only what you'll need, for our journey will be hard. Head west. I'll find you."

"And please," Thoran begged, "ask your spirits to help find my wife."

"Da good spirits are all of our spirits. They come at their will, for their purpose," Zeck said. "We don't *ask* of them. We just do as we're told."

Thoran looked at his new friend, and sternly said, "Don't *ask* them... *tell* them to help!"

Zeck just looked at his friend and smiled. "Take all your weapons, and don't forget that." Zeck pointed at the goblet on the ground. The goblet that was now whole again. "I'll find you." His wings unfolded. And with a mighty thrust, up he went. He hovered for a few clock ticks over the boys and said, "Stay true to your hearts. Be strong for your kin." He lifted himself higher and higher while the boys watched with wonder. He then turned and took to stronger flight. In the blink of an eye he was out of their sight, but he made an ear-piercing call to his brothers. A cry that was heard for miles.

With a heavy sigh, a father said, "Let's get the horses ready and pack up boys. Let's go find your mother." That's what they went to do.

And again, they left without giving any thought to donkey. So donkey did what he had learned to do. He followed them as best as he could.

Forty-Six

Love

The further he drifted from sanity, the closer he cuddled with evil. In the beginning of his bondage, Pitch was deeply sad. He more than merely missed his family— he grieved hard. He ran from them for a good reason, but after being trapped, starved and beaten for weeks on end, despair morphed into anger. He howled endlessly… *"Why haven't they come for me?"* Seena knew the exact moments to throw him bloody bits of meat.

"They knows where ya at," she'd lie to him. "I told 'em myself. But I also tells 'em ya teeth are growing, an cute and cuddly yer not anymoore."

"You lie!" he howled like a wolf.

"No," she calmly fibbed. "They not gonna come fer ya. Ya hungry boy?"

"I am. Please, I am," he barked hard. A thought came to him, and he barked softer, *"I'll be nice to you, if you're nice to me."*

"Nice?" she screamed. "I don't wants nice. I wants someone for me stew. You ready ta get someone for me stew? Someone nice and tasty? Eh ya mangy maggit?"

Pitch knew what she wanted… Grimsdyke wanted the same thing. Someone would have to die. He didn't want that. He didn't want that. But he was so, so hungry.

Meanwhile, Thoran and his sons had been traveling west for four days. Traveling by day, they'd go far into the night, resting only when the horses needed. They couldn't appreciate the wonders that surrounded them on the trip, as their every waking moment was spent searching the sky for Zeck and his friends. Thoran was angry—he questioned whether he should have gone right to the King. All they were doing was heading west, no true direction, no solid plan.

On their fourth night, after traveling through a hazy day, they found a cave set into a small hill. The cave went deeper than needed. They camped just far enough inside to be shielded from the elements and made a comfy fire.

On their fifth morning, they surprisingly woke to the sound of Zeck barking, "Up, up, up, up, up boys. Sleep time done, time ta go. Lots ta do." A most wonderful smell hit them hard, and they quickly spied a huge, two-tailed fish, roasting on a spit. "Nuthin like smoked fish in the mornin," he said.

Thoran was relieved to see him, but quickly worried... "Where are your friends?"

From deep within the cave came a shrieking, hissing sound. The boys cried "AHHH," and sprinted out of the cave. Zeck said, "Don't be afraid. He needs to know you're not afraid of him."

"Afraid of what?" six boys asked, while Thoran drew his axe and held it tight. Before Zeck could answer, *he* came.

"His name is Galeron, and he is our friend," Zeck said. All they could do was slowly step back and stare. What came slithering out of the cave they had just slept in was a creature unlike anything in their journal. It came out of the cave...and came...and came.

As thick around as a large oak, and just as long, Galeron was no ordinary serpent. His head was the size of the cave opening. His skin painted a kaleidoscope of earthy colors. Above each eye were two great horns, and as he rose up and towered over all, he gave a nod to Zeck, then to Thoran. His long, wispy tongue tasted the air. He slowly said, "Frrrrrendsssssss."

Thoran breathed deeply. The boys stared dumbfounded. Before

them rose a magnificent creature. A creature whose shimmering skin was covered with scales the size of a warrior's shield, colored with ever changing hues. His colors matched the ground that half its body rested upon, and the sky upon which its other half stretched into. "I hope he's not hungry," Achu said. And Galeron slowly began to laugh...

"Aahhhhaaaaaaa...aaaaaahhhhhhaaaaaaaaa," and that made Zeck laugh, which in turn made Thoran nervously laugh, followed by the rest of the boys. All except Ayell, who thought it just strange.

"Galeron will help us," Zeck said, "He is the last of his kind— of the great rainbow serpents, and he too seeks revenge— for the destruction of his race. And he's been waiting for a long, long time."

"But our journey is far," Thoran said, "And I'm sure the mighty Galeron is swift. But we hoped to fly with your kind."

"And fly you will," Zeck answered. He turned to Galeron and nodded. And from Galeron's back opened four amazing wings, and with a massive thrust, the winged serpent went up, knocking them all about. Galeron hovered high in the air and with delight he sang, "Flyyyyyy. Aaaaaaahaaaaaaa." Then he flew off a short distance away. They watched him land as soft as a feather touching down, and he quickly slithered back to his new friends.

"I'm glad he's on our side," Joyal said.

"What's he eat?" Alvis asked.

Galeron looked at the youngling and smirked— just a bit. He then looked at Zeck. Thoran became a bit worried, as did the boys. Galeron's double pointed tongue tasted the air again. The great serpent answered— "Trrollsssssssss. Orcsssssss. Yummmm, yummmm."

"Trolls?" Shyel asked, "Orcs?"

"Well, he'd probably eat anything," Zeck said, "but he really hates trolls and orcs, so he eats 'em. An there's orcs lurking about." He looked at his slithery friend, "Maybe we go a hunting, eh? Finds you somethin ta eat."

Galeron nodded and simply said, "Sssoooonnn." He raised his head and nodded to Thoran. In turn, Thoran walked up to Galeron and patted him while saying, "It's our honor to meet you, and we thank you for your help."

Galeron nodded once back—"Sssssssseven ssssssave allllll."

Thoran looked at the giant serpent, unimpressed with those last words. He gave only the briefest of nods, with no smile. Galeron lowered his head to the ground and spread out one wing.

"Let's go find that glass and your mother," Zeck said to the boys.

"Can we take that fish with us?" Yawnel asked, pointing at the spit. "I'm hungry."

Thoran and Zeck smiled at each other, and shrugged their shoulders.

"What about our horses?" Alvis asked. Galeron turned his mighty head to the pack. His long tongue licked the air. All were quiet for a few clock ticks. Thoran walked up to the pack of horses, untied the main line and smacked his horse on the rump, sending it trotting. The others followed. "They'll have to fend for themselves. They'll be fine," he answered.

The great winged serpent slowly flapped its magnificent wings and lifted itself and a father with seven brave little men up to the skies, to search for their most loved one.

Running up a path came a simple little donkey. It stopped and watched his family go up in the air on a very strange beast. It noticed the horses were trotting away and thought… again they forgot to feed me.

Forty-Seven

To Lay Me Down

In a deep chamber of a secret castle that rarely showed itself, a beautiful mother lay in a fetal position on top of bits of dead and not-so dead things. The squirming underneath had long stopped bothering her. Few things actually bit her—most just crawled about her: on her arms and legs, in and around her ears, in her hair. Without benefit of light, time was irrelevant.

Rose knew she had been prisoner for weeks because Grimsdyke's beard was long, and when he first took her, he had only rubble. He would visit her every now and then, telling her his plan to stay at Ghastenblood's while he finished his scheme to take over the kingdom. He'd babble about an army and the Black Asylum being his fortress. He always finished by saying—"I could make you happy." He would then walk away, mumbling to himself when she didn't answer.

When they first arrived at the ancient asylum, he beat her, so she was mostly unconscious. She weakened as the days passed. Even after choking down bits of moldy bread, very little strength came back to her. He, or one of his spidery-minions, would sometimes light a candle in the far corner of the musty room. The candle was near a skeleton that shared the room with her. She didn't fear its frozen smile; she feared nothing.

Curled in a corner, she moved little. There was no reason to move. She needed to die. She could only dream that her spirit would rise to seek her family. That was her only hope. The beating of her heart meant nothing. The breathing of dank air meant nothing. And sight itself opened no door for longing. Time didn't pass. Her bond with life was destroyed.

And Myrtle… she found Grimsdyke. Or rather her wolf-beast Fagan found him. The one strand of hair that Myrtle saved was brimming with the distinct stink of Grimsdyke. The trail was strong and clear. And Fagan's sense of smell, like all dire-wolves, was keener than any animal's.

Hidden in the woods, Myrtle sat with Fagan and stared at Ghastenblood's Black Asylum. Its massive walls, thick with solid bark and veiny vines impressed her. She had only seen it in sketchings of old. In person it was more—special. She knew its fabled tale, storied to be a grand palace of misery, and as such, it would welcome her presence. But how did it come to be? And how did that maggot Grimsdyke, *entice* it to appear? She underestimated him. She questioned her spell. She needed to be careful. "Ee not as stupid as ee looks," she said. "Don't knows what he doing here. Don't trust him. Smart maggot. You ready?"

In a low yowl, the dire-wolf growled, *"You said I can eat him— right?"*

"Lets see what ee's doin." She turned to her beast. "Don't do anythin stupit, eh."

The heavy wood door was open. It never closed since it first opened for the Council Master and his guest. Myrtle comfortably walked inside, as if it were her own shack. Fagan followed, sniffing the air and the ground. Once inside, Fagan was slightly confused. At first glimpse, the inside of the great castle didn't look much different from the dark forest— mossy thick trees, musty wet ground—muggy, dank smelling nastiness. He walked up to a bush and did what animals do. While performing his deed, his eyes focused. They went up and up and around. His eyes widened. Fagan was in awe. He stood inside the entrance of a cathedral as large as any of the Seven Castles of Elberon. As a youth, Fagan explored the Sixth Castle and wondered how such a massive amount of stone and mortar could have been fashioned. Inside Ghastenblood, as an old animal, he wondered how a forest of massive trees and vines seemingly melded into walls, windows and in the distance, a grand staircase.

In that main hall, thin light filtered in through windows without glass. Scattered crevices in the walls let slivers of early morning bright come through. "You smell 'im?" she asked.

The wolf did. Grimsdyke's stink was all over. And just as important, the wolf heard him, or heard something shuffling about. Breathing hard, the wolf snarled, *"He's close."*

And he was. Through vines and trees, Grimsdyke watched Myrtle's every move—had been since the night prior when she came to Ghastenblood. Myrtle was quiet as a flea if she wanted to be. But her beast? He was noisy, especially when he ate, which he did after killing a bumbler that prior night. Grimsdyke hadn't slept since coming to the ghastly castle. And last night, he heard the slight echoes of something chomping away. His interest piqued. Through the moonlit forest, he was able to watch the hag-witch and her pet shuffle through the woods, stop a short distance away, and just sit. Coincidence? No, he thought... fate. He smiled, still thinking... stupid maggot. Smart of her not to trust me. Let her come.

And she came. To Fagan she whispered— "Mayhaps you stay here. I shuffle around quiet-like, eh." Her pet slowly blinked and nodded. Feeling less confident as clock ticks frittered away, he didn't mind staying put. Myrtle walked. She made no sound. She took only a few steps, but Fagan could barely see her amongst misty shrubs. When he lost complete sight of her, the hairs on his neck tingled. Feeling uncomfortable about staying put, less comfortable about walking about, Fagan slowly stepped back, wanting to stay close to the door. His eyes darted around. He looked for Myrtle. Backwards he still stepped. His rump bumped into something, something soft. Quickly turning, he sighed, as it was only a small tree-trunk. But he noticed the massive door was no longer open. And he wasn't even close to it. The once grand cathedral now seemed to shrink in size around him. Can't be…he thought…can't be! He stood for only one more tick before making a move to find the one person he thought he'd never, ever need to be close to. But his feet wouldn't move, couldn't move as they had sunk into a soft muck. Or maybe the soft muck rose to grab his feet. He yelped in fright… *"NOOO,"* and he looked at the ground. Fagan gasped as bloody, white scorpion-like bugs came out of the muck and slowly crawled to his legs. *"Myrrrrrtle,"* he howled for the last time, and as he raised his head, what he saw stopped his scream. The first spider-demon was in front of him and two more came from his right. The one that severed his neck dropped from above, onto his back and reached around, finding his throat quickly. His last vision was of his leg being bitten off, his last thought… humans I can kill, monsters I can't.

Myrtle knew that Fagan was dead. Didn't matter. She didn't need him any longer. He served his purpose. He found the Grimsdyke. But if it was a battle Grimsdyke wanted, it was a battle she would give him. Myrtle reached into a pocket and pulled out a small pouch. "Let's git some light on the sitcheeation." She slapped the pouch between her hands. It exploded into a hundred little flames that flittered and fluttered about. The great hallway lit up. The majestic inside of the castle opened up before her. Trees, shrubs, mosses and vines, like stars in the night, her little flames shined. The forest inside that ominous keep, filled with beings of old, who no longer sleep. She looked where spidery beasts were happily devouring Fagan. She put her hand in another pocket and pulled out a pouch. "Where you at Aaaangus Grimsdyke?" she sneered. "I knows you watchin."

From behind a tree that grew out of the grand staircase, Grimsdyke stepped out—"Welcome to my home. We always enjoy having guests," he said.

"Your home?" she asked offended. "Your home it ain't— that much I knows. I don't know how's ya did it, but you too stupit ta know 'ow special dis place be."

"Oh…really. Let's try something, shall we then," he said. "Let's see if my hungry little friends think I'm stupid." At that, as if he demanded it of them, tens upon tens of spidery beasts of all size descended upon the hag-witch.

And she laughed. As well before the spiders could sink a claw in her, the little flames that twinkled and lit the grand hallway sharpened their points and took aim upon the horde, flying hard and finding their mark. Flaming arrows, clever and narrow, flew into the spiders. Some of the leggy demons burst into flames. Some shriveled and screeched, and some turned into running, flaming balls. All other spiders stopped their attack and cowered backward from the witch, who never stopped laughing. "You think these little bugs scares me," she shrieked. "You forgot yur promise. YOU OWE ME SOMETHING, YOU MAGGOT."

Grimsdyke watched spidery things shrivel and burn. Others jumped back from Myrtle. His breathing quickened. Before he could say anything, Myrtle screamed, "IF YA DON'T HELP ME, THEN I DON'T NEEDS YA!" and she threw the second pouch she held at Grimsdyke's feet. It burst into a cloud. The bolt of pain that shot through his head and into his heart was the worst he ever had. His knees buckled, he dropped onto the stairs. Leaping up the stairs, she was on him quickly, grabbing his hair, lifting his head. "Why you think I let you live, when's you just a little maggot?" Hot spit shot from her lips and sprayed his face. "One purpose...dat's why I let you live, one purpose, an you..."

"I found it," he interrupted and surprised her—"I found it."

She stared at him. Tick...tick...tick... and asked, "Where?"

Confidently, Grimsdyke lied, "Behind you." She snapped her head around.

Stupid...he thought. She didn't see him reach into his pocket and pull something out.

Grimsdyke stabbed at the arm that held his hair, stabbed hard and dug in. Myrtle howled like a fierce animal and jumped back. She growled while holding her wound. "What...what?" Then she screamed in pain as her gashed arm started to bubble and drip and started to melt.

Grimsdyke stood. The pain in his head gone, he held up the weapon so she could see.

Myrtle was seething. She slowly stepped backwards down the stairs. Her left arm partially melted away... "Where did you get that!" she cried.

"Oh, this," he said, slowly walking down the steps while she backed away from him. "Well, for the longest time I've sought out how to kill a witch. You in particular." He kept stepping towards her. She backed away. "And I found out your breed are very difficult to kill." He stepped, she backed up. "But I rescued something that not only told me how to bring Ghastenblood to life, but also told me about the talon of a phoenix." He held out the large claw. It sparkled just a bit, and above a whisper, he said, "The talon has its own magic...doesn't it?"

Myrtle knew it did, for the talon of a phoenix has the only type of point that, if wounded with, a witch can't heal from. There are other ways to kill a witch, but the talon has the most deadly point, and another swipe could mean her death. She needed to escape. She would deal with him later.

He knew she would try to flee, so he ran at her. He needed to stab her heart.

She screamed garbled words, "farooch ata adanooee," and the fire-bits that swirled around the great hall flew at spiders, flew at Grimsdyke, and flew at the great arched door that held her in. In the flaming confusion, Myrtle rocked to and fro, spoke a quick chant and ate something. Then she was gone. Grimsdyke dodged the fire-daggers. Some spiders weren't so lucky, and nothing saw Myrtle turn herself into a rat and scamper out of sight. She would have turned herself into a bat, but her one arm was nearly melted away, and a bat can't fly with one wing. It would be difficult enough for a rat to scamper with three legs, but it had to be done. Myrtle found the smallest of holes in a wall and scampered out of Ghastenblood's Keep. When she left, the little flames that swirled about died, and the inside of the castle darkened.

"Go find her," Grimsdyke said to the spiders, and some scattered to try and do just that. But Grimsdyke knew she was gone. He got close enough to wound her, but wasn't able to kill her. That was a problem. She would come after him, but not now. She needed to heal. He had some time. And with that little time, he could build his army. Shaking his head, putting the claw of the phoenix back in his pocket, tired, angry, feeling unsatisfied, Angus Grimsdyke made a decision. He would kill Rose. She would not be his wife. She wanted none of him or his world. So he would oblige her. He went to the dungeon.

The world inside the castle was not like the regal interior of the King's lair in Thundor. Grimsdyke walked along wide mossy floors surrounded by walls and grand ceilings of lichen-covered bark, mumbling to himself. The air smelled of burnt forest, not like the floral incense of the King's palace. The stairs leading down to his new 'cellarium', crunched with dead grass. They did not have the soft muffle of polished wood. He entered her room alone and lit candles. "I have no regrets, Rose. I never have." He propped himself against a wall, crossed his legs, stared at the ground and contemplated, "I can't blame anyone. I'm *proud* of my deeds." He scratched at the slimy walls. "I'm going to kill you, because I don't know what else to do." He walked to her. "You're probably thinking...I could just let you *go*. But I can't. That's not me." He shook his head and took a deep breath. "I have no weapons, my love. Your last weak breath will be taken only by my hands," he said, while opening his palms to her. "I suspect you'll go quietly," he said while he wrapped his hands around her neck. "I could have made you happy," he whispered as his hands tightened. "I'll do this slowly, and there will be pain." He was smiling.

Rose watched him with half-closed eyes as his hands slowly squeezed her neck. Her mind reached for fond memories but found none. The image of Grimsdyke's face wouldn't allow visions of her beautiful family to shine through. She cared no longer for her life. Rose craved only to dream. She forced a sigh through his grasp, and welcomed her last breath and the dark that came forth. And as it came, it brought with it a gift. She allowed herself a final moment of grief after a last heartbeat. And in that last moment, she felt it.

The kick of a child, deep in her womb—a tiny, but potent kick that jolted her heart and made her spirit scream. And in a dimly lit, musty cellar, a place known only for misery and death, she became flush with the heat of an anger reserved only for the Good Mother herself; an anger that can decimate. Her eyes opened; her body tensed and felt none of his hollow strength. She rose with Grimsdyke's hands tight around her neck. "Fighting will do you no..." But Grimsdyke couldn't finish his sentence as Rose's hands were already deep within his neck, and her nails were as sharp as any dragon's claw.

Both stood with hands locked around each other's necks. Rose screamed, "DO ME NO WHAT? You beast. No good?" With her fetus kicking feverishly, Rose's strength multiplied. Her strangle intensified. Her nails fully embedded into throat muscle quickly found bone. Grimsdyke's head shook as Rose's fury swelled. His eyes were wide with terror. His teeth clenched so hard, his molars and crowns shattered. Blood came from his eyes. The speed of her defense humbled him.

And as usual he lied, for he did have a weapon. Letting go of her, he reached into his pocket, grabbed the talon of the phoenix, and swung it around, seeking the back of Rose's head. His aim was true, but the sweet mother had a special sense, as all mothers do. She moved her head ever so slightly, just enough where Grimsdyke's swinging arm grazed only her ear, his arm kept going, thrusting the talon deep into his own throat. A slight rush of rotten air escaped from Grimsdyke's opened windpipe.

Rose let go and stepped back. Grimsdyke held the talon into his gullet and stood for a few clock ticks. He gurgled his last word—

"Happy," then fell to the ground, twitching.

She stood there for only one click before deciding not to take any chances. She pulled the claw from his throat. His eyes still stared at her. She plunged his weapon into his heart: twice, three times, then a fourth, and pulled it out, satisfied. She spit on the twitching Grimsdyke. She looked at the talon, and noticed it wasn't a knife. She ran, needing to find her family. She had to go up and out. She looked for a way to escape. The stairs out of the dungeon were easy enough, but once she was up in the hallway, her world became a confusing labyrinth of woodland greenery, just like a corn maze she had played in as a child.

She ran, and angry sounds filled the air. First, the shrieking screams of the spider-demons looking for she who killed their master. Then the louder crunches and moans of the castle itself, angry that the Grimsdyke couldn't properly feed it the soul of a pure one. So Ghastenblood would hide itself again and take her pure spirit with it. She ran and ran. Behind her there were spiders of all shapes and sizes. She ran and ran, praying that the last door upon which she came would open. And it did. Her prayer was answered. The window in front of her was an opening to *her* world. And the spider-elf that dropped from the ceiling, onto her back, bit down and clung to her as she flung herself towards the glass-less window…

Forty-Eight

The Colors of the Rainbow...

f lew through the air, and on its broad back, carried part of a family. The winds were warm and the sky was clear. Galeron's wings beat slowly and strong. It amused him to hear the boys croon "oooohs," and crow, "haha's," as he sliced through odorless clouds. His long tongue darted from his smirk and tasted the air. He slowly shifted his head back and forth to catch a peek at the ground. The boys and Thoran watched with fascination at the magnificent panorama of their world passing below them.

Yawnel asked, "How *long* do you think Galeron is, Pa?"

"He looks like he could swallow our whole cottage," Achu added.

"Well," their father said, "by my guess, I'd say he's forty, maybe fifty yards long." He laughed. "And I'd agree— he probably could swallow our cottage."

"Do you really think we'll find her, Pa?" asked Yawnel, "It's been so long."

"And Pitch. Poor boy, something must have happened, something bad," Shyel said as Ayell slowly bobbed his head and rocked back and forth.

Thoran sighed, confidently looking at his third born, "She's alive Yawny. I know it. Just like I'm alive, and you're alive— she is, too." But the husband did worry. "I don't know about Pitch. We have to trust The Good Mother's taking care of him."

Coming from above, Zeck gently landed on Galeron's back. He carried a sack and quickly opened it, handing out apples and other type of fruits. He said, "My friends will be coming soon, more ta help."

"How far to the magic glass?" Alvis asked.

"Mirror!" Grumel corrected.

"Well, getting there's just da first part," Zeck said. "Then's we has to find it. I brought da map to me elders. They thinks it's deep in da ground. Under a mountain marked on dat map."

"This could be like picking a clivet off a hairy dragon. It might be impossible," Thoran said, shaking his head.

Zeck half-hopped to Thoran, "We'll find it," he said, "you have friends. We'll find it and we'll find her."

In a sudden jerk, Galeron twisted his head, his tongue briskly sniffing the air. "Aaaaaaahhhaaa," he cried, "Trolllllsssss, yummm, yyuuummm," and with a wide sweeping arc, the rainbow serpent and his passengers smoothly began to descend from the skies.

"Looks like he's gonna feed," Zeck said, "We goin' huntin men."

"Papa?" his boys asked.

Thoran answered, "It's okay, boys. We have to trust him." But Thoran was very worried. His complete trust was placed in beings he knew only for a few days. He gravely missed his wife. He knew no other course of action.

Forty-Nine

Seena's New Pet

At the bottom of a hole, Pitch was crumpled, whimpering, *"So, so hungry. So, so hungry."*

Seena grunted, "Come with—dog." Pitch raised his head, barely wanting to move. The witch dumped a pouch of something into his hole. Pitch looked up. His eyes were met with a fine dust. He sneezed. Seena jumped in the hole. It was a tight fit, but she didn't land on him. In one swift, easy move, she grabbed Pitch and threw him up. He landed hard with a thunk and rolled once. Looking at the woods, he didn't even think about escaping. She was next to him, "Looky over there," she pointed. "We'll starts ye out small."

A small doe stood at the edge of the forest. "Little ones, little ones, tasty and fresh," was all she cackled. Pitch was up, uncontrollably moving faster than he had ever moved in his life, not feeling the ground beneath his feet. Landing hard on the little deer, he had no thoughts as he viciously fed. The meal lasted only minutes.

His belly was full. He looked at Seena with much less disgust.

"Us gonna take a little trip. Somethin's brewin," she said, "One of da old one's, calls herself Merrrrtle. She callin together a coven. Somethin' special-like happening. Mayhaps we go see what's about. Never been to a coven. Don't needs to waste me time, tho'. Don't needs to palaver."

Pitch looked at her while licking at bits of young venison caught in his teeth. He knew Myrtle very well. He licked his lips and growled, *"I don't care."*

She laughed. "Then mayhaps we go see yur friends, eh?"

He looked through her and barked low and simple, *"I have no friends."*

She grabbed him by his scruff, stared into his face, smiled and said, "I don't takes it personal-like."

He followed her into the woods and again growled low and deep, *"I have no friends."*

Fifty

Rose...

J umped through a window of Ghastenblood's Castle and fell. A spider-demon clung about her back. Its pincers barely held into her. She lightly tumbled. The shades of greens, browns and blacks of the forest jumbled through her weary eyes. The spider-demon broke her fall. She crushed its shell, and it let out a last hiss as she rolled off. She rested, her cheek comforted by the cool fresh earth. Breathing hard, she heard the crunching of the castle as it undid itself. She gently turned to look at it, watched its thick twines uncoil, and smiled as great branches cracked and unlocked to become leafy limbs again.

Cloudy...she thought...maybe it's mid-day? The forest stayed calm for only a few clock ticks, and it moved again. From all sides around her, they came. Her weary, weary mind watched as the spider-demons surrounded her. Am I dreaming...am I dead? But wait! she wondered. These aren't spiders. Trying to focus harder, she squinted ...dragon-elves? They had spears. From behind her, one made a sound. She spun her head towards it.

"Smells it, can ya, eh? Smells it?"

Rose thought...No, not dragon-elves.

A second one uttered, "Another." It chuckled and banged its spear to the ground. Then louder, "Another," and all cheered, snarly gnashing their teeth. Cheers of all types, arms and hands holding crude spears flailed about, whoops and hollers of the nastiest kind filled the air. Rose covered her ears and bowed her head, praying... Wake up, wake up, wake up.

"Quiets!" the first one screamed. They stopped, but shrieking gracklers could be heard in the distance. It walked up to Rose. She looked at the creature.

"Give it up when it comes out," it said, "give her up, an maybe we wont's eat ya'."

She didn't understand. Rose looked around. There was an army of them around her. A third spoke from behind. Rose swung her gaze to it. "She's are's," it said. "She be for us to have." The crowd of creatures became restless.

"We ne'er had two of 'em," a fourth said from the crowd.

"Let's jest eat 'er," a fifth said.

A sixth whacked the fifth on the head, "Can't eat 'er. Babe's not old 'nuff yet. Smell is fresh."

Suddenly, Rose knew what the creatures were talking about, but she was even more confused. Rubbing her belly, she had forgotten about the little one that had kicked her out of her stupor. She held her breath. She no longer felt the baby's kicking. Sensing the concern on her face, the first blood-troll laughed while saying, "Don'ts you worry me pet, our little-uns alive. She jest restin. TAKE HER," it screamed. Like water flowing strong, they descended upon her, lifting her up. She floated along their bony fingertips. They passed her about, through the crowd of trolls, chanting, screaming joyous sounds.

Rose thrashed, but to no avail. She moved as if she were a puppet, staring up. Above her, a seven-shades-of-gray cloudy sky was a background to the swaying treetops that clapped their approval of the forest scene. Below her were scores of ecstatic blood-trolls, all moving as one towards something. How can she be a seventh, her mind cried… how? Rose couldn't remember how many she lost in her womb. She couldn't think straight. A chant from somewhere in the pack, "ONE FUR THE DAY, ONE FUR THE NIGHTS, TWO LITTLE SEVENS, SCREAMIN AN' THEY FIGHTS." More whoops and screams. Then all chanted, "One for the day, one for the nights— one for the day, one for the nights, one for the day, one for the nights." She was passed about their outstretched arms, bouncing and bobbing atop a sea of creatures.

Remembering Grimsdyke's weapon, Rose tried to move her arm, but the trolls controlled her every movement. She couldn't get to her pocket. She screamed, "NOOOOOO," and they stopped. No sounds echoed through the woods. The fifteen or so that held Rose stood their ground. Scores of others stepped back from them. In a hushed chant they began, *"one for the day, one for the nights— one for the day, one for the nights."*

Rose was gently placed on the ground. There was nowhere to run. An army of snarling animals surrounded her, and their chanting grew even more hushed. A troll stepped forward— "Eight full mooons from now, she come's out. She be easy to has, not like this one," and the ground rumbled next to Rose, startling her.

A small hole caved in. A red mist seeped up from it. The ground crumbled inward. The hole grew. Sounds came from the widening crevice. Within a few clock ticks, the hole was wide enough for Rose to easily fit through. The mist melted away, grunting was heard, and from the hole popped out three blood trolls holding ropes. They looked at Rose and snickered. One whispered at her, "one for the day, one for the nights." The three pulled on their ropes. Up and up and out came a child, bound and dirty. Tattered and torn, the little prisoner's vacant stare couldn't hide her identity. Her cute little nose was just like her mother's. Rose knew. The child was the baby in Jillian Sheef's belly, so many years ago—Rose began to weep. Hearing a mother cry, little Flower broke out of her trance and meekly smiled. "It's okay," she squeaked out, "Papa said it's gonna be okay." Rose cried even harder. She tried to get up, to go to the little one, but many pairs of twig-like fingers quickly held her back.

"Very cutes, eh? She likes ya," a troll said.

"Maybe yur little nits'll play dolls, eh?" one laughed, sending the army of them laughing, whooping and chuckling with joy. "Rope," one screamed.

Knowing full well what their chanting meant, and what was about to happen, Rose swiftly reached into her pocket and grabbed the talon of the phoenix, ducked and swiped at whatever was in back of her. The talon sliced true across the chests of three trolls. The celebration stopped as the three stumbled back, holding their open wounds—grayish matter bubbling between their fingers. They fell back on their rumps. The crowd's chanting became low whispered hisses.

"Ya shouldn't a done that," one growled.

"This was supposed ta be an easy one," said another, and pointing to Flower, "get that little thing down." The ones that brought her up, jumped back in the hole, still holding the ropes. With a painful, tiny grunt, little Flower Sheef was pulled hard, back into the deep ground. Rose swung around in quarter-circles, slashing the talon in mid-air. The army hissed and clacked their teeth at her.

"We not gonna, kill ya—but ya gonna' wish we did." They came at her hard. She stabbed once, twice, but there were too many. They jumped and grabbed at her. She was taken fast and twirled in rope, as if spun by a giant spider. The talon cut into her hand, and both hands were useless as they were tied tight to her body, save for two fingers that escaped the rope. Some strands of her hair also evaded the wrapping. No part of her body could move. They barely left a slit for her to breath. The army of trolls screamed with excitement. Again they passed Rose above them, each craving to touch their prize. They screeched loudly. They hollered in victory. They didn't hear what came from the dense woods.

From the brush, and with Zeck atop his head, Galeron lifted two-thirds of his self up and screamed, "YUMMM, YUMMMM." Scores and scores of terrified yellowish red eyes watched the great serpent rise. Their confused eyes darted from one to another, and up. They knew what this beast was in front of them. But why? How?

Thoran and the boys hid behind Galeron's tail. They weren't expecting the army of beasts that rustled before them. "Stay together," their father whispered. "Aim true if attacked!"

Galeron turned quickly to his friends and said loud, "Sheildsssss," and the scales near his tail slightly lifted. Ayell knew what to do— he grabbed and pulled a scale. It came off with a quick snap! The others followed suit and within two clock ticks they had armor.

Only Zeck knew that the mass before them were blood-trolls. He didn't have the time to wonder why they gathered. He too was surprised at their number and had to act. He flew hard at them, breathing fire like he hadn't done in decades. A row of trolls turned into flaming screamers. They broke from the pack and ran into the woods, beating themselves about the head, trying to put out flames. A tremendous turmoil spread about the woods.

Galeron lunged hard and scooped up six in his mouth. In one swift move, he knocked his head back and swallowed them. His thick skin bulged with trolls trying to escape, his strong throat muscles squeezing the life from them. He lunged again at the crowd.

Zeck flew about, spewing fire. In great frustration, trolls scattered about. Two screamed, "FORM A LINE, FROM A LINE!" Many counter-attacked, throwing spears that bounced off Galeron's strong skin.

Thoran and his boys were trying to stay hidden, but were at the ready to fight. This is not our battle...Thoran angrily thought...I should have stayed far back from his feed. They're smarter than ogres. He looked for an escape route, but knew it was too late for second-guessing. Spears landed close to them. They would have to defend themselves.

In the confusion of the clash, Rose was dropped. A troll spotted humans hiding by the serpent's tail. Humans? It yelled..."GET HER BELOW! AN TAKE OFF!" Rose was quickly dragged to the hole. Some trolls jumped into the hole, many more fought. From their vantage point, the boys and Thoran let their arrows fly fast and true. They shot at easy targets.

Only Ayell noticed something was being dragged. Only Ayell saw the little demons taking someone tied and struggling. Someone with black *squiggly* hair! Only Ayell spotted the bloodied fingers sticking out from the wrappings. A rush of heated emotions made him gasp. The wriggling prisoner was dropped into the hole. His mind raced... squiggly hair. And it was a finger! Was it a ring finger that was bloody? Ayell ran. Ran from the safety of his family— from the safety of Galeron. He ran without thinking. Thoran screamed after him— "Noooo.." His brothers shouted as one—"AYELL!"

Hearing his friends, Zeck turned and watched Ayell jump into the hole. While swallowing a mouthful of squirming food, a confused Galeron also watched the quiet youngling run and leap in the hole. Zeck flew in a wide arc. To Thoran he roared, "STAY WITH YOUR FAMILY!" and like a flash, he dove into the hole after Ayell, spitting bits of fire.

The blood-fiends had what they wanted. There was no need to lose any more. They would retreat.

Galeron had fed enough. He slithered, spread his great wings and with mighty whacks to the ground, crushed everything he could. Trolls fanned out into the woods, all thinking... there are many ways to get below the ground.

Running to it, Thoran stared at the hole, as did his sons. Before their eyes, the ground around the hole crumbled, closed in, and the hole was no longer. They stopped in their tracks and gulped. As quickly as the battle began, it was over. A man, six boys, and a giant serpent stood, panting hard. "Papa?" his boys asked, confused as to their next move.

"DIG!" Thoran screamed, and they made haste, chopping at the ground with all their might. Galeron let them dig, but knew otherwise. In his heart, so did Thoran.

Galeron looked on, "Friendsssssss..."

"NO!" Thoran blared. Then with clenched teeth, "Do not say the words." Thoran would not leave his first born.

Below the ground, the trolls were at home. Within the hole and down and down, were tangled roots and sharp ledges. Ayell fell hard and rolled off the first ledge, onto a second, third and fourth before he was able to get his footing. Zeck was quickly by his side, "WHAT'RE YOU DOIN'?" he shouted. With all his might, Ayell silently shouted while searching, "MOMMA." The hole above closed. With it went all light, though Zeck watched his mouth, felt his plea. "Rose?" he said in the dark. The blood trolls were here for her? The thought hit him hard. "Hold on." Zeck grabbed Ayell and dropped down, spitting fire above them, fire that caught dangling roots. They fell through a partly lit tunnel. Below them was dark. Dropping and dropping, Zeck's wings thwacked the ledges. He continued to spit fire above. Before long, there was no more tunnel. They were in an echoing chamber, with hisses of blood trolls filling the air. Zeck hovered for only a clock tick, then spat a mighty glob of fire. The glob caught a giant root, sending the dry, wiry anchor bursting into flames. A vast cavern opened before them, a cavern filled with the crooked tentacle-roots that fed the majestic trees above.

Within the web of roots, hundreds of yellow eyes glinted and darted about, reflecting the flames. A muffled grunt was made. Zeck and Ayell spun their heads toward the sound. "Why you lookin for this?" a troll confidently asked, patting its wrapped prisoner. There she was, not twenty feet from them. Ayell saw her bloody fingers slightly move. He prayed it was his mother.

The human and the dragon-elf were trapped in their lair. "Ya gonna' burn down heah," another said. "No ways out for ya. Only fa us." The fire slowly spread. "Not much air here," a third said. "Smoke'll kill soon 'nuff."

A fourth said, "We come back later, eh? After they cooked up nice'n crispy, eh?"

Zeck and Ayell looked at each other. Ayell forgot that on his back was the sack holding Dagon's journal, the goblet and the candleholder.

He reached for it, but didn't know what good it would do them. Where's my bow? His mind cried…where's my axe?

In the forest above, Galeron lifted his head and slowly tasted the air. He tasted smoke. He felt the hot ground. Thoran and his boys frantically dug. They didn't make much progress. The last Rainbow Serpent searched the forest.

In the depth below, Zeck hopped a bit away from the flames he created, perching himself and Ayell on a large root, close to Rose. His lightly flapping wings stirred smoke that filled the upper part of the cavern. Ayell was sweating heavy. "That's his momma," Zeck said, "let him see her before he dies." The crackling of the fire was slightly louder than the grunting of blood trolls, or maybe Zeck and Ayell were just too close to the flames.

"His momma?" a troll asked. "His momma. Well, well. Well— jest a quick peek. We got's ta get her out a here." It pointed at Ayell, "You don't matter none. Ya little sistah, she's fer us."

Ayell looked to Zeck. His eyes pleaded…what does he mean? Why did he say that? Zeck could only look at his little friend and pray for a miracle from The Good Mother. He searched for an escape. With each clock tick, the chamber shrunk as it filled with smoke. A troll cut the rope from Rose's face. The moment her eyes were set free, she saw her first born, and he saw her. She watched him mouth the words, 'Momma'. The spectacle around him meant nothing. She saw only his face, and he saw only hers. I must be dreaming… she thought…and it's beautiful.

A troll put its face to Rose's and happily said, "Eee's da last thing you'll see. Ee'll be dead soon an we gonna burn ya eyes out!" Through crackling flames, trolls laughed, another shouted, "We be back when's ya done cookin." Rose was roughly taken—Ayell watched her being pulled through the jungle of roots. Smoke clouded their world. Zeck wrapped his wings around Ayell. "She loves you very much. All ya's," he said." Everything gonna be okay. Tis okay." Ayell began to cry, as did Zeck.

Thunder came from the land. Galeron wrapped the whole of his body around a majestic oak and pushed the air under his mighty wings harder than he ever had. The oak was ripped from the land with the force greater than a hurricane, and with it came its stout and sturdy roots. And on those roots were a dragon-elf and a boy. Zeck and Ayell were lifted hard from the ground.

Galeron twisted and heaved the great tree, though before the tree was fully tossed away, Zeck dropped from his perch and flew Ayell to firm land, dropping him at the edge of the new hole. Zeck continued down.

Inside the crater, the mass of trolls screamed in turmoil and pure anger. Never had they fought such a battle. They scattered and descended deeper. Zeck flew down, fists clenched, breathing fire. He flew straight at Rose, dropping at her as if he were attacking. It's the only way to save her...he thought. His fire-breath met all those that held her. Spears whizzed through the air. He landed on Rose hard and prayed his talons didn't find her skin. Trolls wailed and hollered. Zeck took to flight. He had her! Up and up he went, past dangling roots, dodging spears and rocks that flew swiftly by. He held Rose tightly. Her weight became threefold when a spear entered his chest. He slumped only slightly. The pain was great, and with all his might, he flew.

In the battle for survival, anger turns into the ultimate weapon. Ayell jumped back into the hole to help save his mother, followed by his father and six brothers, again screaming after him. Jumping from ledge to ledge, amongst roots and vines, they moved as swiftly as weathered warriors, shooting arrows, throwing axes, and stabbing knives. Thoran spied Zeck flying with —his wife? His heart stopped. How? How? He cried, "Rose," and the blood trolls screamed louder, yelled and fought harder. A troll blew a horn, summoning his brethren that lived even deeper to come up—come up to battle. Grumel's axe found that troll's head, splitting it wide open.

Some trolls cowered. Many more took aim as the sky darkened and Galeron's massive head entered the hole while he screamed, "INSSSSSSIIIDDE!" His mouth opened wide. The great serpent's tongue lashed out and grabbed Zeck and Rose, then recoiled, bringing them in him. Thoran and his boys sprung and swung on roots while shooting arrows, each jumping in the open jaws and grabbing onto fangs for dear life. Galeron closed his mouth, protecting his friends. His massive body shook and shimmied as he made way from the hole. The trolls pursued. Galeron spread his wings and took to flight as the army of blood trolls emptied from the hole, roaring with anger, shrieking for revenge. The great winged serpent flew.

Miles and miles away, in a field of fresh flowers, Galeron landed, opened his mouth, and his friends slowly crawled out. No one spoke—the battle was too fresh in their minds. Thoran carried his sleeping wife and set her gently on the soft ground. He stroked her dirty hair. The boys and Zeck circled them.

"We have ta keep moving. We have ta take flight," Zeck said. "Da trolls won't stop till they gets what they think is theirs. They'll be here soon." He looked at Thoran. "They'll be *here* soon." Thoran knew. Somehow, miraculously, Rose had a little girl growing inside her. He tingled with happiness, shivered with exhaustion. And monsters were coming for his family.

"What's theirs Papa? What's Zeck mean?" Shyel asked.

"Where ya think that council man is?" Achu asked, "Why can't we wake Momma?"

Tenderly, Thoran said, "We need to find someplace to rest her. She'll wake soon. She's had it harder than us—I'm sure."

Thoran would soon tell the boys that their mother was with child. And the child was a girl—a very, very special girl. He would tell them they were being hunted. So their fight was not finished, the battles were not over. "Where should we go?" he asked anyone.

Zeck looked at Galeron. Galeron looked to the sky, closed his eyes and nodded his head.

"Can't we go home Pa?" Yawnel asked.

Thoran looked around at his family, his friends. She's with us... he thought... she's really back with us. He looked at Galeron, then to Zeck, smiled, closed his eyes and took a deep breath. "No...not yet, son." Another breath. "Not yet." He looked at his boys and thought... they'll need their swords.

Zeck remembered something Dagon had said, a long time ago... "The Good Mother, always—demanding, isn't she?" He looked to the great rainbow serpent again and smiled.

A vision exploded in Galeron's mind; he also remembered something. A time when he was very young. At barely seventeen strides long, and from a cave he always played in, his old sorcerer friend, Mortron, called to him.

"Come little one, quickly!" Galeron followed Mortron deep into the cave, deeper than he had ever gone. Mortron's staff lit the way, a staff Galeron knew to be made of dragon's- eye.

Far under the land, Mortron turned to his slithery friend... "You'll know when to come back for this," and he threw his staff into a hole that magically appeared. The light followed the staff, and like the blowing out of a candle, was gone. "Don't be afraid," Mortron said in a calm voice, a voice that softened the cold darkness. "Remember the Witch's Prophecy," and Mortron jumped into that same hole while chanting ominous words that echoed through the darkness:

"Rise he will, the time unknown,
the sap of Terron, through mother's bone,
His heart to beat, fear all to be,
land, sky and mist, none to see,

The Seven's task, defend or fall,
The hearts, the pillars, the love, the all."

Mortron was never heard from again. Galeron remembers missing his friend, and had forgotten the tale of Terron. He was very surprised at the memory, upset at the force with which it had come back. A mighty chill shook his body. His friends felt that shudder.

It would be many, many days before Rose would wake. And when she did, she floated swift upon the back of a great serpent. She was with her family... and a dragon-elf? And when spoken to, she would only smile, as she believed it was all a dream.

"Isn't *this* amazing Momma?" Joyal asked while waving his arms. "Why don't you answer us?"

She missed her sister. But *this* was nice. So she, her husband, and her seven brave little men, rushed through tender clouds. She sensed they were in a hurry.

And as long as she was with her boys, she would be at ease.

To The Readers:

I appreciate your time and thank you for any and all support. Drop me a line at lsdubbleyew.com, let me know your thoughts, this is all new to me and I love hearing feedback.

I'm hard at work on the second book and am very stressed as the story unfolds before me. Scary new worlds are sprouting, new and creepy creatures are growing, and dramatic characters are scheming.

And our brave, seven little men? Well…they're just getting started. They and their family will be put to life's greatest tests.

Thank you for spending some time with me.

L.S.W.

CPSIA information can be obtained at www.ICGtesting.com
Printed in the USA
BVOW042213271212

309308BV00001B/40/P